MISSING
GLA

BY
LENA DIAZ

Published in Great Britain 2015
by Mills & Boon, an imprint of Harlequin (UK) Limited,
Eton House, 18-24 Paradise Road, Richmond, Surrey, TW9 1SR

ISBN: 978-0-263-25326-9

46-1215

Harlequin (UK) Limited's policy is to use papers that are natural, renewable and recyclable products and made from wood grown in sustainable forests. The logging and manufacturing processes conform to the legal environmental regulations of the country of origin.

Printed and bound in Spain
by CPI, Barcelona

Lena Diaz was born in Kentucky and has also lived in California, Louisiana and Florida, where she now resides with her husband and two children. Before becoming a romantic suspense author, she was a computer programmer. A former Romance Writers of America Golden Heart award finalist, she has won a prestigious Daphne du Maurier Award for excellence in mystery and suspense. To get the latest news about Lena, please visit her website, www.lenadiaz.com.

Thank you, Allison Lyons and Nalini Akolekar. Thank you to my mom, Letha McAlister, who got such a kick out of this story. This book is dedicated to my friend and fellow suspense author Sarah Andre. Thank you for self lessly giving me your time, ideas and encouragement. This book would not have been written without you.

Chapter One

Jake aimed his pistol and flashlight through the chain-link wildlife fencing that marked where civilization ended and the Florida Everglades began. Behind him, his black Dodge Charger sat on the shoulder of a remote section of Interstate 75 that Floridians affectionately called Alligator Alley. With good reason. Alligators infested the swampy areas along this east-west corridor connecting Naples to Hialeah.

He swept his flashlight up and down the ditch behind him. Did alligator eyes reflect in the light? He sure hoped so. That might be the only way he'd see the hungry reptiles creeping up on him, looking for a late-night Jake-snack.

Not for the first time, he questioned his sanity in searching this dangerous area at night. But when a rare black panther had darted across the road in front of him and he'd skidded sideways to avoid it, he'd noticed a reflection in the beam of his headlights through the wildlife fence—a reflection that just might be the car Calvin Gillette was driving when he went missing three days ago.

In theory, if Gillette had crashed, the cable barrier system should have kept his car from sliding under the fence into the woods. And hitting one of the cables would have triggered strobe lights and an automatic notification to the Department of Transportation. But the system wasn't foolproof. A few months earlier a minivan hit a pole and went airborne, flipping over the cable without touching it and sliding under the fence into a canal. Jake figured if it happened once, it could happen again. And the few clues he had about Gillette's disappearance all led him to this same area.

A few minutes later, his search paid off. He found deep tire tracks in the wet grass. He hopped the ditch and pressed against the chain links—loose and floppy as they'd be if a car had hit the fence. Excitement sizzled through him. He stepped over the cable and slid through to the other side.

Grateful he'd worn boots for this search, he trudged across the damp ground to a thick stand of pine trees and palmetto bushes. Not anxious to go much farther in the dark, he braced his shoulder on one of the trees and used his flashlight to search for that elusive reflection of metal he thought he'd seen from the road. And suddenly, there it was, behind some bushes, too big and shiny to not be man-made. But without knowing for sure that it was a car, he didn't want to raise an alarm. Which meant he would have to go into the swamp.

It was times like this when he seriously wondered if he should move forward with his planned career change from police officer to private investigator. He was on leave from his police job to give the private sector a try, which was why he'd recently moved south to this unpredictable, dangerous, land-that-time-forgot section of his home state.

Tightening his hold on his pistol, he stepped past the

line of pine and oak trees and—for the first time in his life—officially entered the Everglades. The difference in temperature struck him first. It was much cooler here, the musty, woodsy scent a welcome change from the thick humid air by the road. He'd expected the ground to be wet, slippery like the ditch by the fence. Instead, it was dry and springy beneath his boots, not all that different from the woods behind the house in Saint Augustine where he'd grown up, just a few blocks from the Atlantic Ocean. But where he'd come from he'd hear waves breaking against the sand, seagulls crying overhead. Here, the night was filled with the deep-throated bass of frogs, and a hissing noise that could have been either insects or cranky reptiles warning him to get out of their territory.

Keeping an eye out for panthers and gators and whatever else thrived in this foreign but starkly beautiful section of Collier County, he continued forward. When he rounded the clump of bushes where he'd seen the reflection, he discovered what he'd both expected and dreaded to find—a car, its dented roof, crumpled hood and crushed front bumper broadcasting the wild ride its driver had endured before the car slammed against an unforgiving tree.

The paint was scratched all to hell, but there was no mistaking the color or the make and model—a maroon Ford Taurus. A glance at the license plate confirmed it was Gillette's. The day he'd gone missing, it had been raining off and on for hours, which explained the dried mud caked on the half-buried tires. The ground must have been like wet cement when he'd crashed his car in here.

Fully expecting to see a body slumped over the

wheel, Jake moved to the driver's door. But when he shined his light inside, he didn't see Calvin Gillette or anyone else. The car was empty. The now-deflated air bags must have saved the driver's life. If there'd been any footprints on the ground beside the car, they'd been scrubbed away by the rain and encroaching swamp before the heat of the past few days had wrestled the water back to its normal boundaries. So where was the driver? Had he gone looking for help and got lost?

He shoved his pistol into the holster on his belt to free his hands. In lieu of the gloves he'd have had if he were on active duty as a police officer, he yanked his shirt out of the waistband of his jeans. Keeping the cloth over his fingers, he opened the driver's door and grabbed the keys from the ignition. A moment later he popped the trunk. Except for a useless flat tire and some crumpled beer cans, it was empty.

Time to get the local police out here. He pulled out his cell phone as he peered through the driver's-side window, hoping to see some receipts or a map, anything to indicate where Gillette was headed before the crash.

Bam! The window exploded in a tinkling rain of glass. Jake dropped to the ground. A second bullet slammed into the door.

He cursed and scrambled around the front of the car, taking cover behind the wheel. He drew his gun again, aiming at the dark scrub brush and live oak trees where he'd seen the muzzle flash from the second shot. The moonlight cast deep shadows across the clearing, but he didn't try to grab his flashlight that had fallen on the ground. He wanted to draw the shooter out, but not by giving him a well-lit target.

"Police!" he yelled. "I can see you hiding behind that

bush. Come out, hands up, or I'll shoot." He waited, crouched down, both hands gripping the gun. No sound. No movement. Half a minute went by.

Time to give his prey some incentive.

He aimed his pistol well above where the gunman had to be hiding and squeezed off a shot. It boomed through the clearing, hitting a small tree branch, sending a shower of leaves down to the forest floor.

"The next shot will be lower. And there are sixteen more rounds where that one came from."

Silence. Even the croaking frogs and hissing insects had gone quiet.

"Threatening to shoot me is a lousy way of thanking me," a voice called out, a distinctly *feminine* voice with a velvety Southern accent that had Jake raising his brows in surprise.

Had he stumbled across a beauty pageant queen in these woods? Or a debutante? He could easily picture the owner of that silky voice wearing a floor-length gown, sitting on a wraparound porch in the Carolinas, sipping a mint julep.

When the woman stepped out from behind the bushes, reality sucked the air from Jake's lungs. If there was such a thing as an *anti*-Southern belle, this astonishing creature was the physical embodiment of it.

Her curve-hugging blouse was Pepto-Bismol pink and was tucked into an equally pink collection of veils, or scarves, forming a semblance of a skirt that hung past her knees. Below the skirt was the only part of her outfit that wasn't pink—a pair of green camouflage combat boots. She was probably somewhere in her mid-twenties, and at least a foot shorter than Jake. Her waterfall of blond curls hung to her hips, sparkling like burnished gold in the moonlight filtering through the trees. A stray warm breeze lifted one of the gold locks and fluttered it against the muzzle of her rifle, which was pointed up at the dark sky overhead.

Jake pocketed his cell phone that had fallen by the tire before grabbing his flashlight and shining it on her. If she hadn't just tried to shoot him, he'd have been hard-pressed not to smile at the utterly adorable picture she presented.

He forced himself to focus on the fact that she'd just shot at him. Twice. She was dangerous, at least while she was holding that rifle.

"Toss the weapon," he ordered.

"That's not a good idea. There are all kinds of dangers in these woods, especially at night."

"Now."

She let out a dramatic sigh and pitched the rifle onto the ground.

"Kick it away from you."

"Seriously? Do you know how expensive that gun is?"

He didn't bother to respond to that ridiculous statement.

She pursed her lips, not at all happy about his dictate. But she must have realized she didn't have a choice because she gave the gun a healthy kick. It slid across the pine needle-strewn forest floor and slammed against the car's rear tire.

Jake hopped to his feet and quickly closed the distance between them. "Who are you? Why did you shoot at me?"

She squinted and waved toward his flashlight. "Mind pointing that thing somewhere else?"

He relented and turned it just enough so it wasn't directly on her face.

She cocked her head, studying him. Her emerald green eyes were startlingly similar to the panther's eyes he'd seen reflected in his car's headlights earlier. Her outfit reminded him of the carnival gypsies he'd seen at local fairs, except for all the pink. Anyone else might have looked ridiculous in the flamboyant clothes. But, somehow, on her they looked…enchanting. If he'd seen her in a bar he'd be begging for her number and hoping to wind up sharing breakfast with her the next morning.

"Who *are* you?" he repeated, lowering his weapon. The little sprite certainly wasn't a threat to a man his size.

She braced her hands on her hips and tilted her head back to meet his gaze. "A local, which you obviously are not."

"That syrupy accent of yours doesn't make you sound like a local, either." He cocked his head, mirroring the same look she'd just given him. "But what makes you think *I'm* not a local?"

She snorted in a completely unladylike manner. It was hard for Jake not to grin and to maintain his serious look.

"Oh, please," she said. "You're oblivious to the dangers around here. You might as well wear a neon sign that says 'city slicker.'"

Her delightful accent was as intoxicating as her curvy figure. His fingers itched to slide around her tiny waist and pull her against him just to see how the two of them would fit. He gave himself a mental shake. Now was not the time to let his attention wander. He needed to focus. Finding this woman near Gillette's car couldn't be a coincidence. She must know something about what had happened. Maybe she'd even been a passenger in his car. That thought had Jake glancing around the clearing, his shoulders tensing. Was Gillette hiding in the trees, watching?

"Were you in that car when it crashed?" he asked. "Do you know the driver?"

She smiled as if she had a secret. "You said you were a cop. Show me your badge."

"My name is Jake Young. I don't have a badge because I'm not—"

She whirled around, kicking his feet out from under him so fast that he didn't have time to react. He landed on his backside, blinking up at the dark sky in shock. His flashlight rolled a few feet away, shining its light in a crazy arc. Before he could move, the little firebrand was on top of him holding the tip of a very large knife to his throat.

The last time anyone had gotten the drop on him had been…well, *never.* When the knife pricked his skin, his earlier amusement and distraction vanished in a flood of adrenaline and anger.

The hell with this.

He knocked the knife to the ground and rolled over in one swift movement, trapping her beneath him. Shackling both her wrists in one of his hands, he forced her arms above her head, using his body to pin her to the ground. But as soon as he felt her soft curves pressed to his and breathed in the flowery, feminine scent of her, he knew he'd made a tactical mistake. Especially when the breeze blew one of her silky curls against his face. *She* wasn't the one who was trapped. *He* was, trapped in a sensual hell of his own making. He silently cursed himself a dozen ways to Sunday.

She just tried to shoot you. She's not your potential next girlfriend. Get a grip.

"Let's start the introductions over," he growled, more angry with himself than her. "I'm Jake Young, from Lassiter and Young Private Investigations. And what I was trying to say earlier is that I don't have a badge with me because I'm on leave from my police detective job in Saint Augustine. I don't have jurisdiction around here. But that doesn't change who *you* are—the woman who's about to be arrested for attempted murder when I call the Collier County Sheriff's Office."

Her soft pink lips curved in an amused smile. "Oh, you think so, huh?"

"I know so."

In answer, she wiggled beneath him and tugged her arms, trying to free them.

A cold sweat broke out on his brow at his body's instant, unwelcome response to her sensual movements. He swore and shifted his weight, hoping she wouldn't notice her effect on him.

"Who are you?" he repeated between clenched teeth.

"Let me go and I'll tell you."

"So you can shoot at me again, or kick my feet out from under me, or stab me? I don't think so."

She huffed out a breath. "You're looking at this all wrong. I didn't shoot at *you*. And the only reason I knocked you down and pulled my knife was because I thought that you'd tricked me when you yelled 'police' and then said you didn't have a badge. What's a girl to think? I'm vulnerable, in a secluded area, with a stranger

I believed was pretending to be a police officer. I have a right, a duty, to do whatever I can to protect myself."

He laughed without humor. "It's a little late to pull the helpless female act. Now *that's* a lie if I've ever heard one."

She beamed up at him as if he'd given her a compliment.

"Your name," he demanded.

"Like it really matters. My name is Faye Star."

Faye Star? He let the name sink in as he studied her more closely. "Miss or Mrs.?"

Her sinfully luscious lips curved in a suggestive smile. But her eyes were like a road sign flashing a warning, *danger ahead.*

"For you, it's definitely Miss," she purred.

He ruthlessly tamped down the inappropriate tingle of awareness that shot straight to his groin.

"Miss Star, for the last time, why did you try to shoot me?"

Her brows drew down as if he'd insulted her. "If I was *trying* to shoot you, you'd be dead right now. Like I said, I wasn't aiming at you."

"Right. How stupid of me to think you *were* aiming at me since you shot out the window and hit the side of the car where I was standing just seconds before."

"I shot *exactly* what I wanted to shoot."

"The car?" He didn't bother to mask the sarcasm in his tone.

"No, silly. The snake." She rolled her head to the side, angling her chin in an effort to point. "Over there."

He followed the direction she'd indicated. Lying under the driver's door of the car was the longest, fattest snake Jake had ever seen. Its head had been blown clean off. And its enormous body was sliced in half.

The breath hitched in his throat. He blinked in shock, again.

"That's a boa constrictor," she said, "in case you don't recognize it. It's not native to these parts but there are plenty of the buggers around. People dump them in the swamp after their *harmless* pets grow too big and eat the family dog. It was hanging on a branch above the car and dropped down when you were looking through the window. I saved your life. This is the part where you're supposed to apologize. And let go of my wrists. And get off me."

He shook his head, grudgingly admiring her skill with a gun. He'd have been hard-pressed to make those two shots himself if the snake really had been falling as she'd said. He climbed to his feet, pulling her up with him.

"You could have shouted a warning instead of almost shooting me."

"I told you, I always—"

"Hit what you aim at, yeah, got it. You still could have missed."

Her eyes flashed green fire.

"I'm going to release you," he said. "But be warned. If you go for your knife it won't end well."

She glanced longingly at the thick, six-inch blade lying on the ground a few feet away. Where she'd hidden the thing he didn't even want to know.

She shrugged. "I'll get it later."

"Don't count on it." He let go of her wrists.

She frowned and tossed her long mane of hair out of

her way, before crossing her arms beneath her generous breasts. "What are you doing out here?" she asked.

"Investigating the disappearance of the man who owns that car. And I'm the one asking questions. What are *you* doing out here? Since I don't see any cuts or bruises, I'm going to assume you weren't in that car when it crashed. But I didn't notice any other vehicles parked beside the highway, either."

"I live around here."

"For some reason that doesn't even surprise me. Where? In a tree house?"

Her eyes narrowed dangerously. "As a matter of fact, no." She fluttered her fingers over her shoulder, the moonlight glinting on the half-dozen rings she wore. "A few miles that way."

"Uh-huh. And you just happened to be wandering through the Everglades at ten o'clock at night."

She shrugged. "I couldn't sleep, so I went for a walk."

At his skeptical look she added, "A *long* walk."

"Of course you did." He retrieved his gun from where it had fallen when she'd kicked his legs out from under him and pulled his cell phone out again.

"What are you doing?" Her voice sharpened as if in alarm.

He gave her a curious glance. "Calling the police. Is that a problem?" He shoved his gun in the holster at his waist.

"It is if you're trying to have me arrested. I told you I wasn't shooting at you."

"Call me an idiot, but I believe you about that. I'm calling to report that I found Calvin Gillette's car. They'll need to process the scene and get some men out here to search for the driver."

Some kind of emotion flickered across her face, so quickly he couldn't identify it. Anger? Fear? Or something else?

"Did you see the man who drove that car?" he asked again.

A low rumble sounded from the direction of the bushes where Faye had emerged a few moments earlier.

Jake yanked out his gun and shoved Faye behind his back as he whirled around. Was the panther still out here, stalking them? Or was that more of a curse than a growl? Was Gillette hiding in the trees, armed, ready to make sure Jake didn't make that call?

A full minute passed in silence. No more growls or curses. No rustling of leaves to indicate anything, or anyone, was there. He cautiously straightened and turned back to Faye.

She was gone.

So were her knife and her rifle.

Damn it.

He clenched his hand around his pistol. The one potential witness to whatever had happened to Calvin Gillette had just disappeared. She'd probably orchestrated that growl to distract him. Maybe she was a ventriloquist and a gypsy fairy all rolled into one.

The growl sounded again, closer, vibrating with malevolence.

Jake sprinted to the car, yanked the door open and jumped inside.

Chapter Two

After notifying the Collier County Sheriff's Office about finding Gillette's car, Jake was told there weren't any available units to respond yet and that he should sit tight and guard the scene. He waited, sitting in Gillette's car, watching the woods in case the anticipated panther showed up. But the cat never appeared. Neither did the police. Had he known it would have taken all night, he would have gone home and gotten a much better night's rest than he had in the car—panther or no panther.

While waiting for the police, Jake had given in to the urge to search the car, carefully using his shirt as a glove. But he'd found nothing. He'd also called his client to update him on his progress.

By the time the police arrived and managed to cut through the chain link and get their teams into the clearing, the sun had been up for over three hours.

Jake shifted his weight against the pine tree behind him. The police wouldn't let him accompany them as they searched the woods for Gillette, so he was stuck here waiting, and watching the crime scene techs process the scene. But the hurried manner in which they were working had him clenching his jaw so tightly his teeth ached.

"Something bothering you, Mr. Young?" Scott Holder, the Collier County deputy in charge of the scene, said as he stopped beside him.

"It just seems as if your men are in an awful hurry."

Holder crossed his arms. "You're not from around here are you?"

Really? This again? Jake was tempted to check whether he was wearing a sign around his neck that said "Outsider." He shook his head. "No, I'm not from around here, not originally. I just moved from Saint Augustine a couple of months ago. Why?"

"If you knew this area, you'd understand how to interpret the signs."

So they were back to signs again. "Meaning?"

"Meaning, if you look at the branches that were broken along the path the car took to get in here, you'd see they're turning brown. They aren't freshly broken. This crash happened several days ago, probably the same day the driver went missing."

He seemed to be waiting for Jake to say something. "I understand what you're saying, but what's that got to do with processing the scene?"

Holder smiled the kind of tolerant smile one would give a toddler. "Any clues outside the car that could have helped us figure out where the driver went have been washed away in the heavy rains we've had. So there isn't much point in spending hours and hours scouring the mud. As for the car's interior, we'll process that back at the station. But I haven't seen anything that will help with the investigation. Where Gillette disappeared to is just as much a mystery now as it was when his friend reported him missing."

Jake still didn't agree with going so fast when processing a scene. But he bit back any further comments. He couldn't afford to make enemies of local law enforcement. His long-distance business partner, Dex Lassiter, wouldn't appreciate it if Jake's first big case in their joint venture damaged their chances of cooperation from the police on future cases.

Holder crossed his arms and braced his legs apart as he watched his men combing the ground beside the car for clues. "We looked for Gillette that first day and couldn't find head nor tail of him. And I certainly never expected he could have crashed out here without triggering the cable warning system. What led you to this location?"

"Incentive."

Holder raised a brow in question.

Jake smiled reluctantly. "I need to pay my rent, on both my apartment and my new business. The man who hired me to find Gillette is my first well-paying client. So, I've been busting my hump to figure out what happened. I interviewed dozens of people in Naples near his home and figured out that he'd driven down Alligator Alley the morning he disappeared. I became a pest at the rest areas asking commuters if they'd seen a maroon Ford Taurus the day he went missing. A handful of them thought they may have seen his car. I was able to narrow it down to a five-mile section of highway."

Holder had the grace to flush a light red. "Reckon we could have done the same, but our resources are limited with a heavy caseload. And it never occurred to me that he could have crashed his car out here without triggering the cable system."

Jake didn't bother to remind him that it had happened once before. He sympathized with Holder's position.

He knew all about budgets and manpower and prioritizing cases.

"I don't remember you telling me the name of the client who hired you," Holder said.

"That's because I didn't." And he didn't intend to. Quinn had been very specific about that. He didn't want to risk a leak that could spook Gillette if he somehow heard that the FBI was actively looking for him.

Holder's mouth tightened but he didn't press the issue.

Half an hour later, the CSI team finished its work, and the tow truck driver began the laborious job of winching the car out of the woods using the long cable attached to his truck parked on the shoulder of the highway.

Jake accompanied Deputy Holder to firmer ground and they both watched from beside Jake's Charger as the Taurus was hauled up the slope. Less than an hour later, the deputies who'd been searching the woods for Gillette emerged from the trees and climbed up on the shoulder to confer with Holder. Jake figured they'd found something, or were requesting more equipment. Instead, Holder clapped a few of them on the back and signaled to the DOT crew waiting by the fence. The workers immediately rolled the chain link into place and began refastening it to the poles.

"What's going on?" Jake asked.

Holder turned to him. "The search is over. They didn't find a trail, nothing to indicate where Gillette might have gone. They went all the way back to the marsh. We'll do some flyovers in a helicopter, put out the word on the news, but there's nothing else we can do here."

Frustration had Jake's hands tightening into fists at

his sides. Gillette was a seedy character who lived under the radar, taking odd jobs for cash. And he was rumored to be a petty thief in addition to the background Quinn had supplied. But that didn't mean he shouldn't get the same attention a more affluent or socially prominent person would receive in the same situation.

"I don't understand," Jake said, trying again. "You know he has to be around here somewhere. He couldn't have just vanished."

"If I thought there was any chance he was still alive, or that we could locate his body, I'd throw everything I had at him. But I don't, and none of my men do either."

Jake tamped down his anger. He didn't know this area, its dangers. Maybe Holder was right, even though everything about this felt wrong.

"Then what do you think happened to him?" Jake asked.

"The same thing that happens to anyone lost out here this long—gators, snakes, other wild animals. More than likely his remains will never be found. We had a DC-9 crash into the Everglades just west of Miami years ago. Barely left a trace to show it had ever existed. You have to respect the environment around here and understand how it all works if you're going to thrive or survive."

There was no mistaking the hard glint in Holder's eyes, or his harsh undertone. The double meaning behind his words was clear. *Jake* needed to respect the Collier County Sheriff's Office if his *business* was going to thrive. Jake gave the deputy a curt nod, letting him know he got the message.

The remaining emergency vehicles and DOT truck headed out, leaving Jake and Holder alone on the shoulder beside their cars. What little traffic had backed up at this noonday hour was quickly getting back to normal.

"Did your team find anything useful that would at least explain why Gillette was driving east down Alligator Alley?" Jake asked.

"Not yet. My guys will process the evidence back in Naples, search his apartment again and interview a few more people. I'll also have some officers canvass the rest stops and recreational areas on I-75 for potential witnesses. If we find anything, I'll give you a call."

"What about the potential witness I already told you about, Faye Star? Are you going to interview her?" At Holder's exasperated look, Jake said, "I know you think Gillette's dead, but until I know for sure, I have to keep investigating. I think she might know something, or she saw something."

Holder let out a deep sigh. "Faye Star? Can't say I've ever heard of her. Did she give you an address?"

"Only a vague direction. She wasn't exactly cooperative. She waved her hand southwest and said she lived a few miles 'that way,'" Jake said. "Without a car she can't live far from here. She certainly didn't walk all the way from Naples. Are there any towns nearby?"

"Not really." He rubbed his jaw, looking hesitant. "I suppose you could try Mystic Glades."

Jake pulled out his cell phone and opened up a map on his screen. He typed in the name of the town, but nothing came up. "I'm not finding it. Mystic Glades you said?"

"You won't find it on any map. It's unincorporated, not even a real town. It's more like a collection of houses and a few businesses that just kind of popped up in the middle of the swamp. It was created using leftover buildings that housed construction workers when Alligator Alley was being built decades ago."

"Is it back toward Naples or the other way?"

"Other way. About ten miles east, around mile marker eighty-four."

"Ten miles? I don't think Miss Star would have hoofed it back that far at night in an area this dangerous."

Holder shrugged. "There's nothing else around here that I know of, although I suppose it's possible. You said she was uncooperative, didn't want to talk to you. Well, maybe she had an ATV. She could have pushed it until she was far enough away that you wouldn't hear the engine when she turned it on."

"Maybe so. But I'm still not sure where this Mystic Glades is located. I've been up and down this highway since yesterday morning. I don't remember a town close by, even an unincorporated one."

"It's a bit back from the road, sheltered in one of those tree islands in the saw grass marsh, right where it starts to get really wet and the cypress trees begin. There's a road, of sorts, leading off Alligator Alley to the town. Or so I hear." He fished his keys out of his pocket, seeming anxious to leave.

"What do you mean, 'so I hear'? You've never been there?"

"Nope. Got no reason to. I'll call you if we find anything on Gillette." He hurried to his car before Jake could ask him any more questions. If Jake didn't know better, he'd think the idea of going to Mystic Glades had Holder…scared. But that didn't make sense.

The deputy's tires kicked up dirt on the side of the road as he took off. He headed down the highway to make the turn toward Naples, leaving Jake alone, just like last night—minus Gillette's car. And minus the mysterious woman calling herself Faye Star.

He shook his head, thoroughly confused and aggravated over Holder's lack of interest in helping him. But searching the woods where Gillette's car was found, when the experts deemed it too dangerous, wasn't an option Jake wanted to pursue on his own. However, finding Faye Star was like a godsend, a bonus. He'd bet money that she knew more about the crash than she'd told him. And she just might be able to lead him to Gillette, assuming Gillette was still alive. Jake sure hoped so. He was acting as a pseudo-bounty hunter on this case. And if he couldn't produce Gillette, his fee would be cut in half.

A few minutes later he was driving toward mile marker eighty-four, searching for a road to a town that wasn't even a real town.

The traffic was light, but Jake still kept an eye out for other cars and trucks. Alligator Alley was notorious for accidents. The eastern portion in Broward County was hemmed in by acres of saw grass that lured drivers into boredom and inattention. This western portion was just as monotonous, with its endless miles of pines bordering the highway, hiding the beauty of the marsh, canals and tree islands behind them.

But the deadliest ingredient to the crashes was the high speeds. Jake didn't want to become a statistic because some driver hitting the hundred-mile-per-hour mark didn't realize how slow Jake was going until they were on his bumper. For that reason, he pulled to the shoulder whenever he saw a fast-moving car coming up from the rear.

It took two passes and a full hour before he found the entrance to the nearly hidden road. It was where Holder had said, but so hidden he'd never have found it without specifically looking for it. And even though he was heading east, he had to make a sharp 180-degree turn right after a guardrail and drive parallel to the highway on a steep incline beside the wildlife fence to follow the road. It would have been the perfect spot for a speed trap, because no one up on the highway could see it down here.

When he reached a canal that ran beneath I-75, the dirt road turned the opposite way, directly toward the wildlife fence. As he neared the fence, it slid open to allow his car through. It must have had an electric sensor. But since it was right by the area where wildlife was funneled beneath the highway, it was unlikely any of the critters would have a reason to go near this section of the fence. The design of this little road seemed genius—almost completely hidden but still maintaining the integrity of the protective fences to keep drivers on the highway safe from wild animals running across the road.

About eight miles later he'd driven through several groves of oaks and pines, through a small raised section of road surrounded by saw grass, and then back into a thick tree island with bogs and marsh on both sides of the road. But he still hadn't located the illusive town. And for some reason the GPS map in his car was going nuts, its directional arrows blinking off and on. One moment it appeared he was traveling south, the next moment the GPS said he was going north. The crazy thing was completely useless. He tried punching up a map on his cell phone but there were no bars, no connection. He cursed and shoved it back in his pocket.

He was debating performing a three-point turn to head back to the highway when a black blur ran across the road in front of him. He skidded sideways, narrowly missing a panther—just like last night—and barely managing to keep his car from sliding into the marsh.

The wild cat bounded into the woods on the south side of the road, or at least, the direction Jake *thought* was south. Apparently the endangered panthers weren't quite as rare as they were alleged to be in this area. Either that, or the same animal was stalking him.

He shook his head at that fanciful thought and straightened his car out. He decided to give it a few more minutes before giving up and turning around, so he started forward again. He rounded a curve and slammed his brakes. The Charger shuddered to a stop. Ahead of him, a small, faded wooden sign shaped like an alligator declared the scattering of wooden buildings barely visible through the trees behind it as Mystic Glades.

But he didn't need the sign to tell him he'd arrived at his destination. Just like last night, a little pixie was standing there staring at him. She was in the middle of the road, in a breast-hugging lavender top, her lavender skirts flirting with the tops of her mud-caked combat boots.

And just like last night, she was pointing a rifle at him.

Chapter Three

Faye couldn't believe her dumb luck and incredibly bad timing as she aimed the rifle at the grille of the black Dodge Charger. With the sun peeking through the trees behind her, she couldn't see the driver through the glare on the windshield. But she didn't need to. She'd seen that same car parked on the highway last night as she'd pushed Buddy's ATV along the edge of the trees. She knew exactly who it belonged to—the incredibly hot, but potentially dangerous cop playing at private investigator, Jake Young.

Pointing a gun at him wasn't the smartest decision she could have made. But as soon as she'd seen him rounding the curve she'd panicked. She'd tossed her purple backpack behind a tree and brought her rifle up. Now she had no choice but to "bravado" her way through this second meeting, and hope it was their last.

The engine cut off and the driver's door opened.

"You might as well crank that engine and go back where you came from." She tightened her fingers around the gun's stock. "This is private property."

"You own the whole town?" he quipped as he stood.

It took her several seconds to remember what they were talking about after she saw those broad shoulders again and those yummy muscular arms, that rock-hard-looking chest tapering to his narrow, powerful hips. *Yum.* Everything about him, from his dark, wavy hair to the boots he was sensible enough to wear out here, had her fighting not to drool. But now wasn't the right time for those kinds of thoughts. And without knowing *why* he was trying to find Calvin, it was too dangerous for her to even consider being his friend, much less anything more intimate.

What a shame.

She cleared her throat and hoped she hadn't stared long enough for him to realize what she'd been thinking.

"We're all family here in town, more or less," she said. "I speak for everyone when I tell you that you're not welcome." *Unfortunately.*

"I just want to talk. I need to ask you about Calvin Gillette." He stepped out from behind the open door.

Faye almost whimpered. In the daylight, he looked even better than he had last night. Too bad she had to make him leave.

"I don't know who you're talking about," she said, trying to think of how to make him *want* to go. She debated shooting the car's radiator. But that would just disable it and give him an excuse to continue into town. And she really couldn't stomach shooting such a fine car. It was exactly the kind of car she'd have chosen if she could afford one, and if she had a driver's license. All shiny, glossy black with an engine that rumbled and purred like a well-fed cat.

"Now, why don't I believe you?" he said.

"Not my problem."

His boots crunched on the dirt-and-gravel road. She swung her rifle, following his progress.

"Stop right there," she ordered.

He continued as if he didn't think she'd really shoot.

Would she? Not normally. But desperate times…

She brought the rifle up to her shoulder and centered a bead on his chest.

He stopped about ten feet away, his eyes narrowing. "How about pointing that thing somewhere else before one of us gets hurt."

"It's pointed right where I want it. I'm going to start counting. If you don't turn around and get back in your car by the time I reach five—"

He charged forward.

She was so surprised, she froze. He was almost on top of her before she swung the rifle a bit to the left and pulled the trigger, hoping to scare him into stopping.

Bam! The rifle cracked, barely missing him, just as she'd planned. But instead of stopping, he lunged forward and wrenched the gun out of her hands. He tossed it away and glared down at her, his dark eyes smoldering with fury.

"Give me one reason not to call the police to arrest you for shooting at me. Again," he demanded.

She craned her neck back to meet his gaze. "Because your cell phone probably won't work out here anyway?"

His eyes narrowed to a dangerous slit.

"Okay, okay." She held her hands up in a placating gesture. "Don't get so worked up. I wasn't shooting at you. I missed on purpose."

The skin across his jaw whitened beneath his tan. Obviously the man had no sense of humor and took things far too seriously.

"You're one of those ill-tempered Aries, aren't you?" she accused.

"Sagittarius," he snapped. "And just how is that relevant to you *shooting at me*?"

His declaration that he was a Sagittarius surprised some of the sting out of his insult that she'd ever miss something she aimed at. She automatically reached for the chain around her neck, but stopped before pulling it out. "No reason. None at all." She smoothed her hands down her skirts and tried to gauge his mood.

He took another step toward her, bringing them so close she could feel the delicious heat from his body. But her attraction to him was dwarfed by the formidable anger evident in every line in his body. He was as tense as a wound-up spring, ready to snap. And she was, unfortunately, the object of that anger.

If he were anyone else, she'd sweep his legs out from under him and go for her knife hidden in one of the many secret pockets in her skirt. But she realized two things at once. First, he didn't seem like the kind of man to fall for the same trick twice. And second, if she didn't hightail it out of here, right now, she might be in real trouble.

As if sensing she was about to flee, he grabbed for her. She ducked beneath his arms, taking advantage of their difference in height. She ran as if a whole nest of hungry gators was after her.

He shouted some impressively colorful phrases and took off in pursuit, his boots pounding against the hard ground, his long strides rapidly eating up the distance between them. But she figured she had the advantage. He might be spitting mad, but she firmly believed her very survival was at stake, which made her feet fairly fly.

There was only one place of refuge with him so close: his car. She skidded around the open driver's door and jumped inside. She slammed it shut and punched the electric lock just as he reached her and yanked on the handle.

He leaned down, silently promising retribution as he glared at her through the window.

"Open. The. Door." His deep voice vibrated with anger, pounding through her skin like a hammer against a nail.

She shook her head, her long hair flying around her face. "Not a good idea."

"Now."

Did he think making his voice sound as if he wanted to tear her apart with his bare hands would make her more inclined to remove the only barrier between them? That was the problem with a Sagittarius—too unwilling and impatient to slow down and look beneath the surface to all the subtleties of a situation before jumping into action. Then again, sex with a Sagittarius lover, especially with a Libra—like her—could be explosive and make that overbearing nature superhot.

Counting on the fated attraction between their astrological signs to help her out, she aimed her most seductive smile at him.

If anything, his glare got worse. *Oh, dear.*

"Open the door, Miss Star."

"Not until you calm down." She added a contrite smile this time. But since being contrite wasn't in her nature, she wasn't sure she'd succeeded.

He stared at her for a good long while, as if he was considering all the different ways he could torture her before he killed her. Then he shoved his right hand into his jeans pocket. When he pulled his hand out, he dangled something in the air for her to see.

Keys.

Shoot. She hadn't even thought about starting the car or she'd have realized the keys weren't in the ignition. She tightened her fingers on the steering wheel, desperately considering her options. Jake Young didn't know her connection to Calvin or he'd have used her legal name instead of "Star." Which meant, he probably wasn't the man Calvin had called her about when he'd taken that disastrous, ill-fated trip down Alligator Alley on his way to Mystic Glades.

But if Jake wasn't someone from her and Calvin's past trying to find them, who was he working for? Had Calvin gotten into "new" trouble in Naples? Was that why someone was after him this time? It certainly was preferable to the alternative, and might mean that Jake wasn't a threat to *her.* Well, except for the part where he wanted to find Calvin, and she wasn't about to help him do that. And the part where she'd shot a gun around him several times now, and the stubborn man refused to understand she wasn't shooting *at* him.

Sunlight flashed off the keys in Jake's hand as he shook them out, making them jangle as if he were a prison guard about to take an inmate out for his last walk before his execution. Or *hers.* His lips curved in a feral smile. He pointed to the small black rectangle on his key chain—an electronic key fob.

Faye's breath hitched in her chest.

Jake poised his thumb over the unlock button.

She poised *her* finger over the lock button on the inside of the door.

They faced off like two duelers at dawn, trigger fingers cocked and loaded, each waiting for the other to flinch.

Click. The door unlocked.

Click. Faye locked it again just as he grabbed the door handle.

Click.

Click.

Click, click, click, click.

His eyes narrowed.

She licked her lips, focusing on that damn thumb of his on the key fob.

Click, thump. He managed to unlock the door and lift the handle a split second before she pressed her button again.

Game over.

She scrambled over the middle console, cursing when her left knee slammed against the gearshift, sending a sharp jolt of pain down her leg. She fell on the slippery leather of the passenger seat, fumbling for the opposite door handle. She pulled it and shoved the door open.

"Oh no, you don't," he growled.

She felt, rather than saw, him lean inside to grab her from the driver's side. She pulled herself toward the opening and dived like a world champion. There was a tug against her waist, a ripping sound, and then she was free! She rolled out of the way a split second before he landed on the ground where she'd just been.

She was already splashing through the marsh, sprinting for the cover of trees, when she heard his bellow of rage behind her. It wasn't until she'd entered the much cooler air beneath the pines and knotty cypress, and felt the rush of air against her thighs, that she realized what her narrow escape had cost.

Her skirt.

JAKE STARED AT the surprisingly heavy handful of soft purple fabric in his hand. He supposed he should feel guilty. But once he'd recovered from his anger that Faye was getting away, he'd been too busy enjoying the view of her toned, gorgeous backside adorned in a lacy purple thong to do more than sag against his car and enjoy the show.

He shook his head in disgust. How had everything gotten so out of hand? He retrieved the rifle the half-naked pixie had pointed at him earlier, unloaded it and pitched the shells in the back floorboard of his car. Then he carried both the gun and the fluff of material to the tree line where she'd disappeared.

Taking devilish delight in knowing she'd have to spend hours cleaning it to make the gun usable again, he shoved the barrel of the rifle into the muck beside the road. With the butt of the gun standing up in the air, he was about to drape the skirt over the top when something heavy banged against the rifle. He felt along the fabric and found a hidden pocket, a deep pocket that contained the wicked-looking knife she'd threatened him with last night.

The evil-looking blade winked in the sunlight as if it were laughing at him. He carefully ran the rest of the fabric through his hands. But although he found more hidden pockets, they were empty. He draped the ruined skirt over the end of the rifle and added the knife to the rifle rounds in his floorboard.

He got back in his car and headed toward Mystic Glades again. He was just passing the alligator-shaped sign when he spotted something purple off to his left beside a tree. He braked and got out, drawing his pistol in case Faye had somehow managed to get past him to the other side of the road and had another gun hidden… somewhere.

When he reached the tree he discovered it wasn't Faye hiding there. It was a purple backpack that so perfectly matched the color of her outfit it had to be hers. He crouched down and rummaged inside, cataloging the contents: bottles of water, power bars, a towel, a first aid kit. Not the kind of supplies someone generally carried for a "walk." It was exactly the kind of supplies she might have if she were trying to find someone who'd gotten lost in the wilderness after a car wreck.

FAYE HAD RUN a good long way before she'd reached firm, dry ground. After finding a relatively clean-looking log, she perched on it to wait. She didn't know how long she sat there. But from watching the way the shadows moved, she figured it was at least an hour, long enough that Jake would have given up by now and gone back to Naples.

To be certain that he was gone, she'd have preferred to wait longer. But time was a luxury she didn't have. She couldn't afford to waste any daylight. Searching at night had proved far too dangerous, in more ways than one. So she wasn't going to do that again. But how could she search for Calvin if Jake Young was hanging around?

The battery on Calvin's phone had died yesterday while he was talking to her and he was hopelessly lost. He couldn't even give her any landmarks to help her find him. After surviving that horrendous crash, he'd foolishly headed *into* the woods instead of to the highway. His excuse was that he was afraid he was being followed, and he didn't want to risk being seen. But Faye wished he'd at least have waited until she got there. She could have found him that first night and she wouldn't have backtracked last night to restart her search and run into Jake Young.

Her only comfort was that Calvin had packed supplies as she'd instructed—something she always encouraged anyone to do before venturing into the Everglades—and he had the basics he needed to survive. Well, assuming he didn't step on an alligator, of course. Or get bitten by a snake. Hopefully he'd heard enough of her own ventures in the 'Glades to know what to look out for. But no amount of book smarts could trump experience.

The sun was high in the sky now, about midday. She couldn't wait any longer, especially since she didn't have any weapons to protect herself out here. She was breaking all her own rules by being in the marsh without survival gear.

After a careful look around for predators, she jogged back toward the road. When she finally reached the archway over the entrance to Mystic Glades, she was relieved that the black Charger was gone. But discovering her ruined skirt fluttering in the breeze on top of her upside-down rifle, its nose shoved deep in the bog, had her cursing long and hard. If Jake were here right now she'd lob her knife, end over end, to bury itself in the dirt at his feet just for the pleasure of making him jump.

Wait, her knife. It had been in the skirt. She grabbed the fabric and groaned. It was far too light, which meant Jake had found—and taken—her knife. That was one more sin she could add to her growing list of grievances against the man, Sagittarius or not.

She tied the ragged edges of her skirt around her

waist. It was a disaster, but at least it covered her bottom. It took three tugs of the rifle before the mud released it with a big sucking sound, making Faye stumble backward and reigniting her anger.

A car rumbled up the road. Was Jake returning already? She rushed behind the nearest tree. The car came around the last curve and she relaxed. Not Jake. It was Freddie, probably with cases of moonshine in her trunk to stock up before Callahan's Watering Hole opened for business later tonight. Four more cars passed to and from Mystic Glades. Practically a rush hour for the amount of traffic that normally went up and down this road.

Most of the locals relied on swamp buggies for transportation and headed through the saw grass marsh behind town to barter and trade goods with others who lived the nomadic lifestyle. But it was occasionally necessary to make the long drive down Alligator Alley to bring back more substantial supplies, to exchange mail or even to go to a traditional job. Some of the town's inhabitants worked on the Gulf Coast in Naples. Others worked for the DOT, keeping the wildlife fencing and roads in good repair. Still others worked at the rest stops along I-75.

Faye did none of those things. She lived above the little shop she ran, The Moon and Star. Thankfully, with the orders she received from her catalog, she made enough money to pay Amy to help her part-time. Amy was at the shop right now. Faye didn't want to open herself up to questions about her state of undress. But she didn't have a choice.

She hadn't had a reason to bring her keys with her this morning, which meant she couldn't go in through the back door. She'd just have to keep to the trees so no one would see her until she reached the store. Then she could duck inside, make up some kind of story to placate Amy, and go upstairs to shower and change. After that, she could start another search. But first she needed to retrieve the backpack she'd hidden before Jake Young drove up.

After making sure no more cars were coming in or out of town, she raced to the other side of the road. She reached for her backpack. It wasn't there. She frowned. This was where she'd tossed it, wasn't it? She turned in a slow circle but didn't see the flash of purple anywhere. Instead, she saw muddy boot prints. She hadn't misplaced her backpack.

Jake Young took it.

Cold dread snaked up her spine. Did he understand the significance of what she'd had in that pack? He might be a greenhorn but he didn't strike her as dumb. After finding her at the crash site last night, and seeing the supplies she had in her pack, he had to have connected the dots. He had to know she'd lied and that she was trying to find Calvin.

She pressed a shaky hand to her stomach. Okay, no reason to panic. Not yet. Think this through. All she knew for sure was that a private investigator was trying to find Calvin. But he hadn't mentioned anything about finding *her*. If someone from Tuscaloosa had hired him, they'd have wanted both her and Calvin, wouldn't they? But Jake hadn't tried to grab her…or *kill* her. Which meant he didn't know about her connection with Calvin, and he wasn't sent by any of Genovese's associates.

So far, so good. That had to mean that whoever had hired Jake was from Naples. The worst that could mean, unless Calvin had done something really bad he hadn't admitted to since moving to this area, was that he'd skipped out on some debts. Maybe a finance company had hired Jake to deliver a summons to take him to court.

Okay, that would be bad, too. That would put Calvin in the public eye again, which would make it easy for their enemies to find him, and her. Shoot. No matter how she looked at this it was bad. There was only one thing left to do.

She looked at the archway over the entrance to Mystic Glades, sorrow heavy in her heart. This was her home, the only place that had ever felt like home. But from the moment she'd met Jake Young, this was no longer her sanctuary. It was no longer safe to stay, either for her or the people she loved. It was time to leave. Time to find a new place to hide.

Chapter Four

Jake balanced his ladder-back chair against the wall behind him in the office of The Moon and Star, listening to his slightly inebriated new friend, Freddie, regale him with stories about a certain little golden-haired pixie. Since his latest run-in with Faye, when she'd nearly shot him—again—Jake didn't feel even a little guilty about the lies he'd told her friends. Both Freddie and Amy, the young girl taking care of customers out in the main part of the store, now believed Jake and Faye had dated in the past and that he was here to surprise her.

She'd be surprised all right, especially since his car was hidden behind the shop so she wouldn't know he was here until it was too late for her to avoid him.

Freddie—which Jake assumed was short for Fredericka—licked a drop of whiskey off her shockingly red lips and held the bottle up to top off Jake's already half-full shot glass.

He hurried to cover the glass with his hand. It was still too early for him to indulge in more than the few sips he'd taken to keep Freddie talking. And he needed to keep his wits about him for the inevitable confrontation coming up with Faye.

"Thanks, but I've had plenty."

Freddie shook her gray-streaked, faded orange hair in bewilderment and topped off her glass with more of the amber liquid. "No such thing as plenty when it comes to quality refreshment." She tossed the whiskey back in one swallow, her throat working and her eyes closing as she obviously enjoyed the burn. "Ain't nothing like Hennessey, my friend," she said when she opened her eyes. "I was saving that bottle for a special occasion. And this is definitely a special occasion, meetin' Faye's beau."

That formerly nonexistent guilt started niggling at Jake's conscience. He didn't want to go overboard with his fabrications and disappoint Freddie once she found out the truth. Apparently, in the thirteen months that Faye had rented this store and upstairs apartment from Freddie, she'd never once dated. Which seemed to make Freddie all the more eager to bring the two of them "back together."

"Now, Freddie," Jake said, "I didn't exactly say I was her *beau*. I just said we used to be special friends back in high school."

For perhaps the dozenth time since she'd started tossing back shots, Freddie giggled. Jake didn't think he could ever get used to hearing that particular sound coming from a husky, bear of a woman who looked as if she could arm-wrestle just about any man and win—including Jake.

"I know what 'special friends' means," Freddie said, punctuating her statement with air quotes. "I had a few special friends back in my day. Why, when I wasn't much younger than you must be now, I had a *very* special friend, Johnny Green." She shook her head and finger-combed a strand of hair that had escaped her ponytail. Her faded blue eyes took on a faraway look as she began to describe, in lurid detail, exactly what she and Johnny used to do that was so special.

After a decade as a cop and being in all kinds of crazy situations, there wasn't much that could embarrass Jake. But he could feel his cheeks growing warm, listening to the graphic descriptions Freddie was using to describe things Jake really didn't want to hear about. Especially from a woman old enough to be his grandmother. He was about to beg her to stop when the bell over the front door rang.

Saved by the bell. Thank God.

The low hum of feminine voices told Jake that Amy and Faye were talking to each other. Amy was supposed to tell Faye that Freddie was in the back and needed to see her. That little twinge of guilt reared its ugly head again. Amy couldn't be a day more than eighteen and had been incredibly easy to fool with his lies. And here he was, corrupting her and getting her to lie, too.

There was probably a special place in hell waiting for him right now.

"Freddie, what are you doing back there?" Faye called out. "Is there a problem at the bar?"

"Nope, I'm just testing out my newest whiskey before I open tonight," she yelled back. As if to prove her point, she tipped her glass and drained it.

"I hope you haven't been waiting too long." Faye's boots clomped on the hardwood floor as she approached the back room. "You wouldn't believe the morning I've had so far. I tore my skirt, lost my knife, and my rifle is ruined. I had a run-in with a mean-tempered city slicker who doesn't know his ass from an alligator. It took a lot longer than I expected to get rid of—"

When she reached the doorway, her feet stopped faster than the rest of her. She had to grab the door frame to keep from pitching forward. She was still dressed in her lavender top. And her torn skirts were hanging provocatively low on her hips, held in place by two veils tied together. Her ever-present rifle was in her right hand, pointing up at the ceiling. The fact that she wasn't pointing it at Jake was probably only because she was too stunned to react. Or, more likely, she was worried it would backfire with all that dirt and mud crammed into the barrel, assuming she'd even managed to find more ammo after he'd unloaded it.

Not eager to test his theories around a trigger-happy woman like Faye, Jake dropped the front legs of his chair to the floor and grabbed the rifle out of her hand.

She blinked as if coming out of a daze and aimed a wounded look at her friend. "What is *he* doing here?"

"I think what you meant to ask," Jake teased as he set the muddy rifle in the corner, well out of her reach, "is why is Freddie drinking with a mean-tempered city slicker?"

Faye flushed a light red.

Freddie slammed her shot glass down and twisted around in her chair, looking behind her. "What city slicker? I don't cotton to none of them."

Jake grinned. Winning Freddie to his side had been easy. Faye was proving to be a lot more challenging.

"I was just telling Freddie that I'm an old friend of yours," he said.

Faye's eyebrows shot up. "You are? I mean, you were? Telling Freddie that?"

He nodded. "I told her some of those old stories about our high school days in Mobile."

She went a little green. She had no way of knowing that Freddie was the one who'd told him where she'd gone to high school and that Jake still knew precious little about her.

"I also told Freddie how we planned on going to the University of Florida together but you ended up going to Florida State University instead. Funny thing is, I guess I got that wrong. Freddie said you didn't go to FSU."

Her face went from green to sickly pale. She glanced at Freddie, obviously wondering exactly how much she'd told Jake. "Um, no, no, I didn't. Freddie, can you give us a—"

"University of Alabama, wasn't that it?" Freddie wiped a trickle of whiskey from her chin, smearing her makeup like a brown streak of mud. "That's where you went to school, right? 'Cause that's where you and Amber met." Freddie smiled up at Jake. "Amber Callahan was my niece. She and Faye used to come here every summer between semesters. Seems like the whole town watched Faye growing up into the fine woman she's become. She and Amber both graduated from UA."

"Explains the accent." Jake lifted his glass in salute. "Roll Tide, roll." He downed his shot of whiskey in one quick swallow. The urge to cough and wheeze was overwhelming, making his eyes water. But he managed to cling to his dignity, just barely, and make it through the storm. Good grief the stuff was strong. He suspected the name on the bottle had nothing to do with the contents and prayed he wouldn't go blind drinking what had to be a homemade brew. It certainly wasn't Hennessey.

He cleared his throat and met Faye's look of impending doom with a smug smile.

"Faye, Faye," Amy yelled from the other room. "Sammie's in trouble out front. CeeCee has him wrapped up tight and it doesn't look like he has his alcohol with him."

Faye whirled around and ran down the hallway toward the front of the store.

Jake cursed and ran after her. CeeCee? Alcohol? He couldn't begin to imagine what he was about to see.

He caught a mind-numbing, lust-inducing view of Faye's gorgeous derriere as she raced out the door, her short, ruined skirt lifting up behind her before the door shut in his face. He yanked it open in time to see her pulling on the silver chain that hung around her neck. She lifted it out of her shirt and there were three small pouches hanging from it. She unsnapped the red one and dropped to her knees.

Right beside a man with an enormous snake wrapped around his neck and chest.

Ah, hell. Jake grabbed his gun and dropped to his knees beside her and a small group of people who'd gathered around the man being squeezed to death by the snake.

"Someone find the snake's head so I can shoot it without shooting this guy," Jake ordered.

"No," the man writhing in the street choked out. "No one kills CeeCee."

Everyone looked at Jake as if he'd just threatened to shoot a baby, or kick a dog.

Faye spilled the powdery contents of the red pouch into her hand. "Bubba, there's his head, against Sammie's throat. Grab it, hold it."

Two older men, probably both in their fifties, reached for the snake's head at the same time.

"Not you," Faye said, motioning to one of them. "The other Bubba."

The stronger-looking of the two grabbed the snake's head and forced it back away from Sammie.

"Hurry," Sammie whispered.

Faye leaned toward the snake.

Jake grabbed her around the waist, holding her back.

"I'm not letting you near that thing," he bit out. "It could kill you."

She gave him a surprised look. "I know what I'm doing. Let me go before CeeCee squeezes so hard Sammie has a heart attack."

He hesitated.

"Trust me," she said. "At least with this."

Since everyone was staring at him as if he were the devil, he reluctantly let her go.

She immediately slathered the red powder on the snake's nostrils and head. "Okay, everybody jump back. Bubba, release CeeCee."

Jake swung Faye up in his arms and backed away from the now violently twisting snake. Faye blinked up at him, confusion warring with some other emotion on her face.

"Catch him, Bubba," Sammie yelled. "I need to wash him off or he'll hurt himself."

Faye and Jake looked back at the street, but everyone had scattered. They were all running toward the trees between two of the buildings, including the man who'd had the constrictor wrapped around him just seconds earlier.

"I guess Sammie is okay." Faye laughed.

"This happens a lot around here?"

She grinned. "Often enough for me to always carry a

pouch of snake repellant. I've told Sammie to keep some rubbing alcohol in his back pocket to use if CeeCee ever confuses him with food. It works almost as well as my repellant. But Sammie tends to forget."

Jake carried her into the store. "Sounds to me like he needs to let his pet go before it kills him."

"That pet is the only reason he gets up every day. It's what he lives for now that his wife is gone. He's all alone except for CeeCee."

He grunted noncommittally and headed down the hall.

Faye stiffened as he neared the staircase that led to her apartment. "You can put me down now. I'm not in any danger, not that I needed you to rescue me in the first place."

"You're welcome," he grumbled.

She rolled her eyes.

He started up the stairs.

Her eyes widened in panic. "Wait. What are you doing? Put me down."

He tightened his hold. "Not a chance. We need to talk. No guns. No knives. And no man-eating snakes. Just you, me and the truth."

Chapter Five

Faye tensed in Jake's arms. She waited until he reached the top of the stairs and set her down to open her door. As soon as he let her go, she rushed inside and whirled around to shut and lock the door. He shoved his boot in the opening, blocking her efforts. There was no way to win against his superior strength, not in a direct confrontation without any tricks. She reluctantly stepped back and let him inside.

Her skirt slid dangerously low. She was forced to grab the tattered edges and retie the veils holding it together. Her face flushed as Jake's gaze followed the movement of her hands, lingering on her exposed tummy before sliding past the skirt to her naked thighs.

She'd flirted with him the first time she met him. But that had been so she could distract him and escape. Maybe he thought it was okay to stare at her like this because of how she'd acted last night. If he were anyone else, she'd have decked him already. But even though she was worried about his investigation, and what his presence here meant for her, she couldn't ignore the punch in her gut every time she looked at him. Attraction sizzled between them. Why did she have to be so turned on by a man whose very presence threatened her entire world?

She stepped back to put some much-needed distance between them, and so she could meet his gaze without craning her neck back at an uncomfortable angle. "How did you figure out where I lived? And how did you manage to turn my friends against me in just a few short hours?"

"Mystic Glades isn't exactly a big city. I drove down the main street and as soon as I saw a shop called The Moon and Star, I figured it had to be yours. When I pulled up front, Freddie came out of the bar across the street. I think she thought she was protecting you by asking me why I was there."

"Let me guess. That's when you lied and told her I was, what, your girlfriend?"

"I might have hinted at something like that. Freddie and Amy both thought the idea was sweet and helped me surprise you. Don't be mad at them."

"Oh, don't worry. *You're* the one I'm mad at, not them. You might as well turn around right now and leave. You're trespassing."

In answer to her edict, he kicked the door closed behind him. He moved farther into the center of the tiny living room-kitchen combo. "You live here? Above the store?" He peeked into the guest bedroom that opened off the right side of the living room. It was empty, except for the twin bed and chest of drawers that had come with the place.

"Where I live isn't any of your business."

As if she hadn't spoken, he crossed to the left side of the living room to *her* bedroom and went inside. He flicked the ballerina-pink comforter on her bed before examining the collection of figurines on her dresser. When he picked up the centaur holding a set of scales, she marched forward and plucked it out of his hand. Had she really found him appealing a minute earlier? She never could stand a bully. And she resented him forcing his way into her private sanctuary. She carefully set the figurine back on the dresser.

"Get out," she ordered.

His smile disappeared in a flash. The cold look that replaced it had her shivering inside and wondering if his earlier smile had been a ruse to make her let down her guard. It would certainly explain how he'd gotten past Freddie's prickly exterior. She couldn't believe it when she'd found her friend drinking with Jake as if they were old buddies.

"Get out, or what?" he said. "You'll call the police? I know I can get service here. I did earlier, down in your office, when I was surfing the internet." He pulled his cell phone out of his jeans pocket and held it out to her. "Be my guest. After they get here, I'll tell them to search their databases for Faye Star. How long do you think it will take them to figure out that Faye Star doesn't exist? And how long before they get curious to find out *why* she doesn't exist?"

The blood rushed from her face, leaving her cold. "That's crazy."

"Is it? I can't find your name in any official databases, not here in Florida." He arched a brow. "Of course, I haven't checked Alabama yet. Maybe I need to surf the web a little more."

Her fingernails bit into her palms. "What do you want from me?"

He stepped closer, crowding her back against the dresser. “I want the truth.”

Faye reached her right hand behind her, quietly pulling one of the drawers open a crack to grab the knife inside. “What truth?” she said, stalling for time. “You’re looking for the guy who drove that car, right? Well, I don’t know where he is. That’s the truth.”

“I don’t believe you.”

“I don’t care.” She fumbled behind her in the drawer.

Jake cocked his head. “What’s wrong, Faye? Can’t find your knife?”

She stilled and dropped her hand to her side. “What did you do, search my apartment before I got here?”

“You’d better believe I did. Self-preservation. I’ve learned never to underestimate you. It was easy getting Freddie to let me up here. I just told her I needed to use the bathroom.”

They faced each other like two boxing opponents, each waiting for the other to make the first move. But Faye knew that fighting him wasn’t an option, not without a weapon and a clear avenue of escape. Even if she managed to drop him to the floor, she wouldn’t have any way to get past him and out the door. The bedroom was too small. All he’d have to do was reach out and grab her as she jumped over him to get away. She chewed her bottom lip in indecision.

Jake’s anger seemed to evaporate as he looked down at her. “I know you’re hiding from something, or someone. That’s easy to figure out. But I’m not here to expose your secrets or dig into your past. I’m here for one reason, to find Calvin Gillette. And I believe you’re the key to finding him. If you’ll talk to me, and help me, I promise I won’t do anything that will jeopardize your life here. I won't tell anyone where you are." He smoothed her hair out of her eyes, then placed his hand on her shoulder and gently squeezed. "Help me, Faye. Please."

It was so tempting to believe him, to believe the gentleness of his touch, the plaintive appeal in his words. She would love to trust him, ease her own burden by letting him share it. She needed to find Calvin, too. Was it possible Jake wasn't really a threat? That would mean she didn't have to leave Mystic Glades, leave her friends.

"Who are you working for?" she asked. "What does he want with…Gillette?"

"I can't tell you that."

"Does he want to harm him?"

Jake's jaw tightened. "I'm not in the business of finding people and turning them over to someone who's going to hurt them. The answer to that insulting question is a definite 'no.'"

His defensiveness seemed genuine. Maybe the client who'd hired Jake was a friend of Calvin's trying to find him for some reason she didn't know about. Maybe Calvin had overreacted and had gone on the run thinking he was in trouble when he really wasn't.

"What makes you think I know this Gillette guy? Or that I can help you find him?" she asked, trying to sound nonchalant.

He dropped his hand to his side. For some reason, the disappointment on his face sent a stab of guilt straight to her heart.

"I found the backpack. You were searching for him this morning, just like last night. Can we skip past the lies now?"

"What makes you think it's my backpack?"

His mouth tightened into a firm line.

"Okay, okay." There was no point in denying this particular accusation. If he'd searched her apartment for weapons then he'd probably noticed a few other things, such as that she had the same style of backpack in her closet in many different colors to match her other outfits. And that the bottled water and power bars in the purple backpack were the same brands as the ones in her pantry. She tried to bluff her way into a new explanation.

"I admit it. The backpack is mine. But only because I found that car a few days ago and realized the driver was probably hurt and wandering the woods and needed help. I've been searching for him, to help him, not because I know him."

"I think you can come up with a better lie than that."

"I'm not lying."

"Right. You were concerned for a stranger, so concerned you've spent the past few days searching for him. But you weren't concerned enough to call the police or to tell any of your friends here in town so they could help you find him. Try again."

She crossed her arms. "Why are you trying to find this guy? Who hired you?"

He seemed to consider that question, then nodded as if he'd decided it was okay to tell her. "My client is Quinn Fugate. He's Calvin's brother, different fathers, different last names. He only found out recently that they were related and is trying to connect with him. He'd tracked Calvin down through another investigator to Naples. But a friend of Calvin's reported him missing before Quinn could hop on a plane and go see him. The police gave up searching for Calvin after the first day.

That's why Quinn hired me. And that's why I need to find Gillette before he dies out in the swamp. I'm here to help Gillette. That's all. Nothing more."

Hope had her staring into his eyes, trying to gauge the truthfulness of his words. He *looked* as if he was telling the truth. His story sounded plausible. And the name Quinn Fugate meant nothing to her, which was a relief. It *was* possible Jake was telling the truth. She honestly didn't know if Calvin had a brother or not. Based on their shared past, it was entirely possible. And right now, there was no way to ask him. But wouldn't it be wonderful if Calvin had a family he'd never known about, a family that wanted him after he'd been alone for so long?

Was Jake telling the truth? He certainly looked sincere, and he sounded sincere. What if he was lying? What if he wanted to use her to find Calvin? She could try to shake him, continue her search alone. But that wouldn't stop him. He'd be out searching, too. Maybe he'd even bring others to help. That would make it even worse for Calvin, to have more people looking for him.

So what were her choices? Search alone—assuming she could manage to get away without Jake following her. Or combine their resources, search together. That way she could keep an eye on him. Wasn't that better than knowing he was out there somewhere, but not knowing where? What was that saying, keep your friends close, your enemies closer?

"Faye?" He watched her intently, waiting for her decision.

"You want me to help you find this guy, the one who was driving the car?"

"Calvin Gillette, yes." He sounded disappointed

again that she wouldn't admit she knew him. "You said you were worried about him, a *stranger* out in the 'Glades, and you wanted to help him. Together we might do better than either of us is doing apart. You can take me around town to ask some questions, see if anyone has seen Gillette. That might narrow down our search area. Once I find him, I deliver the information about his brother. Then it's up to him whether to pursue it or not. My job is over at that point."

"You won't tell anyone outside of Mystic Glades that I live here?" she asked.

He pressed his hand to his heart. "As long as you don't try to shoot me again, I have no reason to tell anyone about you."

She put her hand on top of his, feeling his pulse leap beneath her fingers.

He cleared his throat. "Um, what are you doing?"

"I'm trying to read your spirit, see what kind of man you are inside."

He opened his mouth to say something.

"Be quiet."

His brows rose but he didn't say anything.

She closed her eyes, leaning toward him, feeling his warmth flow through her. Reading people, knowing their true nature, was something she'd always had an instinct for. She didn't know if it was a sixth sense, or just that she paid more attention than most people. But as long as she could touch someone, and listen to the way their body attuned itself to hers, she'd always believed she could read the good inside them.

A sense of calm flowed over her. She smiled as she opened her eyes. "You're a good man, Jake Young. I can feel it inside you."

His eyes widened. "You can?"

"Yes, I can. And I trust you. I'll help you find Calvin."

"Calvin? Not Gillette this time?"

She shook her head. "No. I still have my secrets, but I admit that I know him. And I want to find him, before something bad happens out in the swamp. We'll work together. Deal?" She held out her hand.

He hesitated, but finally took her hand in his and shook it. "Deal."

That increasingly familiar tingle of awareness shot through her. She tugged her hand from his and waved at her torn clothes, the smears of dirt on her arms. "I need to shower and change. And then I think we should sit down and plan our search. I've spent days going in circles without any success. I'd rather lose the rest of the daylight we have today figuring out a plan than searching for a few hours and coming up with nothing again."

She waved her hand toward her bedroom doorway. "You can set up in the guest room for tonight. If you don't have extra clothes I can borrow—"

"I always keep a go-bag in the trunk of my car. I'll run down and get it. It's got everything I'll need."

JAKE PITCHED HIS go-bag on the ground and slammed his trunk. He uttered a few choice curse words and leaned back against his car, guilt riding him like a double-edged sword. He'd done what he came here to do. His job. He'd somehow, inexplicably, gained Faye's trust. But instead of feeling a sense of accomplishment, he was drowning in a sense of betrayal.

How could she just touch him and decide he was a "good" man? Why the hell would she trust him so completely after just meeting him? How she'd managed to survive this long with such a naive way of looking at the world around her was beyond him. The woman needed someone to watch out for her, to protect her from the evil in the world.

And to protect her from men like him.

He shook his head in disgust. He'd moved to Naples for a fresh start, and here he was about to hurt someone all over again. If there was some way to go back in time and not take this case, he would have. But he'd signed a contract, accepted the money. And even though he hated what he was about to do to Faye, it *was* the right thing to do. He just hated that he was the one doing it.

He grabbed his bag and went back upstairs. The shower was still running. Faye's soft voice sang some kind of tune he'd never heard before. He'd half expected her to have disappeared again by the time he'd come back inside. And part of him had wished she had.

Enough. He did have a job to do. It was time he did it. Although he'd already performed a cursory search earlier when he'd used the bathroom excuse to go up to her apartment, he performed a more thorough search now. He snooped in every drawer, every closet, even beneath the cushions on the small couch and chair in the main room.

The little pixie wasn't much for keeping things neat and tidy. Her belongings seemed to occupy whatever space they happened to land in when she was finished with them. But the kitchen was spotless, the small bathroom off the guest room shiny and smelling like fresh lemons. At least there weren't any more weapons hiding anywhere, unless they were in her bedroom and he hadn't found them earlier. He'd have to be careful until he had a chance to more thoroughly search that room.

Pausing by her bedroom door again, he listened, assuring himself she was still in the shower. He crossed to the couch and plopped down to make a quick call.

"Special Agent Quinn Fugate," the voice on the line answered. Static reminded Jake of the unreliableness of cell phones around here.

"Quinn, it's Jake Young."

"Hold on."

Jake heard office sounds: ringing phones, people talking. Then a door closed and the sounds faded away.

"Sorry about that. We've got a bad connection and it's too noisy to hear you in the other room," Quinn said. "Go ahead. Have you found Gillette?"

He chose his words carefully, not willing to paint himself into a corner if things didn't go as planned.

"Not yet, but I have a good lead. I'm convinced he was on his way to a town called Mystic Glades when he crashed his car."

"Mystic Glades? Never heard of it."

The bathroom shower shut off. Jake lowered his voice to barely above a whisper. "It's about eight miles south of mile marker eighty-four on Alligator Alley, the stretch of I-75 that runs across the lower part of the state from the Gulf Coast to the Atlantic."

The door to the bedroom opened. Faye stepped out wearing a pink terry-cloth robe that would have been conservative except that it barely came to the tops of her thighs. His pulse slammed in his veins just thinking about what she might be wearing underneath—or *not* wearing. But the suspicious look she gave him as he held the phone had him rushing to cover his tracks.

"Got to go, Mom," Jake said. "Call you later."

Chapter Six

Jake had to quicken his stride the next morning to catch up to Faye as she hurried down the stairs to the store. She might have agreed to work with him to find Gillette, but she obviously wasn't planning on making it easy. He didn't mind so much if it meant she'd sashay that gorgeous rear of hers in front of him in tight jeans. Her mouthwatering chest was cupped in an equally tight, green lace top that had him struggling to meet her gaze whenever she was facing him. Today was going to be a study in both pleasure and torture at the same time.

They'd gone over a crude map last night, marking off the areas she'd already searched. He'd shown her how to mark off the areas in a grid pattern to make the search more efficient. She'd seemed grudgingly impressed. But before they searched anywhere, they were going to talk to some townspeople as he'd suggested, and see if anyone had seen Gillette. Faye hadn't wanted to let anyone know about him, but she understood that time was of the essence now, and if someone could help narrow down the search area, that increased the odds of finding him alive.

Jake followed her through the short hallway toward the main room that made up the store. But as they passed the office they'd been in yesterday, she turned around and pulled him inside. She closed the door. The click of the lock had Jake's brows rising.

"What are you doing?" he asked, wondering if she'd maybe changed her mind about helping him with the search.

"We need to decide how we're going to play this." She placed her hand on his chest.

His pulse immediately sped up. He took a wary step back, forcing her to drop her hand. "What do you mean?"

She closed the distance between them again. "Yesterday you told Freddie and Amy that you and I had a past…a relationship. I actually think that's a good idea. If we keep up that ruse, people here will be more inclined to talk to you, to answer your questions."

His mouth went dry. "You want to pretend we're, what, lovers?"

"Is it really that far-fetched? We're obviously both attracted to each other. It wouldn't be a stretch to convince people we're lovers, at least not on my part." She ran her fingers down his chest and hooked them in the top of his jeans.

He stumbled back until the wall stopped him from backing up any more. Faye smiled and stalked forward until her breasts were pressed against him.

"What's wrong, Jake?"

"I, uh, we don't know each other that well. I don't think this is a good idea." He clamped his mouth shut. Good grief. He sounded like a girl. His words rang false, too, since all he wanted to do was grab her and crush her against him. He tried, really hard, not to let his gaze dip to the cleavage pressed against his ribs.

He failed miserably.

She smoothed her fingers up the side of his neck to play with his hair. He shuddered before he could stop himself.

"We'll have to come up with a story about how we met," she said. "Something not too complicated so we don't get tripped up on the details, right?"

Making up a cover story. Now this was something he could do. He grabbed on to her suggestion like a drowning man grabbing a life preserver. "When Freddie told me you went to high school in Mobile, I told her I went there, too. So we'll have to stick to that."

"Hmm. Maybe. Where *did* you go to high school?" she asked.

"Nease. It's in north Saint Johns County, right outside of Saint Augustine." What the hell was she doing to the back of his neck? Her fingers were drawing little circles that shot heat straight to his groin.

Her eyes lit up. "Nease? Did you know Tim Tebow? The football player? He went there, right?"

Irritation flashed through him. What was it about women and Tim Tebow?

"Never met him. I graduated quite a few years before he came on the scene."

"Bummer." She chewed her bottom lip. "*Quite* a few years, huh? Just how old are you?"

"Why?"

"Because we're trying to pretend we went to school at the same time. I don't think we can pass for having been in high school together, unless you got held back a few years. How about college? People go there at all different ages. I graduated just a few years ago. How long ago did you graduate? Or did you even go?"

He narrowed his eyes. "Yes, I went to college. And

yes, I graduated. But you do have a point about the age difference. I didn't think about that when I told Freddie we both went to high school in Mobile."

Faye waved her hand in the air—unfortunately, not the one that was doing sinful things to the back of his neck. If she didn't stop soon he might set back civilization thousands of years and throw her over his shoulder like a caveman.

"Don't worry about it," she said. "I doubt Freddie remembers much about the conversation. She was well into the brew by the time I got here yesterday."

He pulled her hand down and captured it against his chest out of desperation. "Okay. So we met in college. I was a senior who started a little late, if anyone asks. And you were a freshman. Will that work? University of Alabama, right? In Tuscaloosa?"

Her smile faded. "Just how much do you know about me?"

"Not nearly enough. Just what I tricked out of Freddie. What did you study in college?"

She looked as if she was still wondering what all Freddie might have told him, but she answered anyway. "Biology, with a focus on ecology and plant and animal studies."

"I suppose that makes sense."

She frowned. "What's that supposed to mean?"

"Just that you seem so at home outdoors. It makes sense you would have studied plants and ecology."

"What about you? I'm guessing something like exercise science. I can totally see you as a trainer at a gym, or with a professional football team."

This time it was his turn to frown. "Because?"

She waved her free hand toward him. "Look at you.

Six foot, what—one, two? With muscles…everywhere. You were probably a quarterback, right?"

He rolled his eyes. "No, I wasn't. I didn't play football. And I studied criminal justice. Now there's just one more little detail we need to take care of."

He put his hands on her shoulders, intent on pushing her away. Instead, she slid both her arms up around his neck and locked them together. "Jake, quit fighting this…thing between us."

"We're…working together. We should keep it professional."

This time it was her turn to roll her eyes. "If we're going to say we're lovers, we have to be comfortable kissing, right? To be convincing? If you won't kiss me, I can't help you."

His gaze dropped to her lips. "So, this is part of our… professional relationship then?"

"Sure. Whatever. Just hurry up and kiss me."

His last shred of resolve to do the right thing snapped like a tattered thread. He swooped down and covered her mouth with his. Her mouth opened and she deepened the kiss, taking it from warm to molten in the space of a breath. She pulled him closer, standing on tiptoe, pressing her soft breasts against him as her tongue tangled with his. Heat raced across every nerve ending in his body, numbing his brain to logical thought.

He slid his hand over the curve of her bottom, lifting her up off the floor, fitting her softness to his hardness. She moaned deep in her throat, demanding more, feathering her hands through his hair. She lifted her legs and wrapped them around his waist.

The shocking heat of her against him made him stumble. He cursed against her mouth. She laughed and kissed him again. He turned and pressed her against the wall, ravenous for the honeyed taste of her, the sweetness of her surrender, the savageness of her response. He drank in her every touch, every sexy little moan, every seductive slide of her body against his.

Her hair swept across his hand on her bottom, teasing him with its velvety softness, curling around his fingers. An erotic image of that beautiful hair sweeping over his naked body had him tightening painfully against her.

A bed. He had to find a bed. Or maybe the desk would work. He couldn't wait long enough to find a bed. He had to have her now. He whirled around and sat her on the desk, standing between her legs, breaking the kiss just long enough to reach for her shirt to pull it up over her head.

But she wouldn't let him. She was too busy fumbling with his belt buckle, trying to unfasten it. He looked down at her fingers working his belt loose, and that brief moment of lost contact between them was just enough for the haze of lust to allow his brain to switch back on. What was he doing? This was crazy, wrong on so many levels. She trusted him, and he was betraying her with every breath he took. He couldn't cross this one last line. Once she found out the truth about him, she'd hate him forever. And he'd deserve it. He had to put a stop to this, even if it killed him.

He grabbed her hands and trapped them between his. She looked up at him in question.

"We have to stop," he whispered, barely able to force his voice past his tight throat. "You deserve better than this, a quickie in a backroom office. Amy could discover us at any moment. And we should be out there trying to find Gillette."

She blinked as if just realizing where they were, what they were doing. The fog of passion in her eyes dimmed and she dropped her hands. Her face flushed with heat, but instead of withdrawing or shoving him away, she grinned. “Wow. That was…hot.”

He laughed and pressed his forehead against hers. “You’re like a breath of fresh air, you know that? And way hotter than hot.”

“Yeah, I know. It’s the hair, isn’t it?” she teased, as she refastened his belt.

In spite of his renewed good intentions, he couldn’t resist running his hands over the silky mass. “Trust me. The entire package is sexy as hell, with or without your gorgeous hair.”

She grinned, apparently liking that. “Well, thanks for stopping. I guess. Because I sure wasn’t going to. But you’re right. The desk isn’t exactly comfortable. Next time, we might want to plan the location better.” She gave him an outrageous wink and shoved him back so she could hop down from the desk.

“I’ve got to check with Amy about her schedule and make sure she can cover the shop.”

And just like that, she was gone.

It took Jake several more minutes before his breath returned to normal and he was capable of walking again. Together, he and Faye were like a torch and gasoline—he wasn’t sure which one was which. All he knew was that he had to keep his hands off her. He couldn’t risk something like this happening again. Which meant the next few hours, or days, were going to be sheer hell.

A few minutes later, with his libido safely under control again—or so he hoped—he left the office and entered the main shop. He hadn’t paid much attention to the store yesterday. But since Faye was on the other side of the room talking to Amy, he took a look around. It was one large rectangular room, with deep, plush royal blue carpet on the floor. Matching blue walls contrasted against the bright white molding on the large picture windows on each side of the door. A long counter ran along the back right side of the store. There wasn't a cash register anywhere that he could see, but Amy seemed to have taken up residence behind the counter, so that was probably where people would make their purchases.

Amy gave him a friendly wave. He returned her wave and crossed to the left side of the store to wait by one of the big windows. After looking at the little round tables of displays throughout the room, and the glass shelves that ran along the walls, he still wasn't quite sure what the shop sold.

There were two round racks of clothes in one corner, consisting mostly of colorful veiled skirts and form-fitting tops, the kind Faye liked to wear. But other than that, and a window display of jewelry that appeared to be homemade, most everything else seemed to be jars and glass bottles with silver or gold stoppers, or polished round stones and little velvet bags with gold drawstrings decorating nearly every available surface.

He studied the jewelry in the window then wound his way among the tables, touching the stones, turning them over. He picked up a tiny red velvet bag and tugged the drawstring open, expecting to see powder like Faye had used on CeeCee yesterday. Instead, inside was a vial of amber-colored liquid. He wiggled the little gold stopper open and sniffed. It had a subtle, flowery scent.

"Be careful with that, unless attracting other men is your goal," Faye said as she joined him.

He wrinkled his nose and put the stopper back on the vial.

She laughed and returned it to the red pouch.

"You're saying this is a love potion?" he asked.

"Not love, exactly. More like an aphrodisiac. It attracts men. I can make you a good deal on one of these, if that's what you're interested in."

He raised a brow. "I think I've already proved where my interests lie." He stepped away from the table, way the hell away from the red pouch.

She laughed again and set the bag on the table. She picked up a gold one instead and tossed it to him. "Here. On the house."

"What is it?"

"It does the same thing as the red one, except that it attracts women. Just in case you want to spice things up in that department."

He dropped the pouch on the nearest table. "Thanks, but no thanks. I don't need any help."

She paused by another table and smoothed her hands over a blue velvet bag. She sashayed seductively to him and slid it into the front pocket of his jeans. "Trust me on this," she breathed. "You'll thank me later."

He groaned. "You're killing me."

Her green eyes twinkled with delight.

Desperate to reengage his brain and to stop thinking about what Faye might look like naked, he waved his hand to encompass the shop. "Is that what this place is all about? Woo-woo love potions?"

She huffed as if he'd just insulted her. "To the uneducated, my powders, lotions and potions might seem 'woo woo,' as you called it. But there's science behind every one of them." She reached down her shirt and pulled out three small pouches hanging from the chain around her neck. "This red one, as you know, is a snake repellant. A very effective one. The gold one is a combination of an antibiotic and a blood coagulant, a clotting agent. If you have a deep cut and can't get to a hospital right away, it might save your life." She dropped the pouches back beneath her shirt.

"What's the purple one for?"

She shook her head and stepped to the door. "You said you wanted to ask the townspeople if they've seen Calvin. Now's your chance. Let's go."

As Jake walked down the wooden boardwalk along the main street with Faye, he couldn't help thinking Mystic Glades would have made the perfect old town in a spaghetti Western movie. Well, minus the oak trees and occasional palms that seemed to fill every space of green between the shops and homes. But the buildings were all wood, like an Old West town, with a wooden sidewalk instead of a paved one. And the stores bore fanciful names such as Callahan's Watering Hole directly across the street from Faye's shop, and Stuffed to the Gills. Jake had expected that one to be a seafood restaurant. But Faye told him it was a taxidermy business. Beside it were Bubba's Take or Trade—a general store of sorts—and Gators and Taters, the only restaurant in town.

"Where is everyone?" he asked. They hadn't passed a single soul since leaving her shop. And there hadn't been any customers in her store the entire time he'd been there.

"Most are at work, in Naples or other places. As you can tell there's not a lot of opportunity to earn a living right here. The few shops we have, like mine, are popular mostly on weekends."

"If everyone's at work right now, then where are we going?"

"SBO, where the few people in town at this time of morning hang out."

Feeling completely out of his element, he followed her as she crossed the dirt road to the other side. "SBO?"

She pointed to the gold lettering on the dark-tinted floor-to-ceiling window that formed the front wall of the building in front of them and went inside.

"Swamp Buggy Outfitters." Jake read the words on the glass. "What the hell is a swamp buggy?" He shook his head and hurried in after her.

The answer to that question met him as soon as he stepped inside. A dune buggy on steroids rested on top of a man-made mountain of rock ten feet from the door. The tires were enormous and just about as tall as Jake. The body of the buggy was a collection of steel pipes with a flat steel platform resting on top. The engine was secured beneath the platform between the two front tires. Metal steps would assist the passengers to the bench seats on top of the platform, just behind the driver's seat. A dark green vinyl tarp attached to metal roll bars shaded the seats. And every inch of the monster was painted in brown-and-green camouflage. Jake had never seen anything like it.

"It can be yours for thirty-six five."

Jake turned around and had to look up to meet the eyes of the man speaking to him. He had a reddish-brown beard at least a foot long and a bushy mustache that curled at the ends. The top of his head was bald.

"You in the market for a buggy?" the man said.

"What exactly would someone do with it?"

He laughed. "Faye did say you weren't from around here." He waved up at the buggy. "That's about the only way to get through some of the more marshy areas of the Everglades, without worrying about stepping on a gator. You're too high to worry about much of anything up on that platform. Of course if it gets too swampy you have to switch to a canoe or kayak, or even an airboat. Got plenty of canoes and kayaks if you're interested. Only got one airboat and that's mine. Got an ATV, too, but again, that's mine. Of course, everyone borrows it around here from time to time, so it more or less belongs to the town."

Jake looked past the buggy to the canoes hanging on the back wall. Some were suspended from the ceiling. The shop wasn't all that large, but every inch was crammed full of just about everything you'd need outdoors, including tents, sleeping bags and one entire wall of fishing poles. "I'm surprised you don't have hunting rifles in here, too."

"I would but there wouldn't be any point. Too much competition."

"Competition?"

"Locked and Loaded, the gun store at the end of the street."

"Ah." Jake hadn't seen that store, but he hadn't traveled the entire length of the street, either. He held out his hand. "I'm Jake Young, as you already know. I'm a...friend of Faye's." He looked past the man to where Faye stood near a tent display, speaking to a group of about ten men sitting on folding chairs. All of them were nearing sixty years of age, or more.

The man shook his hand in a tight grip that made Jake want to wince.

"Buddy Johnson. And from what I hear, you and Faye are a bit more than friends." He winked and slapped Jake on the back.

He coughed and stumbled forward a few feet.

Buddy laughed and waved for him to follow him over to the others. "Come on. Faye sent me to get you."

Jake suffered through the round of introductions. He'd never met so many Bubbas and Joes in one place before. There was no chance he'd keep them straight. When the introductions were done, he put his arm around Faye's shoulders and tucked her against his side. She put her arm around his waist, much to the delight of some of the men who grinned and whispered to each other.

Faye waved toward two of them. "Joe and Bubba said they may have seen the man you're looking for, honey. Bubba, tell Jake what you told me."

Heat flashed through him at her easy use of the endearment and the way her fingers absently stroked his side. This woman was dangerous in so many ways.

The man she'd called Bubba scratched the white stubble on his jaw before replying. "Two days ago, I was out near Croc Landing when I saw a guy back in the trees and palmettos. Medium build, short brown hair, about five-eight or nine. I remember him because he had a backpack but no gun that I could see. I figured he was an idiot tourist with no common sense and a lousy sense of direction. I was going to see if he needed help finding his way back to wherever he came from, but as soon as he saw me he ducked behind a tree." He shrugged. "Obviously he didn't want my help."

"Where's Croc Landing?" Jake asked.

"Southwest of here, about six miles," Faye said. "Joe, you saw the same man just yesterday, right?"

"Yep. The clothing matched what Bubba said earlier before your Jake came over here—jeans and a dark blue button-up shirt." Joe adjusted the faded orange-and-black Miami Marlins baseball cap on his head. "About four clicks south of where Bubba saw him. Deep in the marsh. I figured the same as Bubba, that the feller was lost. But he took off as soon as he saw me. Definitely didn't want help."

Faye smoothed her hand up Jake's chest. "That has to be Calvin. If someone else were lost out this far there'd have been a story on the news, maybe a missing tourist from an airboat tour. But I haven't heard of anything like that."

He covered her hand with his to maintain his sanity. Her warm fingers were practically burning a hole through his shirt and had him wanting to pull her behind the tent and kiss her senseless.

She winked, obviously enjoying his discomfort. How was he going to keep his hands off her for the rest of this case?

"He didn't seem hurt?" Jake asked.

Both Joe and Bubba shook their heads.

"He has supplies in that backpack," Faye said. "He's obviously lost but doesn't trust any strangers to help him. He must be using a compass. That would explain why he keeps going south instead of north back to the highway."

The men around her all nodded as if what she'd said made perfect sense.

Jake was still wondering about her statement, that Gillette "has" supplies, instead of "*probably* has" supplies. How would she know he had supplies?

"I don't understand," he said. "A compass would make him get more lost?"

"Compasses go crazy around here," she explained. "Just like a lot of electronic equipment, GPS trackers, cell phones. There's something about the swamp in this area that makes things like compasses unreliable. In order to find your way around, you have to rely on landmarks and the sun or stars."

"Do you mind if I ask why anyone would actually choose to live in a place like this, in the middle of nowhere?"

The friendly looks on the men's faces faded. Faye gave him an aggravated look.

"What?" he asked.

She grabbed his hand. "Come on. Let's get out of here before Buddy decides to use you as target practice for his fancy new crossbow."

They'd just reached the street when the Buddy in question leaned out the door. "Faye, hold up. You going out past Croc Landing to look for that fellow right now?"

"We're leaving as soon as I grab my gear from the shop."

"Hang on a sec." He disappeared back inside. A couple of minutes later he hurried back out holding two dark green backpacks. One of them was noticeably larger than the other. Buddy heaved it at Jake, who staggered back when he caught it against his chest.

"This thing weighs a ton," Jake said.

Buddy arched a brow. "I might have accidentally distributed the weight more in that pack than Faye's. My bad." The sour look he gave Jake told him it wasn't an accident. He handed the much lighter-looking, smaller pack to Faye. "Those packs have everything you need in case you get caught out past sundown. I'd consider it a favor if you take them. You can let me know how the new gear holds up. There's a tent in the pack your man's holding. Do you need any weapons?"

"Of course not. I'm packing." She slid her arms through the straps of the backpack and buckled the strap that tightened it against her waist. She stood on tiptoe and kissed his cheek. "Thanks, Buddy. You're a sweetheart."

He flushed and stepped back. "Be careful, darlin'."

"Always."

Jake rolled his eyes and hoisted the heavy pack onto his shoulders, fastening the straps the way Faye had done. If his pack weighed less than sixty pounds, it wasn't by much.

Faye waved goodbye to Buddy and grabbed Jake's hand. "Come on." She started down the street, away from the shop.

"My car's back that way," he said. "From what your friends told us, Gillette was at least eight miles away yesterday. He could be a lot more than that by now."

"Cars can't reach Croc Landing. It's all marsh."

"We're going to hike the whole way?"

She gave him an exasperated look. "Do you always complain this much?"

He clamped his mouth shut and pulled her to the boardwalk as a car went by, the first he'd seen since he'd been there. They continued toward the end of the street, passing several more shops. When he saw the church at the very end, he couldn't help but laugh.

Faye shot him a death glare.

He coughed and forced the amusement off his face until she turned around and started walking again. He would have loved to snap a picture of the sign above the church, but he figured Faye would probably drop him on his ass again if he did. So, instead, he made a mental note to tell Dex about it the next time they spoke. His business partner would get a real kick out of a church called Last Chance advertising "over five hundred saved" just like a fast-food restaurant advertising how many burgers it had sold.

The street dead-ended behind the church, but Faye didn't even slow down. She headed into the trees, with Jake hurrying to catch up. Fifty yards in, the solid ground ended and the marsh began.

Faye stopped and faced him. "Take off the pack."

He didn't question her dictate. This was her domain and he was more than willing to take the heavy pack off. He unclipped the strap at his waist and slipped out of the shoulder straps. The pack dropped to the ground with a solid thunk.

She crouched down and opened it.

Jake swore when he saw what was inside on top. Rocks. Big, heavy rocks like the ones used to build the fake mountain where Buddy's swamp buggy was perched back at SBO. He counted ten rocks before Faye finished taking them out and then handed the pack back to him.

The weight had easily been cut in half. He slung it onto his shoulders and fastened the straps.

"How did you know?" he asked.

"By how heavy it seemed when Buddy threw it to you. I figured he was teaching you a lesson in manners. Lesson learned?"

He let out a deep breath. "Lesson learned."

"Good. Let's go. It'll take most of the day to navigate to Croc Landing. It's in the most treacherous part of the swamp and hard to reach. If we don't find Calvin there, I want to get a good distance from the Landing to a higher, safer spot before dark."

He looked out over the marsh, wondering how deep it was and whether there were any alligators hiding in the mud. "Can't we borrow Buddy's swamp buggy and make it there faster? And safer?" He'd much rather be higher up where nothing could bite him.

"That swamp buggy costs more than I'd make in two years running my shop. I'm not about to ask him to loan it to me. And I'd have to go the back way, around the main waterways, to get there. I've never been that way on my own."

Jake sighed with disappointment. "Okay. Then how do we get to Croc Landing? On foot?"

She headed past him and bent down beside a pile of leaves. After fumbling with what appeared to be a plastic buckle, she swept the leaves back, which turned out to be part of a camouflaged tarp.

Jake groaned when he saw what was underneath.

Faye gave him a smug look. "Come on, city slicker. I'm going to teach you how to navigate a swamp in a canoe."

Chapter Seven

The canoe slid quietly through a cluster of lily pads, their yellow flowers perfuming the air with each dip of Jake's oar into the water. The knobby knees of cypress tree roots stuck up out of the swamp beneath the canopy of branches over the shallows. Faye loved the swamp, with its musty smells and constant chorus of singing birds and frogs, and the occasional bellow of an alligator. She would often spend an entire weekend out in the bog, with just her canoe for company, taking in the sights, enjoying the freedom. But this time, she wasn't alone. And she was finding, to her surprise, that sharing the majestic world of the Everglades with Jake was even more fun than usual.

When she pointed out birds or plants, naming them, explaining about their habitats and how they fit into the ecosystem, he listened intently, asking questions and seeming to enjoy the marsh as much as she did as his understanding of it grew. She hadn't expected that from a man who'd spent most of his life in the city or walking the beach. He'd surprised her in other ways, too, such as how well he was doing with the canoe.

She'd been half teasing when she'd said she'd teach him. She'd assumed he'd been canoeing at least a handful of times in his life, just maybe not in a swamp. She'd been shocked to find that he'd never even been in a canoe.

In spite of that shameful admission, he'd been a quick learner. Faye had planned on paddling at first to show him how. But Jake had been horrified by that idea. He wasn't about to sit and do nothing while a woman did the work. His old-fashioned ideas were silly to Faye, but she also thought it was sweet. And she thought it would be fun to play along and see how many times he'd get them stuck on a submerged tree or mired in mud before he admitted he needed her help. Surprisingly, he hadn't gotten stuck even once. He followed her instructions to the letter, and was soon paddling them down the waterway like a pro.

She would have liked to sit there facing him, admiring the way his muscles bunched in his arms with each powerful stroke of the paddle, but she had to navigate. Which meant facing away from him, calling out orders to turn, slow down or speed up.

Croc Landing turned out to be a disappointment for Jake, who'd expected to see dozens of the reptiles sunbathing on the banks of the waterway. Instead, the bank was deserted, which suited Faye just fine.

"I thought you were afraid of alligators," she said.

"Let's go with respectful. Wary. But as long as we're inside the canoe, we're safe. So I thought it would be cool to see a bunch of them on the bank."

"Since we have to step out on that bank, I'm happy there aren't any around right now."

He looked at the water with renewed vigilance. "Good point. If it's called Croc Landing, why are we talking alligators? Aren't there any crocodiles around here?"

"We get a few crocodiles but they thrive more in the saltwater marshes. Mostly we have alligators."

"Then why is this place called Croc Landing?"

"Because 'Croc Landing' sounds better on a tourist pamphlet than 'Gator Landing.'"

"Ah, the almighty dollar at work. I didn't see any tourist fliers in Mystic Glades. Does Buddy take people out on his airboat?"

She laughed. "I'm pretty sure he'd be insulted if you asked him that. He doesn't like the idea of tourists traipsing through our precious 'Glades. It's the airboat tour companies a bit farther south that sometimes bring people up as far as Croc Landing. No one in Mystic Glades would dream of welcoming people from the outside."

"Your friends at SBO seemed pretty nice to me. And Freddie and Amy were nice, too, even though I'm an outsider."

"Yeah, but we lied and told them you were with me. Makes a big difference." She pointed to the right where she wanted to land the canoe.

Jake speared the water with the oar and guided them toward shore. "You didn't grow up in Mystic Glades, right? But they accept you as one of their own. That's because of your friend, Amber Callahan?"

She nodded, some of her fun with the canoe trip evaporating. "Yes."

"I don't remember meeting her. Does she help Freddie in the bar?"

She half turned, looking back at him. "Amber and I lost touch with each other a few years ago. She stopped returning my letters. When I…needed to move to a new place, I came to Mystic Glades, hoping to reestablish our friendship. But when I got here I found out she'd gotten lost and died out in the swamp. That's why my mail went unanswered."

Jake winced. "Sorry. I didn't mean to bring up unhappy memories."

She nodded, and forced thoughts of Amber away. "Over here." She pointed to a place that seemed to offer the easiest access to the "beach," such as it was.

The bottom of the canoe ground against the shallows until the nose wedged into the sand. Faye reassured herself there weren't any reptiles waiting to pounce on her from the water before jumping out of the canoe. She held it steady while Jake moved to the prow. He hopped out and together they pulled the canoe up the incline about twenty feet from the water's edge. They stowed it beneath an oak tree and covered it with the tarp.

Faye pointed out some landmarks—twisted trees and groups of rocks—that they could use to find the canoe on their way back, rather than rely on the GPS on Jake's fancy cell phone.

Two hours later, after hiking through the area around the Landing in concentric circles and finding nothing, Faye called an end to the search.

"I think it's safe to say he's not here. We'll make camp for the night and head out to where Joe thinks he saw Calvin in the morning. It's a bit of a hike."

By the time they reached a good camping spot, the sun was sinking low on the horizon. But Faye was pleased with their progress. They had a good, relatively safe area to set up camp for the night and could resume their search for Calvin in the morning. On foot and with only a limited knowledge of the area from the few times he'd been to Mystic Glades, Calvin wouldn't make nearly as good time as Faye and Jake. She was confident they'd find him before the next day was out.

As with the canoeing instructions earlier, Jake was a quick learner at how to set up camp. Soon they had the small dome-tent up and some netting erected between the trees near the tent to dissuade small animals on foot. Little bells on the netting would alert them if something got caught in the net, or if something bigger was on the prowl.

Jake surveyed their temporary home. "What about alligators? Will the nets stop them?"

"Doubtful, but we're pretty far from the water. We should be fine here."

He didn't look as if he believed her. He patted the pistol holstered on his waist. "Hopefully I won't have to use this."

She pulled up her pant legs to reveal her knife strapped on the outside of one boot and her pistol strapped on the outside of the other. "I've got us covered."

He gave her a lopsided grin and shook his head. "I wondered where you were hiding those when you told Buddy you were packing."

"A girl's got to protect herself."

He glanced up at the tree limbs hanging over their campsite. "What about snakes?"

She flicked the silver chain around her neck. "Snake repellant. I grabbed a new bag before I left the shop."

"That's fine for an emergency, but I'd rather not get close enough to a snake to use that."

She laughed. "Don't worry. If you get attacked I promise I'll help you fend off the snake."

"What if you're the one who gets attacked?"

"I'll just have to trust you to save me."

He nodded, his expression serious. "I won't let anything happen to you."

She slid her hand up his chest. "See that you don't."

He took a quick step back, forcing her to drop her hand. "Since I don't see a bathroom or a porta-pottie around here, I'm going to take a walk."

Disappointment shot through her. She'd felt freed last night, at peace with her belief that he had a good soul, that she could trust him. She'd decided to pursue the incredible chemistry between them and just enjoy being with him for however long they had together. But every time she tried to initiate anything more than a casual touch, he pulled away. It had practically taken her attacking him back at the store to get him to kiss her.

But, oh my, did he know how to kiss once he'd let himself go.

She sighed at the memory and pointed to a break in the trees to the west. "You go that way and I'll go this way." She grabbed a latrine kit from the pack and tossed it to him. "You're a smart guy. I'm sure you can figure out how to use that."

JAKE DIDN'T STOP until he was a good fifty yards from their campsite. He found a clearing on a slight rise and checked the bars on his phone. Only two—hopefully that would be enough. He took another minute to scout the nearby bushes and trees looking for snakes and alligators, but he seemed to be alone. Then again, a hungry reptile could be hiding in the dirt nearby and he might never see it. Just to be safe, he pulled out his pistol and set it on a fallen tree log beside him as he sat with his phone.

He absently studied the latrine kit while he dialed Dex Lassiter's number. The green vinyl bag contained a small hand shovel, an equally small roll of toilet paper and antibacterial hand wipes. He laughed and set it aside.

"Lassiter," the voice on the phone answered.

"Dex, it's Jake."

"Well, it's about damn time. I was seriously considering reporting *you* as a missing person. I haven't heard from you since you found Gillette's car."

"I know, I know. I've been busy." He quickly summarized what had happened since then. "Faye thinks we'll find Calvin sometime tomorrow. I don't have a lot of phone time, so you'll have to relay the information to Quinn for me."

"No problem. Is Faye armed?"

"When is she not? She's got a gun and knife strapped to her boots."

"We should call Holder. Get some backup."

"Quinn gave strict instructions to keep this on the down low. And if Holder makes the catch—"

"We don't get paid. Yeah, I know. Still. I'm not sure the danger is worth it."

Jake tapped the log beside him. "Faye has a good heart. She loves animals and plants, and risks her life to help people. Yesterday she saved a man from a boa constrictor. She's not dangerous to anyone."

"Tell that to Genovese."

Jake tightened his hand around the phone. "Yeah, about that. How much do we really know about the case other than what Quinn told us?"

Dex groaned.

"What?" Jake demanded.

"You're falling for her."

"Shut up. I am not. I'm just curious. The woman I've met doesn't mesh with what we've been told. I'd like to see some details from the case. Just get the file and double-check that no red flags go up, all right?"

A bush rustled behind him. He jerked around. Was that a shadow? A deeper black than the rest of the darkness as the sun slid lower in the sky? He grabbed his pistol and stood. "Faye? Is that you?"

"Jake, you okay?" Dex asked.

He waited but didn't hear anything else. The shadow no longer seemed to be there. Were his eyes playing tricks on him?

"Jake?"

"I'm still here. Thought I saw something. You're going to look into the case, right?"

Dex groaned again. "Okay, okay. I think it's a complete waste of time. But since you're the one out there putting your life on the line, the least I can do is get Quinn to email me a copy of the case file."

"Sounds good. I'll try to call you tomorrow but I don't know when I'll be able to get away or have cell coverage. Don't freak if you don't hear from me right away."

He ended the call and answered nature's call before starting back to camp. That dark shadow he'd seen, or thought he saw, had the hairs standing up on the back of his neck. He stopped a few times to listen and peer into the underbrush. But he never figured out what had caused that shadow. Unless it was his overactive imagination.

When he reached the campsite and stepped over the netting, Faye was kneeling by a small fire, stirring a pot on top of a metal rack. Her long hair was twisted into a thick braid hanging down her back.

She looked up in question as he sat beside her. "You were gone awhile. I was about to come looking for you."

"I took a short walk, looked around."

Her brows rose. "You find what you were looking for?"

He was careful to keep his expression blank so he wouldn't give anything away. "I didn't see any tracks from Gillette, but I did get the feeling I was being watched. Thought I heard some bushes move as if something big had passed behind them. Are there any bears around here?"

She smiled and turned her attention to stirring the mouthwatering soup or stew that was in the pot. "We've got some black bears here and there, but they're typically too afraid to go near people. There are some foxes out here, too, raccoons, even an occasional bobcat. But those are rare."

He bent forward to get a better smell of the food. "Would a bobcat trigger the bells and netting we've got strung up?"

She pushed him back. "Patience. It's almost done. And no, probably not. A bobcat would just jump out of a tree on top of us."

He looked up at the branches hanging over them.

Faye laughed. "For such a large man, you sure are skittish."

"I'd just prefer not to become a meal for some predator while I'm out here. That's not the way I want to go out."

"Get the bowls and spoons, will you?" She pointed

to a small cloth lying in the dirt with the dishes sitting on it next to some bottles of water.

He handed her the bowls one at a time as she ladled out the meal. While they sat down to eat, he handed her one of the water bottles. She nodded her thanks.

"This smells incredible." He took a large spoonful of the stew, which was full of potatoes, carrots and chunks of meat. "Wow, that's amazing. Best beef stew I think I've ever had. What's the brand?"

"Brand? You think this came from a can?"

He paused with the next spoonful halfway to his mouth and eyed it suspiciously. "It didn't?"

She shook her head. "Nope."

He put the spoon back in his bowl, untouched. "Did you catch, skin and cook a rabbit while I was gone?"

She laughed. "No. Buddy gave us some stew his wife made. It's Grade A, Uncle Sam-inspected, one hundred percent pure beef. Relax."

He grinned and quickly emptied his bowl, and a second one after that. Faye showed him how to clean the dishes without water and tightly store them and the empty plasticware that the stew had come in so that animals wouldn't smell it and be attracted to the food.

After turning on a small battery-operated lantern, Faye put the fire out. Jake had wanted to keep it lit to scare critters away. But Faye had insisted on dousing the flames to ensure they didn't accidentally start a marsh fire. He reluctantly agreed and helped her stow everything back in their packs, all ready for the morning. The only thing left was to go to bed.

The tiny tent would barely sleep one, let alone two. Jake didn't think he'd be able to get any sleep with Faye lying that close to him. And even if he did, he was worried he might be drawn to her in his sleep and do something he'd regret. Well, *regret* might be too strong a word. He'd love nothing more than to finish what he and Faye had started in the back room of her store earlier today. But it wasn't right, not when almost everything that came out of his mouth was a lie.

"We should probably take turns on watch," he said, "just in case some animal wanders too close."

She picked up the lantern and took his hand in hers. "That's what the nets and bells are for. Plus we'll zip up the tent. Don't worry. I'll protect you." She tugged him toward the tent.

"I'm the one who'll protect you," he grumbled but didn't argue anymore.

Even with the vents in the tent, it was too warm to get inside the sleeping bags. Jake lay on top of his. He kept his clothes on, both out of respect for Faye and to add an extra layer of protection between them if he reached for her in his sleep.

Faye had no such concerns. After taking off her boots and setting her knife and gun at the foot of the tent, she shimmied out of her tight jeans, leaving her in her lacy green top and—oh, God—matching lacy green thong. With a tiny lime-green bow.

His mouth watered at the thought of that delicate, little bow, of grasping it with his teeth and tugging it down, down, down. Realizing where he was staring, he forced his gaze up to meet hers. She smiled, a slow, lazy smile that promised things that made him almost whimper out loud.

No, she's off-limits. She doesn't know you're working for the FBI. It's not right to make love to her with so many lies between us, especially since there's no way we could ever be together once the truth comes out.

He shuddered and rolled over, scooting as far away from her tantalizing heat as possible. "Good night," he rasped through his tight throat as he clutched his pillow to keep from reaching for her.

A deep sigh met his statement. "Good night." The lantern went out, plunging the tent into darkness.

FAYE ROLLED ONTO her back and stared up at the complete blackness of the tent roof above her. The base of the dome-shaped tent was about seven feet long and four feet wide, and yet so far Jake had managed to keep his long, thickly muscled body from touching her in any way. Frustration was making her curl her nails into her palms.

She knew he wanted her. Just as he knew she wanted him. So what was the problem? Was he sleeping? She didn't think so. His breathing wasn't the deep and even breathing of someone off in dreamland. If anything, his breathing was too carefully controlled, as if he was trying not to think about her lying beside him.

Not sleeping together, or rather only *sleeping* together and doing nothing else, was probably the wisest choice. He didn't know about her past, that it was like a ticking time bomb waiting to explode if the Tuscaloosa police figured out where she was. And she didn't really know anything about him other than he was a police officer trying his hand at being a private investigator, trying to find the one person who could blow her world apart.

No, making love to the incredibly attractive, delicious-looking Jake Young made no sense whatsoever. But since when did chemistry between a man and a woman ever make sense? Right now, at this moment, all that mattered was that she was on fire for him. And she knew he was on fire for her. If everything went to hell in the morning, so be it. But, tonight, for the first time in thirteen months, she just wanted to feel, to enjoy having a man desire her and hold her in his arms. For once, she wanted to let her worries and fears melt away and live in the moment. She wanted this, *needed* this. And thanks to the condoms she'd discovered that Buddy had included in her backpack—she was completely prepared.

She sat up and made quick work of her braid, finger-combing her tresses until they hung past her hips to the tent floor. She remembered the way Jake had plunged his fingers into her hair this morning when he'd kissed her. He liked her hair, and she would ruthlessly take advantage of that.

Next she shimmied out of her thong. Just the whisper of the material against her as she pulled it off was almost too much for her nerve endings to take. The way Jake had stared at the bow on her panties had made her clench with need and anticipation. That same need rose up in her now as she pulled her shirt over her head and tossed it to the foot of the tent. Her necklace followed. Lastly she unhooked her bra and added it to the pile of discarded clothes.

Shoot, the condoms. Where were they? In her jeans. In her wishful thinking earlier when he'd left camp for his "walk" she'd slid three of the foil packets in her pocket. She scrambled to the end of the tent to find where she'd put her jeans.

"Faye? Is something wrong?" Jake called out.

She found the foil packets and clutched them in her hands. “Not anymore. Or at least, not for long.”

“What? Did you hear something outside the tent?”

She could hear him moving behind her. She turned around just as the lantern light clicked on.

He was sitting up, the light in his hand. His jaw dropped open, his eyes widened, and he went still as a statue.

Faye looked down at the shiny foil packets clutched in her right hand. There was no way he couldn’t see them, or not know what they were. She was completely naked, her breasts jutting out, her hair hanging down around her hips. What did someone say in a situation like this?

She cleared her throat and smiled. “Um, surprise?”

Chapter Eight

Faye stared at Jake, just three feet away, waiting. His eyes swept down her body, lingering on her breasts, the apex between her thighs. But he didn't move. She wasn't even sure he was breathing.

"Jake. *Say* something."

"Can't," he choked.

"Then *do* something. I'm starting to feel a little silly here."

His eyes finally rose. "You're absolutely exquisite," he whispered, his voice ragged, raw.

Her belly tightened at his words. "I'm still feeling silly since I'm the only one here without any clothes. I'd appreciate it if you'd take your clothes off. I've got something else for you to wear."

He frowned. "What do you want me to wear?"

She held up one of the condom packets.

He visibly shuddered. But he still didn't move to take her.

"Jake?"

"You don't know me," he whispered, for some reason looking completely miserable.

"I know what I need to know," she said. "You're strong, smart, protective even when you don't need to be. You're a great listener even though I probably bored you to death on the canoe trip."

He shook his head. "You weren't boring."

"I want you, Jake. Don't make me beg."

"I'm going to hell for this."

"Take me with you."

He reached for her and lifted her onto his lap, straddling him. He sank his fingers into her hair and shook his head in wonder. "I've never seen a more beautiful woman."

She sank against him, her breasts flattening against his chest as she wrapped her arms behind his neck. "You say the sweetest things."

He crushed her to him, devouring her in an open-mouthed frenzy as if he was dying and she was his only hope of salvation. Their kiss this morning had been mild compared with the heat they generated now. His lips moved against hers, stoking her desire higher and higher, making her moan deep in her throat. She could kiss him forever and never get enough. He was like a master craftsman plying his trade, wrenching every ounce of pleasure her body was capable of feeling, and then bringing her up another level until she thought she'd go out of her mind for wanting him. Her entire body pulsed with need, an ache of longing so deep she thought she'd die if he didn't make love to her right then.

She wrenched her lips from his and reached down between them, desperate to feel him. She whimpered at the feel of him through his clothes. "Take. These. Off," she demanded.

He swallowed, hard, and gently set her down on the sleeping bag. He unbuttoned his jeans but he was moving much too slowly. She shoved him down onto his back and went to work on his zipper, then yanked his pants down his legs, shucking them off and tossing them behind her.

He laughed, then sucked in a deep breath when she shoved her hands beneath his boxers. She stroked his velvety soft skin, reveling in his hardness. She bent down and kissed him, tasted him.

A guttural curse escaped his clenched teeth. He grabbed her and pulled her up his body and captured her lips with his. When he finally broke the kiss they were both struggling to catch their breath. He yanked off his shirt and went to work on the Velcro straps of his bullet-resistant vest.

Faye blinked in surprise. "Why are you wearing that?"

He looked at his vest, as if surprised himself, and shrugged. "Habit. I always wear it when I'm working a case." He quickly discarded the rest of his clothes then pulled her against him, skin against skin, softness against hardness as he worshipped every inch of her body with his mouth.

She was about to beg for mercy when he finally settled himself on top of her at her entrance.

"Wait, wait," she cried out.

He shuddered and stilled against her. "Please don't say you changed your mind," he begged.

"What? No, no. Hell, no." She giggled and grabbed one of the foil packets. After rolling the condom onto him, she gave him one long, exquisite stroke. "Now," she said. "Now, Jake."

But he didn't take her. Instead, he kissed her again as his hands slid all over her body, stroking, kneading, feathering across her skin until she thought she would die from the pleasure of it. Every nerve ending in her body seemed to be at a fever pitch, ready to explode.

She tore her mouth from his and reached down between them to position him again. "If you don't do it now," she whispered against his lips, "I'm going to shoot you."

He laughed and surged forward, thrusting inside her. She threw her head back in ecstasy at the feel of him stretching and filling her. She scored her nails down his back and lightly bit his shoulder as he plunged into her, harder and faster. She matched his rhythm, wrapping her legs around him and trying to pull him in deeper.

Every movement of him inside her, every stroke of his hands against her between their bodies, every touch of his lips against her skin sent her higher, and higher until she didn't think she could possibly go higher. And then he took her there, up, up, up, whispering in her ear, telling her how he loved her body and what else he wanted to do with her as he shuddered and plunged into her over and over again.

Her climax washed over her in an explosion of feeling that had her screaming his name and sinking her nails into his shoulders. He rode her through her climax, drawing it out, sending her up and over the edge even as the last waves of her first climax were still rippling through her. She screamed again. He tightened inside her and this time he followed her, clasping her against his body as wave after wave of ecstasy crashed through both of them. They collapsed back against the sleeping bags in an exhausted but thoroughly sated, boneless tangle of arms and legs.

Faye lay there, her breaths rattling out of her as her heart struggled to stop racing and calm down to a natural rhythm again. Sweat slicked her skin and beaded between her breasts, slowly running down her belly. Behind her, Jake's labored breaths came quick and fast like hers and she could feel his heart pounding against her back.

"Wow," she finally managed. "I've never, ever…"

"Me, neither." His voice was husky and deeper than usual, sending a delightful shiver straight to her core.

He wrapped his arm around her waist and pulled her tighter against him, spooning his body to hers. She loved the feel of his lightly furred chest against her back. In fact, she loved everything about him. Plus, he was a Sagittarius and she was a Libra. Had fate brought them together? She automatically reached for the purple velvet pouch on her necklace before remembering she'd taken it off.

His fingers lightly stroked her belly, warming her all over, making her feel cherished, and for the first time in her life…*loved.* Loved? She stiffened at that ridiculous thought. No one could care about someone that deeply when they were practically strangers.

His arm tightened. "What's wrong?"

"I just…we don't even know each other, and here we are…"

His deep sigh sounded near her ear. "I know. You're right. I shouldn't have—"

"Oh yes, you should have. No take backs. No regrets. That's not what I'm saying."

"Then what *are* you saying?"

"I want to know more about you. I'd like to know more about the man who just blew my mind."

He laughed, his hot breath washing against her neck. He trailed his fingertips up to that same, sensitive spot and stroked her skin, making her shiver. He pressed a quick kiss to her there.

"What is it that you want to know?"

"Where are you from? Do you have a family?" She sucked in a breath. "Do you have a girlfriend?"

He scooted back and gently rolled her over so she was flat on her back looking up at him. His eyes were dark, his expression intent.

"If I was in a relationship with someone, what we just did wouldn't have happened." He gently smoothed her hair back from her face. "I grew up in North Florida, in Saint Augustine. I don't have any family, not anymore."

She slid her hands up his chest, delighting in the way his muscles flexed beneath her hands and the way the crisp hairs tickled her fingers. "Not anymore?"

"My parents died a long time ago. It was just me and my sister for years. But she's…gone now."

His voice was flat, as if he was trying to mask his pain, but she saw it in the tension around his eyes, and the lines of concentration on his brow. She cupped his face and brought him down closer so she could kiss the worry lines away.

"I'm sorry for your loss," she whispered. "What happened?"

He rolled onto his back. She figured she'd asked him too sensitive, too personal a question. But then he reached for her and tucked her against his side, her breasts snugged up against his ribs. She sighed with contentment and rested her hand on his chest.

"She married my best friend," he said, his voice barely above a whisper. "A couple of years later, there was a home invasion. She was killed."

"Oh my gosh, I'm so, so sorry. What happened to her husband?"

"Rafe? He survived. He was knocked out, shot, but he made it. Shelby didn't."

She traced the lines of his stomach muscles. "You blame him. Why?"

He shook his head. "No. I don't blame him. I did, for a long time. I let hate and resentment build up inside me to the point that I made some very bad decisions. It almost cost both of us our lives. And it took a very special person, his new wife—Darby—to eventually bring us back together. But even though he forgave me, I couldn't forgive myself. I needed a fresh start. So when an old college friend contacted me about starting a private investigation firm with him, I took leave from my police job to jump at the chance, see if it was worth giving up my law enforcement career for good. So here I am. What about you? Did you come from a large family?"

She stiffened, her hand going still on his stomach.

He put his fingers beneath her chin and turned her head to look at him. "I'm not asking as an investigator, Faye. I'm asking as the man who just made love to you, the man who genuinely wants to know more about the extraordinary woman that you are. If it makes you uncomfortable talking about family, tell me something else. But don't shut down. Don't push me away."

She doubted there was any way for him to truly separate himself from his job, but the intimacy between them created by him sharing about his past had her wanting to share with him, as well. She carefully waded through the pieces of her life in her mind, picking out what she could share without giving up the secrets that could destroy her.

"I never had a family, not a real one. My parents died when I was too young to remember them. I was put in foster care, starting in Mobile. I was shuffled from family to family, place to place."

"You were never adopted?"

"No. I've always been a bit…headstrong, and odd I suppose, compared to most people. I didn't fit in with the picture of the perfect daughter that families were looking for."

He hugged her close and pressed a kiss on her forehead before lying flat again. "I'm sorry, Faye. That had to be so hard."

"Early on it was, but in my later years, at the last foster home, I met…another girl, close to my age. We both loved animals and plants and exploring. We wanted to save the environment and educate people about the precious habitats around them. We became each other's confidantes, like real sisters."

"What was her name?"

"Doesn't matter."

He gave her a brief hug. "Okay. What happened to her? Is she okay? Do you still see each other?"

"After college, we went to work together, contracting out for major landscaping jobs. I used my education in plants and ecology to design the most amazing gardens. And she used her architecture background to add the hardscape. And yes, we do occasionally see each other, though not as often as I'd like."

After a few moments of silence, he seemed to understand that she wasn't going to say anything else. She couldn't, not without telling him too much, not without endangering herself. He turned on his side, facing her. His mouth dipped down to her shoulder. He lightly sucked, sending heat flashing through her.

He kissed a trail across her collarbone before pulling her in for a deep, mind-numbing kiss that had her melting all over again. When he hardened against her, she broke the kiss, looking down in shock.

"Already? You can't possibly—" she started to say.

"With you, yes, I can," he answered back.

She grinned. "Jake, remember the blue velvet pouch I put in the pocket of your jeans? Trust me when I say that you *really* want to get that." She licked her lips, slowly, deliberately.

He dived for his jeans.

JAKE CAME AWAKE SLOWLY, reluctantly. He didn't want to open his eyes and face the repercussions of last night. Making love to Faye had ranked up there with one of the most incredible experiences of his life. Especially after they'd opened that blue velvet pouch. He shuddered just thinking about it.

But even though making love to her had been practically life altering, it was also one of the dumbest mistakes he could have made. Nothing had changed to make it okay to use her in that way when she had no idea why he was really here. When they found Gillette, she was going to hate him. And he wouldn't blame her one bit.

Perhaps knowing that he could never hold her again was the real reason he lay on the sleeping bag resisting getting up. He could sense the sunlight, knew it was morning and that he needed to get on with the hunt for Gillette. But if he got up he'd have to let go of

Faye. And doing that was harder, much harder, than it should have been.

He ran his hands over her silky hair and slid his fingers in it. Or at least, he tried to. Her hair felt silky, soft, but he couldn't distinguish the individual strands like last night. And her hair was…warm?

Hot breath panted against his face. A sandpapery tongue licked his neck.

Jake's eyes flew open. He stared into a pair of deep green eyes. But they weren't Faye's.

They belonged to a black panther.

He scrambled out of the tent, expecting to feel the panther's claws at any moment, raking down his back and slicing his skin open. He'd just cleared the tent entrance when the panther tackled him from behind, its heavy body knocking Jake to the ground.

He twisted around, aiming a punch at the panther's jaw. But his fist met nothing but air. The panther had jumped off him and bounded across the clearing. Jake scrambled to his knees to see where the animal went. His veins turned to ice when he saw Faye walking toward him from the trees. The panther was headed straight for her.

"Faye, look out!" Jake grabbed one of the small branches from the cold fire pit from last night and ran after the panther.

Faye's eyes widened with alarm.

Oh, God. He wasn't going to reach her in time.

"Faye!"

The panther jumped at her. Faye disappeared beneath a black ball of fur as she fell to the ground. Jake reached them and pulled back the branch like a bat, ready to let it fly.

"Don't hurt him!" Faye yelled, rolling with the panther out of Jake's reach.

Jake stopped with the branch up in the air, blinking down in shock. Faye was on her knees, her arms around the panther's neck, glaring at him as if he was the bad guy.

"He's harmless. Leave him alone," she said.

He slowly lowered the branch, his heart slamming so hard he could feel each beat. "Harmless?" he choked. "He's a wild animal. He attacked me in the tent."

She rolled her eyes. "He probably cuddled with you and licked you. He certainly couldn't have attacked you." She pulled his mouth open. "See, no teeth. No claws, either, except on his hind legs. And I don't see any claw marks on you to justify you threatening to hit him." She hugged the panther and stroked it as if it were a large house cat. "There, there, Sampson. It's okay. Don't be scared."

Jake should have felt ridiculous standing there naked while Faye hugged a toothless, clawless panther as if it were a domestic house cat. But all he could think about was the sheer panic and overwhelming fear when he'd thought she was about to be mauled. Everything else had faded away. All that mattered was reaching her in time to save her.

He'd been willing to sacrifice his own body to protect her, instead of taking the extra few seconds to retrieve his gun from inside the tent, which would have been a hell of a lot smarter than grabbing a tree branch. But he hadn't wanted to risk those extra few seconds. He'd fully intended to wrap his arms around the wild cat and give it something else to chomp on if that would keep Faye from getting hurt and give her time to get a gun to protect herself.

"Jake? Jake are you okay?" She shoved the cat away from her and stood. She looked him up and down, as if searching for injuries. "What's wrong?"

He strode over to her and grabbed her shoulders. "What's *wrong*? What's wrong is that I thought you were about to be hurt, or killed. And I was too far away. My God, I couldn't reach you, I couldn't…" He closed his eyes briefly and swallowed. When he opened them again he looked at the panther, lying on its side, calmly licking its fur. "Next time one of your 'pets' is skulking around, warn me," he bit out.

He stalked back toward the tent to get dressed.

FAYE'S MOUTH DROPPED open as Jake strode away from her, his golden skin gleaming and rippling with muscles in the morning sunlight peeking through the trees overhead. His anger showed in every step, every jerky movement of his beautiful body until he disappeared into the tent.

It hadn't even occurred to her to tell him about Sampson. The cat often followed her on her jaunts through the woods. But he usually stayed closer to the store so he wouldn't miss a meal. She and Amy fed him ground-up meat every day out the back door. The cat tended to be shy around strangers, with good reason. Its past as an abused circus animal still made it skittish. She'd never expected him to show up with Jake here.

And she'd never expected Jake would get so upset, all because he thought she was going to get hurt. She couldn't help but smile. Her instincts about him had been right. He was a good man. After everything that had gone wrong in the past few years, finally everything was starting to go right. When she and Jake found Calvin, they'd tell him about the brother he never knew he had. And then they could all return to Mystic Glades together.

Chapter Nine

Getting over his earlier scare about the panther hurting Faye was proving to be more difficult than it should have been. Jake sat silently through their breakfast of beef jerky, granola bars and water. Faye kept giving him questioning looks, but he just couldn't say anything. He still wanted to shake her.

He'd never been so scared in his life. And that scared the hell out of him. He was losing his perspective, getting too attached. He couldn't deny that now. And that made this trip even more dangerous than it had started out to be.

After packing their gear, they headed out, searching in a grid pattern southwest of where they'd made camp. Nearly three hours later, they found what they'd been looking for—footprints. According to Faye, who was a much better tracker than Jake could ever hope to be, the prints were recent, made in the past day. It was unlikely anyone else would be in this area except for Gillette.

They headed through the trees, occasionally trekking across broad swaths of saw grass marshy areas. Jake kept his gun holstered close at hand, expecting to step on an alligator any minute. But Faye seemed to know exactly what she was doing. She knew the signs to look for, and their jaunt was largely uneventful.

As they neared the edge of another "tree island" and were about to step under the shade of a group of pine trees, Jake put his hand on Faye's shoulder. He'd had enough of the tension and uncomfortable silence between them. And it was time he set it to rights.

She turned with a question in her eyes.

He'd meant to apologize, but instead he framed her face in his hands and kissed her. It was a soft, gentle kiss, at first anyway. But it seemed that any time he touched her he couldn't control himself. He groaned low in his throat and deepened the kiss, crushing his lips to hers. And in spite of how surly he'd been all morning since the "panther incident," she responded with just as much enthusiasm as she had last night.

When he realized he was thinking about pulling her down to the filthy ground and making love to her right there, he forced himself to end the kiss and step back.

"Wow," she said. "What was that for?"

"For being an ass, I suppose. I'm sorry about getting so angry with you earlier. I just…when I saw—"

She pressed her finger against his lips. "Don't apologize. You were upset because you thought I was going to get hurt, and because I didn't tell you about Sampson. I understand, and you're right. I should have told you about him." She stood on tiptoe and pulled his head down to hers so she could press a quick, soft kiss against his lips. "Thank you for caring. It's been a long time since anyone did."

That soft admission sent another punch of guilt straight to his gut. "How did you end up with a pet panther?" he asked, desperate to change the subject.

She took his hand in hers and tugged him along into the trees as they continued to track Gillette. “There’s a panther preserve not far from here. I did the touristy thing there and learned about Sampson, how he was rescued from a circus, how he’d been abused. I kind of fell in love with him. He was so sweet and it was so sad that he couldn’t fend for himself against the other panthers. He had to be kept separate. I guess I visited so much he grew attached to me. Somehow he escaped and ended up here. I walked into my apartment and he’d climbed through the window and was sitting on my couch.”

Jake shook his head and held up a branch for her to walk underneath it. “That had to be scary.”

“More than you realize. I screamed and scared us both. He ran out the window. It wasn’t until then that I realized which cat he was, and that he was harmless and just looking for company. I figured he was hungry, too, unable to catch and eat anything himself. So I went into town the next morning and bought a meat grinder and some raw meat in case he came back. A week later he did, and he’s been coming back ever since. Amy or I usually feed him once a day, but sometimes we don’t see him for several days.”

“It never occurred to you to call the panther preserve people and have them come pick him up?”

“Oh, sure it occurred to me. But I discarded that idea as soon as I thought of it. He was lonely there. I was lonely here. We made a great team.”

He shook his head, smiling. “I think I saw him that first night. He ran across the road in front of my car. That’s what made me see Gillette’s car back in the woods.”

“Huh. Strange.”

"Or fate."

She glanced up at him, probably wondering whether he meant because he'd found the car, or her. Since he wasn't quite sure himself, he didn't say anything.

She stopped and pointed off to their right. "It's getting too dry here to show prints, but see those broken palmetto fronds? I think he ran through there. Those aren't easy to break, so he must have been in a hurry or might have even fallen down."

"Maybe Sampson was chasing him."

She laughed. "Maybe."

Twenty minutes later the trail of broken twigs and bent branches ended at the beginning of a bog.

"He couldn't have crossed this without a canoe," Faye said.

"Because it's so deep?"

"Because it's full of snakes and gators." She turned around. "I don't see a return path."

Jake immediately shoved her behind him and drew his gun. He pointed it up in the trees closest to him, squinting against the late-morning sun. "Gillette, we know you're hiding. I'm going to start shooting up into the trees if you don't come down in the next ten seconds."

Faye put her hand on his forearm. "Threatening to shoot trees again?"

He shrugged. "It worked with you. Why not with him?"

She laughed. "You don't need the gun. He's not dangerous."

Jake knew better. But at the insistent pressure of Faye's hand on his arm, he relented and lowered his gun to his side. He didn't holster it, though. There was only so far he was willing to go.

She nodded her thanks. "Calvin. It's okay. You can come down. Jake's a…friend. It's safe."

Jake looked up at the trees, studying each branch. There, about fifteen feet up the tree closest to them, he saw Gillette. Wearing jeans and a black T-shirt, he blended in almost perfectly. Jake edged his pistol hand slightly back behind his thigh so it wasn't obvious he was holding a gun if Gillette hadn't seen it earlier.

"All right," Gillette said. "I'm coming down."

He wasn't much of a tree climber, or at least, he wasn't as good at getting down as he was going up. Faye ended up talking him through it, telling him where to place each foot. By the time he reached the bottom branch, just a good five-foot jump to the ground, he was shaking so much that pine needles were falling down around him.

Faye looked to Jake for help. He couldn't have planned it any better. He sighed as if helping Gillette was an inconvenience, instead of an opportunity. He holstered his pistol before reaching up and yanking Gillette's leg. The smaller man tumbled out of the tree with a frightened shout, landing on a pile of pine needles and rolling to a stop against the base of the tree.

Faye's gasp of outrage turned to an indignant shriek when Jake tugged Gillette's hands behind him and cuffed them together before hauling him upright.

"What are you doing?" Faye demanded.

"I thought you said he was a friend," Gillette accused, aiming a glare at Jake.

"He is. He's a private investigator. Let him go, Jake."

He shoved the handcuff key in his front jeans pocket. "Sorry, Faye. I truly am." He patted Gillette down but didn't find any weapons. He forced him to sit on the forest floor. Jake put his foot on the chain between the cuffs so Gillette couldn't get up. Then he did one of the hardest things he'd ever had to do. He pulled out his pistol, and pointed it at Faye.

"Toss your gun, and your knife," he ordered. "Over there in the bushes."

Her face went pale. "Why? What are you going to do?"

He could have handled her anger. But the flash of fear in her eyes cut him deeply. "Stop looking at me like that. I'm not going to hurt you unless you draw your gun on me."

Confusion creased her brow. "I don't understand. I thought you were going to help me find Calvin, to let him know about his brother."

"I don't have a brother," Calvin said. "What are you talking about?"

"You do. The man who hired Jake to find you is your brother. When you were put in foster care, you must have had a brother and never knew it. He's trying to find you now. Isn't that right, Jake?"

He fisted his left hand beside him. "That was a cover. To get you to lead me to Gillette. The gun, Faye. And the knife. Throw them into the trees."

She aimed a wounded look at him before bending down and freeing the weapons. She tossed them into the grass. When she straightened, she wouldn't even look at him. Her face had gone hard, and was so pale it worried him.

"So much for my instincts that you were a good man," she whispered brokenly.

He winced.

"Now what?" she asked, her voice sounding wooden.

"I suppose you're going to kill us. It's a good plan. No one will find our bodies out here."

Gillette jerked forward, trying to pull away. Jake shoved his shoulder and slammed him facedown onto the ground. He kneeled beside him with his knee in the middle of Gillette's back to keep him from moving.

"Enough," Jake said. "I'm not here to hurt either of you. I'm a private investigator. I didn't lie about that. I'm under contract to the FBI to find you two so you can face charges in Tuscaloosa."

Faye's brows drew down in confusion. "Charges? What charges?"

"We didn't run from any charges," Gillette insisted.

"No, but you did run. The charges were filed *in absentia*. You're both wanted for murder."

"Murder?" They both said the word at the same time and with the same degree of shock.

Either they had excellent acting skills, or they were truly surprised. A niggle of doubt swept through Jake, but he forced it away. They *had* run. Innocent people didn't run. Or use an alias, as Faye had done.

"Calvin Gillette, Faith Decker, you're both under citizen's arrest."

Faye's eyes widened at the use of her legal name. Handcuffing her was what he should do next. And he'd brought along an extra pair for that purpose. But he couldn't bring himself to do it. Dex was right after all. Faye had gotten under his skin. He'd do his job, take her in, but *he* wouldn't be the one to cuff her. Hopefully he could get a signal out here. Because taking both of them back by himself, with only one of them cuffed, could get messy. He pulled out his phone to call Holder.

"Don't," Faye said, a sense of urgency in her tone.

"Please, Jake. For me. Wait. Hear us out. Something's terribly wrong here. Neither of us has killed anyone. I swear."

He steeled himself against the pleading tone of her voice. "As many times as you've lied to me, swearing doesn't hold much weight."

She flinched. "Fair enough. Looks like we've both been lying to each other, though. Was last night a lie, too?"

"Don't," he said. "Don't go there. This has nothing to do with that and you know it."

"Do I?" She looked away, but not before he saw the sparkle of unshed tears in her eyes.

Damn it.

He tried the phone. No service. Of course.

"We have a right to know who's trying to frame us," her broken voice called out to him. She sounded so hurt, so lost, it was torture not to go to her and pull her into his arms.

"No one's trying to frame you. I'm working for Special Agent Quinn Fugate. He's been following your case out of the Birmingham, Alabama, field office. But the crime took place in Tuscaloosa. The victim was Vincent Genovese."

"Genovese? Calvin and I *worked* for him. We didn't *kill* him."

"Don't tell him anything," Calvin warned.

"Remember the sister I told you about? My foster sister?" Faye asked. "I wasn't completely honest. It was a brother, not a sister. Calvin was the one I was talking about. He's the one I started a landscaping business with. That job I told you about, renovating gardens on a massive estate, that was Genovese's estate."

"Shut up," Calvin called out. "Don't make yourself a target, Faye."

Jake pressed his knee harder against Gillette's back. Gillette grimaced but didn't say anything else.

"Tell me what happened, Faye," Jake said.

"We'd heard rumors about Genovese, that he might be part of organized crime. But we didn't think there could be any harm in taking the job. And we really needed that job. We were fresh out of college, broke, with student loans coming due. It was just a few months of work, and it was on the up-and-up. We were just redoing the gardens. So we took the job. And it worked out great, at first. But when you're outside all the time, you start noticing patterns, the people who come and go. You hear conversations you aren't meant to hear, see things you aren't supposed to see."

"Damn it, Faye. Shut *up*," Calvin swore.

She ignored him and started across the clearing toward Jake. He tightened his hand around the pistol and watched her warily. He couldn't let her get close enough to flip him or pull some other kind of trick. No underestimating this time. But could he pull the trigger if he had to? He honestly didn't know.

"Genovese would have us come in the house sometimes, for meetings in his front study. We'd review architectural drawings, gain approval for the garden plans. He paid us in cash out of his wall safe. That made us both uneasy, but we took it."

"Faye," Gillette cried out.

Jake leaned down close to him. "Interrupt again and I'll gag you. Go on, Faye."

She stopped and flicked a glance at Gillette. "My point is this. We knew Genovese, liked him, had no reason to hurt him. We were both working the day he was killed. Someone shot him while he was in the front study. But, Jake, you have to believe me. Calvin and I didn't pull the trigger. Someone saw the killer. There was an eyewitness."

"Quinn didn't mention that."

"That's because the person who saw Genovese get shot didn't tell the police."

Jake looked down at Gillette. He already knew what was coming. "And who is this supposed eyewitness?"

She drew a shaky breath. "Me."

Chapter Ten

Jake was still reeling from Faye's declaration about witnessing Genovese's murder. He didn't know what to think, or what his next steps should be. The only thing he was sure of was that he wanted more details, because the sincerity in Faye's voice resonated inside him. This time she wasn't lying. He was *almost* sure of it. But then why had she and Gillette gone on the run? Why was she using an alias? Who were they hiding from?

He kept his pistol in close reach on the ground beside him where he could grab it if he needed to. He'd sat Gillette up against a tree about ten feet away. Then he and Faye had shucked their backpacks and left them in the grass before sitting down across from each other so they could talk.

"From the beginning," he said.

She braced her hands on the ground beside her. "There's not much to tell. I was planting flowers around the base of some shrubs outside the window to Genovese's study. When I finished, I gathered my tools and stood to go put them in the gardening house at the back of the property. I was facing the window and saw Genovese arguing with another man. The man had a gun in his hand. I froze. I couldn't move. And then he just…

shot him. I think I must have screamed or moved or something. The shooter jerked around and raised his gun. I ducked down and the window cracked above me."

Jake put his hand on hers. "He tried to shoot you?"

"Yes. I dropped my tools and ran."

"Where were *you*?" he called out to Gillette.

"I was outside, too, on the other side of the house. I heard the shots, and one of the maids screaming. I ran inside and found a group of servants standing around Genovese. One of them had already called the police."

"Did anyone else see the shooter?"

They both shook their heads.

"Okay, what happened next? The police came? Did you both give statements?"

"Yes," Faye said. "But I didn't tell them I actually saw Genovese get shot."

"Why not?"

She clasped her hands together in her lap. "I was too scared. I'd seen enough while working there to know that if I said anything I could end up dead like Genovese. The man who shot him wasn't a very nice man. We think he was into organized crime, like Genovese. Calvin and I had both seen him several times. We'd heard things, and knew he was dangerous. He always had two other men with him, bodyguards, except for that day. He must have snuck onto the property, because his car wasn't there, and neither were his men. I think he'd planned to kill Genovese. But he didn't plan on anyone seeing him. I knew I had to get out of there or he'd come back and find me. That's why we ran. As soon as the police let us go, we were gone."

The certainty in her voice, and Gillette's answering nod from the other side of the clearing, had him feeling frustrated. "But you talked to the police. You could have told them what you saw. They could have protected you."

"Like they protected her in foster care?" Gillette called out. "We know all about police protection."

Everything inside Jake froze. All kinds of horrible scenarios about what Faye might have suffered as a young girl flashed through his mind.

She entwined her fingers with his. "Don't look at me like that. It's not as bad as you think. We had some…rough times growing up. There were some… bad homes. But Calvin was always there to defend me, to protect me. I owe him so much. Even when the authorities didn't believe our claims about the abuse, or attempted abuse really, Calvin was there for me. We stuck together, defended each other. That's the only way I survived."

She pulled her hand back. "But that's not the point, is it? The point is that neither of us had any reason to trust the authorities. After Genovese died, and his killer shot that bullet at me, barely missing, Calvin and I knew we had to disappear. I came back here, to Mystic Glades. Calvin moved around a lot, eventually settling in Naples. Everything was fine until last week, when he saw one of the killer's men. He panicked and called me and was on his way here when he crashed his car."

"Who is he? The man who killed Genovese?"

"Kevin Rossi."

Jake tried to place the name, but it didn't sound familiar. Then again, he wasn't from Alabama. "Okay, okay. The problem is, if you're telling the truth, you have no proof."

"But we do. At least, we can prove *we* didn't shoot

anyone. The police tested us to see if either of us had fired a gun. They tested all of us, everyone who worked on the estate."

"A GSR test, gunshot residue?"

"I believe that's what they called it, yes. We were all cleared."

Jake carefully watched both of them, looking back and forth. He wanted to believe what she was telling him. But he sensed there was something more to the story, something neither of them wanted to share.

"You said you used to come to Mystic Glades during the summers. Did you use your real name or your alias back then?"

She gave him an aggravated look. "I'm not using an alias. Faye is my nickname, and Star is my middle name. My full legal name is Faith Star Decker. To my friends, I've always been Faye Star. But on legal documents I have to use Faith Decker." She took his hand in hers again. "Jake, I'm telling the truth. Neither Calvin nor I have done anything wrong."

Jake shook his head. "Gillette is known as a petty thief in Naples."

She flashed an irritated glance at Gillette, sitting against the tree. "I'm not surprised. He's been known to stretch the law a bit more than he should. But he's not a murderer." She squeezed his hand. "If you take us to Naples, make us go to court, you could be signing our death warrant. Rossi would find us. I have a new life in Mystic Glades. And Calvin can come here, too, or start a new life somewhere else. We can be safe again. All you have to do is walk away, pretend you never met me." Her voice broke and she tugged her hands back from him. "Pretend you never met Calvin. We can both go back to our lives the way they've been for the past thirteen months."

That little catch in her voice had him wanting to pull her into his arms again. But he couldn't do that. Not yet. Things weren't as simple as she naively believed them to be.

"Faye, if I hadn't come along, someone else would have. What about all of your friends back in town? What do you think could happen to them if the mob really is looking for you and they eventually find you?"

Her lips tightened.

Jake turned his attention to Gillette. "If you were trying to find Faye when you crashed your car, why didn't you let the two men you saw in the woods in the past few days take you to her? Instead, you hid out."

"I didn't know who they were. They could have been working for the killer."

Jake swore. "This is one hell of a mess. What did you do to bring attention to yourself back in Naples? Or did you go back home, to Tuscaloosa, and got spotted there? Did you bring the FBI and Rossi back here? Faye would have been better off if you'd stayed way the hell away from her. She's not safe anymore, you've got that right. But not because of me. Because of you."

Gillette glared at him and shoved himself to his feet. Jake grabbed his pistol and jumped up at the same time as Faye.

"Stop it, both of you," she said. "None of this is resolving anything."

"You've got that right," Jake said. "The only way to fix this is for all of us to go back into town, to Naples. We'll sit with Deputy Holder and talk this out. I'll notify special agent Quinn and he can arrange for some

US Marshals to come down here to protect you." He looked at Faye. "If you testify against the man you saw, and he's in organized crime, you could go into WitSec, the Witness Security Program. They'll give you a new name, a new life, and you won't have to worry anymore. You'll be safe."

She shook her head, her blond hair bouncing around her shoulders. "No. I can't do that."

"Why not?"

She shot a glance at Gillette. He looked away.

Jake grabbed her shoulders. "Am I a fool again to believe what you've been telling me? You've lied so many times, I'm not sure what to believe. Part of me wants to buy everything you just said, but you and your 'brother' are holding out on something. You haven't told me the full story. There's obviously another reason you don't want to go to the police. What is it?"

Her eyes filled with misery. "I'm so sorry, Jake."

Her apology, and the sudden quiet in the glade, had him whirling around.

Gillette crashed into him like a small bull, knocking him to the ground. Jake swore and reached for his pistol. But it wasn't there. It was still on the ground where he and Faye had been sitting. He tried to grab Gillette, but the smaller man rolled out of the way and jumped to his feet.

A shrill whistle echoed through the clearing.

Jake looked behind him. Faye was the one who'd whistled. He braced his hands on the ground and shoved himself to his knees. Something hard crashed against him again, knocking him back down. Warm, thick fur brushed against the side of his face. Sampson had jumped on him from one of the nearby trees and had his paws wrapped around him like a blanket.

"Get off me, Sampson," Jake ordered as he tried to shake the cat off.

Another shrill whistle sounded. Sampson licked the side of Jake's neck as if in apology, then leaped off him and bounded back into the trees.

Jake jumped to his feet, then froze.

Faye stood in front of him, just out of his reach, pointing his own gun at him.

"I'm truly sorry," she said. "But you've left me no choice. Toss me the keys to the handcuffs."

"Don't do this," he said.

"I have no choice," she repeated. "The keys."

He tossed them to her.

She caught them in her left hand, her right hand never wavering as she held the gun on him. Gillette immediately sidled over to her like a snake, turning his back so she could unlock the cuffs.

"What are you going to do?" Jake asked.

"We're leaving," she said as the handcuffs dropped to the forest floor.

Gillette rubbed his wrists, aiming a glare at Jake. "Give me the gun. I'll make sure he doesn't try to follow us."

"Shut up, Calvin. You've caused enough trouble as it is," she said.

His mouth tightened but he didn't say anything else.

"You've got everything you need to survive out here for a couple of days in your pack," she said to Jake, motioning toward where he'd set the bag earlier. "You remember the way we came. Just go back the same way. Keep the sun to your right. Don't try to travel at night.

It's too dangerous. I'll leave the canoe for you. Since you won't have to go slow to search for anyone on your way back, if you hurry you could make it to Mystic Glades before dark."

"And where will you be?" he asked.

"Gone. Calvin and I will find somewhere else to hide."

"Hiding isn't the answer. Don't do this. Please."

"I'm sorry, Jake. There are things you don't understand."

"Then explain them to me. Let me help you."

She shook her head. "You can't help me. I'm in too deep. We both are. Now close your eyes."

"I'm not closing my eyes."

Gillette picked up a thick, broken piece of branch from near one of the pine trees and hefted it in his hands. "I can take care of that."

"Touch him and I'll shoot you, Calvin. I'm not joking."

He gave her an irritated look and dropped the branch.

"Close your eyes, Jake," she repeated. "Please."

He sighed heavily and closed his eyes.

"Now count to twenty before you open them again."

"This is ridiculous," he grumbled. "We're not in elementary school playing a game of hide-and-seek." He opened his eyes. Faye and Gillette were gone.

Chapter Eleven

Jake sat on the same log he'd sat on yesterday afternoon, when he'd called Dex after he and Faye had stopped to set up camp. He'd managed to backtrack to the same spot, but he wasn't so sure about his ability to find the canoe—assuming Faye really had left it for him—and figure out how to get back to Mystic Glades. And just like yesterday, he was on the phone with Dex.

"I still can't believe I let her distract me, and Gillette got the drop on me. Stupid, stupid, stupid."

"No arguments here," Dex said.

"Thanks, buddy."

"Any time. So, basically, the bad guys got away, after blaming some phantom named Kevin Rossi for their crimes. We're out a boatload of money, meaning I'm going to have to pump more of *my* money into this venture to keep it afloat. And you're lost. Did I miss anything?"

"Other than the fact that you might need to pay my rent for a few months, nope. That pretty much sums it up."

Dex groaned. "You're killing me."

"You're the money man. You knew the risks when you decided to partner with me."

"In other words you don't feel sorry for me."

"I don't feel sorry for millionaires."

"Billionaire."

"No one likes a bragger."

Dex laughed.

"All these trees look the same to me. Faye did say keep the sun on my right side. But since it's noon and the sun is directly overhead, that's not too helpful."

"You want me to call search and rescue?"

"You're kidding, right? Holder called off the search at the accident site in just a few hours, and he had a good starting place for the search. If you ask him to look for me somewhere within a fifteen-mile radius of Mystic Glades, he'll probably laugh you off the phone. No one seems to even know where Mystic Glades is except the people who live there."

"Sounds like an awesome place."

"You have no idea." He picked up a rock and tossed it at a dark spot near a tree. When nothing moved, he relaxed, a little. Maybe that *wasn't* a gator hiding under the bushes. Then again, maybe it was, and it was waiting for him to come a little closer. The whole area was giving him the creeps. He was seeing predators everywhere he looked.

"Seriously, man. You need me to call the cops?" Dex asked.

If the person who'd stranded him out here had been anyone but Faye, he'd say yes. But telling the police she'd left him here could make things worse for her, if that was even possible. He didn't want her hit with more charges.

Gillette was the true one to blame. He was a bad influence on Faye. He'd protected her when they were younger, which made her feel obligated to protect him now. Whatever the two of them were *really* running from could be laid at Gillette's door. Jake would bet his last bullet on it.

"Don't call the cops yet. I'll make a go of trying to find my way back. I've done okay so far. She left me the backpack. I've got plenty of food and water. And a tent if I don't make it back tonight. She even left my gun, which was a surprise. Obviously she wasn't trying to leave me defenseless out here."

Dex snorted. "No, she just left a townie in the middle of the wild, knowing he probably will never find his way out. Those supplies won't last forever. Neither will the battery on your phone."

"I've got a solar charger or it wouldn't have lasted this long. Not that it works in more than a handful of places out here anyway. The cell service is ridiculous. But I'm okay. For now. Tell me what you've found out since our last chat."

"Nothing surprising." A keyboard tapped in the background as Dex went to work on his computer. "Okay, first, I decided to look at Quinn, just to set your mind at ease. He's exactly who he says he is—a special agent with the FBI on the verge of retirement. And his record is as good as he boasted. There's hardly a blemish on it, except for Genovese. That case went cold within hours of the murder. Quinn's story that he was hiring us on the side because the Bureau wouldn't pump any more money into the case seems accurate. He really just wants a clear record when he retires."

"Okay. Why was the FBI involved in the Genovese case in the first place? It was just a murder, if there is such a thing as 'just' a murder."

"Good question. I wondered the same thing and dug in a bit. Because of Genovese's occupation as resident mob guy and head of organized crime in Tuscaloosa and everything within a fifty-mile radius, he was already under investigation by the FBI. They were trying to break into his operation for a couple of years before his death, trying to get a guy on the inside, although I couldn't get any details on that. Quantico wasn't pleased when Genovese got whacked. They were left with nothing after spending considerable resources on him. They decided to cut their losses and move on, which is why they left the murder investigation to the locals. Not that *they* did much, either. Genovese didn't have any family to push them to keep the case open. All his assets went to charity. No one seems to care about finding his murderer."

"Except Quinn."

"Except Quinn, yes. If he solves the murder, it doesn't rehabilitate the case against the mob the FBI was going for, but at least he ties up the loose ends and can get credit for solving the murder. For someone with a twenty-five-year career, something like that can be pretty important, I would imagine."

Jake rubbed the ache starting between his eyes. "Okay, did you find anything else about Faye and Gillette?"

"Not much more than we knew when we started. I did confirm they both basically grew up in foster care together. And I may have bribed a clerk at UA to give me the name of one of Faye's roommates so I could ask her some questions."

"Bribed, huh?"

"Looks like I'm flying to Tuscaloosa for dinner when this case is wrapped up."

Jake laughed. "I hope she's worth it."

"She sounded gorgeous on the phone."

He laughed again. "I'm sure she is. What did you find out?"

"The roomie said Faye basically had two really good friends—Amber Callahan and our friend Gillette. Faye didn't open up much to her, but the roomie said Faye was really tight with Gillette. He got into trouble, petty, stupid stuff. And she was always there to bail him out, sometimes literally. He has a record, most of it juvenile types of crimes. I got the impression Faye was like a mother hen, or even a bulldog when it came to being loyal to him."

Jake thought back to the incredible night he'd spent with her, and then how quickly she'd turned on him to save Calvin. He laughed bitterly. "Yeah, you didn't have to tell me that. I know where her loyalty lies." Certainly not with him. He kicked at a dried branch lying near the log, smashing it in two.

"Is there something else you're not telling me about what happened out there?" Dex asked.

"Nothing I'm going to share."

"O…kay. We'll just move along then. Assuming you can find your way out of there without me calling in the troops, what's our next course of action? Should I get Holder to put out a BOLO for Gillette and Star?"

Jake stood and did a slow turn again, making sure he wasn't about to become prey to something sneaking up behind him, before sitting back down on the log. "I wouldn't have a clue what to tell them to be on the lookout for. Gillette, as far as I know, doesn't have another car out here anywhere. And Faye didn't have one at her shop. For all I know, they're escaping by canoe or on foot. And knowing Faye, I don't see her going down the highway back to civilization. She'll take advantage of her knowledge of the Everglades and come out the other side, probably south of here, closer to the Big Cypress Preserve or the Tamiami Trail."

"Then we're just going to do, what, nothing?"

"You can look into Rossi."

"The phantom killer. Waste of time, but okay. Back to my original question. What else are we going to do, if anything?"

"Give me a minute." He scrubbed the stubble on his face that he hadn't shaved because he'd forgotten to bring his razor. He wasn't coming up with any amazing strategies, so he decided to play it by the book, to work it the way he would if he was undercover as a detective in Saint Augustine. And he'd use his knowledge of Faye to guide him—assuming he ever made it back to civilization and found her. "Okay. This is what we're going to do."

After listening to Jake's plan, Dex said, "That's it? That's the brilliance you came up with?"

"You got something better?"

"No. But I haven't been a police detective for the past ten years, either."

"Bite me."

Dex laughed and ended the call.

With a rough plan in place, he shoved his phone back in his pocket. He stood and looked around again, trying to get his bearings, trying to remember where he and Faye had emerged from the trees yesterday before going back in where they made camp. He considered himself to be observant. He'd been trained to remember things like hair color, height, approximate weight, even the clothing someone was wearing. He could look at a crowd of people for just a few seconds and remember how many men and women were in the crowd, even the mix of ethnicity, all as part of his training as a police officer. But remembering which clump of trees he and Faye had walked through was an entirely different skill set he apparently did not possess.

The sun was still high overhead, which meant he had several hours of false starts if necessary before he lost the light and had to give up for the night. Might as well start right now.

He picked what he thought might be the right direction and headed out. A few hours later, he was back in the exact same spot, cursing whoever had come up with that saying that lost people often went in circles. *He* certainly had. He took a deep sip of water, shoved the bottle back in his pack, then started out in what he hoped was the *real* right direction. Again.

"Don't go that way unless you want to walk to Key West," a soft voice called out.

He drew his gun and whirled around. Faye stood about twenty feet behind him, her expression a mixture of sadness and regret as she slowly lifted her hands in the air.

FAYE STOOD INSIDE her bedroom, relieved to be clean and dressed in a fresh blue skirt and top, but not at all pleased she would have to knock on her own door for Jake to let her out. Not that she could blame him for shoving a chair up under the handle so she wouldn't disappear again while they both took showers. He was furious with her for letting Calvin go and had barely spoken on the trip back to Mystic Glades.

He was waging a war within himself about what to do with her. He'd admitted that the policeman inside him wanted to call Deputy Holder and the FBI agent who'd hired him and have her arrested. But he hadn't. Not yet. She suspected, she hoped, the part he wasn't telling her was that the lover she'd shared herself with didn't want to turn her in. He *did* seem surprised and confused over why she'd come back for him.

The answer to that was easy. She couldn't have lived with herself if something had happened because she'd abandoned him in the swamp. She couldn't have done that to anyone, but especially not to Jake. Somehow he'd managed to work his way past her defenses to the point where she was willing to risk her life just by being with him, when she should have been running somewhere safe as Calvin was doing at this very moment.

She smoothed her skirts, flipped her hair back behind her shoulders and knocked on the door. Boots echoed on the hardwood floor from the living room. The chair on the other side scraped against wood before he opened the door.

He braced his arms against the frame. Neither of them said anything for a moment, facing off like the adversaries they'd become.

"You hungry?" he asked, his voice sounding strained.

The suggestion of food elicited an immediate growl from her stomach. She slapped her hand against her belly. "Apparently I am."

His lips curved in an *almost* smile. After this morning, she was grateful for that much at least.

He stepped back and waved his hand toward her

eat-in kitchen. A mixed salad sat in the middle of the table. Sandwiches sat on a plate beside it.

"Based on the frightening lack of meat in your refrigerator," he said, "I'm guessing you're a vegetarian of some kind. All I could find for sandwiches was cheese. But it's better than beef jerky and granola bars. Hopefully."

"I eat cheese sandwiches all the time. It looks great. Thank you."

He surprised her by pulling out her chair for her before taking his own seat. Since both of them had skipped lunch and dinner in their rush to get back to Mystic Glades before nightfall, they were both hungry and ate quickly. Faye didn't mind. It meant no stilted conversation and that she could eat without being grilled with dozens of questions. But as soon as she finished her last bite and put her fork down, Jake did the same, as if he'd been going through the motions of eating just until she was done.

With both of them helping, the cleanup went fast. Too fast. Soon there was nothing left to do except sit on the couch and start the interrogation.

They both sat sideways, facing each other.

"Go ahead," she said. "Get it over with. Ask your questions."

"What's the real reason you came back for me?" he asked. "What's the catch?"

She stiffened. "No catch. I never intended to leave you stranded. As soon as Calvin was safe, I went looking for you."

"Again, why?"

If he couldn't figure out that she cared about him, she sure wasn't going to tell him. "Because you're a human being. I wouldn't leave anyone out there to fend for themselves. It wouldn't be right."

His eyes searched hers, as if he could divine the truth. "That's the only reason?"

"Of course. What other reason would there be?"

His mouth tightened, making her wonder what he'd expected her to say.

"Where's Gillette?"

"Gone, where no one will find him."

He cursed and shook his head. "He's a fugitive, Faye. He needs to face up to his past."

"We're both fugitives, according to you. But neither of us has done anything wrong."

He put his hands on her shoulders and pulled her toward him. "Faye, I found him once. I'll find him again. But if you help me, it would make things easier on you. I can tell the Feds you cooperated. That might help your own case."

She tugged his hands off her shoulders and sat back. "Make things easier on me? In case you haven't figured it out yet, that's not the kind of person I am. I don't hurt other people so I can take the easy way out."

He blew out a frustrated breath. "You went to college for four years. You had a future ahead of you, and you gave it up to hide out in Mystic Glades. I don't buy your fear of policemen as the only answer. There's something more. What did you and Calvin do that makes you too afraid to go to the cops even though you think a killer might be looking for you?"

When she didn't answer, his brows drew down like a dark cloud. "Faye, I can help you. But you have to trust me. You have to open up to me."

"By telling you where Calvin is? So you can have

him arrested for a crime he didn't commit?" She shook her head, her lip curling with disgust. "We may not be blood-related siblings, but I have more loyalty to him than that. I would never trade my safety for his. I thought you would understand that since you knew what it was like to lose your only sibling."

He winced as if she'd hit him, immediately making her regret her harsh words. But what was done was done. She needed to convince him to leave so she could leave, too. She was trying to put a brave face on everything, but in reality, she was terrified. Her past had already caught up to her, and she had to get out of here before it was too late.

It wasn't that she didn't trust Jake to help her. She believed he'd do everything he could if she let him. But that would only put him in danger. And even though she wasn't a murderer, she wasn't completely innocent. If he found out what she *had* done, he'd have to make a choice. And she was very much afraid that keeping her secret was a choice he wouldn't make.

He sat there a long time, watching her, perhaps waiting for her to change her mind. But she'd already made up her mind. Nothing could make her risk Jake's life to help her out of a mess of her own making. He deserved better than that.

Finally, he stood. And without another word, he left the apartment.

She blinked in surprise. Was he letting her go then? She ran to the window at the end of the living room and looked down into the street. Moments later, Jake's black Charger turned out of the side alley beside her store, out onto the main drag. He didn't look up at the window as he drove by. And soon, he passed through the gates of Mystic Glades and disappeared from sight.

She sank down to the floor, stunned. He was letting her go. Tears pricked the backs of her eyes. *He's letting me go.* He'd forced his way into her life, into her heart, and he was letting her go. She wrapped her arms around her knees, and for the first time in a very long time, she stopped being strong, stopped trying to bottle up her frustrations, her fears, her regrets. The tears flowed freely, branding hot tracks down her cheeks and falling to the floor.

A long time later, when the room had gone dark around her, she drew a shaky breath. She went into the bathroom and washed her face. She was ashamed that she'd allowed herself to sit there so long feeling sorry for herself. She didn't have time for that. Staying here was no longer an option. The past had caught up to her and Calvin.

They'd had a terrible fight after leaving Jake in the swamp, the same fight they'd had several times over the past few months. Her answer to his question remained the same as it always had—no. He'd been furious, but there was nothing he could do about her decision. She took him to a friend's cabin near the highway. The last she saw of Calvin, he was staring at her from the passenger seat as Eddie drove him back to Naples to collect his things. The plan was for Calvin to get a bus ticket and find his own place for a new start. A few months from now, when they were both settled and Calvin's anger cooled, they'd contact each other through email and reconnect. They'd both apologize and everything would be fine. That was the constant cycle of their relationship.

She sighed and started packing another one of her

backpacks. Eddie had been insistent that she didn't need to pay him for taking Calvin to Naples. But he didn't make much money and she knew he couldn't afford the gas. Since neither she nor Calvin had cash on them, she'd promised to return later. She would stop at Eddie's place first, then continue south to the Tamiami Trail. Maybe she'd keep going all the way to the Florida Keys. It was probably beautiful this time of year. And she could probably get a job waiting tables at any number of tourist traps down there. It wouldn't be her beloved Everglades, but she could think of worse things than living near the ocean every day.

Since she couldn't be sure that Jake wouldn't change his mind and come back, possibly bringing the police with him, she couldn't risk taking the extra time to say goodbye to her friends. She'd have to tell Amy, of course, since she took care of the shop. And she'd have to make sure Amy continued to feed Sampson every day. But other than that, it was time to go.

The grief over leaving her friends, and leaving Mystic Glades, clogged her throat. But she couldn't give in. She had to hurry.

She hid another knife in the sheath sewn into the folds of her skirts. The knife and pistol Jake had made her toss back in the woods had ended up somewhere in the muddy bog. She hadn't taken the time to try to find them. She regretted that now. Hopefully she wouldn't get into a tight spot where she needed a gun.

Her money situation wasn't great, but thanks to the generosity of her "adopted" Callahan family, she'd be okay for several months before she'd start getting desperate. By then, hopefully she'd have a new job—one that paid cash under the table and didn't require a Social Security number.

She took one last look around, then headed downstairs.

JAKE HAD TAKEN a gamble. Based on Faye's pattern, he was assuming she would run again after he left. The gamble was that he was betting she wouldn't be watching out the window for his car to turn around and drive back through the main entrance of Mystic Glades. As soon as he'd driven back inside, he'd turned a sharp left and parked his car behind one of the other businesses off the main road, a bookstore called Between the Covers.

He hopped out and hurried back toward The Moon and Star, keeping to the backs of the shops, close to the tree line. He'd just tucked himself behind a thick live oak behind Faye's store when the back door opened. She stood in the doorway with Amy. They said something to each other and hugged. Faye had her backpack on, and from the tears streaming down Amy's face, it was obvious Faye had no intention of coming back.

She jogged to the edge of the trees, only ten feet from where Jake stood watching her. She waved at Amy and disappeared with a flick of her deep blue skirts.

Chapter Twelve

Faye was moving fast, so fast that Jake had a hard time keeping up with her. Not that he couldn't outrun her. His legs were much longer than hers. But to make his way through the unfamiliar terrain of the Everglades, at night, without getting stuck in a bog or crashing through the low-hanging tree limbs and alerting her of his presence slowed him down far more than he'd anticipated. Hopefully he'd catch her before she got so far ahead that he couldn't hear her.

He followed her for over two hours, something he couldn't have done if the moon wasn't so bright. But then again, if the moon wasn't bright tonight he'd have never let her take off into the woods. He'd have had to come up with a new plan.

She rarely stopped to catch her breath. He was usually gasping for air by the time she did. He considered himself to be in excellent shape, but he wasn't in the habit of running marathons.

There were a couple of times when he lost her and started to panic. But since she obviously didn't think anyone was following her, she made no attempt to be quiet or disguise her tracks. He watched for broken branches and footprints as she'd done when they'd been searching for Gillette together, and he was able to pick up her trail again.

When they started on their third hour, everything suddenly went silent. Jake hurried forward until he could see her and ducked behind some bushes. Thirty feet ahead, she stood in what appeared to be as much of a yard as one could have out in the marsh. In front of her was a tiny building, one of the smallest houses Jake had ever seen. But it was well kept, with a lean-to on the side that sheltered the car parked there. She looked around, as if to make sure she was alone, before knocking on the door.

"It's Faye, Eddie," she said. "Can I come in?"

A full minute went by. No one opened the door. She knocked again and tried the doorknob. The door cracked open a few inches.

"Eddie?" she called, before stepping inside and closing the door.

Who the hell was Eddie? Was Calvin in there with him?

Jake checked his phone, hoping to call Dex again and give him an update. But unsurprisingly, there wasn't any service.

A scream sounded from inside the house.

Jake vaulted over a bush and sprinted for the door, pulling his pistol as he went. The door burst open just as he reached it. Faye ran outside, practically knocking him down as she barreled into him.

He grabbed her arms, steadying her. "What's wrong? Are you hurt?"

She blinked, her shock at seeing him overriding the shock of whatever she'd just seen. Her brow wrinkled in confusion. "Jake? What are you doing here?"

He lightly shook her. "Are you hurt? You screamed."

Her eyes widened. "Oh my God. Eddie. Someone… someone killed Eddie."

He grabbed her wrist and pulled her behind him toward the door.

"No, I'm not going back in there." She tugged, trying to free herself.

"And I'm not leaving you alone out here. We're sticking together. I won't let anything happen to you. Come on."

She swallowed hard and allowed him to pull her inside. He quickly cleared the main room, checking behind the couch and chair, the only places big enough for anyone to hide. The tiny kitchen to the left was completely open. There weren't any doors on the cabinets. He shut the front door and locked it before shoving her down on the floor beneath the window.

"Don't move. I mean it, Faye. Don't go outside, and don't move from this spot. Promise me. And for once, mean what you say."

Her shoulders stiffened, just as he'd intended. He'd insulted her to get her angry, to snap her out of the shock she was sliding into.

"I won't go anywhere," she bit out. "Promise."

Hoping she really was telling the truth, he swung his pistol out in front of him and headed into the tiny hallway. To his left was a bathroom, empty. He steeled himself for what he was about to find in the only other room. He crouched down, and kicked the door open. It slammed against the wall as he ran inside, sweeping his pistol back and forth.

Ignoring the gory scene on the bed since the man there posed no threat, he checked the closet and beneath the bed before holstering his gun. There wasn't any point in checking the man's pulse. He didn't have one. His throat was slit from ear to ear.

Jake pressed his finger against one of the man's wrists just because it was one of the few places not covered in blood. Warm. Which meant the killer might still be close by. He tried his phone again as he headed back into the main room. Still no service. He put it away and knelt down in front of Faye.

"Did you see anyone else when you arrived?" He gently swept her hair out of her eyes.

"No. No one. Just you. *After.*" She shuddered and pressed her hand to her throat as if struggling not to gag.

He nudged her chin up to get her to look at him. "You didn't kill Genovese."

Her eyes widened. "You believe me now?"

"Yes. You would have thrown up all over the crime scene. You don't have it in you to kill anyone."

"You picked a great time to start believing me."

He smiled sadly. "Sorry about that. Sometimes we city slickers can be a little slow. Who was Eddie?"

She gagged again and clapped her hands over her mouth.

Jake grabbed her and ran with her to the kitchen, reaching the sink just in time. He held her hair back from her face as she retched over and over, until there was nothing left in her stomach to throw up.

"Deep breaths, baby," he said. "Slow, deep breaths."

She gave him a startled look. He realized what he'd just said. Calling her "baby" wasn't exactly keeping his professional distance.

He sighed and grabbed the towel hanging from the stove handle. He wet it beneath the faucet and handed it to her. While she washed her face and rinsed her mouth, he made another quick circuit around the room, hoping to find a landline so he could call the police. There wasn't one.

Faye met up with him in the middle of the main room. "You followed me here?"

"Yes." There was no point in denying it.

"I should have expected that." She looked toward the bedroom and shuddered again. "I won't fight you anymore. I'll go with you into town, tell the police everything I know."

"Why? Why now? Because of Eddie?"

"Yes, because of Eddie. He didn't have any enemies, nothing of value to steal. He's dead because of me, because I thought I could outrun my past. But obviously I can't. And I can't risk anyone else getting hurt. I'll turn myself in."

If she'd told him that a few days ago, he'd have jumped at her offer. But suddenly *he* was the one who was hesitant. He wanted nothing more than to grab her in his arms and carry her somewhere far, far away. Where she wouldn't have to face the ugliness of being arrested and going through a trial. Where he wouldn't have to worry about whether she was adequately protected if Rossi came looking for her.

For that matter, Rossi could be outside right now, waiting for her to come back out.

Jake tugged her over to the couch and pressed her down on the cushion. He sat beside her and took her hands in his.

"How does Eddie figure into this? What's his connection to you and Gillette?"

"This morning, when Calvin and I got away from

you, I brought him here. I asked Eddie for a favor, to take Calvin to a bus station. Calvin insisted on going to his apartment first. He said he had to grab some of his things. After that he'd go to the station by himself, go somewhere far away and lie low for a while. But Eddie can't…couldn't…afford the gas for a trip like that. He doesn't have much money. So I told him I'd stop here tonight and reimburse him for a tank. That's all. There's no other connection."

"Calvin went back to his apartment? Didn't he say that he saw one of Rossi's thugs prowling around Naples days ago? That's why he left in the first place, right?"

Her eyes widened in dismay. "Yes. He'd left in a hurry, though. So he didn't have many of his belongings with him. I didn't think about him being in danger going back. He was just supposed to run in and out, a fast trip. Do you think someone might have been watching his apartment?"

"I think it's a real possibility."

She jumped up from the couch. Jake stood in front of her, in case she tried to go out the door.

"We have to get out of here," she said. "We have to warn him. There's a good spot for cell service about three miles north of here. If you can…get Eddie's keys, we can drive there. We can call the police from there, too."

"All right. Wait here and I'll check Eddie's pockets for the keys."

"Faye," a voice called from outside. "Get out here."

"That's Calvin!" She stepped around Jake.

He grabbed her before she could run to the door. "Wait. Let me talk to him first."

Her brows creased. "Why?"

"Because we're in a secluded area, with one dead body and three live ones. And since neither you nor I killed Eddie, do the math."

She glared up at him. "Calvin didn't do this."

"Humor me. Let me check out the situation first."

She crossed her arms and plopped back down on the couch. "Go ahead."

He flattened himself against the wall and peeked out through the blinds. Relief shot through him as he viewed the scene outside. For once, one of his plans was working out. Not exactly the way he'd planned, but he'd take it. Unfortunately, Faye wasn't going to be happy when she realized what had happened.

He crossed to the door and pulled it open. "Come on. Let's go."

"I thought you wanted to talk to him first."

"I've seen what I need to see. It's safe."

Confusion warred with relief on her face as she hurried out the door with him. Guilt reared its ugly head again as Jake watched her eyes widen in shock. He hated that she was upset. But at least the worst was over. She was safe now. That was what mattered.

Calvin stood ten feet away, his hands tied in front of him with a white nylon rope. Another length of rope circled his waist, like a long leash. And behind him, holding the other end of that leash, with a rifle pointed at Gillette's back, was Quinn Fugate.

"It's good to see you, Quinn," Jake said. "Dex called you?"

"Yes, he did. Early this afternoon. I got into Naples just a little while ago. I was going to go straight to that Mystic Glades place Dex told me about. But I stopped by Gillette's apartment first. Guess who showed up? I followed him out here and, well, you can see what happened." He flicked the end of the rope.

Gillette stumbled but righted himself. He swore beneath his breath.

"Oh my God, oh no, oh no," Faye whispered, from behind Jake. She tugged on his shirt.

He turned back to look at her. She was shaking, pale, even worse than when she'd seen Eddie.

He was shocked at how terrified she looked. Then it dawned on him why she was so scared. Regret shot through him. "Honey, it's okay. I'm sorry. I know how bad this must look. But it's okay. The man who has Calvin tied up is an FBI agent. That's Quinn Fugate. Everything's okay. Calvin isn't in any danger."

She shook her head violently back and forth. "That's not Quinn. That's Kevin Rossi, the man I saw shoot Genovese."

Chapter Thirteen

"Toss the pistol," Quinn ordered.

Jake reluctantly pitched his gun into a group of palmetto bushes a few feet away. Faye started around him as if to run to Gillette. He grabbed her, forcing her behind him.

"Don't move," he ordered.

"I have to do something," she whispered. "He's going to kill Calvin."

"Making yourself a target isn't the answer." He looked over his shoulder at her, waiting until she gave him a reluctant nod before facing Quinn again. "What's this all about? You hired me to find these two. Job done. All we have to do now is go into town and work on that extradition order."

Quinn laughed harshly. "Did you think I didn't hear Miss Decker tell you I was Kevin Rossi? You can drop the act. We all know I'm the one who killed Genovese. He and I had a professional disagreement that unfortunately couldn't be settled any other way."

"Professional disagreement?" Jake asked, stalling for time as he tried to think of a way to end this without anyone getting killed. Unfortunately, nothing was coming to mind.

"Playing dumb isn't your forte, Mr. Young. Obviously I was playing both sides of the fence, undercover for the FBI supposedly trying to get the goods on Genovese, while at the same time forcing Genovese to sock away money in a special account for my retirement. It was working beautifully until my boss started demanding results. I had to end the arrangement and cover my tracks. Still, even then, everything would have been fine except that Miss Decker was in the wrong place at the wrong time, and she and Mr. Gillette stuck their noses where they didn't belong. Now I'm forced to remedy the situation."

Stuck their noses where they didn't belong? Obviously there was still more to the Genovese story that Faye hadn't told him. Which put him at a disadvantage. It was tough to bluff or negotiate his way out of the situation if he didn't know the facts. He curled his fists in frustration. "Why now? You got away clean."

"Clean? Not exactly. These two took something that belonged to me the day they ran away. It's a ticking time bomb. I've been agonizing over it ever since, worrying it would surface some day and destroy me. Thanks to Mr. Gillette's stupidity, using an old credit card of his in Naples, I finally got a lead. But my boss is already suspicious of me, so I couldn't follow up on my own. Thanks to you, Mr. Young, I can be in and out of here and log just a couple of sick days back at the office. No one will be the wiser and I can finally retire without worrying." He flicked the rope in his hand like a whip.

Calvin grimaced when the rope snapped against his back. He stumbled forward a few steps. "He wants the journal, Faye. You have to give it to him or he's going to kill me."

Her fingers curled into the top of Jake's pants.

"What journal?" Jake asked. "What makes you think either of them have it?"

Quinn pointed his rifle at Jake again. "While I appreciate that you found these two for me, that's where your usefulness ends. Did you think it was a coincidence that I hired an investigator new to the area, with no family ties? If something happens to you, no one's going to be crying over it and pushing for an in-depth investigation. So if I were you, I'd *shut up*." He swung his rifle back toward Calvin. "The journal, Miss Decker. Where is it?"

"It's not here. But I can get it for you," she called out.

"Where, *exactly*, is it? In that little town of yours, Mystic something or other?"

"It's hidden in the swamp, a full day's hike from here," she said.

"Step out where I can see you." Quinn's voice was calm, cold. His gun hand was just as steady as his voice.

"No," Jake said.

The rifle jerked back toward him. Jake swore and grabbed Faye, diving to cover her just as the rifle boomed through the clearing. The shot kicked up dirt just inches from where they'd been standing. He glared at Quinn.

"That wasn't necessary," Jake growled.

"I disagree. Help her up and push her over here beside her cohort or I'll shoot again. And this time I won't miss."

"Get ready to run," Jake whispered to Faye. "When I stand up, run to the trees as fast as you can. I'll draw his fire."

"No! He'll kill you. And I can't leave Calvin."

He helped her to her feet. "Just do it. Trust me."

But instead of running, she moved away from him just as Quinn had ordered, flashing Jake an apologetic look.

Damn it. He knew she meant well, that she thought she was protecting both him and her brother. But she'd just made everything that much harder. Now Quinn had three clear targets instead of two.

"Thank you, Miss Decker," Quinn said. "Your cooperation is noted and appreciated. I assume you have a cell phone, Mr. Young. Toss it to me."

He pulled his phone out and pitched it squarely at Quinn's chest, hoping he'd lose his grip on the rifle trying to catch or deflect it. But the phone hit him and dropped to the ground. The rifle didn't move. His mouth twitched with amusement.

"Good try." He stomped his heel on the phone, crushing the display.

"A day's walk to the journal. Is that correct, Miss Decker? Or are you making up stories?"

"I'm telling the truth. I hid it in a hunting cabin deep in the swamp."

"Hmm. Not the most ideal of situations, considering I don't know this area. And I certainly don't want to trek through a filthy swamp to find the thing. But then again, that's why I have leverage." He flicked the rope again. Calvin grimaced.

"I'll be generous. I'll give you twenty-four hours to retrieve it and meet us back here. If you aren't back by this time tomorrow night, with the journal, Calvin dies. If I see any signs of law enforcement poking around, or hear any chatter on the police channels—about me, the journal or anything remotely suspicious in the area—

Calvin dies. If you do *anything* to alert anyone or try to get help, he dies. Understood?"

She nodded and held her hands up in a conciliatory gesture. "I understand. Please, don't hurt him. We'll get the journal."

Quinn's brows quirked up. "We? You said *you* know where the journal is. Did anyone else help you hide it?"

"No, I buried it, months ago when I first got here."

"Then you can *unbury* it by yourself." The rifle boomed. The bullet slammed into Jake, sweeping him off his feet. White-hot pain flashed through his body. His lungs seized in his chest. He crashed to the ground, his head cracking against the hard earth. The last sound he heard was Faye screaming.

JAKE RESTED ON the floor in Eddie's main room. He didn't know which was worse—his throbbing headache, the sharp jabs of pain every time Faye pressed her wet cloth against the lump on the side of his head, or the weight and chill of an ice pack sitting on top of his bruised ribs.

"Quinn?" he asked.

"Gone." She pressed the cloth against a particularly sensitive spot, making him wince.

"I'm okay. You can stop now." He pulled her hand away from his head.

"Thank God you were wearing a bulletproof vest." She feathered her hands over his bare skin as if still searching for a bullet hole between his ribs.

"Bullet-resistant. Not bulletproof. But it still packs a punch."

"Do you think your ribs are cracked?"

"All I know is they hurt like hell."

She repositioned the ice pack against his side. He sucked in a sharp breath.

"Sorry, sorry." She dropped the ice pack to the floor and pressed the wet cloth against his head again, sending another sharp jab of pain shooting through his skull. "You've lost a lot of blood. Do you feel light-headed? Can you breathe okay? If you have a broken rib and it punctured a lung—"

He winced and grabbed her hands. "Stop worrying. I'm breathing fine and the bleeding has mostly stopped. I never would have given much credence to your woo-woo science before, but I have new respect for the pouch of medicine you carry on your necklace."

She frowned at him. "Woo-woo science? Maybe I shouldn't have wasted my very scientific powder on you after all." She tugged her hands away and plopped the cloth on the floor beside the ice pack.

He pulled her hand back to his mouth and pressed a quick kiss on it. "I didn't mean to criticize your woo-woo science. Thank you for helping me."

She rolled her eyes. "You're welcome."

"How did you manage to get me into the house?"

"Leverage and physics. I rolled you onto a blanket and used it to drag you inside. It wasn't that hard really, except for getting you over the threshold. I think I may have bumped your head a few extra times doing that. Sorry." She bit her bottom lip in sympathy.

"I'm pretty sure the threshold isn't what's making my head throb right now. Remind me again what exactly happened."

"We need to get you to a doctor. Your memory is pathetic."

"My memory is bound to be fuzzy since I was

knocked unconscious." He tried to sit up. Faye braced her shoulder beneath his and helped him scoot his back against the wall with his knees drawn up in front of him.

"Thanks." He winced. "You said that Quinn had left. Are you sure he's gone?"

"I heard his car going down the road back toward the highway. And he didn't stop me when I was pulling you in here. So, yeah, I'm sure."

"The last I remember," he said, "Quinn was asking about a journal. What was he talking about?"

"Can we discuss this later, after we get you to a hospital? We'll take Eddie's car. And..." She swallowed hard. "Then we'll go to the police and report Eddie's murder, and tell them about Quinn and Calvin."

"I may not remember everything, but I'm pretty sure Quinn would have said something about *not* going to the police. I doubt he's going to make exceptions for hospitals, too. We can't risk your brother's life by outright defiance against his instructions."

She sat back on her heels. "You're right. He said no cops or he'd kill Calvin. He gave us twenty-four hours to get the journal and bring it back here."

"Then we need to get the journal. *After* you tell me what it is."

She cocked her head, studying him. "I don't understand. Why would you, a cop, even consider *not* calling the police in this situation? I would have expected that to be the first thing you'd want to do."

His mouth thinned. "I know what it's like to lose a sibling. And I also remember the cold, dead look in Quinn's eyes. He's not bluffing when he says he'll kill your brother if we don't follow his instructions. Faye?"

"Yes?"

"The journal?"

She sighed. "It's stupid. I told you earlier that Genovese paid our wages in cash from a safe in his study. Well, Calvin apparently paid a little more attention than I did to the lock combination Genovese used when he opened the safe in front of us."

"I think I know where this is heading. After the shooting, Calvin took something out of the safe before the police got there."

"A leather-bound journal."

"Stealing from a mobster isn't the smartest thing he could have done. Even a dead mobster. No telling who else might be interested in whatever's in that journal."

"I know, I know. It's been a constant source of arguments between Calvin and me ever since. I didn't discover what he'd done until we were on the run. By then it was too late to return it without associating our name with the journal. I was afraid that whoever is listed in it would come after us."

"What exactly does it contain?"

"Initials, dollar amounts, dates, account numbers, descriptions of agreements and deals. Pages and pages full of things like that. At the back there's some kind of index written in code. I'm pretty sure it's the key to figuring out the names that go with the initials."

He whistled. "Sounds to me like you've got a gold mine the FBI would love to get its hands on. Did you make any copies?"

"No. I just wanted it gone. And I was afraid Calvin would try to use it to blackmail some of the people in the journal, which would have made everything worse. So I stole it from him and hid it. I wanted to destroy it, but honestly, it seemed too important to destroy. I worried something might happen later on and we'd need it. Thank God I kept it."

"It would have been better if you'd turned it over to the police in the first place."

"Easy to say now. Obviously I didn't think so at the time."

"Sorry. I'm not trying to place blame. Let's just get it and figure out our next steps."

"Are you sure we shouldn't go to the police?"

"If we do, and Calvin pays the price, I don't want to bear that burden the rest of my life. Let's at least start out doing what Quinn said, to buy some time until we can figure out a plan. Okay?"

She leaned in and pressed a soft kiss against his lips. "Okay."

He motioned to his shirt and vest lying a few feet away. "Put the vest on and I'll fasten the straps."

"Uh, no. Not happening. That's *yours*. You're the one who's going to wear it."

"Faye, with Quinn out there somewhere, I'm not about to wear a Kevlar vest while you have nothing to protect you. That's not even negotiable. And we're wasting time we don't have arguing about it."

She shot him an exasperated look and tossed him his shirt while she grabbed the vest. A few minutes later, he was trying to hold back his laughter as she glared at him.

"It's too big. I can hardly move in this thing." The vest extended several inches past her shoulders, practically swallowing her. It hung almost to her knees. "There's no way I can hike through the marsh like this. It's more of a hazard than protection. I can't wear it."

He grudgingly agreed and put the vest back on. He

felt like a heel, but there was no sense in neither of them wearing it. Hopefully it wouldn't come to a gunfight so it wouldn't matter. He didn't bother putting it under his shirt this time. He just strapped it on over the top.

He reached for the holster on his hip. Empty. "My gun, did Quinn leave it where I threw it in the bushes?"

"Unfortunately, no. He took it with him. And he took my weapons, too, even my pocketknife I had stowed inside my backpack."

"What about Eddie? Don't all of you marsh-people have guns all over the place?"

She smiled her first real smile since Quinn's arrival. "While I don't appreciate the disparaging marsh-people comment, you're absolutely right. We do love our firearms out here." Her smile faded. "It goes against my nature to claim helpless female, but I really don't want to go into Eddie's room to look for a gun. Would you mind?"

"No problem." He headed into the tiny hall and opened the bedroom door. The tableau inside had turned from dark red to brown already and was beginning to smell. He held his breath as much as he could and performed a quick search. But apparently Eddie wasn't like everyone else out here. There wasn't one single gun to be found. Then again, maybe Quinn had taken Eddie's guns after killing him. Calvin had known Faye would come back here tonight to give Eddie gas money, and Quinn must have forced that information out of him. Poor Eddie. All he'd done was help a friend and he'd paid for it with his life.

Jake returned to the main room and perched on the couch. "Sorry, nothing."

Faye chewed her bottom lip. "I searched the kitchen and under the couch cushions. I even looked in the oven.

I suppose he could have a gun in his car. It's worth a look."

"I'll do it. Wait here."

"No. You've got sore ribs and a goose egg on your head. I'll do it."

He blocked her at the door. "I've also got the vest. Unless you want to put it back on?"

She held her hands up in surrender. "You win."

After a quick look out the front blinds, he was reasonably certain they were alone. He hurried out to the carport and searched Eddie's Honda Civic. Nothing. He decided to check the backyard just in case Eddie kept a shed with something useful in it. He grinned when he saw what was sitting behind the house. Finally, something was going their way again.

Chapter Fourteen

"I can't believe Eddie was so poor and still had this sweet ATV." Jake waited for Faye to slide off the seat behind him before he dismounted.

"I'm not surprised." Faye turned on the flashlight she'd had in her backpack and looked around to get her bearings. The clear sky and bright moon illuminated quite a bit, but it was still treacherous to be this deep in the 'Glades at night, even with a powerful flashlight. She really wished she had her gun and her knife.

"Why aren't you surprised?" He pocketed the keys to the ATV and joined her.

"A lot of people have them around here. It's almost a necessity. I borrow Buddy's ATV sometimes. It's nearly impossible to reach some of the more remote areas without one. It sure saved us a lot of time. We're ahead of schedule."

"Why would you need to go to remote areas out here?"

"Because that's where the most beautiful parts of the Everglades are hidden. There are pristine waterways and saw grass marshes that stretch for miles and miles, untouched by man, just bursting with life. You wouldn't believe the gorgeous flocks of snowy egrets that live out there. Or the incredible plants and flowers. It's breathtaking."

She flushed when she realized he was staring at her. "What? Am I gushing too much?"

He smiled. "Not at all. I enjoy hearing you describe this place. You really love it, don't you?"

"What's not to love?"

"Oh, I can think of a few things. No electricity. No roads. No bathrooms."

"We have all of those back in town, in Mystic Glades."

"Spotty phone service. Internet that fades in and out. Should I continue?"

She gave him an aggravated look and aimed her flashlight off to the right, toward a dark scattering of rocks and downed trees. "That's where we need to go."

"Looks like an obstacle course."

"Yep. We can't use the ATV anymore."

He groaned as if she was taking away his favorite toy. Which, judging from the way he'd grinned when they'd begun their trip, she probably was.

"I don't suppose there's a canal near here. And you've got a canoe hidden away in a strategic spot we could use."

"Uh, no. Fresh out of canals and canoes at the moment. Are you going to start complaining again? I thought I worked those greenhorn complaints out of you when we were looking for Calvin together?"

"Apparently not." He held up a low-hanging branch. "After you."

She murmured her thanks and they started the last long leg of their journey. The terrain here was much rougher than what they'd gone through before. But that's why she'd originally chosen it. She and Calvin had hiked several times through the 'Glades during those summers with Amber, but not through this area. When she'd hidden the journal, she'd wanted to make sure it was somewhere that he'd never been, somewhere he wouldn't think to look.

The path they were following gradually became even rougher as the pines that had outnumbered the cypress trees gave way to almost nothing but cypress. The tree roots bumped up out of the wet ground all around the base of each tree, spreading out for several feet, like knobby knees just waiting to trip her and Jake. They were forced to slow down and carefully pick their way along the path so they wouldn't fall. They often had to splash through shallow water, or make wide circuits around bogs to find drier land.

Jake glanced up at the dark sky. "These trees are blocking most of the stars. Are you sure we're headed in the right direction?"

"Positive. Everything looks familiar now. We're close."

"How close is close?"

"Maybe another hour."

He groaned. "At least tell me this 'hunting cabin' is kept up and has luxuries like, you know, walls."

She laughed. "Yes, it has walls. And a bed. And a rain-water capture system that filters and supplies water to the kitchenette. It's practically the lap of luxury."

"You didn't mention a bathroom."

"I brought latrine kits."

He shot her a disgruntled look. "Who owns the cabin? I want to complain."

"Buddy."

"Which one?"

She gave him a good-natured shove. "Buddy Johnson, the owner of Swamp Buggy Outfitters. If you're through complaining, we'll be on our way."

An hour later, just as she'd predicted, the cabin she'd told him about came into view. At least, for her it did. She stopped and leaned back against a thick cypress tree.

Jake paused and turned. "Something wrong?"

"Just appreciating how observant you are, Mr. Police Officer Private Investigator Guy."

His hand automatically went to his holster, which of course was empty. He frowned and scanned the woods around them, turning in a full circle. "What do you see?" he whispered.

"The cabin," she whispered back.

He quirked a disbelieving brow and studied the woods again, more slowly. When he saw the structure, he gave her a rueful grin. "You could have mentioned it was camouflaged."

"And spoil my fun? Not a chance." She hurried past him, down the side path that led to the only door. The wood on the little cabin had been painted brown and green to match the trees around it, and nets held dried tree branches against the sides, making it blend in with its surroundings.

She turned the doorknob, but before she could push it open, Jake pulled her back.

"Is it supposed to be unlocked?" he asked, his voice low.

"It's called hospitality. Anyone out this far is welcome to use it. Especially hunters, thus the designation as a 'hunting cabin.'"

He didn't crack a smile at her teasing. "If Buddy

wants to help strangers that way, why camouflage the building in the first place?"

"I didn't say it was for *strangers*. Everyone in Mystic Glades knows about this place. If there are any strangers out this far, trust me, they're up to no good."

"Drug runners?" he asked. "I hear they use the Everglades as a drug route."

"So far I've been lucky enough that I've never bumped into any out here. I've heard stories about people using the canals to make their getaway. We've had more than a few meet their end with an alligator or constrictor because they thought jumping into a canal was a good way to escape the cops."

He took her flashlight, gently shoved her behind him and went inside the cabin first, apparently to search for bad guys. She thought the gesture was sweet, but she didn't wait for him to search the place. She could already tell it was empty. It was only one room, with nothing but a full-size bed against the far wall.

Jake frowned, obviously not pleased that she hadn't waited outside. He stepped past her and bolted the door.

"Mind shining the light over here?" Faye asked.

He pointed the light into the kitchenette. It didn't boast a pantry. There was just a cabinet beneath the sink for things like dishwashing liquid and cleaners and one cabinet attached to the wall next to the door. Inside were a few plates and cups, and two shelves of nonperishable food and some bottled water. It didn't look as if anyone had used the cabin since the last time she'd been here, which meant there was plenty of water and they could snack on crackers and peanut butter. Or she could whip up a can of tuna fish with some of the packets of mayonnaise if Jake wanted some.

"Shouldn't we dig up the journal before we get too comfortable?" he asked.

His bald statement brought the reason for their trip sharply back into focus. She'd been trying not to think about what was at stake while hiking through the marsh. It had been easy since she'd had to concentrate on watching out for predators and trying not to break an ankle by tripping over any downed trees. But now, all of that faded away.

"I'll grab an extra flashlight." She moved a box of saltines to the side and grabbed one of the flashlights from the back. She cracked open a fresh pack of batteries and made sure the flashlight was working before closing the cabinet. "The journal is buried behind the cabin. There should be some tools hanging on the back wall outside, including a shovel. Once we get the journal, I think we should try to get some sleep. The ATV put us way ahead of schedule. And I really don't like being out here at night. We've been lucky so far, but this is hunting time for some of the bigger predators. We can wait here until dawn."

"Works for me. Ready?"

She blew out an unsteady breath. "I guess so. When I buried that thing, I never intended to dig it up again. I'd hoped it wouldn't ever come to that." She pulled back the dead bolt and headed out the door with him beside her.

Jake grabbed the shovel from the back and she led the way between some cypress trees a good thirty feet from the cabin. She stood in the small cleared area and lined up the old, rotted palm that she'd used as a landmark, with the cypress to its right, before pacing off four steps. She used her boot to scrape an X in the soil. "This is it."

Jake broke ground. "How wide and how deep?" He scooped out a shovelful of dirt.

She frowned at how moist it looked. "A foot wide should do. And only about a foot down. I couldn't go much deeper. The high water table would have flooded the hole."

It took him only a few minutes to widen the hole to the required twelve inches. He scooped out more dirt to deepen the hole. Faye kept her flashlight aimed at the ground where he was digging. He'd gone only half the required depth when his shovel made a sucking sound.

A feeling of dread swept through her. "Please tell me that's not what I think it is."

"Mud." He lifted the shovel out and deposited a gooey, wet pile of dirt beside the hole.

"I chose this place because it's on higher ground and over fifty yards from the nearest bog. It should have been dry." Her fingers curled painfully tight around the flashlight as Jake scooped out two more shovelfuls of mud, the last one so wet that oily black water dripped from it.

His shovel thumped against something hard. He tossed the shovel aside and dropped to his knees to finish digging by hand. Faye helped him, scooping out handfuls of the dripping mud. And she prayed harder than she'd prayed in a long time.

"It's in a plastic bag inside a metal box. It should still be okay. Right?"

Jake glanced at her but didn't say anything.

"I've got it." He cleared mud from the corners of the metal box she'd buried over a year ago. It took some tugging, but the cement-like mixture finally gave up the fight, releasing the box with a giant sucking sound. He wiped the globs of gooey earth away from the top and sides and set the box down in front of Faye. "You do the honors." He held a flashlight and waited.

She hesitated, offering up another quick prayer. Her fingers shaking, she flipped the latch and opened the lid.

"Oh, no." The entire box was filled with the same goo as the hole where it had been buried. "It's in plastic," she repeated. "It will be okay. It has to be." She scooped her hands inside. "I can't find it. It's not here." Panic made her voice a high-pitched squeak.

"Here, let me." He took the box and turned it over, shaking it to let the mud drop to the ground. When the box was empty, he set it aside. He sloughed off layer after layer of mud until, finally, something shiny reflected in the light. He pulled the piece of plastic up, letting the remaining clumps of mud fall to the ground. What once had been a gallon-sized plastic Baggie keeping the journal clean and dry was now bloated and dripping at the seams.

Completely full of mud.

Faye shook her head in horror.

Jake laid the bag on top of the ground and tore it open. The edges of the journal finally came into view. He slid his hand beneath it and picked it up. The pages dropped out in big, wet clumps. Only the leather binding was intact.

"I'm sorry, Faye. Whatever was printed on these pages is gone. The journal is just a soggy mess."

"Gone?" She shook her head. "No, it can't be gone." She pushed his hands aside and feathered her fingers over the top of the mass. She gently tried to peel off what seemed to be a page. It shredded like wet toilet paper. A sob caught in her throat. Her eyes clouded with tears.

"Maybe if we dry it out we'll be able to see something," Jake offered, his voice gentle. "I noticed a small tabletop stove in the kitchenette. We could put a pan on top and set the papers in it, turn the stove on low. When the moisture is out, we might be able to dust off the dirt and still read something."

She latched on to his words like a skydiver desperately deploying the backup shoot when the primary one failed. "Yes, yes, that could work. We'll dry them out." She shoved her flashlight into her pocket and scooped her hands beneath the soggy mess, lifting it free of the mud.

Jake put his hands around her waist and pulled her up. He led her back to the house and inside the kitchen, where she deposited the glob of papers on the counter.

"I'll fill in the hole so no one steps in it and sprains an ankle. Be back in a few."

She nodded, barely noticing the door closing behind him as she grabbed a pan.

JAKE STARTED FILLING in the hole, not that it mattered. It wasn't as if there weren't a thousand other holes out in this wild land just waiting to trap an unsuspecting ankle. But he'd needed an excuse to get away for a few minutes. He couldn't bear to see the despair and hopelessness in Faye's eyes. He'd never met a more capable, strong woman. To see her brought down like this was just…wrong.

And now, with nothing to bargain for her brother's

life, and with no weapons, and no way to get help, how was he supposed to protect her? He'd had a vague plan in place when he followed her to Eddie's house. But that plan had mostly consisted of Dex keeping everyone informed—including Deputy Holder, and unfortunately, Quinn Fugate.

Jake had finally admitted to himself last night at Faye's apartment that he was in over his head out here and needed backup. Dex was supposed to arrange that. But without any way to contact him, even if backup came, they wouldn't know where to go. And what if Quinn saw the police before Jake could get to him? He'd kill Calvin.

Or would he? Jake tried to put himself in the crooked FBI agent's shoes. Quinn was risking everything to find that journal. It must have had some incredibly incriminating entries to justify that risk, something that could put him in prison for a long time, or even send other mob guys after him. Calvin was his leverage to get the journal. So he couldn't afford to kill him and risk Faye giving the journal to the police.

Quinn would have to wait until he saw Faye again before doing anything about Calvin, even if he saw police presence. And if Faye didn't arrive back at Eddie's at the agreed-upon time? Jake shook his head. Quinn still wouldn't kill Calvin. He couldn't lose his only bargaining chip.

With the journal destroyed, the only way to keep Calvin alive was to keep him and Faye apart and hope that Holder showed more interest in the situation than he had at the crash site—because Calvin's survival just might come down to the decisions Deputy Holder made.

Keeping Faye from her brother wasn't a task Jake

looked forward to. But hopefully she'd listen to reason and come around to his side of thinking. Either that, or he'd have to trick her.

He smoothed the mud and dirt over the top of the hole and stowed the shovel at the back of the house. He did a quick circuit around the perimeter to make sure there weren't any broken branches or footprints that would indicate Quinn had decided to head into the swamp after all and had somehow followed them. With everything looking okay, he headed inside and locked the door.

When he turned around and saw Faye, he swore beneath his breath. She was sitting in the floor in the middle of the room, a foil pan in front of her with a clump of brown and black inside it. He knew even without asking that the little stove-drying experiment had been a failure. He could tell by the tears coursing down her cheeks.

Faye lifted her head, her expression so bleak it took his breath away. "What am I going to do?" she whispered brokenly.

The desolate look in her eyes, the broken sound of her voice, slammed into him with the force of a hurricane. He'd seen that same desolation in his own eyes when he'd looked in the mirror the day his sister died. He'd choked on those same words, felt the same sense of hopelessness, of loss. The feeling that the world would never be normal again, that he couldn't survive without the one person he cared about the most.

She choked on a sob and covered her face with her hands, leaving muddy tracks down her cheeks.

Ah, hell.

He stepped over the pan on the floor and scooped her into his arms.

Chapter Fifteen

Faye had taken care of Jake, after he was shot. Now it was his turn to take care of her. He set her on the countertop in the kitchenette and gently washed the mud from her hands with a wet washcloth. He washed away every smudge and smear from her tears, every trace of dirt from her face, her arms, her hands, even her legs as she stared off into space. But even though he spoke in low, soothing tones the whole time, trying to get her to react in some way, she acted as if she didn't even know he was there. Tears continued to silently trace down her cheeks.

He rinsed out the washcloth. He'd already washed the mud off himself as well, and there was nothing left to do. She'd refused to drink from the bottle of water he'd offered her, and turned her head when he tried to give her some of the crackers he found in the cabinet.

"I wish I could tell you everything's going to be okay," he said. "But I honestly don't know what's going to happen in the morning. All I can promise is that I'll do everything I can to keep you and your brother safe. Even without the journal. We'll leave early, scout around, come up with a plan long before we get to Eddie's house for the meeting with Quinn."

She blinked and focused on him for the first time since he'd found her staring at the ruined journal, sitting in the middle of the floor. "Why?" she whispered.

He waited but she didn't say anything else. "Why, what?"

"Why would you risk your life to help me? This goes way beyond being hired as a private investigator. I think it's safe to say Quinn's not going to pay your fee anymore." She fingered the silver chain around her neck, something she often did, without even seeming to realize she was doing it.

He grinned. "I suppose it's that whole damsel-in-distress thing. I'm a sucker for a woman in need."

His attempt at humor fell flat. She didn't even smile. What was he supposed to say? Admit that he cared about her? It was crazy to care about someone so fast. He didn't trust it, especially a relationship based on so many lies right from the start, on both sides. Until a few hours ago, he'd thought she was wanted for murder and he was ready to turn her in. And now he knew she was innocent of murder, but she'd stolen that journal. And she was always trying to cover for her brother. For all he knew, she could still be keeping more secrets. He didn't even know if he could trust her. So, why was he helping her? He couldn't answer that. Because he really didn't know.

Since she was still staring at him, waiting, he slid his hand under the necklace to turn her attention. "Are you ever going to tell me what's in that third pouch? The purple one?"

She glanced down and pulled the necklace out from between her breasts. Red, gold and purple pouches hung on the end. She pulled the top of the purple bag open, took his hand and emptied the contents into his palm. It wasn't a bottle with some kind of potion or powder as he'd expected. Instead, it was a pewter figurine, about two inches high.

Both their flashlights were on the countertop, standing on end, pointing up at the ceiling to light the kitchenette. He picked one of them up and shined it on his palm.

"I remember this. It was on your dresser in your bedroom."

"Yes."

"It's a centaur, right? Half man, half horse. Something to do with astrology, I think."

"It's a zodiac symbol. Usually the centaur carries a bow and arrow. Instead, this one is carrying a set of scales."

He turned the little figurine in the light. "Ah, so he is. Like the scales of justice."

"Or scales to balance out the elements, colors, nature…love. That figurine was given to me many years ago, when I had my palm read."

"Read? Like, someone told your future?" He turned the figurine over, impressed with the detail carved into the horse.

"Yes."

At her somber tone, he looked up from the figurine. Her beautiful green eyes captured his. He cleared his throat. "What does the figurine represent then?"

"My fate. The scales and the centaur are linked. One can't exist without the other. The scales are for Libra. The centaur is for Sagittarius."

He grinned. "I'm a Sagittarius."

"And I'm a Libra."

He laughed, but when she didn't laugh with him, he sobered. "Wait? You believe this woo-woo stuff? You think, what, that…you and I…are somehow…fated? What does that even mean?"

She grabbed the figurine and shoved it back into the pouch. "That's the second time you've disparaged my beliefs, and what's important to me." She jumped off the counter and headed toward the bed, her bare feet slapping against the floor, blue skirts fluttering out behind her.

He swore softly. How had she gone from completely nonresponsive to being upset with him in the span of a few minutes? He flicked off one of the flashlights. He brought the other one with him and followed her.

"I wasn't trying to make fun of your…beliefs, or whatever. You kind of threw me with the fate stuff. Are you trying to say something here? About you and me?"

"Not necessarily." She yanked the covers back and slid into bed.

He noted that this time she didn't strip down as she had back in the tent. He sighed and pulled the covers back on his side. When they were both settled, he switched off the flashlight and set it on the floor. He lay on his back, staring up at the dark ceiling.

"What does 'not necessarily' mean?"

She made an aggravated noise and fluffed her pillow. "It means somehow my fate is tied in with the fate of a Sagittarius. Whether it's a good fate or not, I couldn't say. The only thing I'm sure of now is that it's most likely a different Sagittarius than you. Good night." She turned on her side away from him, dismissing him.

He scowled. He didn't believe one bit in her spiritual nonsense. So why did it tick him off that she'd decided *he* wasn't the Sagittarius tied with her fate? He scrubbed his stubble, which was really starting to drive him crazy. He couldn't wait until he was back in civilization again so he could take a real shower and shave.

After several moments of silence, he let out a long breath. Who was he kidding? When this was all over, if they survived, he was going to miss the crazy town of Mystic Glades and all its crazy people. And the person he'd miss most of all was the crazy woman next to him. But she wasn't going to miss him. Of that he was certain. Because once she found out tomorrow that he had no intention of letting her anywhere near Quinn, she was probably going to hate him.

AFTER ONE OF the worst nights of Jake's life, sleeping on a lumpy, far-too-small mattress beside a woman who kept huffing and arching away from him every time he got too close, he was more than happy to see the sun's first rays peeking through the blinds.

Using a latrine kit was just another fun thing to add to what he was sure would be a miserable day. By the time he and Faye were both ready and had stowed their dirty clothes and toiletries back in their packs, the sun was up enough for them to be able to navigate without the help of flashlights. It was time to go. Thank God.

Faye stood beside him at the door. Her golden hair was captured in a braid for a change, focusing attention on her beautiful eyes, which were as deep green as the bodice-hugging skirt outfit she was wearing. If they were talking right now he'd tell her how gorgeous she was. But so far she hadn't said a word to him, and he refused to be the first one to break the silence. Childish, maybe. But he was in a foul mood and wasn't ready to back down or even apologize at this point.

He grabbed the bolt, ready to slide it back and open the door.

She put her hand on his forearm, stopping him. "Wait. We've been running around so fast getting ready that we haven't even had time to make a plan. How are we going to ransom my brother without the journal?"

They hadn't had time to make a plan because they weren't *talking* to each other, not because they were running around so fast. Then again, since his plan was to keep her going in circles today and he was going to do everything he could to sabotage their progress, what was there to discuss?

"We've got several hours of hiking ahead of us and then a long ride on that cherry ATV. We can figure out a plan on the way."

She didn't look as if she agreed with him but she didn't argue. She adjusted one of the straps on her matching green backpack—which meant she'd actually unpacked her backpack from yesterday and had repacked everything into the new one, all so her outfit would match. He barely managed to hold back a grin over that. She squared her shoulders, and her jaw, as if she were about to march out to face a firing squad.

She was brave. He'd give her that.

He slid the bolt back and pulled the door open just a crack to make sure there weren't any gators, snakes or panthers lying in wait. The coast was clear, so he shoved the door back and stepped outside.

Faye closed the door behind her and took the lead without a word.

They headed down the same path they'd traveled

yesterday, going slowly to avoid the bumps of cypress roots and soggy marsh encroaching from the woods. So far they'd been lucky not to encounter any rain, which was unusual during the summer. But the sky was cloudy today, as if they might get an afternoon thunderstorm or two.

The path wound around a thick clump of trees. A metallic ratcheting sound echoed through the 'Glades.

Jake grabbed Faye to pull her off the path. He jerked to a stop. The muzzle of a rifle was pointing directly at his head from about ten feet away. And the person holding it was Quinn, a cruel smile curving his lips.

"Hello again, Mr. Young. You're looking fit for a dead man. Kevlar?"

He grudgingly nodded.

"Should have thought of that. Take it off."

"What are you doing here?" Faye asked, sounding panicked.

"I thought I'd do you the courtesy of saving you the long trip back. And since I threw a tracking device into your backpack when I searched it last night, it was pretty easy to find you."

Jake swore. Electronic devices never worked for him out here, but of course they'd work perfectly for Quinn. When Faye told him last night that Quinn had searched her pack, he should have thought to look for some kind of tracker. Unfortunately he was still fuzzy from hitting his head and hadn't been thinking clearly.

Quinn waved toward the other side of the path. "I also brought our friend Calvin along to make the exchange easy."

Faye sucked in a keening breath when she saw her brother, a few feet to the right of the path, the white nylon rope wrapped around his waist securing him to a tree. His hands were behind him.

"The vest, Mr. Young."

Jake pulled his shirt off over his head, grimacing when his bruised ribs protested the movement. He tossed his shirt aside and dropped the vest onto the ground.

"Excellent. We're almost done here." Quinn edged over, putting more distance between him and Jake, stopping next to Calvin. He swung the rifle to point at Calvin's head. "Give me the journal, Miss Decker, or your brother dies."

Chapter Sixteen

"Stop, stop, please," Faye pleaded. "There was an accident. I—"

"Faye, don't," Jake whispered.

"An accident?" Quinn demanded.

Ignoring Jake's warning, she said, "I buried the journal in a metal box, only a foot deep. I thought it would be safe. But the marsh must have crept in during the rains. The journal was ruined. But that's okay, because it means you don't have to worry that someone will see the information. The evidence is gone."

Jake inched closer to Faye, slowly, so as not to draw Quinn's attention. He should have come up with an alternate plan before they left the house, just in case something like this happened. But it was too late. All he could hope now was to try to get Faye to safety before all hell broke loose. He took another step, another…

Quinn's face paled. He shot a quick glance at Calvin. Calvin narrowed his eyes, his face flushing a bright red. Jake's gaze fell to the ropes around Calvin's waist. Was it his imagination or had they drooped?

Quinn cleared his throat. "What about the account numbers in the journal? There were offshore accounts listed in there. Accounts that can't be touched unless someone knows those numbers."

"I… I didn't know that. This is my fault, not Calvin's. Please don't hurt him."

"Did you make a copy?" Calvin spoke for the first time since the standoff began. His tone wobbled with anger, not fear. Faye must have noticed it as Jake had, because she frowned, her brow wrinkling in confusion.

"No, no I didn't make a copy."

"The money then," Quinn said, sounding nervous. "When your brother took the journal from Genovese's safe, he also took two hundred thousand dollars in cash out of that safe. He said when you two were on the run, you tricked him and stole both the journal and the money. Where's the money now?"

Jake waited for Faye to deny what Quinn was saying. Calvin must have lied to Quinn, to save his own hide somehow, to focus attention on Faye instead. But the miserable look on Faye's face when she glanced at him sent a jolt of dread straight to his stomach. No. No, not possible. She couldn't have stolen that money. There had to be another explanation.

"I don't have it anymore. It's gone," she said.

She didn't have it anymore? Jake clenched his hands into fists beside him. If she had taken that money… No, no, she hadn't taken it. She wasn't that kind of person. He didn't believe it. He *couldn't* believe it.

"It can't be *all* gone," Calvin said.

Quinn glanced at him. If Jake didn't know better, he'd think Quinn looked…scared?

"I'm telling the truth. I don't have the money."

Calvin roared with rage. The ropes binding him fell away. His hands came up from behind him. He was holding a pistol, Jake's pistol. Jake lunged for Faye, throwing her to the ground as the pistol went off. He rolled with her, pulling her behind a tree.

"I need those account numbers, sis!" Calvin yelled. "And I want that money!"

Jake clamped his hand over Faye's mouth when she would have replied. He shook his head in warning and peered around the side of the tree. He jerked back. The bark exploded where his head had been.

Faye's eyes widened. She mumbled something against his hand.

He leaned down and whispered in her ear. "Quinn's dead. Your brother shot him. I think he must have gotten the drop on Quinn before they got here. The rifle had to be empty or Quinn would have fired. And Calvin has my pistol. His ropes weren't really tied. It was all an act. We have to get out of here before he kills us both."

She shook her head in denial and dived away from him. Jake grabbed her, pulling her back behind the tree as the pistol boomed again. She sagged against him, her eyes wide with shock.

"You owe me, Faye! I protected you the whole time we were growing up. You owe me!"

Calvin's wild rantings told Jake just how desperate he was. Which meant he was extremely dangerous. Jake carefully peeked out from behind the tree. His blood ran cold when he realized what was happening. He jerked back behind the cover before anyone saw him, before any of the three men saw him. There were two others with Calvin now. Was that how he'd gotten the drop on Quinn?

Jake sifted through the facts as he knew them. From what Quinn had said, he'd watched Calvin's apartment and grabbed him, and forced him to take him to Faye. That's how they'd ended up waiting at Eddie's, because Calvin knew she was going to return there last night. Maybe some of Calvin's thug friends had seen Quinn grab him. Maybe they'd followed them and after the standoff with Jake and Faye, they'd overpowered Quinn and come up with a new plan. Calvin must have promised them a cut of whatever Faye gave them. Either that's what had happened, or Calvin had somehow planned this all along. Somehow Jake couldn't see Calvin being that smart.

Not that any of that mattered. Not now.

"We have to get out of here. I need you to trust me," he whispered in Faye's ear.

Another bullet cracked into the tree where they were hiding.

She swallowed hard and nodded. He dropped his hand from her mouth.

He looked around, judging the distances from each tree, mentally planning a path that would give them the best cover. He didn't tell her about the other two gunmen. That would only make her more scared than she was right now.

"Okay, we're going to run, fast. Stick with me. Don't stop or slow down to look back. Just do what I do. Got it?"

"Got it," she whispered, her voice breaking.

After picking up a piece of decayed wood lying on the ground, he grabbed her hand and pulled her upright, using the thick cypress as cover.

"Get ready," he whispered. He tightened his hand on hers and threw the wood to the other side of the path.

Gunshots echoed through the trees as Calvin and his men fell for the diversion.

Jake yanked Faye's hand and they took off running.

FAYE CROUCHED BEHIND a rotted tree stump, folding her arms in against her body to keep them from showing and making her a target. She couldn't see Jake anymore, or—thank God—Calvin. Jake had learned a lot in the past few days following her as she was tracking Calvin. Now he was off making noises, bending tree branches, doing whatever it took to create a false trail and lead her brother farther and farther away from them. They'd argued before he left, because she wanted to lay the trail. She was afraid he'd end up lost. He'd rolled his eyes and told her he wasn't quite as useless as she thought and had ordered her to stay put. His order rankled. But he hadn't given her a chance to argue.

She slumped farther down, covering her face with her hands. How naive had she been to believe she could change Calvin by taking the journal and the money? Every few months he'd called her about the money, begging her to give it to him, yelling at her, threatening her. But she'd never really thought he would try to hurt her.

The arguments had gotten worse and worse in the past few months. She should have realized how desperate he'd become. He must have gotten himself into trouble with some thugs, or a bookie. She'd always known he didn't have the same values as her, but she never would have expected him to actually kill anyone. And to turn on her—especially over money. He had to be really desperate. That's all she could think. He wasn't himself, wasn't in his right mind.

Some branches clicked together off to her left. She

stilled, watching. Jake stepped from behind the tree across from hers, motioning for her to follow him. His gaze darted toward the trees on the other side of her.

She jumped to her feet and ran to him. He grabbed her hand and hauled her close.

"You okay?" he whispered.

"I'm as good as I can be, given the circumstances," she whispered back. "What do we do now?"

"You were a good teacher about the marsh. I followed your instructions and led Calvin off a good ways in the opposite direction and circled back to you. I've found another path, more or less, that will take us toward Mystic Glades, if you're right about the direction you told me."

"I am. I know this area. I know the way back home."

"Okay. Let's go. Lead the way. I wouldn't want to get us lost."

She smiled a sad smile. She appreciated his teasing since she knew he was trying to keep her spirits up. But knowing this particular jaunt through her precious Everglades was because her own brother was trying to kill her…the horror of it was almost beyond what she could handle.

When they reached a small clearing, she pointed to their right, directing him the way they needed to go. He started off ahead of her, as was his habit since this nightmare had begun. If they were going into any trouble, he wanted to be the first one facing danger. Before meeting him, she hadn't even realized men that… good…existed.

Something moved off the side of the path in front of him. She drew in a sharp breath and grabbed his arm.

He stopped and raised a brow in question.

She held her finger to her lips and pointed.

A moment later, an enormous constrictor slithered across the path right where they would have been if she hadn't stopped him.

"Was that what I think it was?" he whispered.

"Boa. Just like CeeCee."

"Great. Are there very many more of those around here?"

"Probably."

He shuddered, then winked to let her know he was kidding. Her greenhorn was actually getting more comfortable with the critters in the 'Glades. She grinned back at him.

He started to lead the way but again she stopped him.

"What? Another snake?" He studied the path as if a whole family of boas was about to wiggle through.

"No. This is the way I'd normally go to get back to town. But I think we should go back a different way. It won't be as fast. But it might be safer. If we keep heading straight, we'll end up hemmed in by some waterways on one side. Which would be fine if we didn't have to worry about…about my brother. We could get trapped with nowhere to turn. And going into the water to get away is not an option. Trust me on that."

"Alligator snacks?"

"Alligator snacks." She waved her hand to the left. "If we head back that way we can circle around this section of the swamp and get to higher, drier ground. Then we can move back toward town again."

He gave her an admiring look. "You're teaching me to get around in the marsh like a native Mystic Glades guy. And it looks like I'm teaching you to think like a cop. We make a good team. Let's go. I don't know how long my fake trail is going to fool Calvin."

CALVIN WASN'T FOOLED very long at all. Neither were the two men with him. Jake spotted all three of them picking their way through the treacherous boggy soil, driftwood and scrubby pines that dotted this part of the 'Glades, several hundred yards out. The sun had glinted off Calvin's rifle, which he was betting was loaded now. That flash of light on metal had given Jake the warning he needed to throw Faye and himself down behind a fallen tree before they were spotted.

"There are *three* people after us now?" she whispered, her eyes going wide.

"Actually, there've been three after us since the hunting cabin. I didn't want to alarm you. I'd hoped we could outrun them before you found out."

She lightly punched him in the arm. "I'm not a delicate flower. We're a team. Remember? If we're going to survive we need to communicate better."

"Yes, ma'am. We need to get moving again. Which way?"

She looked around. "Well, we can't cut back toward town the way we were going to go, not without going through Calvin and his men."

"Then we circle around them."

She shook her head. "Can't. This is the only clear area, the highest ground around here. If we go to the left or right of him and those men, we'll end up in gator territory."

Jake peered over the top of the fallen tree again. "Well, we can't stay here. They're heading straight for us. Which means—"

"We head deeper into the 'Glades, and try not to get trapped with the swamp at our backs. Exactly what we were trying not to do." She chewed her bottom lip.

He put his hand on hers. "As long as we watch each other's backs, we've got a chance."

She nodded. They crept toward the trees, staying low so the fallen log would shield them from Calvin's sight.

Another handful of hours found them out of breath and trapped, just as Faye had feared they might be. Jake stood a few feet back from the murky edge of the canal that blocked their way. Behind them, Calvin and his henchmen were still on their trail. Now that Jake knew what to look for, he was able to catch sight of them in the distance every once in a while, and the distance between them was closing. One of the gunmen was obviously a skilled tracker and was able to follow their trail even though both Faye and Jake were doing everything they could not to leave one.

If Jake's guesstimate was right, their pursuers would reach them in about an hour, or less. He stared out over the water, fifty feet across. A quick swim. In and out, just a few minutes, and they'd be on the other side. He scanned the water and the bank on both sides. Not a gator or snake in sight. Just a few egrets and pelicans sunning themselves on the other side of the canal. No ripples in the water to indicate anything sinister lying in wait beneath the surface.

"You sure there are gators in here? Maybe it's the wrong time of day and they're off in their nests somewhere, sleeping."

She snorted. "I grew up in Alabama and I know more about alligators than you do. I thought you were a Florida native?"

"I am. I grew up in a subdivision. By the ocean. The closest I ever get to amphibians is the zoo."

She laughed. "They're reptiles, not amphibians. And trust me. By the time you see them out here in the 'Glades, it's usually too late. The water is *full* of them. And they can hide in the mud so well you might never see them. Don't even think about going in the water."

He glanced nervously at the muddy bank around them, then back at the water. "I'm not sure we have any other options."

"Did you see the movie *Jaws*?"

"Sure. Killer shark. Eats everything in sight."

"No one saw it until it was too late. Picture that waterway full of killer sharks. Do you still want to go for a swim?"

"Okay, okay. We aren't going into the water."

"Maybe I can try reasoning with Calvin. He can't really intend to hurt me. He loves me. Maybe he's just… confused."

"Yeah, shooting Quinn was probably an accident. He *accidentally* pretended to be tied to the tree and *accidentally* shot Quinn in the head. I'm sure he feels awful about it and will be happy to sit and talk with you."

She shot him a glare. "You have a better idea?"

"Plan B."

"Which is?"

"*You* hide and *I* take out the bad guys."

"They have guns. How are you going to take them out without getting shot? Even if you could sneak up within fifty yards of them, that golden tan of yours will make you a gleaming target. And how am I supposed to hide with this?" She flicked her bright green skirts, which swirled in the warm breeze.

"Good point. I don't suppose you'd consider going naked?"

She gave him a droll look.

He grinned. "Didn't think so." He turned around and looked down at the rich, dark mud. Her earlier reference to the movie *Jaws* had other ideas swirling through his head. "Ever see that movie *Predator*, with Arnold Schwarzenegger?"

"Yeah. Why?"

"Plan C."

Chapter Seventeen

Faye reluctantly handed Jake the veils she'd cut from her skirt. Without the veils, she was left with the lining, which resembled a short, black miniskirt of sorts, barely coming to the tops of her thighs. Thankfully she hadn't gone commando today or Jake would be catching glimpses of a lot more than just her legs while she sat on the muddy bank beside the water.

"You owe me a new skirt," she grumbled. "I still don't know what you want to do with the veils. Or why we're sitting here in the mud."

In answer, he tied the ends of two of the veils together and tugged them tight. "Homemade rope, just in case I get lucky and sneak up on one of those gunmen before he sees me."

She swallowed at his reference to the gunmen, only too aware that they were closing in on them. "And the reason we're in the mud?"

He shoved the veils in his pockets before reaching down and scooping up two large handfuls of the black goo. "You gave me the idea earlier. You said gators can hide in the mud. We're going to cover our bodies with this and blend in with our surroundings, just like in the

Predator movie." He leaned toward her and slapped the mud on her calves just above her boots.

She stiffened in surprise, but that surprise quickly turned to heat at the feel of his hands sliding over her skin to the sensitive spots behind her knees. When her calves and knees were covered, he grabbed more of the mud, this time dabbing it on more gently and massaging it into her thighs. She should have made him stop. She could certainly put the mud on without his help, but God help her, she couldn't have asked him to stop if a whole posse of gunmen were on their trail. His fingers on her skin felt too good, reminding her of their first meeting, when he'd pinned her to the forest floor. She'd been shocked at her body's answering response to the stranger that night, and had later wondered if she'd imagined the jolt of attraction that had zinged through her core.

Nope. She hadn't imagined it.

The teasing amusement on his face gave way to a taut tension as he continued to rub her legs. His fingers slid higher, higher. She closed her eyes, reveling in the feel of him, waiting, wondering just how high he would go. Wondering just how high she'd *let* him go.

His hands suddenly left her. She barely refrained from voicing her disappointment. He came back with more mud, for her arms this time, and then he moved behind her.

"We can stuff your braid under your shirt, but the gold color still catches the sunlight."

"Go ahead," she said, dreading this part. "You might as wall blot it with mud, too."

He leaned close to her ear. "Sorry about this."

"Me, too."

He rubbed the mud into the blond strands, turning them dark. Then he slid his hands down the back of her neck, and around to the front, stroking her throat. His breath came in short gasps near her ear, and she realized he was just as affected as her.

His hands stilled, and then he was in front of her again. "There, you're effectively camouflaged," he said, his voice tight, husky. "You should put some on your face. I don't want to risk getting it in your eyes."

His Adam's apple bobbed in his throat as she leaned down, purposely allowing her shirt to gap as she scooped up some of the mud. But instead of using it on her face, she dropped to her knees and plopped it onto his bare chest.

He sucked in a breath. "What are you doing?"

"Covering that gorgeous gold skin of yours. If you're going looking for bad guys, you need to blend in with your surroundings, too."

He gave her a tight smile as she slid her hands across his chest, his shoulders. When she trailed her fingers down his abdomen, he sucked in another breath, then coughed as if to cover it up. She moved to his back, only then allowing her smile to escape. She was enjoying this way too much, especially since time was running out. But then again, if this was her last moment on earth, wasn't this the best way to spend it? Enjoying the feel of a warm, sexy man beneath her fingertips?

Yes, that's exactly how she wanted to spend her last moments. She wanted far more than that, but she'd have to settle for what she had time for. She quickly finished his back and his arms, then moved to the front again. She studied him up and down.

"I missed a few spots," she announced. She grabbed

two more handfuls of mud then faced him on her knees just inches from his body. She stared up into his eyes as she rested her hands against the golden skin right above the front of his waistband.

His pupils dilated and his gaze dropped right where she wanted it, her lips. She slid her fingers up over the planes of his chest, over his shoulders, to the back of his neck. Then she licked her lips.

That was all the invitation he needed. He dragged her to her feet and then his mouth crashed down on hers, ravishing her, devouring her as one hand cupped the back of her head and the other slid down over the curve of her bottom, pulling her against his hardening length. His tongue swept inside her mouth, teasing, tasting, setting her nerve endings on fire.

He moaned deep in his throat as his fingers slid down, down, kneading her bottom, approaching the very core of her, but stopping just short, with the material of the skirt between his wicked fingers and where she wanted him most.

He suddenly tore his mouth from her and grabbed her shoulders with both hands.

"Don't stop," she breathed.

He shuddered and pressed an achingly quick kiss against her lips. Then he was slapping more mud in her hands.

"This is insane," he said. "We don't have time for this. Hurry up and put the mud on your face. You have to cover all of your skin." He grabbed a handful of mud for himself and scrubbed it onto his face as he ran to the top of the small swell of land, apparently to look for the gunmen.

The sensual haze Faye had been in died a quick death

as she stared down at the no-longer-quite-so-appealing mud in her hands. She squeezed the goo through her fingertips in frustration, then closed her eyes and rubbed the mud across her face.

JAKE QUIETLY EDGED through the trees and bushes, careful not to step on any of the dead wood that might snap and announce his presence to one of the gunmen. He still couldn't believe he'd kissed Faye with three gunmen after them. Kissed? Hell. He'd practically consumed her. He'd been one heartbeat away from tearing that erotically tiny miniskirt off her and devouring her right there in the mud. He should have known from experience that the moment he touched her silky legs he would be lost. He should have stopped right then, but his desire to keep touching her was fanned into a wildfire when he felt her pulse leaping beneath his fingertips and knew she was just as turned on as he was. He shook his head, disgusted at himself for losing control when their lives were on the line.

Something snapped in the bushes about twenty feet away. He ducked down, peering through some low-hanging branches and using a tree for cover. He waited and watched, carefully controlling his breathing to make as little noise as possible.

Another snap followed. Leaves crunched beneath someone's foot as the person moved toward him. Branches clacked against each other and leaves lifted as a small branch was shoved out of the way. One of the men who'd been with Calvin stepped into view, his gun in front of him as he scanned the area.

Where was Calvin? And the other man? Had they split up? That would make things easier for Jake, but more dangerous for Faye if the others were out searching for her. He had left her concealed in a hollowed-out tree, bushes tucked in and around her. He'd stood a foot away and tried to see her and couldn't because of how well the mud made her blend in. But what if she made some kind of noise? A cough? A sneeze?

Worry squeezed his chest, but he forced it away. He had to focus on the most immediate threat, the man right in front of him. Twelve feet. Eleven. Ten. Jake timed the man's footfalls, tensing, waiting. The man drew even with the tree where Jake was hiding.

Now!

He jumped up and slammed his foot against the man's knee and chopped at his Adam's apple at the same time.

The man's scream of pain died in a painful wheeze. He dropped to the ground and clutched his throat. His gun went skittering across the ground, but Jake didn't have to worry that his prey would fight him for it. The man was too busy fighting to breathe through his bruised trachea.

Jake grabbed the gun and checked the loading before sliding it into his holster. Relief surged through him at having a weapon again. He yanked out a length of the green veils from Faye's skirt and dropped down beside the gasping man.

"Stop fighting it," Jake whispered. "You'll be okay if you relax. Hold your breath, then start breathing again, slowly."

The man's eyes widened with alarm when Jake rolled him over and tied his wrists together behind his back. When he was satisfied the man wouldn't be able to break free, he rolled him back over, grabbed the back of the man's shirt, and dragged him to the nearest log.

"Relax, relax, in, out, in, out," Jake coached, hoping he hadn't hit the man harder than he'd planned. He didn't want to kill the guy, even if he deserved it. He secured the man's wrists to one of the thick branches on the log and knelt down in front of him with another wad of cloth from Faye's skirt.

"I'm not going to kill you, all right? Look at me," Jake ordered, keeping his voice low so if the other men were nearby they wouldn't hear him. When the man finally focused on him, Jake nodded. "There you go. You're breathing better. Just relax and the pressure will ease and let more air in." He waited, watching.

The air rattled out of the man's mouth in one last wheeze and settled into a more normal pattern. The panic left his face. Jake waited, holding the wad of cloth. The man suddenly opened his mouth as if to scream. Jake jammed the cloth between his teeth and whipped another veil around the man's mouth, tying it behind his head to keep the gag in.

The man fought the gag, his face turning red. But other than a guttural moan against the cloth, he couldn't scream. His breaths were coming in and out just fine now.

"I'll come back for you, once it's safe." He leaned in close. "Stay alert. I don't think there are any gators in this far from the water, but who knows."

The man's eyes widened and he looked around, as if a gator was about to lunge at him.

Jake grinned and melted back into the trees. He hadn't been able to resist baiting the man. It was either that or shoot him, and Jake wasn't in the habit of killing unarmed men, no matter how much they deserved it.

He crept through the trees, his gun in front of him as he searched for signs of the other two men.

A gunshot shattered the quiet, sending birds screeching and flying into the sky.

Oh God, no. Faye!

He took off in a sprint, his arms and legs pumping as fast as he could go.

He broke through the trees near where he'd hidden her, pistol drawn.

Half a dozen uniformed Collier County deputies drew on him.

He skidded to a halt, raising his hands in the air.

"Hold your fire!" someone yelled. "That's Young, one of the good guys."

Deputy Holder had yelled that order. The deputies stood down, holstering their weapons. Jake holstered his pistol and ran to Holder, who was supervising another officer handcuffing Calvin's other henchman. Dex had come through after all. He'd sent in the cavalry.

Jake turned in a fast circle, taking inventory. "Where's Gillette? And Miss Star? Did you already take them back to town?"

Holder frowned. "This guy was the only one here when we arrived. We haven't seen Miss Star."

Chapter Eighteen

A scream sounded from somewhere behind them, followed by a huge splash.

Oh God, no.

Jake took off running toward the sounds.

"Wait," Holder yelled. "Remember police procedure, Young. Don't go running in without assessing the situation!"

Jake didn't stop, even when he heard more shouts and people running after him. Holder didn't know what Jake knew. He didn't know about the canal. And the alligators.

Please let me get to her in time. Please.

He burst from the trees, onto the muddy bank of the canal, drawing his pistol as he ran. As if in slow motion, his mind's eye saw everything at once—Calvin ripping off Faye's necklace with its gold, red and purple pouches and throwing it into the water; Faye's golden curls flying up as he shoved her under the surface; two alligators sliding into the canal with barely a ripple, headed straight for Faye and Calvin.

"Let her go," Jake yelled. He aimed his pistol, his finger tensing on the trigger.

Calvin yanked Faye up in front of him, holding her

as a shield. Water streamed off her hair like a waterfall. She sputtered and coughed, grabbing Calvin's arm that pressed against her throat.

"Let her go," Jake repeated, entering the water. He kept his pistol in his hand, but pointed it away from Faye. He didn't have a clear shot at Calvin.

"Get out of the water," Holder yelled behind them. "There are two gators coming up fast behind you."

Calvin turned his head, but kept Faye shielding him from Jake's and the officers' guns. "Shoot them," he yelled, his voice sounding panicked. "Shoot them or I swear I'll feed her to them."

"No," Jake yelled. "Holder, don't. You'll hit her. I've got this." He ran farther into the water, off to one side, and shot at the ripples where he thought the gators had gone under. One of them surfaced and hissed but turned back to shore.

"I don't know where the other one is. Calvin, for God's sake, get out of there."

"I'm not going to prison," he yelled, jerking back and forth, looking for the gator, holding Faye clasped to him in spite of her struggles. "Tell the deputies to back off."

Jake looked at the shore. Five deputies stood on the bank, pointing their pistols at Calvin. Holder stood in the water, not far from Jake, his own pistol down by his side as he watched what was happening.

Something splashed. Jake whirled around. Calvin screamed. A massive alligator broke the surface beside him, its jaws snapping, narrowly missing him. He stumbled backward, pulling Faye between him and the gator.

Jake dived into the water. He surfaced next to Faye. He grabbed Calvin's hand and twisted, hard. A sickening popping noise sounded. Calvin screamed and let Faye go. She dropped into the water. Jake grabbed her and jerked her back just as the gator turned and snapped at her.

She threw her arms around his neck, her eyes wide with terror. Jake ran with her back toward shore, as fast as he could move through the water. Holder met him halfway.

"Take her." Jake thrust her into Holder's arms. He turned and rushed back to shore.

Calvin screamed behind him. Jake turned around and swam toward him as fast as he could go. The gator almost seemed to be playing with Calvin. It circled him, without touching. Then disappeared underwater again.

Calvin sobbed and started swimming toward shore. Jake headed straight for him.

Back on the bank, Faye screamed. "Jake! Look out!"

He dived to the side just as the gator surfaced right where he'd been standing. For the space of a breath, Jake stared right into the cold eyes of the monster. Then it was gone, and Calvin was swimming past him toward shore.

He screamed and went under. Jake treaded the water, shocked at what had just happened. One second Calvin was swimming. The next he was…gone. He shook himself and took a huge lungful of air then submerged beneath the murky surface.

FAYE STOOD BESIDE HOLDER, watching with horror as Jake disappeared. She took off toward the water, or tried to. Holder grabbed her around the waist and pulled her back.

"Don't," he ordered. "He risked his life to save you. Don't throw that away."

"Someone has to help him."

He didn't say anything but he refused to let her go.

She stood there, feeling completely helpless, searching the water's surface, frantically looking for bubbles, something to let her know Jake and Calvin were still alive. What was happening out there under the water?

Suddenly the alligator broke the surface of the water with an enormous splash. Jake was glued to the gator's back, his arms wrapped around its head.

"Oh my God, no!" Faye clapped her hands to her mouth.

Jake clawed at one of the gator's eyes and slammed his fist on the gator's nose. It hissed and rolled onto its back, diving beneath the water again with Jake still hanging on. Bubbles broke the surface. Then…blood.

Faye sank to her knees, horrified sobs escaping from her. "Jake, no, Jake!"

Another splash, a shout. Calvin bobbed to the surface, spitting up water, flailing to keep afloat. And then Jake broke the surface beside him. He grabbed Calvin and turned him on his back, then started for shore.

Faye stared in disbelief. "Where's the gator? Where's the gator?"

Holder pointed. "There, look!"

On the other side of the bank, a gator crawled out of the water, hissing as it headed into the grasses.

Everyone seemed to move at once. They all ran to the water, toward Jake and Calvin, who were in the shallows now. One of the deputies shot his gun into the water behind them, scaring off another hungry reptile, turning it toward the other bank.

Two of the deputies grabbed Calvin and pulled him

to shore. His left leg was severely bitten, hemorrhaging blood.

"Get a trauma chopper out here," Holder barked. "Put pressure on that wound."

Faye barely glanced at her brother. She ran straight to Jake and threw her arms around him. "Thank God, thank God, thank God."

He crushed her to him and buried his face against her neck.

JAKE AND DEPUTY HOLDER ducked beneath the Med-Flight helicopter's blades and ran to Holder's squad car parked a short distance away in the middle of Mystic Glades's main street. Faye waved from the chopper window as it lifted off, carrying Calvin to Lee Memorial Trauma Center in Fort Myers. The downdraft buffeted the nearby treetops, sending down a rain of oak leaves and pine needles.

When the chopper was just a spec in the sky, Holder motioned to his car. "It's a long drive to the hospital. I wouldn't mind the company. And I'm a good listener. I can have a deputy follow us in your car."

Jake gave him a rueful look. "Is that cop-speak for I'm about to be interrogated and I don't have a choice?"

"Pretty much."

He laughed. "Then I accept your generous offer. Just as long as we stop somewhere along the way so I can get a shirt."

Holder wrinkled his nose. "Trust me. That's the first stop we'll make."

FAYE CLUTCHED HER hands together as she sat in the emergency room waiting area. Calvin had been in surgery for almost an hour. So far, no one had come out to give her any updates. And her only companion was the Collier County deputy standing on the other side of the room who'd accompanied her on the helicopter. She didn't know if he was here to act as Calvin's guard, or hers. Probably both.

Every time the ER doors swooshed open, she looked up, expecting to see Jake. And every time, she was disappointed. Where was he? Shouldn't he have been here by now? He'd said he'd meet her here when Calvin was being loaded onto the MedFlight. There wasn't enough room in the chopper for him to go with her. But he'd had plenty of time to drive here. So why wasn't he here?

The doors opened again. But instead of Jake walking inside, there were two more Collier County deputies. And they were looking right at her. From the grim looks on their faces as they stopped to talk to the deputy who'd been her shadow for the past couple of hours, she knew she was in trouble.

She turned to the woman next to her, a young, frazzled-looking mother trying to keep her toddler occupied while playing the waiting game.

"Excuse me," Faye said. "I need to call a friend." She pointed to the woman's cell phone sitting on the table between their two chairs. "Would you mind if I borrowed yours? It will just take a minute."

The woman waved toward the table. "No problem, take all the time you need." A delighted squeal had her turning back the other way. "Jimmy, good grief. Get that out of your mouth." She jumped up and ran after her giggling boy, who was now running down the hallway.

Faye picked up the phone and punched in a number. The deputies finished their conversation and the two who'd just arrived moments ago started toward her. Faye clutched the phone. *Hurry up. Pick up, pick up.*

"Swamp Buggy Outfitters," the friendly voice on the line answered.

"Buddy, it's Faye. I need your help. I think I'm about to be arrested."

TURNED OUT, DEPUTY HOLDER had no interest in driving all the way to the hospital. Not after grilling Jake with dozens of questions and deciding he had a whole lot more. He took a detour to the police station and had Jake sit with him in his office to go over everything they'd talked about, again, and to provide a written statement.

"So you don't know for sure whether Quinn or Gillette killed Eddie Stevens?" Holder asked.

"No. He was dead when we got there."

"You and Miss Star arrived separately, though, correct?"

"Yes, and before you go there, she wasn't involved in Eddie's murder. I saw her go into the house and come back out in less than thirty seconds. She didn't have the time, much less motive, to kill him. Besides, the blood was already starting to coagulate when I checked the body."

"Fair enough. Let's circle back to the Genovese murder, in Tuscaloosa. I've been on the phone with the lead detective who worked that case. He confirmed neither Mr. Gillette nor Miss Star…or Decker I suppose…were suspects. There were witnesses who saw both of them at the time of the murder and corroborated their alibis. But he didn't know anything about the journal you told me about."

Jake shrugged. "I would assume that journal was

Genovese's secret. It's not likely he would have told anyone about it."

"True. And you told me both Quinn and Gillette were after Miss Star because of the journal. Is that the *only* reason they were after her?"

Jake shifted in his seat. He'd been trying to answer Holder's questions without implicating Faye in the theft of the money. But there was no way he could avoid a direct question without lying. And lying to a fellow police officer wasn't something he was going to do. He let out a deep breath. "No. That's not the only reason."

He filled in the details about the money, about Quinn's claims that there was two hundred thousand in the safe and Calvin's accusations that Faye had taken the money.

"I'm not really sure what to think," Jake said. "Calvin wasn't exactly in his right mind when he said that. He was under some kind of stress and seemed pretty desperate."

"But you said Miss Star told him she didn't have the money anymore. That sounds like she was corroborating his claim that she took it in the first place."

Jake shook his head. "She was trying to placate a man who was shooting at her. Maybe she was worried he'd be even more out of control if she argued that she'd never had the money in the first place."

Holder leaned back in his seat. "Since you're being forthcoming and not lying, I'll go ahead and share what I've learned and try to clear up the confusion over the money for you. Unfortunately for both Miss Star and Mr. Decker, that two hundred grand in Genovese's safe was one of his eccentricities. His financial adviser said Genovese always kept that much in his safe as his emergency fund. When the money wasn't listed in the estate's assets during probate, the lawyer notified the police. They listed it as stolen."

A sick feeling settled in the bottom of Jake's stomach. "You don't have any proof that Faye ended up with any of that money."

"I don't have to prove it. I just have to provide a jury with reasonable doubt. And trust me. That's not going to be hard at all. Did you know that Miss Star had over sixty thousand dollars of student loans after she graduated from the University of Alabama? And that she paid them off a couple of months after Genovese's death? Tell me, Jake. Where do you think she got that money?"

That sick feeling in his gut became a fiery inferno in his chest. "I have no idea."

"She also started that store, The Moon and Star, not long after Genovese died. Any idea where she got the money for the inventory?"

Jake slowly shook his head. "No."

A knock on Holder's open door had him glancing up in question at the police officer standing there.

"They're ready for you, sir."

"Thanks." Holder shoved his chair back from his desk. "Looks like we're about to get our answers. You're welcome to watch with me if you want."

Jake stood. "Watch what?"

"Miss Star's interview on the closed-circuit monitor. They just brought her in. Detective Davey is interviewing her right now."

By the time the interview was over, Jake felt raw, as if someone had ripped his heart out through his throat and stomped on it. Faye had looked so innocent. She'd sounded so convincing—her tone at least. But her excuses sounded anything but convincing.

I don't know who paid off my student loans.

Freddie Callahan bought the inventory for the store. I didn't have much money when I came to Mystic Glades.

No, I didn't take the two hundred thousand dollars from the safe. Calvin did.

Yes, I took the money from Calvin, but only because he shouldn't have taken it in the first place. I don't have it anymore. No, I didn't spend it. I donated it to charity. I saw on the news which charity Mr. Genovese's estate had donated everything to so I sent the money to the same one, just like the lawyers would have done if Calvin had never taken the money.

No, of course I don't have a receipt. It was an anonymous donation.

Jake had heard enough. He was disgusted with himself for trusting Faye, and for letting himself fall for her. Because there was no question any more that he *had* fallen for her. Only a lovesick fool would have believed the lies she'd told him, especially with his background as a police detective. He should have known better. He did know better. But he'd closed his eyes to all the signs that pointed to her guilt. He'd convinced himself it was all Gillette, when Faye was just as guilty as her brother.

The door on the interview room opened and Detective Davey stepped out, pulling a handcuffed Faye along with him to be processed into the jail.

Her eyes widened when she saw Jake sitting at the desk a few feet away with Holder.

"Jake," she called out. "They're arresting me. Help me. I don't know what to do."

He steeled himself against the panic in her voice. She was a liar, a thief, a criminal. And so damn beautiful it almost hurt to look at her. But he'd never be fooled by that beautiful shell again. Because the woman inside was ugly.

Her brows creased with confusion. "Jake?"

He stood and walked out of the squad room without looking back.

JAKE STOOD IN front of his bathroom mirror and studied his reflection. Freshly showered, freshly shaved, dressed in a clean pair of jeans with his shirt tucked in, he should have felt like a new man. Especially after spending most of the past week hiking through mud and swamps. Instead, he felt empty. Drained.

And guilty as hell.

He kept hearing Faye's voice. Not when she'd asked him for help, but when she'd called out his name. Just one word, four letters, but they'd carried so much fear, pain and ultimately confusion as she realized he wasn't going to help her.

Had he done the right thing? He didn't have a clue. His life had been black-and-white before this case. The lines between good and bad were clear, solid, easy to separate. Now? Now everything was murky and gray. Because even though Faye had lied, so many times, and she'd broken the law, he was making excuses for her. And he was doing everything he could to keep himself busy so he wouldn't jump in his car and drive back to the station and beg for her forgiveness.

His phone rang, the landline in the kitchen, which was the only way anyone could get in touch with him now that Quinn had destroyed his cell phone. He'd have to remember to pick up a new one. Maybe tomorrow. Because tonight he was pretty sure he was going to end up too drunk to go anywhere.

He grabbed the phone on the second ring. "Young."

"Would it have killed you to call your business partner and friend to let me know you're alive?"

He plopped down in one of the chairs at the kitchen table. "Dex. Sorry. So much has been going on. You're right. I should have called."

"You sound like hell."

"I feel like hell."

"Well, maybe this will make you feel better. When you didn't call—after I went to all that trouble to convince Holder to go to Mystic Glades and look for you and save your sorry butt, I might add—I called him for an update. He brought me up to speed. He told me the charges against Faye were dropped."

Jake straightened in his chair. "What? What are you talking about? When did you talk to him?"

"About five minutes ago. Seems that her claim about donating the two hundred grand has been corroborated by the charity. They pulled their records and confirmed the donation was made when Faye said it was, and that it was made in Genovese's name. The Tuscaloosa police were more than happy not to pursue charges. With Quinn as their guy for Genovese's murder, they can close that case and move on."

"But…what about the student loans? Faye paid off sixty thousand dollars' worth, right after that money was taken from the safe."

"No, *Freddie Callahan* paid off Faye's student loans. Some guy named Buddy drove Freddie to the station with a receipt for the payment to prove it. Apparently

Freddie thinks of Faye as a daughter and didn't want her to worry about her debts. But she didn't want Faye to feel beholden to her, so she paid the loans anonymously. She's innocent. All charges dropped. She's on her way back to Mystic Glades right now."

Jake groaned and dropped his forehead against the table.

"Jake? This is a good thing, right? Jake?"

"I'm such an idiot. I totally screwed up. I thought she was guilty."

"We both did. No big deal. Wait. Why does it matter?"

Jake didn't say anything.

"Um, okay," Dex said. "I'm guessing there's a whole lot more to your little trip through the Everglades than you've told me. And I'm also guessing we care what Miss Star thinks now?"

Jake forced himself to sit up. "Yes. No." He cursed viciously.

"All righty then. I'm going to hang up. Call me back when you're in a better mood."

Jake clutched the phone. "I did her wrong, Dex. I hurt her. I don't expect she'll ever be able to forgive me. I don't even want her to. I don't deserve it. I didn't believe in her. But I should have."

"Well, then maybe you need to show her you believe in her now."

"Yeah, right. It's a little late for that. How am I supposed to do that? I didn't believe she was innocent. I didn't believe in *her*, or even what was important to her. I've mocked her belief system more than once. I called it woo-woo science. At least twice."

"Ouch. You're toast."

"Pretty much. I just wish there was something I

could do to make it up to her. She's lost her brother. He's going to prison for a long time. And she's been alone most of her life. She even had this crazy idea about her future, a plan, all because of some fortune-teller." He stiffened. "Wait. That's it. That's what I can do to make it up to her. I can give her back her future, her dreams."

"Uh, hey, pal. I think you might have been hitting the bottle a bit early today."

"Nope. Haven't had a drop. You have that fancy computer of yours handy?"

"Always. Why?"

"I need to you to surf the net for me."

Chapter Nineteen

Jake drove past the alligator sign that announced the entrance to Mystic Glades and drove under the arch.

Bam! Something exploded against his window. He slammed on his brakes. *Bam! Bam!* Two more missiles exploded against the glass, spilling their slimy, yellow goo.

Eggs. Someone was pelting his car with eggs. Awesome.

He turned the windshield washer on and continued down the street. More eggs slammed against the windshield, the roof, his door. But whoever the culprits were, they were hiding so well he hadn't seen any of them. He continued his drive of shame down the street, past The Moon and Star, and parked in front of Swamp Buggy Outfitters.

He got out of the car with the tool he'd bought after Dex had located a store for him. *Bam!* An egg slammed against the side of his head. He clenched his jaw and ignored the sticky slime as it dribbled down his jaw. He marched into SBO.

Buddy was sitting with the other old-timers by a display of canoes. His gaze shot to the egg dripping from

Jake's hair as Jake strode toward him. Buddy stood, his jaw tight when Jake stopped right in front of him.

"Buddy, I need to borrow your swamp buggy."

Bam! White-hot fire burst inside Jake's skull as he flew backward from the force of Buddy's punch. He landed on a display of beanbag chairs that thankfully softened his fall. He held his hand to his throbbing cheek and pushed himself upright just as Buddy and his crew circled around him like a pack of vultures ready to pick his bones, except they weren't willing to wait until he was dead before starting their meal.

Buddy drew back his fist again.

Jake held his hands up in surrender. "I deserved that. I deserved that and a whole lot more. And if you want to beat me to a pulp I'll let you, but not right now. I have something more important to do. And I need your help."

Buddy bobbed on his feet like a championship boxer waiting for an opening. "And why would I want to help a slimeball like you?"

"Because I'm not asking you to help me. I'm asking you to help Faye."

He slowly lowered his fists and gave him a suspicious look. "Start talking."

FAYE STOOD BESIDE Amy and Freddie looking out the front window of her shop toward SBO.

"What do you think he's doing in there?" Amy asked. "And what was it he carried in there? It looked like a cattle prod or something."

Faye shook her head. "I have no idea." She chewed her bottom lip. "He's been in there a while. I hope he's okay."

Freddie snorted beside her. "Quit worrying about

him. Whatever happens, he's probably getting what he deserves. And we certainly don't care." She grabbed Faye's shoulders and pulled her away from the window.

"Wait," Amy called out. "That huge glass window is opening up like a door on the front of the store." She pressed her hand to her chest. "Oh, my gosh. What are they doing?"

Faye and Freddie hurried back to the window. Buddy's brand-new, state-of-the-art swamp buggy rolled through the enormous door out onto the street. Buddy was driving. At least a dozen of his friends were sitting on top of the platform with him. And standing beside Buddy was Jake, holding that crazy-looking pole contraption he'd had when he got out of the car.

The buggy turned and headed down the street, toward the swamp.

"What in the world are they doing?" Amy cried.

Freddie pulled Faye back from the window again. "Like I already said, we don't care. Faye, you said you'd make up a batch of that hand lotion for my friend, Estelle. Well, time's a wastin' and she's not getting any younger."

Faye let her friend lead her to the counter. There was no point in staring after Jake anyway. He'd made his feelings for her—or lack of them—perfectly clear when he'd abandoned her at the police station.

FAYE PATTED ESTELLE'S HAND. "Just put the lotion on twice a day and your hands will be soft and smooth again in no time."

"Thanks, Faye. You're the best." Estelle gave her a hug and headed out of the shop.

Faye slumped against the counter. "Let's close up

early tonight, Amy. I'm worn-out. I don't know what I was thinking opening today anyway. We'll just have to work extra hard this weekend to make up for the lost sales."

"You're the boss." Amy straightened one last row of jewelry in the window display and turned to go. "Faye, wait, wait! They're back. And they're coming this way!"

Faye hurried in from the back room. "Who's back? What are you talking about?"

"The guys. Buddy and…" She bit her lip. "Jake."

The door to the store burst open. Jake stood in the opening, covered from head to toe in dirt and mud. He glanced at Amy and looked around until he saw Faye standing in the hallway. He marched toward her, and behind him Buddy and all of his friends poured inside. They were all grinning and holding rifles. Everyone except Jake.

Faye put her hands on her hips. "Buddy, what did you guys do to him?"

"Nothing, honest." He coughed. "I may have punched him, but that was before."

"Before?" She blinked and looked up at Jake, who had stopped right in front of her.

"Faye."

"Jake." A big glob of mud slid down from his hair and plopped onto the carpet. She winced. That was going to stain.

"I was a jerk."

She looked up at him. "Uh, yeah. You were. What did you and Buddy—"

"I didn't believe you. I should have. I'm sorry."

She leaned over and peered behind him. The entire shop was filling up. Freddie was back, leaning against a display, drinking from a bottle of Hennessey, or whatever homemade brew she'd put in the bottle. Sammie gave her a sheepish wave from the corner by the clothing racks, with CeeCee draped over his shoulders. She straightened and cleared her throat. "So that's why you're here? To apologize?"

"Yes. I mean, no. I came here to give you this." He grabbed one of her hands and covered it with one of his own.

She felt something cold and hard in her palm. He closed her fingers around it.

"I really am sorry. And I'm probably half in love with you. I don't know. All I know for sure is that you deserve better than the way I treated you. I should have respected your beliefs, respected you, believed in you." He leaned in and kissed her cheek. He squeezed her hand in his. "I hope you find the right Sagittarius one day."

He turned around and walked out of the store.

Faye uncurled her fingers and looked down at what lay in her palm. The centaur, holding up the set of scales. The same one Calvin had tossed into the swamp. She blinked at it in confusion.

"He dove into that alligator-clogged cesspit to find that for you." Buddy stood in front of her now. He pointed at the figurine. "He had some fancy-shmancy underwater metal detector. Had all of us stand on the bank and shoot the water to scare the gators away so he could keep diving until he found that. Even so, there were a couple of close calls. Had to drag him out a couple of times or he'd have sacrificed himself to the alligators for you. But he wouldn't quit, wouldn't stop going back in the water until he found that. I don't know what that little figurine means to you, but apparently he thought it meant enough to you to risk his life for it." He cocked a brow. "So what are you going to do about that?"

The other old-timers gathered around him in a circle, grumbling and adding "yeah, yeah" on top of Buddy's statement, as if suddenly she'd become the bad guy in this scenario.

Freddie sidled up to her and put her arm around her shoulders. She dabbed at her eyes and sniffed. "Well? Don't just stand there. Go get him."

Faye handed the figurine to Freddie and ran to the front window. She had to push half the townspeople aside to look out at the street.

"His car is gone! He already left."

"Faye, catch," Buddy called out.

She turned around and caught the keys he threw to her. "Thanks, Buddy!"

"Don't thank me. Just hurry."

She turned and ran out the front door.

HE SHOULD HAVE washed the egg off his car somehow before he'd left Mystic Glades. Jake punched the windshield washer button again. Half the fluid shot up on top of the roof instead of on the windshield, rewetting the egg that had already dried and making it slide down onto the windows. He shook his head in disgust.

Something black ran across the road in front of him. He swerved to avoid it, sliding sideways to a bumpy stop. *Sampson.* The panther stopped at the edge of the trees and looked back. If Jake didn't know better, he'd swear the panther was grinning at him. It disappeared into the swamp and Jake took off again. He rounded the next curve. His eyes widened and he slammed on his brakes again.

When his car shuddered to a complete stop, he sat there staring in disbelief at what was sitting in the middle of the road: Buddy's swamp buggy, squatting like a World War II tank ready to take out anything that tried to pass. And standing in front of it, pointing a rifle at him—as usual—was Faye.

Great. Just great. He shoved the door open. Just as he was getting out, a gooey piece of egg slid off the roof onto his head.

Wonderful.

He sloughed it off, shook his head and shuffled reluctantly to confront the little armed pixie waiting for him. She tossed the rifle down when he reached her.

"You have egg on your face," she said.

He sighed. "Yes. I know. I admit it. I screwed up. I'm a jerk. A slimeball. Or the worst insult Buddy could think of this afternoon, a 'city slicker.' I'm in total agreement with all of the above."

Her brows creased. "What? Oh. No, no, no. I mean, *literally*. You have egg on your face. You… Here. Just, let me…" She reached up and wiped his face. A glob of yellow fell to the road.

"Perfect," he mumbled. "Anything else?"

"Just this." She put her arms around his neck and jumped up, wrapping her legs around his waist.

He stumbled back against his car with her in his arms and plopped down on the hood. "Um, okay, what, *ergmgf*—"

She covered his mouth with hers and scorched him with a searing kiss. When she pulled back, all he could do was wait for the punch line. Because *this* was not what he'd expected.

"Say something," she said.

"I…I don't even know where to begin. I thought you were going to shoot me, not kiss me. I'm getting mixed signals here."

She lightly punched him in the arm. "Are all city slickers this slow? Don't you get it? You were wrong, back at the store."

Now, this was what he'd expected. "I know. I'm sorry."

She rolled her eyes. "You were wrong because you think I still need to find my Sagittarius. Jake, I don't need to search anymore. I've already found my perfect Sagittarius, my fate, my future. You."

He blinked, certain he couldn't be hearing her right. "But I was terrible to you. I didn't believe in you. I left you."

"Oh come on. Seriously? Even if you're a PI, you're still a cop. You have standards. You thought I was a criminal. Did you hurt me by walking out? Yes. But I understood why you did it." She kissed the tip of his nose. "You're spiritually challenged."

"Spiritually…what?"

"You don't understand fate the way I do. And it's only been a few days. You need time to come to grips with everything, to understand that you and I are meant to be together. It's okay. You've come a long way in a short amount of time. I'll be here to teach you what you need to know. I'll be patient with you."

"Faye, sweetheart. I have no idea what you're saying. But I hope what you mean is that you forgive me."

She punched his arm again, a little harder this time.

He winced.

"Of course I forgive you," she said, smiling.

He swallowed hard. "Okay. And the rest of what you said, it means…you're not going to shoot me?"

She let out a big sigh. "It means, *sweetheart*, that it's time for plan D."

He frowned. "Plan D?"

She curled her fingers into the front of his shirt, all signs of humor gone, her emerald green eyes searching his. "That's the part where you fall in love with me."

He stared at her in wonder, stunned at his good fortune, at the amazing, incredible woman who had burst into his life. And completely undone by the love shining in her eyes. For him. In spite of all his faults, in spite of all the mistakes he'd made, she loved him. And all she asked in return was that he fall in love with her.

His hands shook as he cupped her face in his palms. "Too late," he whispered, "I already did that." He covered her mouth with his.

* * * * *

"Where are we going?"

"My place."

She lifted her head and stared, eyes narrowing as if trying to decipher his intentions. Funny, to think of that sort of danger after all the other threats she had faced today.

"I'm not comfortable with that."

"You don't need to be comfortable. You need to be safe. I can make sure he doesn't get to you."

When she spoke, her voice seemed almost sedated, as out of focus as her gaze. "Maybe I could stay with a friend."

"That would just put the friend in the crosshairs."

She rubbed her arms and rocked back and forth. "I can't stay with you all night."

"Lea, think for a minute. You need protection. Nowhere else is safe."

"I could go home."

"To Salt River? He'll follow."

She slapped her hands on her thighs in frustration. "You make him sound like an unstoppable robot or something."

"Yeah. Exactly, but with one important difference. I can kill him."

SHADOW WOLF

BY

JENNA KERNAN

Published in Great Britain 2015
by Mills & Boon, an imprint of Harlequin (UK) Limited,
Eton House, 18-24 Paradise Road, Richmond, Surrey, TW9 1SR

ISBN: 978-0-263-25326-9

46-1215

Harlequin (UK) Limited's policy is to use papers that are natural, renewable and recyclable products and made from wood grown in sustainable forests. The logging and manufacturing processes conform to the legal environmental regulations of the country of origin.

Printed and bound in Spain
by CPI, Barcelona

Jenna Kernan writes fast-paced romantic suspense, Western and paranormal romantic adventures. She has penned over two dozen novels, has received two RITA® Award nominations, and in 2010 won the Book Buyers Best Award for her debut paranormal romance. Jenna loves an adventure. Her hobbies include recreational gold-prospecting, scuba diving and gem-hunting. Follow Jenna on Twitter, @jennakernan, on Facebook or at www.jennakernan.com.

For Jim, always.

Chapter One

Kino Cosen wondered if this trail might be the one that would finally lead him to his father's killer. Ten years he'd waited but he'd never been this close. Smugglers were dying, killed by the Viper. If he just had a little luck, he might finally be at the right place and at the right time.

He pulled the truck to the shoulder of the road on the lands of the Tohono O'odham Nation, which were just two miles from the Mexico border. Waves of heat undulated across the asphalt road as the June sun blazed down on the Sonoran Desert from a clear blue sky. His brother Clay opened the door of the SUV and the heat hit Kino like a furnace blast, eliminating all traces of AC in the time it took to take one single breath. He started sweating as he grabbed his rifle from the rack behind the seat. Clay took his from the opposite side.

Kino left the vehicle to investigate the solitary footprint where someone had stepped from the asphalt before returning to the impenetrable surface. This was the only visible sign of the smuggler's passing. But farther up, he saw more tracks.

His brother slammed the passenger door shut and swore. "And this isn't even the hot part of the year."

"They crossed here," said Kino, pointing to the narrow gap of open ground between two thorny bushes. His brother fingered a bent branch.

Clay, the better tracker, saw things that even Kino missed. He squatted to study the imprints upon the sandy ground.

"Carpet shoes," he said and stood, returning his attention to the unrelenting sun. "If we were home I'd be tracking elk right now instead of men."

"Not men. Man. Just one and these guys can lead me right to him. Then we can head home."

"It won't change anything," said Clay.

"Family first," said Kino, echoing his father's favorite expression.

Clay made a sound through his teeth before backtracking to the vehicle to retrieve their water. When he returned, he handed Kino his bottle and they both clipped the plastic containers to their belts, leaving their hands free for the rifles. Kino also carried his service pistol, a semiautomatic, but Clay would not carry one. It was a difference between them. Kino was the law and Clay an ex-con. Not a felony, but since his release, his brother despised handguns. Their captain, Rick Rubio, had told Clay he could carry, but to no avail.

Prepared to track on foot, they stepped into the thorny brush, following the faint depressions left by the distinctive carpet-soled shoes that marked the trespassers as smugglers. Clay went first and then Kino.

"Another," said Kino, pointing at the slight disruption of the unbroken sand. The indentation was small and circular, definitely a track.

"Good work, little brother," said Clay, slapping him

on the back, making his shirt and bulletproof vest stick to his shoulders. "How many?"

"Three?"

"Four," he corrected, noting the different tracks visible to Clay, even though the group had walked in line and often in each other's footsteps.

Walking was cumbersome because he and Clay wore full SWAT gear, as required even for them, and the standard equipment ringed their narrow hips. The water bottles knocked against their legs with each step, and the portable radios, ever ready, sat heavy on their left shoulders. Kino had left the satellite phone in the SUV. His semiautomatic was holstered around his waist and anchored to his thigh with a wide black strap. On their sleeves was the arrow-shaped tan patch that read Shadow Wolves. In the center was a fierce black wolf with one eagle feather tied to its fur.

Kino and Clay had taken one liberty with the uniform. Neither wore the regulation boots, preferring instead the lighter, higher moccasins that had been specially made for them by their grandmother. They were knee-high and sewn from soft buckskin. The lining was a paper-thin fabric that was totally snake- and thorn-proof. The rawhide soles were equally so. Kino's moccasins had a thin vertical band of beads in a traditional pattern of arrows in red and white, while Clay's sported beaded crosses of black and yellow. Anyone who knew the Apache would recognize the brothers' people instantly by the distinctive tab at their toes. No other tribe wore moccasins quite like theirs.

Kino and Clay were Black Mountain Apache, used to winter snow and cool mountain air. But Kino had put in for a leave of absence to sign on for this mission. Only then had his older brother, who worked for the tribe's cattle association, decided to come with him. As far as Kino knew, this was the first vacation Clay had taken in the six years since Clay's release from juvenile detention—if you could call this a vacation.

They were on temporary assignment with Immigration and Customs Enforcement. ICE's mission was to apprehend smugglers and traffickers along the borders that included the stretch that ran straight through the Sonoran Desert and the Tohono O'odham reservation. Because the Americans had missed things, ICE had formed the only special unit composed exclusively of Native Americans. Sanctioned through the US Department of Homeland Security, the Shadow Wolves were members of an elite drug-tracking force. The unit was composed of the best trackers to be found anywhere.

Their mission was to cut for sign—to look for footprints, spot broken vegetation or tire tracks that might indicate evidence of the traffic that washed drugs into the US from Mexico. That was their official mission but Kino wanted one particular smuggler, the one known as the Viper.

The Shadow Wolves were here on sacred land by special invitation of the Tohono O'odham people. And though they worked closely with the US Border Patrol, they did not answer to them. Border patrol secured borders from illegal entry or illegal products. ICE handled enforcement and removal operations. The Shadow Wolves, numbering only sixteen, were here to see what the Americans could not and to find the ones who were slipping by under their noses.

Kino followed the tracks, his brother trailing behind, both staying well clear of the slight indentures.

"Getting close to the rez," said Clay.

Kino glanced up to take in his surroundings. The land didn't look any different. Saguaro cactus rose above the ground; sage, barrel cactus, rock and sand stretched for miles. But this land *was* different because this side of the road belonged to the Tohono O'odham Nation of Arizona. Sacred land. Indian land.

Kino continued on the trail.

"The border patrol captain requested notice of our location if we enter the rez," said Clay.

"Lucky we don't report to him," said Kino.

It was true. They worked directly under Captain Rick Rubio, an Apache who reported to the field operations supervisor for ICE. Still, if they found illegals, it was US Border Patrol that would be called to detain and deport them.

"Should we call Rubio? He can call Barrow."

Gus Barrow was the pain-in-the-neck overachiever, control-freak captain out of Cardon Station whom Kino avoided when possible.

"I left the phone in the truck," Kino told him.

"I can radio Rubio. He can call BP," said Clay.

"Wait a bit. The O'odham are damned sick of border patrol. You heard the council leader. What's his name?"

"Sam Mangan," said Clay.

"Yeah," said Kino. "He welcomed us personally. Invited the Shadow Wolves onto the rez. They've got no beef with us."

Clay gave a lopsided grin. "Because we're not the ones stopping them every time they want to visit their families in Mexico."

"Exactly. So leave BP out. We might not need them."

Kino pointed to a track. "They're fresh. These guys are close."

"I know that. That's why I want to call in. Captain Rubio said that Barrow wants notice when we cross onto Indian land." Clay snorted and stopped tracking. "You used to be more fun."

Kino paused and pointed at the tracks. "I'm not giving a white man notice that I'm on Indian land. We got permission from Mangan and we answer to Rubio, not BP."

"Fine."

Kino ignored the ire behind the single word Clay spit at him and continued following the tracks.

Clay blocked his path.

"Why do you always do this?"

"Do what?"

"Captain says to coordinate with border patrol, you don't. They say to go left, you go right. Clyne and Gabe tell you to stay home, you come here. They're short-handed as it is. It was a rattlesnake rattle they found. Anyone can get them."

"But not everyone leaves them inside dead bodies."

And, yes, his brother Gabe wanted him home in his absence. And, yes, as a Shadow Wolf, it was his job to find smugglers. But, really, he didn't want them. He wanted the one who was killing them.

"Family first," said Kino again.

"Your family is at Black Mountain and up there in South Dakota. That's where we should be."

"I've got business here."

Because word had reached him that they were finding Mexican smugglers with rattlesnake rattles shoved into the bullet holes in their dead bodies. He'd read the reports. Sometimes the rattles were in the victim's cheek, or the shoulder, the breast or in the belly, right next to the navel. But always, the rattle was there, just like the one they found ten years ago in the body of Kino's father. And Clay knew exactly how Kino had known it was there.

Clay rubbed the back of his neck.

"You gonna help me or what?" asked Kino.

"I should be helping Gabe and Clyne. They're going to the powwow without me."

"This is more important."

Clay gave him a look that told him he disagreed. "Grandma wants us there."

Kino waved his arms. "Why'd you come, then?"

"Not to chase a ghost."

"The Viper isn't dead."

"I wasn't talking about him."

Did he mean their dad, then? Was Clay so willing to let his father's murderer go unpunished? Kino wiped the sweat from his forehead.

"Look. He's here. I can feel it."

Clay sighed and swept his hand forward so Kino could continue along the trail.

They traveled nearly a mile and were climbing a ridge when Clay slowed Kino with a touch.

"Stay down." Clay motioned to the rocky ridge. "Don't give them your silhouette."

Kino nodded, lowering his profile as they neared the top. The prints were fresh. Their quarry was close.

That was when they heard the distinctive pop of four rifle shots. Both men exchanged a glance, hunched down and ran in the direction of danger.

They crested the small incline and fell in unison to

the ground. There, below them, was a red pickup truck. Four men lay motionless on the ground. Another man stood over them, a rifle relaxed in his left hand.

Looked like four Mexicans from appearances and, given their parallel positions, Kino guessed they'd been kneeling then shot execution style. The ethnicity of the one still standing was questionable.

Clay lifted his rifle and took aim.

Kino placed a hand on Clay's shoulder. He knew his brother was an excellent shot. Not as good as Kino, but excellent.

"Wait," whispered Kino. He was already certain, but he wanted to see the man do it and then he wanted that shot himself.

Clay took his finger from the trigger but continued to watch through the scope.

Kino did the same.

"I can't see his face," whispered Clay.

"Damned cowboy hat," replied Kino.

The man was slim, broad-shouldered, obviously fit, and spitting tobacco as he went methodically from one body to the next, checking each with the toe of his boot.

None of the Mexicans moved.

"Rancher?" asked Clay.

"Don't think so. Too light for an Indian. Why is he on Indian land?"

Clay shrugged. "Not border patrol. No gear."

The man wore a white work shirt and jeans cinched at the waist with a worn leather belt that held a knife housed in a black nylon sheath. He also had a pistol holstered to his hip. On his head rested a straw, sweat-stained hat. His truck was old, faded red in color and rusted at the wheel wells. There was a gun rack behind the seat.

The shooter held his rifle in a casual grip. Right-handed, Kino noted. He stooped and recovered four camo-colored backpacks one at a time and casually tossed them into the truck bed. Kino recognized the backpacks as the type often favored by Mexican drug smugglers.

The man tucked the rifle under his arm and reached into his front breast pocket, withdrawing what appeared to be a can of chewing tobacco. The man turned his back as he handled the container. Then he used one hand to retrieve his knife.

"What's he doing?" whispered Clay.

"Not sure." But Kino had a feeling. Hope bubbled in his throat and his body tingled all over. Was this his man?

Clay settled against the earth, getting comfortable.

The cowboy squatted and flipped the nearest smuggler onto his back. He set aside his rifle and used his knife to slice open the camo shirt covering the body.

"Looking for drugs?" asked Clay.

The guy could be raiding the smugglers. There was certainly a living to be made stealing from men carrying drugs. But it was a dangerous game, robbing from the cartels.

The cowboy now had exposed the chest of one of the dead men. Kino could see the bullet wound oozing dark blood.

The man lifted something from the container and shoved it into the bullet hole.

"What was that?" asked Clay.

"It's him," said Kino, raising his rifle to take aim just

as a cloud of dust rose up to obscure his view. "What the hell?" He opened his other eye to see a blue pickup rattle into view.

"More company," said Clay.

Kino took his eye from his scope because it now showed only billowing dust and noted the position of the dead men and the arriving truck. Was it possible that the driver of the blue pickup might not see the cowboy or the dead bodies strewed on the thirsty ground? Or was this the shooter's contact?

As the dust billowed, Kino returned his scope to his target. Waited.

"Tell me what you see," he said to Clay as he searched for his shot. Clay was ten feet to his left and had a different perspective. Plus, by not using his scope, Clay could see the entire picture.

"Looks like a woman. She's waving, pulling parallel. Maybe Native. She's got water barrels in her truck bed. He's stepping out to greet her. Waving, too."

"Contact," he whispered. Two birds, one bullet, he thought.

Kino could see his target already rounding the front of the newly arrived pickup, rifle in hand. He fingered the trigger just as the man stepped behind the cover of the cab.

Kino muttered a curse. "No shot."

"Might be together," said Clay. "Or she's part of the aid organization filling the water stations."

"They aren't supposed to be on Indian land, either," said Kino.

"Tell *her*," replied Clay. "Anyway, if she's unexpected company, he'll kill her for sure."

Kino needed to take the shot but he couldn't see his

target. All he could see across the bed of the red pickup was the passenger door of the blue truck, scratched and dusty, window open. On the opposite side of the seat he saw a woman's figure, the driver, sitting behind the wheel, visible from shoulder to waist through the open passenger window. Shapely, her dark hair was braided in one long plait that hung over her right shoulder. She wore a pale blue T-shirt that hugged her breasts and slim torso. Her face was obscured by the roof of the cab, but her hands were slim, cinnamon brown and bedecked with a silver-and-turquoise ring and wide-cuff bracelet, both Zuni, from the style.

"He's lifting his rifle," said Clay.

The woman's hands extended and left the steering wheel.

"I've got no shot," Kino repeated, his accelerating heart rate now interfering with his aim. All he could see was the man's elbow and the barrel of the rifle.

"He's going to shoot her," said Clay, his voice holding a rare note of alarm.

Kino did the only thing he could think of. He took out her windshield. Glass exploded and his target vanished on the far side of the truck. The woman threw herself across the seat, hands over her head.

Kino shot out the rearview mirror and then the driver's-side mirror for good measure.

"Where is he?" said Kino, scanning the area.

"No sign," said Clay.

A moment later the red pickup began to roll.

"Must have gone under the truck," said Clay, taking a shot at the red truck.

Kino had no target, but he now knew where the guy

was. He started shooting, trying for a lucky hit through the cab of the truck. From beside him, Clay began shooting.

They punctured several holes before the pickup turned to drive away. Kino took out the back window but the gun rack remained in place. The driver never lifted his head.

"Driving blind," said Clay.

And doing a darn good job, thought Kino. He'd managed to get to the road, which was lined with scrub cactus and thick with sage.

"Getting away," said Clay.

"Try for the tires."

Kino had one glimpse of the back of the man's head as he popped up behind the wheel and steered onto the road. The truck veered as Kino fired and missed.

"That was some move," said Clay.

Kino calculated the time it would take to get back to their SUV and pursue. Too long, he realized. The guy would be on the highway before they backtracked.

Kino watched the plume of dust from the truck he could no longer see. Then he directed his gaze at the blue pickup. Ten years and he finally had him, only to have this imbecile drive right into the middle of his shot.

"Call it in," he said to Clay as he bounded down the steep incline to see about this woman, the one with the terrible timing.

Chapter Two

Lea Altaha lay flat out on the truck seat as glass from the windshield showered over her like hard rain. She folded her arms over her head to protect herself from the falling glass. Her arms offered no defense from the bullets that shattered her rearview mirror and then something behind her.

What was going on?

First that guy in the red pickup had pointed a rifle at her and ordered her out of the truck, and the next moment the shooting had started.

Her heart jackhammered in her chest and she breathed in the tang of her terror mixed with sweat.

The engine of the other truck revved. Next came the crunch of gravel as the tires spun, sending sand and rock flying. The guy with the rifle was leaving. Had he been the target of the shooter?

She didn't know. All she did know was that she was staying here on the seat until she knew it was safe.

The shots sounded again, but not at close range. Far off now, she could hear the familiar *pop, pop, pop* of someone taking deliberate aim. The sound recalled her time hunting with her father. But that was where the similarity ended.

Dust poured in through the open windows, the result of the man's hasty retreat. She eased open the passenger's-side door, thinking to take cover under her truck. But the sight that greeted her caused her to give a yelp of fear. Lea stared through the swirling dust at the figures on the ground. Grit coated her mouth and filled her nose. Her skin prickled as the hairs on her neck lifted. Suddenly her mouth was as dry as the desert surrounding her.

There, prone upon the sand, were bodies. All but one was facedown. That one lay with arms sprawled wide, shirt open and eyes staring sightless at the sun. No one could stare like that for long, not without risking blindness. The chest showed a dark wet stain of blood.

Had that man shot him, too?

She shivered with cold, her fingers and face feeling numb despite the heat of the day.

"What's happening?" she whispered to no one.

She crawled forward, sending cubes of glass cascading onto the floor mats and crunching painfully under her knees. The second man lay just as still, but he was prone, his arms spread wide as if in surrender. From her new position she could make out two other bodies.

Lea reached for the door handle and pulled. The solid metal shut with a satisfying thump. She slipped into the wheel well and tucked her knees to her chest. Where was the satellite phone? She scanned the seat where it had been, found it empty and reached for the radio still clipped to the waistband of her jeans.

She got it switched on, despite the fact that her hands were shaking so badly and were so slick with sweat that she could barely hold the thing. She hit the button to transmit.

"Margie?"

Her area supervisor, Margaret Crocker, answered immediately, as if she'd been holding the radio that usually sat on her desk. "Lea! I've been trying to reach you. Radios must remain on."

Lea didn't try to interrupt because there was no use. She couldn't speak until Margie finished and released her transmit button.

Margie's voice crackled on. "Where are you? Ernesta just called in and that means you're alone, again. I've explained this to you. Everyone rides with a partner." Her voice went to an angry whisper. "I can't believe you pulled this today of all days when you know I've got the regional director here! I do not need this."

Finally, Margie stopped talking so Lea could speak.

"Dead," she squeaked. Was that even her voice? It sounded completely unfamiliar to her own ears.

"What? What was that? Repeat."

"He shot them. They're dead."

"Who's dead? Lea, where are you?"

She told her.

"Indian land? What are you doing there? We have no stations there. It's too dangerous. Lea, that's where the cartels are moving."

"I-it's on the map." She blinked, glancing up at the clear blue sky that had no more pity for her than for the migrants who'd tried to cross the desert.

"What map? Oh, no! Where did you get it?" asked Margie. "Are you hurt?"

A man stepped into view, blocking the sky. He looked tough and dangerous.

The radio slipped from Lea's fingers as she opened her mouth and screamed.

The door swung open as the air left her lungs. She scrambled onto the seat, bounced off the steering wheel and smacked into the closed driver's-side door.

"I'm not him," said the stranger. "Look at me. I'm not him."

She did look at him. He had a rifle slung over his shoulder and a pistol in his hand. He wore body armor and an expression of fury. His dark eyes narrowed as she clung to the door latch, deciding if she should run or face him. He looked fit and heavily muscled and far bigger than she was.

"B-border patrol?" she asked, her voice going all airy and breathless. She felt dizzy as she dragged scorching desert air into her lungs.

He gave a quick shake of his head that sent his single braid flashing over his shoulder before it snapped back like a whip. Then he rotated his torso and tapped the patch on his tan-colored shirt. "Shadow Wolves. I'm with ICE. The good guys."

Good guys? Right. To some, he was a worse sight than the cartels. Immigration and Customs Enforcement, the ones who hunted the immigrants like prey. She knew about the Shadow Wolves, of course. Their reputations preceded them.

"Are you injured?"

The humming in her ears made his words hard to understand. He waited for her reply but she only blinked stupidly at him, past the spots that danced in front of her eyes like fireflies. He reached a large hand in her direction and she pulled the latch, falling backward into space and hitting the ground hard. But not so hard that she couldn't roll, which she did, under the truck.

This unfortunately put her at the same level as the

bodies. My God, she thought, this morning they were alive with dreams and a future. Now they were carrion bloating in the heat. How long before the buzzards found them?

Lea began to cry. The passenger door slammed and the man's footwear crunched as he took two steps along the side of the truck. He didn't wear the usual hiking boots or the army boots many of the border patrol officers wore.

Lea stopped crying. She knew those moccasins, or she knew what they represented. The upturned decorative toe-tab marked them and the wearer. The boots were high, to protect against the ever-present rattlesnakes and thorny vegetation, but soft and supple. Cactus kickers, her father called them. The man was not only an Indian. He was Apache, like her.

"How long you gonna stay under there?" the man asked. His voice held a hint of irritation.

She switched to Apache and asked him his tribe.

He squatted, resting on one knee to peer beneath the vehicle at her as he answered in Athabascan, speaking in the formal way of introductions. His voice was rich and deep and held a calm that made it easier for her to breathe.

"I'm Kino Cosen. My parents are Tessa and Henry Cosen. I am Bear Clan, born of Eagle. How are you called?"

"Lea Altaha." Her voice shook only a little now. She hesitated, her lips pressing together as she decided what to say. "My parents are Oscar and Maria Altaha. I am…" Her words fell off. *I am nothing. No one.* The familiar shame seized her but she pushed it away.

"Salt River?" he asked, correctly guessing at her origins.

"Yes."

"I'm Black Mountain," he said. The two reservations were once one but had been divided east to west. Black Mountain had the higher elevation, good water, terrain and plenty of wildlife. But Salt River had more lakes, one formed by the Salt River dam, and so was considered a fisherman's paradise. Both tribes had a cultural center, casino and various other forms of tourism. More important, he was Western Apache, where her rez was a mix of Apache tribes.

SHE MET HIS gaze now, looking into those dark eyes. He wore his hair in a single braid, a traditional style for a man roughly her age.

"I am honored to meet you, Lea," he said and offered his hand.

She took it and he helped her scramble out from beneath the truck. When she was standing in front of him, she realized he was a good deal taller than she expected and far better looking. He had that rare combination of earnestness and intensity in his gaze that held her captive. His features were classic with a broad nose, full mouth and a jaw that looked strong enough to take a hit. Her stomach fluttered as she realized what was happening between them. The heat and absolute stillness seemed to charge the air, like the electricity before a storm. Their clasped hands tightened as they each stepped closer. Oh, this was bad.

She stepped back, breaking the connection between them and wiping her tingling palm upon the denim of her jeans. This was not the time or place for mooning over a man. She rubbed the hand that so recently clasped his across the back of her neck. It didn't ease her discomfort. Was it because he stood a little too close?

The jitters came back and she felt as if someone were running an electric current through her. She leaned heavily against her truck but the heat of the metal made her spring away, straight into his arms. He enfolded her against him and she realized to her chagrin that she could no longer stand without his help because her knees had given way. He opened the passenger's-side door and eased her onto the seat.

She glanced at the carnage all around her and pressed both hands over her eyes. When she removed them, the bodies were still there.

"Someone was shooting at me," she said.

"Yeah," he said. "That was me."

Chapter Three

Kino paused, pistol holstered, rifle slung over his shoulder and body armor sticking to his back as he considered what to do with this woman. He should take her in, but that would mean paperwork and he hated paperwork.

The woman stared at Kino as a mixture of shock and fear played across her features. She was smaller than he'd first judged, smaller than most of the women on his rez. And now, as he looked at her face, he saw that even pale and dusty as she was from her ordeal that her features seemed a blending of Native blood with some other race. Even dirty, there was no denying that she was a beauty.

Lea Altaha seemed to be recovering because color was now rapidly returning to her face. Her eyes glittered dangerously. Kino's body reacted to the challenge in her gaze, though not as he expected. His emotions flicked from anger at her interference to complete awareness of her as a woman. Now, with her color high, her nostrils flaring and her brow sloping down over her large dark eyes, she looked fierce and wild and sexy as hell. The tight T-shirt publicized an aid organization—Oasis—but also served to advertise a killer body. The thin cotton and her tight faded jeans hugged her dangerous curves. She wore high boots, as anyone with sense would out here. She also had a water bottle and a folded utility knife strapped to her tooled leather belt. The buckle was large and silver with a thundercloud symbol on the front. Appropriate, he thought, for clearly there was some kind of storm building between them.

She lifted her hand to point a finger at him as if his words had just registered in her mind.

"You!" She slid from the seat, her voice and posture all accusation as she stood, chin high and brow low. Even angry she was adorable, he thought, like a startled kitten. "You could have killed me."

"I could have. But I was aiming at your windshield." He pointed at the space where the glass had been. "Your rearview and then your side mirror."

And he had hit them all in that order. It was a point of pride, his accuracy with a rifle.

"What is wrong with you?"

"That man was gonna shoot you. Yeah? Like he killed them." He thumbed over his shoulder. "I stopped him."

He judged from her widening eyes that she knew what was behind him.

Her shoulders slumped and the color washed from her face. She started shaking again and leaned back against the seat behind her.

"He was," she whispered. "And you were trying to shoot him?"

Kino's jaw bulged. He took a moment to push down the fury. His chance, come and gone. Would he ever have that chance again?

"I was. Until you blundered into my shot." He

pointed to the ridge of rock some hundred yards back and twenty feet higher in elevation.

She looked at the place he indicated and then at the windshield. Finally she looked at him. Her mouth opened and then closed as she worked it out.

"I blocked your shot."

He nodded.

She was covering her eyes with her hands again. The silver-and-turquoise jewelry on her right wrist and fingers shone bright in the sun. There was no jewelry on her left hand.

Why was he even checking?

He knew exactly why. He was attracted but he had a policy of never hunting in another man's territory. But she was too attractive for him not to notice. Still, he didn't know if he would ever forgive her for bumbling into his hunt. Likely that didn't mean he wouldn't sleep with her if she gave him the chance. He'd have to be dead not to want her. She was stunning, really. The tingle of desire prickled through him. He sighed and forced his thoughts back to the hunt, the important hunt, the one for the Viper.

"Did you get a good look at him?"

She nodded, pressing her hand over her mouth as if trying not to be sick. She gagged but held down whatever was threatening to come up.

"Close your eyes. Think about that face."

She shook her head as if unwilling to remember.

"It's important."

"Because he killed these men?"

Kino waved a hand in the direction of the corpses. "These men are smugglers."

She cocked her head as if she did not believe his

words or understand them. “These men are people, with families.”

He gritted his teeth. “Right. Fine. But the shooter. Please, try to picture him.”

“I don’t have to close my eyes to picture him. I’ll never forget that face. He was three feet in front of me and he was aiming a rifle at my heart.”

“Do you know him?”

“I’ve never seen him before.”

Kino exhaled in frustration. All he knew from his own observation was that the man was white and driving a red truck while wearing a stained cowboy hat. Oh, and that he chewed tobacco. It didn’t narrow the field much.

“What are you doing here?” Kino asked. “There’s not supposed to be any water stations on tribal land.”

She glanced around. “I was just following my map.”

Clueless or a liar? As he tried to decide, Kino took a page from his older brother Gabe’s book. Gabe was the chief of tribal police back on Black Mountain and often said, “If a suspect’s lips are moving, assume they are lying.” If she knew where she was, then she also knew that the tribe had pulled the plug on Oasis and their little water parties.

“Where is your partner? I thought you guys always traveled in pairs.”

“I…I have special permission.”

“That’s bull.”

Her failure to meet his gaze confirmed it. The way she shifted in place and worried the turquoise ring on her index finger made him think that she was lying. If she’d lie about this, she might be lying about not knowing the perp or, worse, she might be working with him.

“Okay. I’m detaining you.”

"What! Why?"

"Because you're a witness. Plus, you're lying to me, Miss Altaha, and I don't like being lied to."

"Okay. Look, I know this area is usually off-limits. But I'm Apache and—"

"Not Apache land."

Kino knew that damned well because border patrol wasn't allowed to be here, either. They had to be invited. That was probably why BP was always pumping their captain for information. Because only the Shadow Wolves had permission to pursue traffickers onto sacred lands.

He glanced at the men lying still and baking with the rocks that littered the thirsty ground. How did anyone live in a place so dry?

"Maybe you were here to meet them."

"I wasn't. I'm here to check this station and add water."

"I thought the O'odham wanted the stations removed from their land."

"Yes, but the migrants—"

"Smugglers," he corrected.

"No. Migrants. They're crossing here and they are dying here."

"Yeah, less security here, no fences. Makes it easier."

"Easier? To cross a desert in June? Thirteen bodies only last week. One of them was a nine-year-old girl."

Almost the same age as his sister, he realized. Lea had scored a point and this time it was Kino who glanced away. But her voice followed him.

"Have you ever tried to cross this desert without water?"

No one could. He gave his own water bottle a flick.

It was only half-full but they always carried extra in the truck.

"Did you ever think that if there were no water stations, they might not be so willing to take the chance? How many come because they expect to find Oasis and missed your water stations by a few hundred yards?"

She pressed her lips together and the corners of her mouth tugged down. "We save lives."

"Maybe. But how many have you cost?"

"You don't care. If you did, you wouldn't be working for the Feds." It was an old resentment that went all the way back to Fort Apache. His people had acted as scouts and trackers. His people had worked with the Americans and had helped them find Geronimo. In exchange they had remained on their land instead of being relocated to Oklahoma. But so had hers. So she had no rights to the "us against them" argument.

"I'm working for myself."

"Shadow Wolf. That's what you are, right? Special consultant, tracking the ones the Americans can't find."

"What's wrong with that?"

"Not our business. The Spanish, the Mexicans and then the Americans. They all tried to take this land. It's ours."

"So why are you helping the Mexicans?"

"They're people. *Not* Mexicans. *Not* illegals. *People.* Women, children, desperately poor who have it so bad back there—" she gestured south "—that they'll take their lives in their hands to cross this. That's who I am helping."

"And drug smugglers and the cartel."

"They have trucks, planes and ATVs."

Kino pointed at the bodies just past her line of sight.

"Not those four. They stopped here, for water. A natural meeting place."

She stared him down. "And a place for hunters to overtake their prey. Always has been. Isn't that right?"

Kino glanced down the road to where it disappeared into the scrub and cactus. Where was his brother and the damned truck?

The buzz of insects dragged his attention back to the bodies. The flies had already found them. Buzzards would be next. He had to call it in.

He lifted his radio and relayed to the captain the important details, including their location. These bodies meant that border patrol would have to be called because they were the ones with the body bags and the refrigerated truck to transport them. His captain was thirty minutes out.

"What are you going to do with me?" she asked.

"I'm detaining you for questioning."

Kino turned to Lea and offered his hand. She took it and slid off the seat, bringing with her a shower of broken glass. Her grip was strong, as if he were all that kept her anchored. He walked her to the rear of the pickup, watching her as she scanned the ground, getting a closer look at the bodies.

"Holy smokes," she whispered.

"Yeah. You're a lucky woman. But you should think about carrying a gun. A rifle at least."

She did not take even an instant to consider it but shook her head.

"A pistol, then. Not just for traffickers. There are rattlers out here. Big ones. And Gila monsters. Though you have to be pretty slow to be bitten by one of those."

She shivered and folded her arms across her as if that could protect her from bullets. It wouldn't.

"If I hadn't stopped him, you'd have joined them. I can get you a rifle, help you pick one out. Teach you how to shoot, if you like."

"No, thank you."

"Why not?"

"I'm a pacifist."

"You're a what?"

"I don't believe in violence of any sort. And I don't believe in shooting at people for any reason." She stared right at him as she spoke, her words an accusation.

The ungrateful thing, he thought. "So you would have just let him shoot you? Wouldn't even fight back?"

"That's right."

Kino shook his head, still disbelieving. How could anyone just stand there and let someone kill them without making even the most basic attempt to save themselves?

"I don't understand," he said.

"Most folks don't."

She dusted away the shards of glass still clinging to the folds of her T-shirt. He retrieved a glittering piece from her hair. Then he lowered the truck gate and grasped her lightly around the waist before boosting her to a seat. His hands lingered on her until she glanced at where he held her. Then he pulled away, stepping back. What was wrong with him?

"The water," she said, looking back at the barrels. "I have to fill them." The clear plastic water tank that occupied the last third of her truck bed looked as though it held 200 gallons or more and she had additional barrels, a pump, hose and electric hose reel.

"Nice setup."

She scrambled to her feet to retrieve the hose.

"Lea?"

She paused, yellow hose in hand.

"This is a crime scene. You can't fill those tanks. Plus, I know from one of the tribal council leaders, Sam Mangan, that the Tohono O'odham requested that all stations on tribal land be removed."

Her shoulders slumped but she released the hose and returned to him, sitting on the open gate.

"Why did they do that? Some of their tribe lives on the Mexico side."

In answer he pointed toward the bodies. "The smugglers leave a mess."

"They're not all smugglers."

"I know that. But they're all uninvited."

"Like the Spanish and the Americans?"

Just then Kino picked up the sound of an engine. A moment later he saw the rooster tail of dust. He dragged Lea unceremoniously off the gate and shoved her behind the side of the truck bed. Then he swung his rifle out in front of him and rested it on the running board, taking aim.

"Stay behind the tire," he ordered.

"Is he coming back?"

Kino gazed through the scope at the approaching vehicle. Was that his brother Clay or the Viper?

Chapter Four

The SUV emerged from the maze of sage and cactus. Kino blew away a breath and straightened as he recognized the vehicle.

"That's my big brother Clay," said Kino.

Lea stood on wobbly legs and he gripped her elbow to keep her from losing her balance. He held her long enough for her to regain her equilibrium and for him to lose his. She was a witness, an aid worker and a pacifist. Any one of those should be enough to send him running in the opposite direction. But they weren't. Not even close. His hand tingled at the point where his fingers circled her bare arm, sending an electric sizzle of heat through him. He told himself to let go and didn't.

Their eyes met and held. She could be only his witness, nothing more. He knew that, because he wasn't getting mixed up with someone who spent her spare time breaking the law and wandering the desert alone without even a rifle for protection.

"You all right?" he asked, his hand relaying the softness and smooth texture of her skin.

"No," she said and reclaimed custody of her arm.

Was she coming to the realization that her efforts might be helping the drug smugglers? That the reason they were in this very spot was because of her water station? Or was she just now realizing how close she had come to oblivion?

"I'm taking you in to headquarters at Cardon. We need a statement."

She stepped farther away and rubbed the place where he had touched her as if to remove all memory of the contact. He noted the flush in her cheeks. Was it the heat of the day or their contact that caused that bloom of color?

"You're detaining me?"

"Until we have your statement. They'll interview you at Cardon."

"Who will?"

"Border patrol."

"I hate those guys," she muttered and then said to him, "I've got to radio Oasis." She patted the back pockets of her jeans and came up empty. Her eyes widened. "Oh, no, I was talking to her when this happened."

She rushed back to the cab and searched for the radio from where it had fallen behind the driver's seat as Clay pulled up, covering them with a fresh wave of grit and dust.

Kino went to speak to Clay, leaving Lea to her radio and check-in.

Clay pulled up in front of her truck.

"Any sign of him?" asked Kino.

"I'm sure there is. Everything that moves leaves a sign. But he was gone by the time I found the access road. What do you want to do?"

What Kino wanted was another shot, to go back in time and have Lea arrive ten seconds later. He looked toward the woman, scrambling in her truck to retrieve her radio. She'd seen the shooter's face. The Viper. She could identify him.

Clay followed the direction of Kino's gaze. "She okay?"

"Shaken."

Clay nodded. "Understandable. So, do we chase him or question her?"

The need to hunt warred with the need to protect this woman who seemed to have no self-preservation instinct of her own.

"Her," he said.

"Okay, then. We can wait for BP and then go cut for sign."

Clay's and Kino's radios came alive simultaneously as their captain called in.

"Clay? Kino? Over."

Clay lifted the radio. "Here, sir."

"Border patrol is requesting you meet them at the closest access point. If you aren't there, they'll miss it."

"No doubt," muttered Kino.

"Yes, sir." Clay glanced at Kino, who nodded. "On my way."

"Can either of you identify the shooter?" asked Captain Rubio.

"Negative. Only witness is Miss Altaha."

"From Oasis?"

"Affirmative."

"Okay. Bring her for pickup by BP in twenty."

"En route."

Clay hooked his radio back on his shoulder and met

Kino's gaze. "I'm calling Councilman Mangan. He'll want tribal representatives here."

"Satellite phone's in the car," said Kino. "I'll get Altaha."

As he turned to collect their witness, he glanced at the four bodies. He had considered them no more than collateral damage, pawns in this game of chess. They weren't the first to be killed execution style, stripped of the drugs and then left to rot. But they were the first he'd really noticed. He had his witness to thank for that.

What had she said—that they were people? He looked at them—really looked for the first time. The men were thin, dust-covered, wearing old trousers and new camo shirts provided for their journey. Their feet were sheathed in the odd shoes sewn from sections of carpet to obscure their prints from trackers like him. They'd been hired to carry a load with promises that it would earn them their passage. Instead they had earned a body bag. They'd been used and discarded, as if they were nothing more than the empty water jugs they had carried. Kino admitted to himself that he had used them, too. For him, they had been just a means to find the Viper.

The discomfort made Kino turn away.

Clay was on the satellite phone, the only sure means of communication in many of the more isolated areas out here. He lowered the phone and turned to Kino.

"Mangan is coming himself with another member of the tribe. They want us to meet them, as well."

"We've gone from trackers to an escort service."

Clay's smile was fleeting. He motioned with his head. "She's crying."

Kino met his brother's look of discomfort with one of his own.

"What do you want me to do?"

"Your witness. You said so." He might as well have shouted, "Not it!"

"Great," said Kino, hoping his captain got here before border patrol so they could get going.

Kino headed to the battered pickup and found Lea wiping her eyes. But she didn't fall into his arms or shatter like the windshield. Instead she met his cautious gaze with one of her own.

"What now?"

"Gotta get you to Cardon Station. They're coming to pick you up."

Lea sighed and followed him to the SUV, where they drove to the highway.

An hour later the rattlesnake rattle had been removed from the one man's wound and all four bodies had been bagged. The Bureau of Indian Affairs—BIA—and the US Border Patrol, the field operations director from ICE, Shadow Wolves captain Rick Rubio and two members of the Tohono O'odham tribal council were all on site. Lea had been transported to border patrol headquarters while Kino and Clay continued to cook out here in the desert heat.

Kino stared up at the sky, counting the minutes the Viper had to escape. But now Kino had something he'd never had before: a witness.

The last to arrive was a representative from Oasis. Their regional director was a guy named Anthony DeClay: a white guy, tall, with a muscular frame evident beneath the pale blue, long-sleeved, button-up shirt he wore. Stitched to the left breast pocket was the Oasis insignia: two crossed flagpoles topped with triangular royal blue flags. The flags were a shorter interpretation of the ten-foot poles and flags that alerted travelers from a distance to the presence of water. Kino glanced from the symbol to the worn circular ring on the opposite pocket.

Was it tobacco or a tin of rattlesnake rattles?

Kino's eyes narrowed as he studied the man now engaged in conversation with one of the tribal council, comparing his body type to the Viper and finding a possible match. The gist of the conversation was the time frame for removal of the water stations from tribal lands. Kino knew that the Oasis organization had many stations set up illegally on federal land and the Bureau of Land Management seemed to mostly look the other way. Kino thought that Oasis made a habit of going where it was not welcome. Oasis claimed it had not erected the stations, but did seem to be maintaining them.

DeClay appeared to be in his midforties with an affable smile and mirrored sunglasses. He was covered with dust even though he'd been in an air-conditioned Ford Explorer complete with water tanks, pump and coiled hose. He dangled his keys off his index finger. Kino noticed the key ring immediately because it included a one-inch rattlesnake rattle encased in clear acrylic. The man fingered the fob as he spoke to the tribal councilman.

Kino glanced at Clay, who gave the slightest nod. He'd seen the fob, as well.

Border patrol captain Gus Barrow joined the conversation. DeClay said that he had not met Lea Altaha yet, as she had been out in the field both times he had been through to check in with their area supervisor, a woman named Margaret Crocker. DeClay explained that he supervised the Oasis program in Texas, New Mexico and now Arizona. He said they had strict regulations about traveling in pairs, a rule that Altaha had apparently ignored. According to the manager, Crocker, Lea's usual partner had recently left the organization. Altaha had been assigned a temporary partner who had called in sick. At that point, Lea had taken her own initiative and picked up the wrong map, the one denoting the stations designated to be removed, and come out here all alone, which was against every protocol they had. She had received no authorization from anyone to be on Indian land and DeClay was not willing to guess if her mistake was accidental or intentional.

The one tribal councilman Kino knew, Sam Mangan, had words with DeClay, telling him to get this station off Indian land today. DeClay promised to remove the barrels immediately and excused himself to make some calls.

Kino glanced again at the two blue barrels resting on their sides on a wooden frame. The two-by-fours and nails had that just-built glow. Strange, he thought. They were not scratched from blowing sand or worn. In fact, the station looked brand-new.

"That station hasn't been there very long," said Kino to his brother.

"Nails are still shiny."

Kino watched DeClay and one of his fellows get the blue barrels loaded. The fact that they could lift them without emptying the water led Kino to surmise that the barrels were empty. But the way the two men carried them seemed wrong.

Kino went to speak to his captain. "I think there might be something in those barrels."

Captain Rubio glanced at the two men hoisting the containers with renewed interest. "Maybe so. Worth a look."

Clay asked permission to cut for sign but their conversation was interrupted by Captain Barrow.

"Why wasn't I alerted to your men's location?" asked Barrow.

"We alerted you," said Rubio.

"After they found the bodies."

Rubio said nothing.

"We're supposed to be coordinating operations," Barrow reminded Rubio. "If your men don't report in and they go missing, we won't have the first idea where to begin our search."

Rubio smiled. "I would."

Barrow snorted. "What if they were shot?"

"That's easier." Rubio pointed skyward. "Just follow the buzzards." Sure enough, the black birds already circled, having smelled the carrion from miles away.

"Yeah, well, I don't like sending my guys home in body bags."

Kino wanted to tell them they weren't his guys but wisely kept his mouth shut.

Rubio spoke again. "That rattle in the wound might link this to the Cosen murder."

"Oh, this again?" Barrow threw up his hands. "Listen, that was ten years ago. And their father wasn't crossing the border—he was found in his home. I know because I looked it up."

"He had a bullet wound in his chest and a rattlesnake rattle plugging the hole," said Kino. "Just like that guy." Kino pointed at the body being stowed in the refrigerated truck.

"Right. So it has to be the same guy. Where's he been for ten years?"

"I don't know. Prison? Or maybe no one noticed the rattles. You don't do autopsies on all the bodies."

"We do on all the ones with bullet holes," said Barrow.

Kino glanced at Clay, who shrugged. For reasons he did not understand, Clay seemed fine with letting their father's killer go free. At least, he wasn't driven to find him. None of his brothers seemed to share his coal-hot need to bring this guy down. Restless spirits haunted the living. That was what his grandmother believed. Kino believed it, too, because his father's murder had haunted him every day for all ten years since Kino had witnessed his death.

Barrow turned to Rubio. "I request a copy of their report."

"Report?" said Clay. Thus far they had been blissfully free from paperwork. That alone almost made up for the heat.

His captain rubbed his neck and glanced at Barrow. "I'll get you something."

"What about my witness?" asked Kino.

"*Your* witness?" Barrow snorted. "You'll be lucky if she doesn't sue your ass. Don't think she'll want to see you again."

"She's the only one who's seen his face," said Kino.

Captain Barrow stopped, turned and glared. "You think I missed that part?"

"No, sir. She can identify him."

"Yeah?"

Kino nodded. "So she needs protection." Unless she was one of them. He pushed that unwelcome thought aside, not wanting to consider Lea as a criminal. But she had broken a lot of rules.

"I've already arranged for tribal to keep an eye on her overnight. She'll be at the station for a while yet. I want to speak to her."

Rubio turned to Kino. "So this guy took the drugs. He's either robbing the smugglers or he was their contact. That makes him local. This is his territory." Rubio looked to Barrow. "Roadblocks?"

"In place. And an APB on the vehicle."

"Sir." Kino spoke to his captain. "I'd like to volunteer to keep watch over the witness tonight."

Rubio's brow arched. "You're a Shadow Wolf, son. Not local tribal police or border patrol. That's not our job and this is not your murder investigation." He pointed at the tire tracks leaving the area. "That's your job."

Kino opened his mouth to argue but his captain gave a slow shake of his head.

"He might come after her," Kino said.

"He might. Tribal or border patrol will handle it. Either way, you're out."

Like hell, he thought.

Chapter Five

Kino should have let it go. But he couldn't. Lea Altaha was the key to the entire thing. He could no more leave her be than he could drop the search for his father's murderer.

"I'd like to help in the investigation. I'm a police officer."

Rubio sighed and looked at Barrow. The border patrol captain's face reddened.

"Not here you're not," said Barrow, looking to Kino's captain for backup.

Rubio's usually impassive face remained unchanged, but his eyes took on a hawkish quality. "BP inspects, detains, deports. ICE enforces and we look for signs."

Barrow's expression turned smug. "Exactly."

Captain Rubio directed his comments to Barrow. "But as a Shadow Wolf? That means he sees things others can't. And to use your own words, we're supposed to be coordinating operations. So I expect to be kept in the loop regarding Altaha."

"Hmm," said Barrow. "Well, I've got to check those barrels and get those Tohono O'odham Indians off the warpa—" He glanced at Rubio, Kino and Clay. "Uh, all right, then."

Barrow walked away.

Clay watched the BP captain retreat. "Was he about to say 'warpath'?"

"Sounded like it," said Rubio. "Americans. Still think they run everything, including this border."

Rubio left them to go talk to the guys from ICE.

Kino met the cold look his brother cast him, a look that said Kino had, unfortunately, acted exactly as Clay had expected. His brother's words replayed in his mind. *They say go left and you go right.*

Barrow had said that Lea was now their witness. Well, Kino needed that description. And that meant he would see her again.

Barrow was already having the barrels pulled down from the Oasis truck.

Kino nudged Clay. "What do you know about their captain?"

"He took early retirement up in Tucson. Police detective, I think." Clay watched Barrow. "Been in charge here a few years. Guys say he's a pain in the butt about procedure and, man, you better be where he tells you or else."

So he had way more law enforcement experience than Kino did. He knew things, had seen things, but he wasn't Apache. He couldn't read sign.

Their captain returned, studying the ground as he approached. "You two think you can find that truck—the one with the missing back window?"

Kino and Clay nodded simultaneously.

"Check in if you find anything."

Dismissed, the brothers climbed back into their SUV. From the twin-tread access road, they could see that the last vehicle leaving this way had turned south. So they turned south. Then they stopped at every turnoff on either side of the road, looking for matching treads.

One small road, that had been leveled once or so within the past six months, had a set of tracks coming from the highway and back into the desert. There had been another vehicle coming from the correct direction and the tread matched, so they followed the matching tread marks and ended up at a small ranch just inside the rez. The truck had pulled in here. A few hundred yards up, they found a squat little house, sheep pens, sheep and a pickup truck with the back window blown out. Clay covered Kino as he stepped out into the heat and examined the bullet holes. They'd found the truck. Now where was the driver?

"I'm calling Rubio." Clay lifted his radio and spoke to their captain.

Then they headed for the modest one-story home that had the appearance of BIA housing written all over it. The bureau's Housing and Urban Development oversaw most tribal housing and Kino recognized the look from Black Mountain. The structure was one floor set on a concrete slab, built from cinder blocks and painted the same drab brown as the sand. Someone had added a porch, which lilted and sagged. The plywood roof had been left unpainted as it darkened and curled. The windows were dirty and the paint was peeling. The yellowing stain on the door had all but worn off, exposing the lower portion of wood to the harsh sun. That was what happened when you had to wait for HUD to do the maintenance. Still, if it was anything like Black Mountain, even crumby housing was scarce.

Clay and Kino hadn't reached the lopsided step when a man appeared in the half-open door. He was middle-aged, tall, slim, with a distended belly that said he liked beer more than food. He was white but the desert sun had burned him to a brownish pink, and the deep wrinkles on his work-worn face showed he didn't spend all his time drinking. Although the red spider veins that covered his cheeks and nose indicated he had an earnest commitment to that pursuit. Kino wondered if he owned a sweat-stained straw cowboy hat.

"Yeah?" asked the man by way of a greeting. He smelled like a brewery.

"We're with ICE," said Kino. "Shadow Wolves Unit."

The man nodded, his smile humorless. "Yeah. I figured. You working break-ins now?"

"Break-ins?" asked Clay.

He nodded again. "Yeah. Two days ago. You guys just getting here now? They're long gone. Why don't you just sit over there by the sheep pen? Bound to be another group along anytime."

A woman appeared behind him, short, round and a Tohono O'odham from the look of her. She wore a bright pink T-shirt that was large and tight, gray sweatpants and a frown.

"What now?" she asked.

"Damned if I know," said the man.

"Your names?" asked Clay.

"I'm Bill Moody and this here is my wife, Arnette."

"This your place?"

"We rent it," he said.

"Did you call about the break-in?" asked Kino.

"Don't have no phone out here." Or electricity, since there was no power line to the house, just the constant roar of a generator somewhere round the back and the propane tank for heat. The yard was a mess, with trash littering the porch and a rusted-out pickup tucked under the carport. But beyond the residence and past the sheep pens sat a solid, clean outbuilding made of concrete with an aluminum roof. The contrast between the two buildings struck Kino as odd, as did the solid padlock on the large garage door.

"Is that your truck?" Kino pointed to the pickup with the shattered back window and numerous bullet holes. It was sitting to the side of the outbuilding with just the front visible from where they stood.

Arnette gave a shriek and Bill swore then headed out toward the truck.

"What happened?" he asked, his arms out and his face a mask of shock.

"Did you lend it to someone?" asked Clay.

Arnette reached the tailgate and fingered a hole. "Somebody shot it up." She turned to them, her jaw open as she panted from her exertions. "I didn't hear no shooting."

"Where do you keep the keys?" asked Kino, fearing the answer.

"Right up there on the dash," said Bill.

Arnette shuffled along on swollen feet. "Right there."

Clay was already searching the ground for sign. Kino noticed the key ring had a red metal fob inlaid with the image of a coiled silver rattlesnake. His eyes narrowed on the key ring and then on Moody.

Kino asked a few more questions and learned that Bill worked in Pima at the auto-repair shop but had the day off. Kino also discovered that illegals were frequent visitors to this place, filling their water containers at the hose and stealing clothing from the line.

"Them illegals even broke in here while she was at church and cooked a meal right there in our kitchen."

"And left a mess," said Arnette.

Clay returned. "Looks like a truck, newer tires. Footprint shows one single male, construction boots, weighs about two-twenty."

Arnette stared at Clay in wonder. "You boys are them? Part of the unit. All Indian? Right? The Shadow Wolves?"

Clay nodded then checked the tread left by Bill Moody. Kino waited for Clay to lift his head and give a shake. But he didn't. He merely shrugged. That meant he couldn't eliminate Moody. Clearly he was wearing different shoes. But his size matched the prints.

"Did you see anyone today?" asked Kino.

"Been inside all day. Threw out my back chasing one of them rams. He got out somehow." He pointed vaguely toward the pens.

Kino looked at Arnette, who dropped her gaze and shook her head.

"Will you call us if you see a guy? Big, white, wearing a cowboy hat." Kino handed over a card.

Moody rejected the card. "I don't got a phone."

"Then find someone who does," Kino said and then held Moody's gaze until the man looked away.

"He dangerous?" asked Moody.

Kino nodded.

Arnette made a sound of discontent in her throat. "Guess I'll start carrying my shotgun again."

Unlike Lea, Mrs. Moody seemed to have no qualms about arming herself against danger.

"That your barn?"

"Garage," corrected Moody. "Sheep don't need no barn."

"You always keep your garage locked like that?" said Kino, pointing at the padlock.

"Told you that migrants come through here. They steal everything that ain't locked down. Sleep in there if they could," said Moody.

"Can we have a look inside?"

Moody's jaw bulged and he narrowed his eyes. "What's this about?"

"Shooting in the desert."

"I don't know nothing about it. And as you can see, the garage is locked. No other way in."

Kino's antenna for lies vibrated. He wanted a look in that garage. But he didn't have cause, so he handed over a card.

"Still, I'd like to have a look inside," said Kino.

Moody's face reddened. "Well, you can't. Now get off my property."

"Thought you said it was rented," said Clay.

"I had enough talking to the both of you. Coming in here with a lot of questions. Why don't you catch the damned migrants instead of bothering us? They're like damned locusts." He hoisted up his pants. "We done here?" asked Moody.

Kino touched his brow in salute. "All done. Thank you for your help."

Moody growled and folded his arms, waiting for them to leave.

"You buy his story?" Kino asked Clay.

"Tracks didn't match. But he is wearing sneakers now and the size and his weight are about right.

Whoever it was, he changed vehicles. Had another behind this building, judging from the tracks."

"Like to get a look inside there," said Kino, thumbing over his shoulder at the building that was too new and too well kept to be on this property.

"Think you need a warrant," said Clay.

"She didn't look at us when I asked if she'd seen anyone," Kino said. "Might want to speak to her when he's not around. Maybe she'll let us have a look inside."

"Come back in an hour," said Clay. "The way he's going, he'll be passed out by then."

"Couldn't she hear someone starting a truck?"

"Not with a generator and television on," said Clay.

"I suppose."

"I saw those other tracks on the turnoff. They're headed south. Same way we're going."

"Could that car be a Ford Explorer?" Kino was thinking of Anthony DeClay, Lea's boss. The one with the new truck and the key ring with the rattlesnake rattle.

"Sure or a Ram or a Toyota, Chevy or Subaru. Can't tell from the tire tread. Only shows the width and tire brand. Not the make. You know that."

They reached their vehicle and Kino settled into the driver's seat. "Let's go talk to Altaha. See if she can give us that description."

"Don't you think she would have mentioned if the guy who pointed a gun at her was her boss?"

"She's never seen him. He said so at the scene. She's been out in the field both times he visited. Love to have her take a look at Moody, too."

"Yeah," Clay said and buckled in. "But that sounds a lot like an investigation and you quit your job on Tribal."

"Leave of absence."

"Yeah, well, Gabe told you there were plenty of dead cases on the rez. If you want to investigate crimes, we could have stayed put."

Kino didn't take the bait. He needed to find out all he could about Lea Altaha. "Call Rubio. Tell them we found the truck and ask what they have on Altaha."

Clay lifted the radio and Kino turned them toward Cardon Station, where his witness would be waiting. Because no matter what Barrow said, Lea was *his* witness and he had a lot more questions.

Chapter Six

Lea was tired, drained, dusty and hungry. All she wanted to do was go home, or what passed for home while she was in Pima finishing her college internship before starting as an anthropologist for the Salt River reservation's historical society.

The border patrol officer paused, looking over what he had typed on the computer monitor. A sheen of sweat made his brown skin gleam despite the churning air conditioner. The stitched name on his forest green shirt read D. Mulhay, though he had not bothered to introduce himself. Where she came from that was considered very impolite.

"Are we done?" she asked him.

"Almost." He scanned the form. "I just need your partner's name."

"I was alone today."

Mulhay typed in the information and then glanced up, studying her in silence for a moment. "I don't mean to tell you your business, Miss Altaha, but you shouldn't be out there alone." He waved a hand in the general direction of the window. "Guess you know that already."

"Yeah."

Mulhay glanced at the glowing screen. "I think that's

everything. I got your number if I need anything else. Oh, Captain Barrow said he wants to speak to you, but he's still at the scene."

"Fine. When?"

"We'll give you a call."

Lea rubbed her forehead, vainly trying to push away the image of the murdered men. The memory made her flesh crawl.

She rose, hesitated and then returned to her seat. "Um, they impounded my truck, so…"

"Oh, I can get you a lift." Mulhay made the call then replaced the handset on the cradle. "They'll let me know when the unit is out front."

"Is it okay if I make a call?" she asked.

"Of course." He motioned to his phone. She lifted her cellular and gave it a little wave. "Oh, fine," he said, turning back to his computer and the report.

Lea called Margie, hoping she'd still be in the office.

Margie told her that Anthony DeClay, the regional director she had yet to meet, wanted to see her first thing in the morning.

"Yes, that's fine."

"He's plenty mad," said Margie. "Especially when he heard you went out there alone. I think he might fire you."

"I'm a volunteer," she reminded Margie.

"Fail you, then. Send you home. The tribal guys are really peeved." She paused. "Lea, you shouldn't have done that. It's against guidelines. And the map you took. It's of the water stations we are removing, not filling."

"We need more water stations. Not less."

"Not up to us. The tribal council wants them out."

Margie hesitated once more then said, "Come in with Ernesta tomorrow and stick with her. She knows the rules."

That really meant that Ernesta followed the rules. Lea knew them, as well. But rules had never stopped her from doing what she felt was right. In this case, that meant filling any blue barrel she could find. "Listen, I'm sorry about the map, Margie. It was just a mix-up. Ernesta was supposed to do the navigating."

"Bring me that map tomorrow and you don't go out until I see Ernesta or Nita."

"Sure." Lea's tone flattened with her spirits. "Can I get another truck delivered to the RV park in Pima tomorrow?"

"Where's yours?"

Lea glanced at Mulhay, who quirked a brow.

"Impounded. Part of the investigation," said Lea.

"Geez. Maybe. I'll see what I can manage," said Margie. "Do you think Ernesta could use hers? We have magnets for the doors."

"I'll ask her," said Lea.

"And tell her I hope she feels better," Margie added.

"You bet," said Lea.

"I'll see what I can do about getting that truck back."

"And repaired," said Lea.

"Repaired?"

Lea described the damage and Margie uttered "Oh, geez" another four or five times.

Margie told her that she'd take care of it and to get some rest. Lea ended the call.

Mulhay watched her. "You're lucky to be alive, you know."

That made her chin begin to quiver, a sure sign that tears were imminent.

"And it's only a truck," he said. "You gonna be okay tonight?"

She knew she wouldn't be, but she gave him a quavering smile, nodded and swallowed back the lump growing in her throat. "I'll be okay."

"Tribal police will be keeping an eye on you tonight."

Lea's phone vibrated. She glanced down to see Ernesta's name and photo fill the screen. She took the call.

"Lea, you home yet?" Ernesta's voice had a definite nasal quality from her head cold.

"Not yet."

Ernesta gave a wet cough that made Lea think the head cold had moved into her lungs. "Boy, Margie was plenty pissed when I called in. How'd it go today?"

She doesn't know. Lea blinked as that realization sank in.

"Not so good."

"Well, see, you need us. Nita got back this afternoon, so she and I are going out tomorrow. You can ride along until your new partner shows up. Friday, right?"

Lea wondered how to tell Ernesta about the shooting and, well, everything.

"Are you well enough to go out?" Lea asked.

"I think so. The cold medicine is helping. Listen, somebody cracked our water pipe outside the trailer, so they had to shut it off. Can we use your trailer to take a shower?"

"Sure. You know where the extra key is?"

"Yup. Thanks."

"Ernesta?"

"Yeah?"

"I need to talk to you. Tell you what happened today."

"Sure. Nita is out getting us tacos. Come by for dinner."

"All right."

Ernesta disconnected and Lea put away her phone.

The border patrol officer took a call and glanced at her as he spoke. "Good. We're on our way." He covered the receiver. "Your ride is here."

Lea rose and the officer followed, standing behind his desk as he returned the phone to the cradle.

"I'll walk you out."

She trailed along beside Mulhay, through the maze of hallways and finally out the main entrance of the new Cardon Station. This was the federal government's answer to the increase in illegal immigration. Though how building a larger detention and processing center addressed the issue she didn't know, unless it was because they now had a larger morgue and an entire refrigerated tractor-trailer fleet to keep the bodies cool.

On the curb, Mulhay directed her to a patrol car and a tall, clean-cut black officer who waited beside the vehicle. But before she could get into the passenger side, a familiar dust-covered SUV pulled up.

The window glided down and Kino Cosen gave her a winning smile that should not have made her stomach tighten, but it did. The seat beside him was empty.

Cosen did not even speak to her, but directed his comments to the two officers.

"I got her."

Mulhay and the other officer glanced at each other then back to him.

"You sure?" asked Mulhay.

"Yeah. Where's she going?"

Apparently she'd become invisible. She was about to object, but a part of her wanted very much to crawl into his car. Much as she might wish to deny it, she was relieved to see him, which made no sense at all.

"She's going to Pima."

"Fine." Kino leaned across the passenger seat and opened the door, then glanced at her and raised his dark brows in invitation.

She didn't know this man well. But she knew where he came from and she knew that he'd done what he'd felt was right to protect her.

Lea walked around to the passenger side with Mulhay trailing behind. She let him open the door, but her attention was already on Cosen.

He gave her a warm smile as she slipped into the cab. She smiled in return. One glance at the gun on his hip made her lose her smile and recall herself. This man's job was to hunt *people* and he clearly thought nothing of shooting at them. He was handsome and fit and he'd shown her a compassion that seemed contrary to her initial impression of him as a badass. But he wasn't like her. No, Kino Cosen was a warrior. She needed to remember that.

Mulhay stepped back. "Take care, Miss Altaha," he said and closed the door.

A moment later they were rolling out of the station.

"Where's your sidekick?" she asked Kino.

"Clay? He had some paperwork to do." He smiled then asked, "Miss me?"

She frowned and refused to answer that. Instead she told him where she lived. He nodded, turning onto the highway.

"So, the RV park." He lifted his brows in speculation.

"Nothing but the best for Oasis." She grinned. "We don't have fancy new housing like BP. Where do they have you?"

"Not in that new housing. We have a place in Pima, on Artists Road. It's Indian housing but it has a shower and the AC works."

Cosen stepped on the accelerator. The air conditioner blew cool on her flushed skin, but it did nothing to stem the heat building between them. She needed to get out of this car because Kino Cosen was not in her future. She would make certain of that.

They rolled toward Pima, Arizona, the only city on the Tohono O'odham reservation.

She tried to keep her eyes on the road but they kept sliding over to the strong, muscular arms that held the wheel. He was still wearing the uniform of the Shadow Wolves, and only now that she was looking closer did she notice the Taser on his utility belt. Her attention quickly fixed on the knife with an antler handle.

"Why do you need a knife when you have all that?"

He touched the shaped horn lovingly. "This? Clay made it for me from one of his kills. I've got another in my moccasin."

She scowled. The man had as many weapons as a porcupine had quills.

"What's wrong?" he asked.

"I'm not used to seeing all this." She motioned at the weapons ringing his waist.

"Really? Don't you have tribal police on Salt River?"

"Yes, but I don't know any of them."

"Then they're not doing their jobs. Community outreach is half the battle. My brother is the chief of police in Black Mountain. Gabe is all about the community. Little League, boys and girls club, schools. He's in the schools more than he's in his squad car."

Chief, a job keeping the peace through force. Lea shook her head in dismay. But maybe he wasn't like that. Maybe back at Kino's home he had a job that didn't involve guns and violence. She held out hope as she asked.

"What about you? What do you do back on the rez?"

"Tribal police, too. I'm a patrolman. Just started, actually. Been on the job ten months. Passed the test on the first try."

Her heart gave a tiny ache and she rubbed her knuckles over her chest. He was a man who lived by violence. She needed to stop hoping otherwise.

Beyond the windows the desert flashed by golden in the late afternoon. She found herself searching for people walking in single file. But there was nothing, no one, that she could see.

"Is Clay on the force, too?" she asked.

He flinched and then shook his head. "No. He works for the tribe's cattle association. And he's a big-game scout for the tribe. Takes out tourists on hunts."

More killing, only this time animals, she thought.

Kino continued. "Just Gabe and me on the force."

"How many brothers do you have?" she asked.

"Three. The oldest, Clyne, is on the tribal council. He's only thirty-three."

"Young for a tribal leader."

"Yeah. Youngest on the council."

"All boys," she said wistfully. "Must have been a handful for your mother."

Kino shifted in his seat and his silence made her

wonder what she had said. Finally he took a deep breath as if she had startled him awake.

"My mom died in a vehicular accident in South Dakota when I was ten. Drunk driver."

Lea's stomach tightened as she absorbed that information. Was this why he had become a police officer, to protect people from such threats as drunks behind the wheel?

"I'm so sorry," she said.

"My mom was a barrel racer. Fast as lightning. She was up there for the big Fourth of July powwow. She also was a dancer—fancy shawl and jingle. She won a lot of contests. She died on the Fourth. I hate the Fourth. Anyway, after that my grandmother raised us."

She wanted to ask about his father but was afraid of what he might say.

Kino wiped his mouth and then gripped the wheel with two hands. "And as for all boys, well, I have a sister. She was with my mom."

Lea found herself gripping the armrest for support, bracing for what she expected him to say next. A child, his sister, dead beside her mother on a highway hundreds of miles from home.

"She survived the accident."

Lea's grip on the armrest slackened and the blood returned to her fingers, but one look at Kino and she was squeezing again.

"What happened to her?"

His mouth pressed tight for a moment and his fingers flexed on the wheel. "That's the thing. We don't know. She was three when I last saw her, trying on her first jingle dress, spinning and jumping to make all those silver cones rattle. That was nine years ago. After the accident, we didn't find out for several days. When we heard, my grandma drove up there with my eldest brother, Clyne. See, my mom didn't have her ID with her. It was back in their camper. So by the time they figured it out and called us…well, my mom was buried and we thought my sister was, too. At the time, they told my grandmother that there were no survivors, but they had made a mistake. My sister survived."

"How could they do that?"

"We don't know. Really, we only just found out that she survived the accident. My grandmother wanted to mark the tenth anniversary of their passing with a small stone lamb to be placed on their headstone. She called the cemetery and found out they only had my mother buried up there."

"But where is your sister?"

"We don't know. All we do know is that the cemetery buried one Indian on Sioux land. One. A woman. My brother Gabe thinks the BIA took Jovanna out of the car. He says the troopers should have called them right off, soon as they saw the child was an Indian."

Lea knew from personal experience that BIA had a long track record of screwing things up.

"That's terrible."

"Jovanna is still lost. If she's alive, she'd be twelve now."

Lea knew what that meant for an Apache girl. The Sunrise Ceremony was approaching—the sacred passage of a girl into womanhood. Lea thought of her own ordeal. Four days of dancing, prayer and instruction. It was one of her fondest memories. But still, even after completing the ceremony, she never felt completely one of them. Would she ever?

"No wonder your grandmother wants her back."

"Yeah. We got to get her pretty quick. My grandmother wants her before next July, so she's sent my older brothers up there to find her."

"I hope they can."

Kino glanced at her. "I still see that little girl in that pink dress. I wish I could have stopped them from going up to that rodeo."

Lea placed a hand on his thigh, feeling the muscle jump under her light touch. A moment later his hand covered hers, fingers entwined.

"Your brothers will find her."

"I hope so. I dream of seeing her at her Sunrise Ceremony. Of beating the drums as she dances." He let Lea go and returned his hand to the wheel.

"Thank you," she said.

"For what?"

"For taking my mind off what happened today. I'm grateful."

He gave a shrug as if it was nothing and silence filled the cab for a moment.

"Why did you come down here, instead of joining them?" she asked.

His wistful expression vanished and his face hardened into an icy determination. "Got business down here, too."

He didn't elaborate and she didn't press. Somehow she felt she didn't want to know this particular business because she knew it had to do with the man he hunted.

"Will you answer one more question, Officer Cosen?"

"I will if you call me Kino."

"Okay. Kino." It sounded right. The unusual name fit him somehow since he was like no man she'd ever met. "Did you really intentionally shoot out my mirrors and windshield?"

"Had to. He was going to kill you, right?"

"Were you trying to kill him or distract him?"

"Distract him."

She breathed away her relief. So he had acted in violence only in defense.

"But only because I didn't have a shot."

Lea cast him a reluctant look. Why had she allowed herself to hope otherwise?

"He deserves killing, Lea."

Did he? Did anyone? And was that really up to him?

She felt a cold wave of fear as the moment replayed in her mind. The gun aimed at her head and the expression of indifference on the shooter's face. In the past, she had considered what she might do if threatened. Then when the time came she had done nothing. It had been easier than she'd expected not to fight for her life.

She stared at the road, lost in her recollections. She had been a pacifist since she was ten, though she hadn't known the name for it then, or that there was an entire group of people who, like her, believed that fighting for any reason or any circumstance was wrong.

Kino had a different world view.

She looked back at him, alert as he glanced in the rearview and then back to her. "How did you know that guy would be there? Did you know about the…bodies?"

"We got a tip from a friend about the smugglers. A trucker. He's from Black Mountain, originally." Kino's expression was stormy again, but she couldn't tell if it was the topic or subject that touched a nerve. "He brings supplies to gas stations along the border. He sees a lot.

This time he saw a line of men cross the road, all in camo."

"Camo. Is that important?"

"The cartels supply their smugglers with camo backpacks and shirts. Makes it harder to see them moving in the rough. They also give them those carpet slippers. Darn hard to track."

She recalled now the odd footgear on the feet of the dead men. She hadn't registered it at the time, but she remembered that they'd looked as though they'd been made to wear for dusting floors. "I haven't seen any of those guys before or ones like them."

"You will if you stay here very long. They're dangerous. If you see them, go the other way and call us."

She nodded and glanced out at the desert, the fading light making the saguaros look like giant sentinels casting long shadows ahead of them. Lea rubbed her hands together, the air-conditioning suddenly as cold as the blood in her veins.

Kino's unit radio crackled on, broadcasting information about apprehensions and calling for transport.

"Do you have to respond to that?" she asked.

"Off duty," he said. "How long you been here?"

"Three weeks. I'm here on an internship. It's my last course before graduating. Community service and some anthropology all in one. I'll be here through mid-July."

Kino cast her an appraising look. "From college?"

"Yes." She let the pride in saying so show in her smile.

"Good for you. I finished police academy, but that's it."

"Better than most." She didn't have to tell him how

many of their people dropped out before they earned their high school diploma.

He asked her about her family and she told him most of it. Not about her mother, of course, or her elder sister. But the rest. That she had two younger sisters and one older. Her father worked for HUD—Housing and Urban Development—fixing all sorts of problems, and her mother worked in the office registering payments and such.

"We got over a thousand people back there in Black Mountain waiting for housing."

"Yeah. It's bad on Salt River, too." She wondered if she should tell him about her dad. No, she decided. It was too sad.

"I'll bet your dad is plenty busy working for HUD," said Kino.

She looked away. HUD oversaw the public housing projects that made up the bulk of all homes on the rez. Most of the housing was lousy and in short supply. Her dad had been part of the solution. He *had* been.

"Yeah. Something is always broken."

"You know, last winter, up on Black Mountain, they had to give away wood because so many of the people couldn't afford it and their pipes froze in the cold. HUD couldn't keep up with all those ruptured lines. It was cheaper to give away firewood."

"Same in Salt River. Plus, somebody keeps setting fires to one of the houses. Just one, but they've burned it down three times. My mom says they can't catch the guy and are considering just plowing it under. But they really need every house."

"It's like the old joke," said Kino. "One guy says,

'The food here is terrible.' And the other guy says, 'Yeah, and the portions are too small.'"

She chuckled at that. "Exactly."

He'd done it again, she realized. Taken her mind away from her troubles. He had a natural way of speaking and an earnest style of listening that put her at ease. She had expected him to interrogate her as the border agent at Cardon had, but he'd kept the conversation casual, sharing some of what he knew about the area as they drove toward town, like where to have breakfast and who made the best coffee. He surprised her by telling her which church he attended, not that it was surprising that he was Christian. Since the Spanish had come with their missions more than five hundred years ago, many of the Apache people were Catholic.

Her stomach rumbled.

"Wow. We need to get you fed," he said.

She realized she hadn't eaten anything since…before she'd left for the water station. Lea pressed a hand over her noisy tummy as the day's events closed in on her again.

This time she couldn't control the shakes, so she gripped her hands into fists.

Kino steered to the shoulder and pulled her into his arms. She needed the strength of him and the solid reassurance of his touch.

"Come here," he whispered and she leaned toward him. He gathered her in.

He stroked her head as she allowed herself the indulgence of tears.

"It's all right. I got you."

If only that were true. But his recent charm was offset by the man she'd seen in the desert, the hard, cold man who hated what she did and what she represented. She pressed one hand against his chest, intending to move away. His grip tightened and she was trapped between the solid muscle of his chest and the strength of his arms. She found this was exactly where she needed to be.

"Give yourself a minute, Lea. You're entitled."

How did a man, no older than she was, get to be so wise? She relaxed, letting him hold her, calm her with the gentle stroking of his hand over her back. He didn't try to kiss her. Maybe, just maybe, he was really a gentleman who was putting her needs above his.

When her breathing lost its hitch, she wiped the moisture from her eyes. He let her go with a kiss on the top of her head. As she pulled back, all Lea could think was how much she wanted to kiss that wide, generous mouth. She stared at him a moment and he sat quietly for her perusal.

"You're very brave," he said at last.

"Brave?" she choked out. "I'm crying."

"You don't need to be brave now. But when you needed your strength, you had it. I saw you face that gunman. Like a true Apache woman."

She was hardly that. Even her Sunrise Ceremony could not change the truth of her origins. "I was terrified."

"But you didn't fall to pieces. And when the windshield went out you dove away from him and took cover. You used your radio to call for help. You survived him. That's not just luck."

What he saw as bravery, she saw as resignation. Acceptance that she would forfeit her life instead of trying to kill the man who would kill her. It was not until the bullets shattered the glass that she had acted.

She lifted her head and stared up at Kino as a question formed in her mind. He had not been close enough to see her lift her radio.

"How do you know all that?"

"I saw you through my scope."

That sent a chill through her. He'd had her sighted, as if she were an elk or bear. He'd watched that man point the gun at her and then he had acted.

"He killed them all, didn't he?"

"Yes."

"Why would he do that? They were just people. They weren't even armed, were they?"

"No. They weren't." Kino looked at her a long minute as if deciding how much to say. "He's been killing all his mules. He meets them, shoots them and takes the drugs. We don't know if he's their contact or if he's robbing them."

"But why? He doesn't need to kill them to take the drugs."

Kino gave a long sigh. "Could be so he doesn't have to transport them to Phoenix."

"Is that what you think?"

He gave a quick shake of his head.

"Why, then?"

"Maybe he likes it."

"Likes it? What? The killing?"

Kino shrugged. "Or…"

She moved to the edge of her seat. "What?"

"No witnesses."

Her heart beat in her throat. "Until now. I saw him."

"And he saw you. That's why I picked you up. I want to keep an eye on you."

"Oh." Did he hear the disappointment in her voice? She had no right to expect that her interest in him was mutual. Besides, wouldn't it be better if he didn't find her attractive? Then, at least, she'd have another good reason not to make more of a fool of herself.

Visions of that gun loomed in her mind, the black center of the barrel staring at her like a soulless eye. She was shaking again. He tightened an arm around her shoulders. Lea clutched at his hand as if she dangled from a cliff. She clung to him as her convictions wavered. It was one thing to hold faith in theory. It was another to place your life where your morals were. She didn't know if she had half the courage he seemed to believe she had.

"You think he'll come back for me?" She met his gaze and saw the concern there.

"I would." He squeezed her shoulder and then pulled away, resting his hands loosely on the steering wheel as his attention flicked to the rearview mirror before he pulled them back onto the road.

He glanced over at her. "You can't go home, Lea. Not until we have a unit in place. Clay is working that out with the tribal police. He'll call when it's safe. Until then, you stick with me."

"I thought you were taking me home."

"Not a good idea."

"You think he might know where I live?"

"Probably not. But it's possible. Let's just be on the safe side. It's your life we're talking about."

"It's possible…" His words sent a shot of adrenaline zinging through her and she stiffened, gasping.

Kino's glance shot to her and then returned to the road, his brows low over dark eyes. "What?"

She pressed a hand over her pounding heart, the beating so fast her chest ached. "He might know!"

"What?"

"Ernesta. Nita. My neighbors. I told them they could use my shower." Lea knew she was babbling, but she couldn't seem to stop. "Their water is off and they know where the key is and they might be there now. I never thought… It didn't occur to me. I have to warn them."

His voice took on that cold, hard edge that frightened her. "What do they look like?"

"Nita is Navajo and Ernesta is from Salt River. Like me."

Kino accelerated down the highway, racing toward Pima.

Chapter Seven

Kino hoped the buzzing awareness was not premonition but just his body's necessary preparation to confront danger. He also hoped that the tribal police had beaten them to the trailer park. He didn't want Lea in the middle of another shoot-out.

"There's no answer," said Lea, her voice frantic as she pressed her cellular phone to her ear. "I tried them both."

Kino said nothing, but focused on driving.

Lea gripped the phone as if it were a small wild animal struggling to escape. "But Ernesta is taller than I am. And Nita is heavier. We don't look that much alike and…and he's seen me close-up. He wouldn't confuse us."

She looked to Kino for reassurance and he had none to give. The shooter might easily confuse them from a distance in the twilight. If he were taking Lea out, he'd do it with a scope. He sure as heck wouldn't walk up close where anyone in the trailer park might see him.

"Would he?" asked Lea.

"We're almost there."

Kino had made only one call, to Clay, requesting he send tribal police to Lea's address.

A call came in on Kino's radio. He grabbed the mike clipped to the loop on the left shoulder of his uniform.

"Kino."

His brother's voice crackled to life. "Unit is on site." Here Clay hesitated. "Kino?"

"Yeah."

"She still with you?"

Kino's body straightened. "Yes."

The silence that followed filled the cab as Kino met Lea's worried gaze.

"The unit called in a 451."

Kino clenched his jaw and then responded. "Roger. En route."

"Units responding," said Clay. "Out."

"What's a 451?" asked Lea, her voice high, anxious.

"It's... Lea, it's a homicide."

She clenched her hands into fists, one still gripping her phone as she pressed them to the sides of her head. "Oh, no. No."

Kino pulled into the RV park to find a wall of red and blue flashing lights. Police units lined the narrow road between the trailers.

"Stay here," said Kino as he exited to investigate, pressing the button on his key chain to lock all doors so that no one could open the door or see past the tinted glass.

He identified himself as a police officer to one of the on-duty officers who told him that there had been a shooting. They had no witness. One body. Two shots.

"Female?" asked Kino.

"Yeah. No ID yet."

"She Indian?"

The Tohono O'odham tribal officer pressed his mouth into a thin line and nodded.

Kino looked at the blue tarp covering the body, certain the killer had taken out the wrong woman. Did he know? He would discover his mistake soon enough. He needed to have Lea well away by then.

"Close range?"

"Doubt it. Lots of expansion. Entry is in the back and exit in front."

Kino wanted to stay, to look at the body and figure out the angle of the shot. To cut for sign. Instead he looked back at his vehicle. Lea was there, watching them, seeing her friend there on the ground just like those men in the desert. He needed to get her out of here.

He returned to the car and pulled away.

"Who is it? Is it Nita? Ernesta?"

He cleared the last trailer and pulled in beside a mobile home.

"I'm not sure." He only knew it wasn't Lea. The relief of that took him off guard.

She reached for the door handle. "I can identify her. I know them both."

He gripped her arm and struggled, but she was small and it was simple to pull her back into his vehicle. She used her arms like a swimmer, trying to free herself, so he gave her shoulders a shake. It got her attention.

"You can't help her."

He met her gaze, trying not to be affected by her tearstained face and the anguish of her expression.

"He might still be here," he said.

Lea stopped struggling and stared up at him with wide, dark eyes. Tears flowed down her cheeks and her chin wrinkled as she tried and failed to stanch the sobs.

"Quiet now," he whispered. "They don't have her identity yet."

"But I should do something."

"You *did* do something. You stayed in the car so he didn't see you."

She glanced frantically around. "Is he still here?"

"Maybe. But if he thinks he got you, that gives us a head start."

"But Ernesta… Nita."

"Gone." Kino turned her to face him and gripped both her shoulders. "You understand? He thought one of them was you, and he took her out. He might be here right now, watching. Don't give yourself away."

Lea went stiff at the thought then pulled the door closed and covered her mouth with her hands as if the air outside had become toxic.

"You told me he'd come." She pounded on his chest. "This is all my fault! You told me and I told them they could use my shower!"

He tried to take her hand but she pulled back, pressing herself to the door as if preparing to throw herself out of the car. She didn't want comfort. She wanted to escape this nightmare—and he could hardly blame her.

"It's not your fault, Lea. I sent a unit. You called her. If you want to blame someone, blame him."

She stilled.

"He came to your house and shot the first Indian woman he came across. We have to get him, Lea. You and I, together."

She slumped in her seat. A moment later they were driving into the gathering darkness.

KINO FELT LEA'S sobs as if they were his own. That had never happened before. But he experienced her pain just as intensely and agonized with the knowledge that he could do nothing to ease her suffering.

Her friend's death proved his belief—the Viper planned to eliminate the only surviving witness of his crimes. Maybe he should have told Lea that she was a target sooner. Maybe then she could have warned her friends. But he hadn't. He had only thought about Lea. He'd have to live with that doubt. But he was sure as hell that Lea didn't need to live with it. She'd done nothing wrong.

He tried to touch her but she pulled away, huddling against the door, as far from him as possible. Why did that hurt him? She was nothing to him but a witness. Right?

But he knew that was no longer true. Somewhere between finding Lea lying in the bits of broken glass this morning and this moment, when she sat weeping softly in the seat beside him, his feelings had changed. She'd gone from being his witness to something more. Earlier he had protected her because he'd needed her. Now he just wanted her safe and wished very much that she had not bumbled into the middle of all this.

"Where are we going?"

"My place."

She lifted her head and stared, eyes narrowing as if trying to decipher his intentions. Funny, he thought, that she would think of that sort of danger after all the other threats she had faced today.

"I'm not comfortable with that."

"You don't need to be comfortable. You need to be safe. I can make sure he doesn't get to you."

When she spoke her voice seemed almost sedated,

as out of focus as her gaze. “Maybe I could stay with a friend.”

“That would just put the friend in the crosshairs.”

She rubbed her arms and rocked back and forth. “I can’t stay with you all night.”

“Lea, think for a minute. You need protection. Nowhere else is safe.”

“I could go home.”

“To Salt River? He’ll follow.”

She slapped her hands on her thighs in frustration. “You make him sound like the Terminator or something.”

“Yeah. Exactly, but with one important difference. I can kill him.”

She sat still as stone, moving her hand only to wipe at her eyes while giving the occasional sniff. He wanted to pull the car over and kiss every tear from her face. Hold her. Comfort her.

You never got over losing a loved one. No amount of comfort in the world could make that right. Kino knew that much. He didn’t seek comfort. Only justice. For him and, now, for Lea, too.

“How could he know who I am? Where I live?” Lea asked, her voice quavering.

He put his mind back on the problem. The only ones who knew her identity were with border patrol. No, that wasn’t right. The tribal police had been called to watch her place. And if they’d used their radios to call the unit, which was very likely, anyone monitoring the police frequency could also have her address. Had they mentioned her name, too? Had the Viper been monitoring police radio frequency?

The people from Oasis knew her address. All of

them, including that tall, white boss with the rattlesnake key chain.

"It's a long list."

"Oasis?"

"Plus border patrol, BLM, ICE, tribal police and anyone with a shortwave radio."

She sank farther into her seat, looking small and vulnerable.

"They don't know I picked you up. Right now you are missing, presumed dead. We need to keep it that way. Will you trust me?"

"You told me to stay put. But he might have seen me with that scope."

"No. He didn't. And if he did, then I'll keep you safe, Lea." He gripped her shoulder and squeezed.

She tilted her head toward him until her cheek brushed the back of his hand. The gentle caress made his body heat and his heart rate rise.

"I will protect you," he said. It wasn't just a promise. It was a vow, just like the one he had made over the body of his dead father all those years ago.

She nodded. "I believe you. But…"

"What?"

She sobbed again.

He reached over and rubbed her back as she made hiccuping sounds, her face buried in her hands.

"I don't want any more killing," she said, her words muffled against her palms.

He withdrew his hand and returned it to the wheel. "I can't make that promise because I'll kill him if I get the chance."

She lifted her tear-streaked face and stared out at the shadowy twilight. Kino wondered what she was seeing. Her friend's motionless body in front of her trailer or the shooter holding her at gunpoint?

His phone vibrated and he took it out to see that the call was from Clay. He swiped to accept and raised the phone to his ear.

"Yup."

In the quiet of the cab, Kino was certain Lea would hear Clay's words, but did not try to prevent her. She should know what was happening. Clay reported that a border patrol officer named Dale Mulhay had been suspended. He was the officer who had taken Lea's statement. According to what Clay had found out, Captain Barrow had told him to keep Lea in custody until he arrived. They were holding Mulhay responsible for Lea's release. They hadn't yet heard that Lea was not the victim, but that would be at any time. Clay said that rumors and speculation surrounding Mulhay's actions were rampant.

"You think he's dirty?" asked Kino.

"That's what I'm hearing."

"He can't be the shooter. He interviewed Lea. She would have recognized him." He could be working with him, though, Kino realized. Was that why he'd ignored the captain's directive and sent Lea into danger? "Can you go talk to Mulhay?"

"If you want me to. Might be better for me to watch your back for now."

"Yeah. Mulhay will have to wait."

"I looked into Moody's background," said Clay. He was referring to the owner of the truck they had tracked from the scene. "His wife is O'odham. She raises sheep and chickens. He's a part-time mechanic. The truck involved in the shooting isn't registered to him and the registration has expired. Truck is uninsured."

"Who is it registered to?" asked Kino.

"Rosa Keene. I've got an address. She's in Tucson."

"Who is she?"

"No idea," Clay said.

"What's her truck doing in Moody's yard?"

"Don't know."

"Ask Gabe to call in a favor. He has friends up there in Tucson. Have an officer visit her."

"All right. But..." Clay didn't finish his thought.

"What?"

"He's on his way north by now."

Kino had completely forgotten about the trip to the Sweetgrass reservation in search of his sister. "He can call a friend en route," he told his brother.

"I'll ask him."

"Anything else?" asked Kino.

"Moody's got a DUI and a prior for narcotics."

"Using or selling?"

"Both."

"What do you think?" asked Kino.

"Best keep an eye on him. He's mixed up in this somehow. Maybe I'll stop by his work and see what kind of shoes he wears. You want me home or what?"

"Can you go check Lea's address for sign?"

"Nearly full dark," Clay noted.

"I know and there are about six units there. But there's a half-moon and I think the shooter used a scope."

"Maybe they haven't fouled the tracks. I'll have a look. You shouldn't go home. Won't be long before they figure out who gave Lea a ride from the station."

"I'll go to Carver's. Call when you get close." Kino disconnected.

Lea pressed a hand to her forehead and then rubbed it down her face. "I don't understand how this could be happening."

They drove through Pima and off Main onto Artists Road. When he got close to his place, he cut the lights and threw the SUV into Neutral, coasting silently past the squat, ugly cinder-block house that was his temporary residence. He saw no one and no vehicles, but he rolled right by and pulled into a house three doors down, gliding into the carport that was built into the front left side of the home. This was Joe Carver's place and Joe would be working all night. He was a Shadow Wolf, Navajo, who had been with the unit for several years.

"Is this Carver's house?" she asked, staring at the home that looked like every other house along the road.

"He's a buddy of mine." He released his safety belt. "I need to check his place."

"Can I come?"

He debated whether she'd be safer in the vehicle or with him. He might be out here with night-vision goggles and a scope sited on them right now. Or he might anticipate Kino's move and be inside that house, waiting to ambush them.

Kino glanced at Lea and knew he wouldn't leave her alone. Whatever was waiting, they'd face it together.

"Stay behind me."

Chapter Eight

Kino slipped out of the SUV. Lea exited a moment later and the cab light slowly faded to dark. Kino released the strap of his holster that kept his personal weapon in place and crept toward the side door. Lea fell in behind him.

"Why don't we just go to your house?" she whispered.

His reply was so quiet it might have been the breeze in her ear. "If it's an inside job, they might be waiting. I need to know it's safe before we go there."

"It doesn't look like anyone is home," she whispered.

Kino tried the door, found it locked and so rammed his shoulder into the wooden frame. The frame cracked and the door swung inward.

Lea gasped. "You broke it."

"No talk now," whispered Kino as he stepped inside, gun drawn. He knew Joe lived alone but it was best to be sure. He pointed to the kitchen floor. Lea nodded her understanding and crouched against the cabinets. He circled through the dining room and down the hall that led to the first of two bedrooms. Nothing moved as he checked the second bedroom and then the small bathroom. Once he'd checked the rooms, he returned to her.

"Clear," he said.

"Lights?" she asked.

"Yeah. Okay." Kino closed the front door and threw the dead bolt.

Kino walked to the entrance and flicked on the switch. The central circular fluorescent light flickered and then snapped on, emitting a soft buzz.

Kino wanted to check his place to see if anyone had been there, but he also wanted to sit tight with Lea until Clay was here to help him protect her.

"Can you put that away?" she asked.

"What?"

She motioned at his pistol. He holstered his weapon and she blew out a breath.

"I hate guns," she muttered and wiped her hand over her mouth.

Kino wondered about her reaction to his semiautomatic as she looked around the room, as if suddenly free to explore.

"Your friend doesn't know you're here," she said.

Kino shrugged. Joe's house looked similar to his, except the kitchen cabinets were a yellowing white laminate instead of beige. The kitchen table was round instead of square but the chairs were just as mismatched. He pulled one out for her and she sat, sagging as if too weary to remain upright. He took the seat adjoining hers and folded his hands on the pinewood surface.

"We stay here until Clay calls. I'll have to help him check our place. In the meantime, I need to know everything you remember about the man who threatened you. I know he's white. I could see that much. Tall and lanky, but muscular. He looked fit."

She nodded. "Yes. I could see the muscles in his forearm bunch."

Kino felt his skin prickle with awareness. He was so close to getting this guy.

Lea started her description. The guy was over six feet tall. He was white with very short hair, brown in color, she thought, but his hat had covered most of it. He had no facial hair, but a heavy five o'clock shadow. He had no scars, tattoos or marks to distinguish him. She hadn't seen his eye color because of his sunglasses, which were like the kind athletes wore, with black rims and blue-mirrored lenses. And she recalled the two deep vertical lines between his brows. He'd also worn a large black watch on the wrist that gripped the rifle.

When she finished speaking she was shivering.

"Age?"

"Forties, I'd say. Maybe fifties. I'm not good at guessing ages."

"Rings? Jewelry?"

Lea spun the turquoise ring on her right finger. "None that I remember."

"Earrings?"

"I don't know."

"What about his voice? Did he say anything?"

"He told me to get out of the truck."

"Accent?"

"He sounded like he was from here, somewhere in the Southwest."

"Anything else?" he asked.

"I don't know. He scared me. Something about the way he moved, the angle of his chin, tucked in like this." She inclined her head and pulled herself up.

"Imposing?"

"Yes. Definitely. And he had a big jaw."

"Square?"

"No. Just big."

"When did you notice the others?"

She pressed her hands over her mouth and shook her head. He wondered if she was going to be sick. Her eyes were closed. Finally she dropped her hands and folded them in her lap, letting her head drop forward.

"Not at first. I didn't see the…bodies until after the shooting. I just saw him. I waved like a fool and called hello. I thought he was from Oasis."

"Why?"

"Because he was already at the water station." Lea tipped her head to stare at the stucco ceiling and inhaled a long breath. Then she returned her focus to him. "He just sort of ambled over, as if there was no hurry. It wasn't until he was right beside my truck that I saw the blood on his shirt." She had her hands pressed over her eyes now and she rocked back and forth as she spoke. "I pointed to the blood and his expression changed. He didn't say a word, just stepped back to lift his rifle. Then he aimed it at my head and told me to get out of the truck. That was when you fired."

"Did he touch your truck? The door?"

"No. I don't think so."

Likely no fingerprints, then, Kino realized.

She lifted her chin and regarded him with big, dark eyes. "You going to find him?"

"That's why I'm here."

"I thought you were here to track smugglers."

"That's why they brought me. But I'm here for that

man. I call him the Viper. He's the man who killed my father."

Lea's eyes widened. "So you're on some kind of vendetta?"

He nodded. "You could call it that."

"What else would I call it?"

"Justice," he said.

She blew away a breath, regarding him. "What are you going to do when you catch him?"

"What do you think?"

She couldn't prevent the brief pressing of her lips and the disapproval that rose inside her. "It's wrong—killing."

"So is shooting four men in the back of the head. I need you to help me find this guy before he finds you."

"I'm not a vigilante," she said.

"I know what you are. You're an activist who saves lost smugglers with your damned blue flags and water stations."

She stiffened and aimed a finger at him. "Look… I'm a human being and I'm trying to keep the Sonoran Desert from becoming a killing field like South Texas. Migrants are going to make the attempt. All Homeland Security has done is drive them from urban centers and out here." She waved dismissively at the kitchen walls. "They can't make it, can't carry enough water to survive, but they come anyway, because it's better to take a chance than to die back there in a civil war."

"You talking about Central America?"

"Yes."

"Why do you care?" he asked.

"Why don't you? Why spend your time trying to

avenge the death of one man when right now, tonight, there are mothers and children out there trying to reach one of my damned blue flags? What makes your dead father's life more valuable than theirs?"

They glared at each other. Finally she leaned both elbows on the table and rested her forehead in her hands. Her shoulders sagged as exhaustion seemed to grip her again. "I thought you were protecting me because… But you just want me to identify this guy so you can shoot him."

In most of his fantasies he used a knife, but she had the gist of it.

"Lea, you have been through a hard time."

She rose. "Hard? She's dead! Because of me!" Lea headed for the door. "I've got to go. I can't have any more deaths because of me. I just can't."

He caught her before she made it halfway across the tiled floor.

"Let go!"

He let her slap at him and he took it until he had hold of her wrists. Then he let her struggle until she worked herself out. Finally she stood blowing and trembling like a spent horse.

Her head sank forward and she rested her forehead on his chest.

"I'm sorry," she whispered.

Kino gathered her up in his arms and rocked, slowly, from side to side, quiet, rhythmic, as he held her. She seemed to fit perfectly against him.

"I don't know what I'm doing," she muttered into the muscle of his shoulder, her words muffled by the contact of her mouth with his body. "What am I supposed to do?"

"Help me," he said. "It's not just my dad. This guy has been at this for years. I don't even know how many men he's killed. And it won't end here. If we don't stop him, he'll just keep going." He walked her back to the table, and as they sat down again, he prepared to tell her what he had not spoken about since it happened.

How a man had come to his house. Everyone had been at church, except Kino, who was sick, and his dad, who stayed back because his youngest son had a fever.

"My dad saw who it was at the door and told me to hide. Hide. I couldn't believe it, but something in his voice made me cold all over. I made it under the kitchen table before someone kicked in the door. The table was like this one," Kino said, resting his hands flat on the wood surface of the table. "But with one important difference. It had a tablecloth. That tablecloth saved my life."

Kino described the argument. About money and drugs. A delivery. A stash house. He didn't understand all of it at the time. Now he did. His father was transporting drugs and some had been missing. Kino had heard the shot and seen his father fall, head turned toward Kino, staring out at him with sightless eyes.

Lea took his hand and Kino looked away, shamed by the moisture that pricked his eyes.

"I saw the shooter squat down. He had on dark jeans and cowboy boots. Black ones. I couldn't see his face—just his legs and hands as he searched my dad's pockets. Then he opened a tobacco tin and picked something out of it."

Kino remembered the long, pale fingers lifting something that looked white, like the larva he'd seen under a rotting log. But when the man had shaken it from side to side, Kino had recognized the sound. The man had tried another before finally settling on one. Then he'd pushed the rattle into the oozing bullet hole in his father's motionless chest.

"That's where they found me. I was still under there when they got back from church. My brothers, my mother and my grandmother."

How long had Lea's hands been over his?

"How old were you?" she asked.

"Eleven."

He looked at her now. Was that horror or pity in her eyes? He didn't know. But something about her had given him the courage to tell her what he would not speak of to the police, his teachers, the counselors, not even his grandmother when she'd found him years later crying in his bed.

The corners of Lea's mouth tightened. "I don't think he'd want you to risk your life to avenge his. He told you to hide for a reason. He wanted you safe."

Kino was about to try to explain why he had to do this. Why he needed justice and, if not peace, at least the knowledge that this killer would not destroy another family.

But his phone vibrated, chiming the tone he'd programmed for Clay. He had a different tone for each of his brothers.

He answered the call on the second ring. "Yeah?"

Lea sat back.

"Any tracks?" asked Kino.

"Too many police vehicles and men tromping all over the place. If there were any, they're long gone."

"Not surprised."

"I met the chief of the tribal police," Clay continued.

"Yeah?"

"New on the job. White guy."

Kino's hairs lifted on his arms and neck. "How old?"

"Midforties. Why?"

"Just got a description of the Viper. He got dark hair?"

"Yeah. So does Bill Moody," said Clay. "Lots of white men here. Everywhere. Right?"

"We need to get Lea to see Moody without him seeing her."

"Okay."

"And we need a background check on the chief. What's his name?"

"Charlie Scott. Charles."

"Can you call Gabe?" Kino asked.

"Already did. Didn't ask about Chief Scott, though. Tomorrow, okay? He's on his way to South Dakota now."

Kino felt a pang of guilt. "How are they?"

"Good. Taking turns driving, like when they used to ride the rodeo circuit."

Kino didn't really remember that. He'd been too young. He only remembered his older brothers disappearing and coming home a week or so later, tired and hungry, but with money in their pockets and new shiny belt buckles.

"Right."

He couldn't say that he'd forgotten again because it would just aggravate Clay. Was it that he was missing the powwow or the rodeo that had his brother so bent out of shape? Still, he needed information on Chief Scott.

"What about Uncle Luke?" Kino asked, referring to his father's half brother, a former US marine.

"He ride rodeo?" asked Clay.

"No, I mean what about asking him to check out Moody or Scott?"

Their uncle, their father's younger brother, was a Black Mountain Apache who had been recruited into the FBI. Kino recalled that more than a few folks on the rez had been against his working for the government, saying things like you could never trust an Indian who worked with the Feds. But Kino trusted his uncle and he owed him.

"Worth a try. I'm on my way. Be there in five," Clay advised.

"Meet you out front."

"Yeah."

When Kino disconnected, Lea stood and he did, too.

"I want you to wait here."

"Alone in the house you broke into. Not happening."

"You're stubborn, you know?"

"I've heard that before."

"It would be safer for you here."

"No. I'm coming with you."

Kino left his vehicle in the carport and walked with Lea to his place. Together they circled the property and reached the street as Clay pulled up.

"No sign of a break-in," said Kino.

Together, with Lea trailing behind, Kino and Clay checked and secured the house. Clay then left them to retrieve the SUV, pulling it into the carport, nose out. In the meantime, Kino rummaged in the refrigerator.

"What are you doing?" she asked him. Just the sight of the carton of orange juice made her stomach gurgle.

"I'm cooking for you," he said.

She couldn't keep the skepticism from her voice. "You cook?"

"I won a chili contest at our powwow last year."

"Awesome."

"But it takes time to make a good chili. You like steak?"

"Yes."

"Not a vegan or something."

She gave a tired smile and a slow shake of her head.

Kino started cooking. He had steaks in the broiler and a bag of fries in the oven before Clay got back. Lea set the table and added ice to glasses. The fries were barely brown and the steaks still rare when they sat to eat. Kino was ravenous and, judging from the speed the food disappeared, so was Clay. But Lea ate slowly and very little.

After the meal, Kino found something for Lea to wear, coming up with a red T-shirt that read Rez Life and a pair of basketball shorts with a drawstring. She headed for the shower, clutching the clothing the way a child would hold a stuffed bear.

Clay watched her go. "That one has 'trouble' written all over her."

"How do you figure that?"

"Just by the way you look at her, brother."

"That's ridiculous."

"Well, you've already eaten, so why are you still drooling?"

Kino scowled. "I'm focused on finding the Viper."

"Sure. Sure." Clay stared at the closed door behind which came the sound of running water. "Still. A man can't live on only steak and justice."

Kino's phone rang and he took the call. After a brief conversation he disconnected and met Clay's inquiring stare.

"The victim's name was Ernesta Mott."

Clay nodded. "You going to tell her?"

Kino rubbed his neck, dreading the task ahead. "Yeah."

"Better you than me."

Chapter Nine

Lea woke, her body stiff and her head aching along with her heart. Ernesta was dead. Was it her fault, as she believed, or the shooter's, as Kino had said?

He had held her and rocked her long into the night. She had drawn comfort from his embrace and strength from his words. She thought he would have stayed all night with her if she had asked, which was why she hadn't. But she'd wanted to. That had frightened her enough to give her the strength to send him away. Had she slept at all?

She groaned and rolled facedown into the pillows, wishing she could stay here, lying in his sheets instead of facing the day. She found the scent of him here and pressed her nose into the pillows to inhale deep. Despite his assurances and the comfort of his now-familiar scent, she could not shake the images of death clinging to her like shrouds.

Lea found the strength to rise and shower, scrubbing her skin in a vain attempt to wash away the horror. When she returned to the bedroom it was to the aroma of coffee. That was enticement enough to get her out of the room and down the hall to the kitchen, where she was greeted with the sight of Clay pouring coffee and

Kino at the stove, spatula in hand as he turned browning potatoes in a black cast-iron skillet.

"There she is," Kino said, turning at some sound or change that was imperceptible to her. She had approached on bare feet on carpet. Yet he knew the instant she entered the room. How did he do that?

Clay wordlessly offered her a cup of coffee, which she accepted. He motioned her to a chair. On the table she added sugar to her coffee and then savored that first sip. It was strong and sweet. Just as she liked it.

"Milk is in the refrigerator, if you take it in your coffee," said Kino, as if it were the most natural thing in the world for Lea to be dressed in his clothing, sleeping in his bed and eating at his table. A tiny part of her wished that were so. The other part wanted her life back.

"I won't ask how you slept. Lousy, I'll bet. Understandable. It will be a while before you get a straight eight."

What made him so sure, so confident that the images burned into her memory would leave her? She lifted a brow and prayed he was right.

She was then presented with an enormous pile of fried potatoes, fresh-made fry bread with honey and enough bacon to take three years off her life. Kino could indeed cook. Why wasn't she hungry?

"Eat," ordered Kino.

She tried.

After the meal, Kino went to get her something to wear that didn't look as if she was preparing to go play basketball. That left her alone with Clay, who sipped his coffee and eyed her over the rim of his mug in the silence yawning between them. Why was it that she was so at ease with Kino and so jumpy around Clay?

At last she could nurse her coffee no more and was forced to try conversation.

"How did you two find out the Viper was here?"

Clay's brows lifted. He looked similar to his brother, although he was taller and rangier. Kino seemed to spend time lifting weights while Clay reminded her more of a distance runner.

"He told you about the Viper?"

"Yes. And how he killed your father."

Clay sat forward, slowly placing the coffee mug on the table surface. "What did he say?"

Lea told him. Clay sat so still Lea found it disconcerting. When she finished he still didn't move. She frowned. "Well?"

"He's never told any of us about that day."

"What? That doesn't make any sense."

"Nevertheless, it's true." Clay cocked his head. "Why you?"

"Because I've seen the shooter?"

Clay shook his head. "No. It's more. I think he likes you."

She gave a harsh laugh. "He doesn't like me. He hates Oasis. Thinks I'm helping the smugglers. Disapproves of pacifists in general and me in particular. And, finally, he doesn't have the first clue what it is like to cross that desert."

"Do you?" he asked.

Lea felt she'd said too much already. "No, of course not. I'm a member of the Salt River tribe." Why had she felt the need to say that last part? It made her sound as though she had something to prove.

"You like him?" asked Clay.

She made a face. She didn't like Kino. But she trusted

him. And she found herself extremely attracted to him. He made her feel safe, while Clay made her jumpy as a frog in spring rain. Lea glanced at the door, wishing Kino was back. "He and I don't see eye to eye," she said. "I don't approve of killing."

"Most women don't."

Lea moved to the counter to refill her cup, feeling Clay's gaze following her.

"What about you? Do you want to kill this man?"

Clay stretched his neck and shoulders and then returned his unsettling gaze to her. "I'm older than Kino. I knew what our dad was. But Kino? He only remembers what he was like around the house…taught him to cook, fish, stuff like that. At home, he was a good father and Kino idolized him. But Dad wasn't one of the good guys. He was away a lot and he didn't spend much time with us. Kino was too young to remember. Me, too, actually.

"Dad was locked up for DWI before I was even born. When he got out, he couldn't find any work. Clyne told me he got arrested again when Clyne was five. Arson this time. Apparently he set a hell of a blaze, hoping to get work putting out the brush fire, which he did, but the fire burned for days. Destroyed a lot of property. I remember him getting out after that one. I was ten. Kino was only six then. He didn't see that dad was using."

"Using?"

"He came out of prison addicted to crystal meth. I heard the police tell Grandma that to pay for his habit he was transporting drugs from the border to stash houses on the rez. Lots of drugs on the rez. You know. Harder to prosecute 'cause it's Indian land. It draws bad people and trouble. Lots of trouble." Clay finally looked away as his eyes took on a distant quality.

"I'm sorry."

He returned his focus to her. "Yeah. Anyway. Dad was…well, ruined by prison or unemployment or alcohol. I don't know which or when. Kino just knows that they took him. Then we meet up with one of the guys working down here, a Shadow Wolf, and he mentions a cartel hit and the rattlesnake rattle in the bullet wound. Kino puts in for a leave of absence and convinces me to come on down here with him."

"You're here to find this killer, too?"

"My dad deserved what he got." Clay ran a finger around the rim of his empty coffee cup. "I'm here for him." He thumbed toward the hall.

That surprised her. "You're looking out for him?"

"Miss Altaha, I lost my dad and my mom. Maybe my little sister, too. I can't afford to lose anyone else."

"I see."

"I'd stop him if I could. But I can't. He's got his jaw locked like a snapping turtle. No use trying to pry him off. So the best I can do is watch his back."

Lea had the feeling that Kino would need that kind of help very soon.

Clay's phone rang, the ringtone a recording of Apache drums and the high song she recognized from dance competitions. Clay picked up.

"Yeah?" He listened and then stood. "Okay, then." Clay disconnected and met her questioning gaze. "Kino convinced the tribal police to meet us at Moody's. He wants to see if you recognize him."

"Who's Moody?"

"We found the Viper's truck on his property yesterday."

"You think it's him?"

"You tell us."

Kino returned, carrying her T-shirt and jeans, now obviously washed, folded and stacked. Someone had taught the Cosen brothers how to keep house, she thought. Kino extended his offering and she looked again at the pile, noticing two unfamiliar items of clothing at the bottom of the stack. A tan-colored shirt like the ones the Shadow Wolves wore and beneath that a bulletproof vest. Her stomach twisted at the reminder of her vulnerability.

"What's this?" she asked.

"You know what it is. I want you to wear it under the shirt."

She accepted the pile, finding the vest much lighter than she'd anticipated.

"Is this really necessary?"

"We'll see."

KINO DROVE THE SUV and they reached Moody's place just behind the tribal police. He planned to kill two birds with one stone here. Lea would remain safe behind the tinted glass where she could see everyone who passed by. He would make sure that included Bill Moody and the new tribal police chief, Charles Scott.

Lea sat in the back between the two bucket seats, wearing her jeans and Kino's shirt, beneath which she wore her T-shirt and his body armor.

She hadn't fought him on that, which made him think she realized the danger. But she showed tremendous courage, quietly doing all he asked. When he'd asked why she was so agreeable, she'd said she just wanted to get this over with.

Why should that bother him? Didn't he want to get this over with, as well? Hadn't he been thinking of this day for years? But once he found the Viper there would be no reason to keep Lea close. No excuse to bring her along or to let her sleep in his bed. Granted, he'd been on the couch, but this morning, when he'd been dressing, he could smell her soft, sweet scent on his pillow. What would it be like to wake up beside her?

He'd never find out because she clearly wanted nothing to do with him and that suddenly bothered him. He'd never felt this protective instinct for any other woman and that bothered him, too.

Clay had called her a distraction that could get them both killed while Kino saw her as the lucky break he'd been praying for. Maybe Clay was right. He was getting too attached to her.

Kino eavesdropped as Lea called border patrol and rescheduled her meeting there. When she dropped the phone in her overlarge front pocket, she looked years older. The US Marines called it the two-thousand-yard stare: that vacant look of battle-weary soldiers.

"You all right?" asked Kino.

"No. And I don't know if I ever will be."

She would. Lea was strong, stronger than she knew.

Two tribal police units and a single ICE vehicle had pulled off just out of sight of Bill Moody's residence to organize.

"You didn't call border patrol," Clay said, looking out the window. It was more statement than question.

Kino met Clay's long stare and shrugged. "We're not

on the border." He aimed his thumb out his passenger window. "Our captain is here."

His friend and fellow Shadow Wolf Nesto Gomez sat in the ICE unit with Captain Rubio. In the backseat was Nesto's dog, Coco. If there were drugs on the premises, Coco would find them.

"Hey, Chief Scott is here," said Clay, pointing to the first tribal unit.

Kino cast Lea one quick glance before exiting the vehicle, leaving the SUV running and the AC on. Lots of guys did that to keep the interior cool. Kino waited for Clay to disembark before hitting the alarm and lock button. Clay approached the chief of police and thanked him for coming. Then he introduced Kino, who shook Scott's hand. Lea would see his face now. Was it him? Was his palm now pressed to the one that had held the weapon that had killed his father?

With introductions made and the plan in place, Kino returned to his SUV, waiting until all the tribal police were moving before opening the door. He stuck his head in and looked at Lea. She shook her head.

"You sure?" he asked.

"Not him," she said. Her voice held complete certainty.

Kino didn't know if he should feel relieved or disappointed. Having the chief of the tribal police involved with the cartels would be very bad business. But it meant he was down to three possible suspects. Bill Moody, Anthony DeClay and Dale Mulhay.

Kino climbed in behind the wheel and took his place at the end of the line of units. They approached without sirens or lights.

Moody's house was within the jurisdiction of the

tribal police. They knocked and Moody came to the door, obviously just out of bed, his pink face still showing the marks of wrinkled bedsheets. His wife appeared behind him and there was an exchange in O'odham that Kino could not follow.

Kino knew that Lea could not see Moody from where he stood on his cluttered porch. But she'd see him when they walked to the outbuilding. Unfortunately, Chief Scott insisted Moody turn over the key and remain on the porch with one of his men while they went to investigate. Inside the building they found three more vehicles. There was a four-seat all-terrain vehicle that could maneuver in places a truck could not. There was also a cart that could hook up behind the ATV.

"Wonder what he carries in that?" asked Scott.

Beyond the ATV and cart sat a new truck, a tan-colored dually with the backseat removed in exactly the fashion used by traffickers transporting quantities of product that had been smuggled over the border. The next two vehicles made Clay let out a whistle of appreciation. The first was a four-wheel motorcycle in camo color. The last was a dune buggy complete with roll bars and metal cage.

"Now, where would a part-time mechanic get the scratch for all this?" asked Chief Scott. Then he called over his shoulder, "Okay, Gomez. Bring in Coco."

The dog entered, pulling on her leash in her effort to search. She gave positive signs on the dually and the cart.

"Arrest him," said Scott to one of his officers.

Kino went along to be sure Moody walked past Lea.

Clay went with him. "If that's him, you'll have to be satisfied with him going to jail."

Kino knew that. "I just want it over."

"I thought you wanted him dead," said Clay.

Kino looked toward their SUV and thought of Lea.

"Yeah, I did" was all he said. But now he wasn't quite so sure.

Moody put up a struggle and, after having his hands secured with plastic ties, managed to get away from the two arresting officers. He was heading straight for their SUV, the last in the line.

Kino caught up to him, grabbed him by the neck and threw him up against the SUV. Moody grunted and his cheek slid against the glass of the rear passenger-side window. He stopped struggling. It was only then that Kino realized that Moody had his forehead resting on the glass and seemed to be peering into the vehicle. Kino felt a shot of adrenaline bolt through him as he yanked Moody away from the SUV.

"Thanks," said one of the officers, taking charge of Moody again. Moody turned his head, met Kino's gaze and smiled. Kino watched him march away between two tribal police officers. Then he pressed his own face close to the glass and saw Lea with her hands fisted to her cheeks. Their eyes met and Kino knew for sure—Moody had seen Lea.

Chapter Ten

Lea was cowering when Kino got into the SUV. He spun so that his shoulders filled the gap between the seats.

"Was that him?" he asked.

Lea shook her head. "Not him."

"Then what's wrong?"

She couldn't put her finger on it, but the way the man had looked at her, with a sort of triumph, had washed her entire body cold. Her mouth had gone dry and her head was still pounding.

Clay slipped into the front passenger seat. "He's dirty. You know a guy living in BIA housing can't afford toys like that. Hell, it took me a year to save up for my boat, and I'm working overtime five days a week."

"Which is why you don't have a girlfriend," said Kino without looking at him. His eyes were still on Lea, sweeping her face, his concern showing in the slight downward tug at the corners of his mouth.

"I prefer my boat," said Clay. "Jason said he'd call us when they run the VINs on those vehicles."

Kino shifted back into the driver's seat and put them in Drive. "Who?"

"The tribal officer we met in the outbuilding. Jason Beach was his name."

Lea listened to their exchange, trying to get her heart rate to return from frantic to terrified. What would happen now?

Kino was talking. "…can't go back to her place. He might have figured out his mistake by now."

"If she doesn't show for work they'll list her as a missing person. Everyone will be looking for her."

Kino glanced at her in the rearview—the problem they needed to solve. "We've got to report in. Lea, I want to see your director. DeClay. I'm going with you to rule him out." He glanced at Clay. "Then we can report in."

"But he knows Ernesta," said Lea. "Surely he can tell us apart."

"At night? From the back?"

From the back? Had that coward shot Ernesta in the back? Lea's shoulders slumped as she sagged in the seat, the belt holding her upright. Ernesta was a wonderful, committed person who'd done all she could to make the world a better place. This was all so very wrong.

"You going to leave her without protection?" Clay sounded astonished.

"No. I'm riding with her."

They'd reached Oasis headquarters in Pima when Clay got a call. He wrote something down and then thanked the caller before disconnecting.

"That was Beach. He said the vehicles are all registered to the same person."

"Who?"

"Rosa Keene."

"That's the same name we got for that old truck. The one he was driving."

"Yup."

"So who is she?" asked Kino.

"I don't know, but Beach says Moody is denying knowledge. Says he was just holding them for a friend who likes to take them out in the desert."

"That's bull."

"Yeah, but Coco didn't find any drug evidence on his property. Beach says that the only place they got a clear signal was in the vehicles and Moody doesn't own them."

"He's going to walk."

"Seems like it."

"Call Gabe. Get him to send someone to Rosa Keene's address. Find out anything he can about her and ask him to call us back."

"He's going to see the state police up there today."

Kino grimaced. The brothers exchanged a look in silence and Clay looked away. He gave a long-suffering sigh and made the call.

Kino left Clay in the running SUV and opened her door. He offered his hand and she walked with him into the offices of Oasis on rubbery legs. She was still wobbly when Margie got up and enveloped her in a warm hug.

Lea breathed in the scent of baby powder and coffee.

"You poor thing. You come and sit here. I heard about Ernesta. Anthony has already contacted her folks. He said you didn't answer your phone. He's pretty worried."

"I shut it off." She hadn't but Kino didn't want her answering.

"Geez, he was gonna call the police today and report you missing."

Just as Clay had predicted.

"Don't worry about the truck. Anthony picked it up

this morning. I'm so sorry I gave you those keys. I had no idea." Margie started to cry.

Kino pulled a tissue off her desk and handed it over with a request to see Anthony DeClay. Margie took them out back where the man in charge of this arm of Oasis stood on a truck bed filling a 200-gallon tank with water. Her tread slowed and Margie got farther ahead of them. Kino gripped her arm.

"Is that him?"

"I can't tell yet." But it looked like the man who had aimed that rifle at her. Same tall, lean frame. Same short brown hair. He wore jeans, construction boots and a long-sleeved, worn denim shirt that was open over his Oasis T-shirt.

Kino released the safety on his gun and returned it to its holster as they moved within ten feet.

Margie was out in front of them, pausing at the truck gate. She called a greeting and the man straightened and flicked off the water nozzle. Lea froze. Kino stopped just ahead of her, not blocking her view, but shielding her.

She stared at those glasses, black frames, blue-mirrored lenses and she couldn't help the intake of breath. But then she looked at his face as he pulled down the shades. He had crow's-feet flanking blue eyes. His jaw was square and he had dimples on each side of his mouth. His ears were small and tucked back.

Lea sagged. Kino slid his hand off his gun.

"This here is Lea Altaha," said Margie.

Anthony DeClay hopped down from the truck, his eyes flicking from Kino to her before he took her hand.

"I'm sorry about Ernesta," he said.

Lea's eyes burned as she nodded.

"And about the truck mix-up. I got ours back." He motioned to the battered blue truck devoid of windshield glass or side mirror. "Hell of a thing."

"Did you get your map back?" asked Kino.

DeClay released Lea. "Oh, yes. It was in the truck. This whole thing could have been avoided, if Lea had checked in with me."

"You hadn't arrived yet and Margie gave me the keys," said Lea.

Margie, flustered now, turned a bright red as she stammered. "I h-hope you don't think I was responsible for what happened to you yesterday. I'm just sick about it."

But she didn't look sick. She looked scared. Her gaze kept sliding from Lea to Anthony and then to Kino. She looked cornered and on the verge of tears.

"We haven't met," said DeClay to Kino. "I'm Anthony DeClay. I'm the director."

The men shook hands, eyes locked, smiles frozen.

"Officer Cosen," said Kino. "I'm the one who shot out your windshield."

They released their grips and regarded each other.

"Who repairs your trucks?" asked Kino.

"A local shop. We try to use local businesses when possible."

"Any chance I could get a copy of the map Lea was using?"

"Oh." He hesitated, hand going to his neck. "That's just the stations we are taking out. Perhaps you heard—the tribal council voted to have us remove the stations on their land."

"Yes, but the Shadow Wolves have permission to

hunt and track on O'odham land and the station on your map was a drop spot."

"That's not connected to us. We're a humanitarian organization. We save lives."

Why did he sound defensive? Lea wondered. DeClay looked positively hostile with arms folded over his broad chest.

"The map is part of our investigation. So I'll need a copy."

"I'll make you one and have my people bring it to Cardon Station."

"You can't make a copy now?"

"Printer is down."

Lea glanced at Margie, whose face was the color of a boiled beet.

"Lea is taking a few days off," said Kino.

She was?

"Of course," said Anthony. "Understandable. But we are short-staffed. We only have three crews. So I'm out in the fields today, too. If there is nothing else, Officer Cosen, we've got work. Important work. They found another body last night. A young woman. She'd sustained an injury. Broken ankle, I'm told. She made it to one of our stations, but, well, it was empty." His gaze went to Lea, as if it was her fault.

Had that been one of the stations she was supposed to have filled? She felt as if someone had kicked her in the stomach.

"I have to get back to work," she said to Kino.

"You have no partner."

"You could help after your shift," the director suggested to Kino.

DeClay regarded Kino, waiting for his decision.

"All right," said Kino.

"Wonderful. Margie will get you the papers you need to sign and we can set you two up."

"Great," said Kino.

"Nice to meet you, Officer Cosen. Welcome on board."

The tension in Kino's body made his usually graceful stride an angry staccato as he followed Margie back into the building. Twenty minutes later Kino was an official aid worker and he and Lea were back in the SUV.

"Why did you do that?" she asked.

"You were going out there again, right?"

"Yes. I have to. People are out there in the desert. They need that water."

"I don't want you out there alone or with any partner but me."

Kino tucked the papers he carried in the visor.

"Margie made me a copy of the rules and regs." His gaze fixed on hers. She knew what he meant. The copier wasn't broken. DeClay had lied.

"I don't know why he did that," Lea said.

"Love to see that map." He started the SUV.

They drove out of Pima and into the desert. The route looked all too familiar.

"Where are we heading?" she asked.

"Back to the scene. I want another look at the scene."

Chapter Eleven

Lea tried to hold down her panic at having to return to the place where she'd nearly died. When they got there, she was surprised to see no evidence of the gun battle. No shattered glass or blood-soaked sand. And no water station. She couldn't even really tell where the men had been. But Kino could. He was already sweeping the site—seeing what, she did not know.

"Where are the barrels?" she asked.

Kino stopped to stand in the place where the barrels had been. "Here. Oasis was told to remove them." His eyes narrowed. "Short-staffed, but they move pretty fast when they want to." He turned to Lea. "You remember any other stations on that map?"

She thought a minute. "Yeah. I had three loaded into my GPS but the thing doesn't work out here. I have the coordinates, though." She looked them up and they returned to the SUV. In twenty minutes they reached the next station on her list. Before they left the vehicle, a call came over Kino's radio from his brother.

"Got some information."

"Go ahead."

"Moody repairs trucks for Oasis."

Lea's stomach dropped. "But he works in town.

Doesn't he? That doesn't mean—" Clay continued, so Lea broke off.

"Moody's already out. He had a lawyer he can't afford. Finally, Captain Rubio wants you back at the station now."

"Be there in twenty," Kino advised. "Anything else?"

"Yeah. Gabe and Clyne got the police report on Mom."

Kino's grip on the wheel tightened. "Go ahead."

"The report did not say 'no survivors.' But the handwriting was rough. What it actually said was 'one survivor,'" Clay revealed. "The officer's retired but Gabe found him. He still lives up that way, I guess. The trooper said he remembered that accident because it was the Fourth and because of the little girl crying. He told Clyne that he called BIA and they took Jovanna at the scene."

"Why would they do that?"

"BIA is in charge of Indian affairs. Our sister *is* Indian. Makes sense."

"So the cemetery people were right? There's only one grave up there?"

"Seems so. Gabe and Clyne saw it and checked with the cemetery office. One body, female. Jovanna is alive, or she was alive after the accident. They are checking hospital records next to see if they took Jovanna there. But I did ask Gabe if he knows someone in Tucson who could visit Rosa Keene. He said he'll try a buddy there. See if they can send a unit to interview her."

"Okay. Keep me posted."

"On Jovanna or Rosa?" asked his brother.

Kino made a face. "Both. Out."

Lea placed a hand on Kino's thigh. "Is that your mother's grave that Clay is speaking of?"

He nodded.

"And your sister might be alive. That's good news."

"Yes. Very good."

"Shouldn't you be up there helping your brothers?"

Instantly she regretted her words as Kino's face went to stone. He swerved to the shoulder of the highway and then skidded off onto a wide stretch of sand. He threw the SUV into Park with more force than necessary and then faced her. She noted the dangerous glitter in his eyes and wondered if this was the kind of man who used his fists to relieve stress. Lea pressed her back to the door as her heart beat in her throat.

"You sound just like Clay." He shot her a dark scowl. "Gabe and Clyne can handle it. They can handle anything."

"Of course they can." She forced herself to speak in a soothing tone and lifted her open hands in a sign of surrender and mollification.

Kino's brows lifted as he stared at her. Then he closed his eyes for a moment. When he opened them, his features were calm and his body relaxed.

"Lea, you haven't known me long. But I want you to understand something about me. I have never and will never, ever, lift my hand to a woman. I fight to protect, defend and apprehend. That's it."

She felt some of the tension leave the muscles in her shoulders and stomach. Her heart continued to wallop her ribs like a caged animal.

"I believe you," she said. "But it's a contradiction. The peace and violence. I don't understand it."

"Everything has two sides, dark and light."

She knew the stories and the philosophy. Man's struggle for the light; his battle with the darkness.

"As for helping? I've spent much of my life trying to keep up with my older brothers. Being told I was in the way or too little to be included. Feeling their frustration as my gran insisted they take me along.

"Clyne is thirty-three. That's thirteen years older than me. He was more like a second father than a brother. Gabe, too. He's nine years older and Clay is four, just old enough to be ten times better at everything and to find me mostly a pest. He's been looking out for me since forever. Still is. Can't stop, I guess. I suppose I don't think they really need my help."

"They do. Of course they do."

"I do feel guilty that I'm not at Black Mountain. Gabe is away and we are always shorthanded. But it's only a month—just a few more days now."

She knew what a difference a few days had made to her mother's sister. The thought made her sad and weary all at once.

Kino pursed his lips and blew out a breath. Then he flexed his fingers on the wheel and gripped it with one hand. The other he extended to her, palm up.

Lea hesitated for less time than she should have before taking his hand. This man had a magnetism she did not understand and could not seem to resist.

Their fingers entwined and she felt the pleasant stirring of need; her body for his. Their eyes met and held.

"I'm close to finding this guy. Close to putting him away. But I need your help."

And then his hand slipped from hers. He seemed to really want her understanding. So she tried. But still she could not comprehend why he was here with his father's ghost instead of with his older siblings looking for his sister.

Why did so many people think that the correct response to violence was more violence? It created an endless circle of aggression.

She stared off to her right at the scrubby plants that might not see rain for another full year. Yet they endured, twisted and stunted as they were. The stark outline of rocky mountains punched upward into the blue sky and there, above it all, shone the unforgiving sun. Who was out there now, without water, thirsty, dying?

This time when he spoke, the earnest, plaintive quality had been replaced by wistfulness. "She's been missing for nine years. She won't even know us."

Lea had reached out again automatically, responding to his pain with a gentle stroking of her hand on his thigh. His leg flinched beneath her fingers and she pulled back. Why did she have the continuous gnawing need to connect with him? Was it just the physical—the longing to press flesh to flesh and to know this man in the most intimate way possible?

She forced her mind back to his concerns. His sister, whom he obviously loved despite his absence and his current priorities.

"How old was she then?" she asked.

"Three."

"She'll remember something. I'm sure."

Kino put the vehicle back in gear and drove them to the coordinates she had given him. Once at the second station, Kino stepped out of the cool SUV and Lea followed. The long-sleeved shirt kept the sun from her arms, and the bulky vest, which did not quite fit even with the Velcro straps cinched tight, allowed some airflow. Still, the nylon pressed down on her shoulders like an unwelcome backpack. That made her think of her mother walking out here with everything she'd owned in a pillowcase, the pack on her back reserved for other things.

Kino stood a few feet in front of the vehicle, but instead of checking the station site for sign, as he had at the first station, he stood with his head bowed.

Lea crossed around in front of the hood to reach him. She rested a hand on his shoulder, which was free of his bullet-stopping vest.

He wrapped her in one arm and tugged her against his side. The flak jacket he insisted she wear shifted and stuck to her breasts and stomach. Still, the pressure of his body against hers made her breasts ache with want.

"You all right?" she asked.

"I should be asking you that question," he said. "How are you managing?"

"Well, I'm glad the director isn't the Viper. That's the only good thing that's happened. I want to get back to work. I feel the same way you do about your job. They are short-staffed and need every aid worker." She gazed up at him, one hand resting on his chest, taking in the slow, steady beat of his heart as she inhaled the spicy scent of him.

"But you'll be leaving eventually."

"Yes, when my internship is done. But not until my replacement arrives."

He'd worn his hair loose today and it brushed past his shoulder blades in a straight black curtain. She wondered if he ever danced at powwows because she would dearly love to see him in his regalia. Just the thought gave her goose bumps.

"I'd like to check this station. Could you just stay still while I cut for sign?"

She stepped back, reluctant to let him go. It felt so natural to be in his arms. She needed to stop that line of thinking because it wasn't natural. She could tell what he thought of her humanitarian efforts and he knew what she thought of his work, too.

Kino spent a few minutes walking in a zigzag pattern, examining a sagebrush branch and squatting to check the ground. What did he see?

Finally he glanced back to her and motioned with his head. She followed him to the barrels. "What did you see?"

"Recent visit. Six men. Smugglers, likely, as they came in heavy, left light. All visited the water station."

She was helping smugglers again, just as he'd accused. Her stomach dropped with her spirits.

"Saw a fiber on that bush from a burlap sack." He pointed to the water barrels. "Curious to take a look in there."

"Oh, they don't open," she said.

He quirked a brow but said nothing. Then he addressed the first barrel, lifting it several inches from the frame and dropping it back into place. It made no sloshing sound.

"Empty?" she asked. "If it's marked for removal, then that makes sense."

He tried the lid.

"Those are glued down. They don't come off," said Lea. "We fill them from the top and the migrants use the spigot at the bottom to draw water."

Despite her expectation, the top popped right off and fell to the sand. Lea gave a little exclamation of surprise as she leaned forward to peer into the barrel, which now rested on its side. The blue container was filled to the brim with plastic rectangular bags about twelve-by-twelve-by-eighteen. Just the right size for transport in a backpack, she realized. Judging from the smell, it was marijuana.

"Bingo," said Kino. He turned to Lea and lowered his shades. "You know about this?"

"What? No!"

"So are these not on the map because they are marked for removal, as your boss states, or because they are using them as drops?"

"This is terrible," said Lea. "If a migrant tries this station, they won't get any water."

"Might be why we're finding so many dead men near certain water stations."

Lea reached for her radio. "I have to call this in."

Kino stilled her hand. "Not yet. Someone will be picking up this stash. I aim to be here when they do."

He took out his phone to call his brother to come out.

"Captain wants us in," Clay told him.

Kino relayed what he had found. Clay said he'd be there with one of the veterans, the Navajo, Joe Carver, whose home he and Lea had broken into last night. He asked Kino to text him the coordinates.

While they waited, Kino's eyes searched the scene.

"I'm going to be waiting when he arrives," said Kino to Lea.

"Who arrives?"

"The Viper."

Chapter Twelve

Kino turned to Lea and his triumph vanished. The need to hunt pushed against the promise he had made to her to keep her safe. Her cheeks had gone pale and a look of terror froze her features. Had he forgotten what had happened to her yesterday or that he'd promised to protect her? She was not military or law enforcement. She did not thrill to the chase. She was a pacifist and he was dragging her straight into a shoot-out. He needed to get Lea out of here before the Viper came in to collect his merchandise.

He sent a text to his brother with the coordinates and asked permission to use Joe's place again.

A few minutes later he received Clay's reply: Carver wants his door fixed.

Kino responded. Glad to. Leaving site.

Clay's text appeared a moment later. Key behind house number.

She peered over his shoulder. "Wish we'd known that last night." Lea seemed to have recovered some of her nerve, but her color was still bad. "So, he's on his way?" she asked.

"Yeah. And we're going."

They backtracked to the vehicle and he headed down

the long empty stretch that was becoming as familiar as the roads around the rez.

"I know why I can't go home," she said as they drove through the midday heat. "But why not your place?"

"We left the station together. Border patrol knows I drove you home. Plus, we might have been seen driving through town."

She hugged her arms around her middle and shivered. "You mean by that guy Moody, at the repair shop?"

Him, yes, Kino thought. He didn't know who bothered him most, Moody or Lea's boss.

"Lea, do you believe what DeClay said about that station being scheduled for removal?"

"I do, yes. Why?"

"Because that map might just be a map of drop sites."

"But then he'd be involved. He'd be working with the smugglers."

Kino met her gaze as her expression blossomed into shock. Her mouth hung open and her pink lips were wet and appealing.

"Lea, you've got to stop trusting everyone and believing exactly what they tell you. Not everyone works on that level."

She folded her arms. "I don't believe Anthony DeClay is a smuggler."

"Or you don't want to believe it." Kino went through the order of events, checking the sequence. Could he have misinterpreted what he had seen? Could Lea have been meeting the Viper? No, he'd seen the guy aim a gun at her. There was only one way to interpret that. Then he'd sent her to the BP station. That was the only time she'd been out of his sight. "What did Dale say to you?"

"Who?"

"Dale Mulhay, the guy who interviewed you?"

"Oh." Lea began to relax. She rubbed her index finger on her upper lip, contemplative now. "Well, he said they might want to speak to me again."

"But the captain told him to detain you until he got there."

"I didn't hear anyone tell him that. In fact, he said the captain wanted to speak to me but was at the scene and that they would call me."

"Did he step out or away from you?"

"Not that I remember."

"Receive a phone call or text?"

She shook her head. "No— Wait. Yes. He called someone to get me a ride home."

"Did you insist on being released?"

"No. He said I could go."

Kino's mind was rolling faster than the wheels.

"Something stinks. I need to speak to Mulhay. Will you be all right at Joe's for a few hours?"

"I would think so."

"You ever shot a handgun?"

She waved a hand. "Of course not. And I won't be shooting one. Not ever."

"I'll show you."

"No. You won't."

He took in her stubborn expression.

"What about a Taser? It just stuns a guy. No harm."

Kino pulled half off the road until the outside tires sank into soft sand. Then he lifted the Taser out of its cradle on his belt and showed her. "See, you just flip off the safety. When you see the orange you're good to go. Just point and shoot."

"Unless it stops his heart."

"That's very rare. You'd have to hold the trigger down to give him a continuous charge and he'd have to have…" He glanced at her horrified expression and stopped talking. "This pacifist thing is a pain in the neck."

"So is your insistence on shooting at people."

"Only if they draw first."

Kino glanced in the rearview and then steered them back onto the road.

She folded her hands in her lap. "I feel so much better."

He got her to Joe's place and used the key Joe had tucked away. Then he gave Lea a quick lesson on home security and reminded her to keep her phone on her at all times.

Lea lifted her phone from her jeans, showing him that she had it. "What I really need is a change of clothes."

"I'll see what I can do. Size?"

She told him and he headed out. "Can I take off the vest?"

"No."

She shrugged, her shoulders lifting and dropping the vest as if weary from the weight. "Fine."

"Call if you need me."

"My phone is about dead. I've got it switched off to save the battery."

"Turn it on." Kino looked at the connection and made a note to get her a charger from the station. "Don't open the door."

She stood there, looking small and vulnerable, with her chin up and her face fixed with a familiar impassive expression.

He knew that look; it was a practiced one. He'd seen it on the face of every girl who had taken part in the Sunrise Ceremony. He had been told that the girls were instructed to show no emotion, only a kind of mental toughness, no matter how difficult the task. Perhaps the ceremony that was designed to prepare a girl for the rigors of life as an Apache woman was more valuable than Kino had ever imagined. Certainly, Lea needed to draw on that inner toughness now.

She did not move toward him, but he moved toward her, tugging her forward into an embrace he hoped would tell her that he would look out for her. She lifted her chin and he lowered his mouth, taking her in a slow, thorough kiss that left them both breathless and Lea clinging to him.

"I'll be back," he murmured.

"I know you will." She stepped away, letting him go instead of begging him to stay. Her face was inscrutable again, her breathing faster.

Tough, he decided as he left her.

"Be safe," she said, closing and locking the door behind him.

KINO HEADED TO Dale Mulhay's place and got no answer to his knocking. Suspended didn't mean house arrest, of course, but the man's car was in the drive and his front door was unlocked.

Kino shouted a greeting from the entrance before he stepped inside. He found Dale in the bathroom, face down on the floor. Beside him was a crack pipe and a clear plastic bag filled with white crystal shards. There was a smear of blood on the toilet lid and on the floor.

Kino dropped to one knee and checked Dale's pulse. He didn't find one.

Kino left Dale where he had found him. Once at his vehicle, he called the tribal police and reported the death. Then he called Clay, who was already at the water barrel station, and told him what had happened. Clay decided to stay put and continue to read sign.

While Kino waited for a tribal officer, he called his uncle. Luke Forrest was his father's younger brother, a full-blood Apache, though born to a different father.

After he'd become a Fed, Uncle Luke had been the one to stand by his nephew at the tribal court, asking for leniency after an arrest. That had ensured that Kino's teenage stupidity hadn't translated into a criminal record and had also made it possible for Kino to become a cop. After the hearing, Uncle Luke had put him to work.

Kino glanced at his left hand thinking he could still feel the blisters. He owed his uncle a lot and now he wanted another favor.

Kino told Luke about the situation and his uncle agreed to run a background check on Charles Scott, Anthony DeClay, William Moody and Lea Altaha. He also asked him to find out all he could about Rosa Keene.

"I'll put my new partner on that one. She just transferred in from North Dakota."

"She?"

"Yeah. That's a first."

"She Indian, too?"

"Nah. White. Really, really white."

Kino smiled and then thanked his uncle, promising to pass on his regards to Kino's grandmother, before ending the call.

The police arrived on scene first, followed by Captain Rubio. Judging from the stiffness at the corners of his captain's mouth, Kino was in for it.

After Chief Scott had all his questions answered, Kino faced Captain Rubio. The sweat that now trickled down Kino's back was only partially to do with the desert heat.

"Did you not get the message that I wanted to see you first thing this morning?" asked Rubio.

"I got it, sir."

"Then you mind telling me why I didn't see you?"

"I was following a lead from yesterday's sighting."

"So I hear." He glanced at Chief Scott, now engaged in conversation with one of his men. Rubio focused on Kino. "Son, if you miss police work so much, you can just head back up to Black Mountain. You signed on here to track smugglers. Not to make arrests or investigate crime scenes—" he signaled a hand in the direction of Dale's house "—or whatever the hell you are doing here."

"Yes, sir." Kino continued, regardless of the reprimand, "It's just that truck—Clay and I tracked it."

"He told me. And he told me about Moody and that you found a drop that I should be investigating right now. He told me because he follows orders and checks in on occasion."

Kino clenched his jaw. He wanted to catch the Viper. But to do that he needed to stay on the job. He also needed to protect Lea.

"I haven't seen your witness yet. Clay says you have her."

Kino nodded, meeting the captain's hard gaze.

"Border patrol wants her in," Rubio advised. "It's not safe out here for her or for you. Plus, they are bringing in a computer specialist to render an image of that guy she saw."

"Yes, sir."

The captain rested a hand on Kino's shoulder. His grip was strong and his eyes intent. "Cosen, I read your file and I'm sorry about your dad. But you're here to track. That's it. You keep this up and it's going to kill you, one way or the other."

Kino stepped away from the man's hand. He'd heard this speech before, most recently from Clyne and Gabe. He didn't believe it. This hunt was what had kept him alive, not the other way around.

"Now, about our business. We've got activity and I need trackers on site. You and your brother. Gomez found a spotter's station and drop truck, so they can't use that vehicle. I need to know where they're going instead."

"Yes, sir."

"Report back to headquarters, find your brother and get to that drop."

Rubio left him then. Kino headed to his vehicle, paused, watched Rubio drive off and then headed back into the crime scene. He wondered if Dale had committed suicide, as it appeared. He found the coroner, who said it could have just been an overdose. The investigating detectives said the drugs had been heroin, not meth.

Dale had been on suspension and was facing dismissal for not following a direct order. The kind of order the captain had just given him. All Kino knew was that Dale was no longer here to answer questions about his conversation with Lea or the orders given by Captain

Barrow. That lead was gone forever. And Kino was treading on shifting sands. He didn't know whom to trust. He only knew that he had to follow orders or face suspension, Lea was in danger, his brother had his back and the Viper was still out there—hunting.

Chapter Thirteen

Lea heard the car pull into the driveway and crept to the front window to have a look. Her heart was jackhammering as she parted the curtain and peeked out to see two vehicles and Kino and Clay heading up the steps.

Her shoulders sagged and she fell back against the solid wall beside the window. She closed her eyes and tried to rein in her galloping heart. She pretended she heard the drums from home: slow, steady and filled with the strength she drew on to keep dancing that long, long night of her Sunrise Ceremony. Yes, her heart was slowing and her energy was rising.

One of them knocked and she pushed off the wall and went to greet them, opening the door.

She couldn't keep from smiling at their return.

Kino seemed distracted and tense. "Have you eaten?" he asked. It was past dinner but she hadn't wanted to impose.

"No."

"I got you some tacos. You like beef?" He handed over a bag. "I got cheese, too, and black bean."

Kino sat with her at the kitchen table while Clay stood quiet vigil by the kitchen window. Kino told her that they had spent much of the afternoon at the drop she had found and then at another stash car.

"What's a stash car?"

"It's a truck, usually, hidden in the desert. Modified to carry the most amounts of drugs possible. In this one, they removed the rear seat to gain more space. It was under a camo tarp near a rocky outcropping. That's normal. They put a spotter up there. When the coast is clear they signal the mules and they come in."

"Mules? They use mules in the desert? Wait—you mean the migrants."

"Yeah. Mules are what they call the smugglers."

"Like they call the ones who lead them over the border 'coyotes'?"

Kino nodded as Lea ate her dinner and he continued with his story. "The captain wants us spotting that site tonight. He's hoping we weren't seen and the drop might still happen. But I'm moving you first."

She stopped eating. "Where?"

"Farther onto the rez. I have a friend who is letting me use his place."

"You trust him?" she asked.

"With my life. His name is Luke Forrest. He's my uncle. He's FBI. I'll tell you about him sometime."

"So this place—it's not border patrol or ICE?"

"Nope. And it's not close to town and will be easier to secure."

"Will you be there?"

Kino cast Clay a glance. Whatever the meaning of the exchange, it was silent and unreadable to her.

"Yeah, I'm staying with you."

"Didn't you say you had an assignment tonight?"

"My assignment is keeping you safe. Tomorrow you

and I are going to that third drop. The one on your GPS. See what we find there."

She didn't like it. Without Kino, who would look after Clay?

"What about your brother?" she asked.

"He's riding with the guy who lives here. Good guy. Experienced. Indian. Neither one will be alone." Kino's phone vibrated and he stood to retrieve it from his pocket. Then he glanced at the display and answered the call. "Uncle, thank you for getting back to me." Kino did a lot of listening, even had one finger in his ear as he paced the room giving an occasional reply. After several minutes he wrote something down and then thanked the caller before disconnecting.

"He got a place?" asked Clay.

"Yes. He gave me the address." Kino lifted the sheet of paper. "Also got some information about Scott. He says the chief of the tribal police has been here a few months, has a clean record, and he is engaged to a Tohono O'odham woman."

"Well, that all sounds good."

"Yeah." Kino rubbed his neck. "All good except for where they met. At the annual Rattlesnake Festival in Oklahoma."

Clay's eyes narrowed. "Well, lots of people go there. You and I have even been there."

"Still…" said Kino.

Lea understood his concern.

"But I saw him before we went to Moody's place," said Lea. "It's not him."

"He could be working with him," said Kino.

"Uncle Luke have any more information?" asked Clay.

"Yes. He checked Anthony DeClay. The guy was

an aid worker in Central America. He has written and received several grants to fund various organizations. He's not married but was once engaged. He went to the University of Texas and had an affair with a fellow student who subsequently dropped out and had a child. DeClay is listed on the birth certificate but has never paid a dime in support. The mother works in Albuquerque for city government. She's of Mexican descent. Her family is upper middle class."

"What about Moody?"

"Dirtbag. Mostly what we know—that he repairs trucks for Oasis."

Both Kino and Clay looked at Lea.

"I've never heard of him. But Margie would be the one to arrange for repairs. I just drive the trucks and fill the tanks."

Lea had finished her meal, or rather, her appetite had left her. So they threw out the remains and the three headed to the door. Lea climbed into the passenger side of the SUV and Kino and Clay paused outside the driver's side.

"You know he's going to suspend you," said Clay.

Kino shrugged. "I don't have a choice. You'll be all right?"

"Don't worry about me. Worry about her. Seems like she's found a nest of rattlers all on her own."

"Yeah. I guess so," said Kino.

"Hey, no calf roping tonight."

Kino smiled and gave his big brother a quick bear hug, and Lea heard him say, "Thanks."

Then Kino was in the SUV and they all headed out into the night. At the first fork, Clay turned his truck in the opposite direction and Lea was alone with Kino.

"Did he say you'd be suspended?"

"Don't worry about it."

"But why?"

"For disobeying a direct order. I'm supposed to be on that hunt tonight."

"But you're staying with me instead," she said, working it out.

He gave her a smile mixed with a deep sadness, and she felt a welling of gratitude. It was just gratitude, wasn't it? Her hand on her knee twitched as she tried to resist the nearly irresistible need to reach across and touch him.

Somehow she managed to keep her hand where it was.

Lea thought of Clay's odd words at his departure and a suspicion rose. She arched a brow at him. "'Calf roping'?"

Kino raked a hand through his hair. "Just an expression."

"I'm pretty sure it's not an expression. Sounds more like code."

Kino sighed, clearly debating something. Well, she wasn't giving up so easily. She placed a hand on her hip and waited him out.

"We call it calf roping. It means sleeping with a woman. And before you go there, we were both in the rodeo for a while and it just seemed funny at the time."

"Hmm. Do you always talk in code?"

"It's common. Police radios aren't secure. Border patrol's, either."

"What other code words do you use?"

"Well, if I tell you they won't be codes."

She cast him an irked look.

"Okay, okay. Here's one. If we mention our mother's name it means we're in serious trouble. All my brothers use it."

"What's her name?"

"Tessa."

"Have you ever had to use it?"

He'd never been in that much trouble. But this hunt felt different. He was certain he would find his father's killer. But after that…he was not certain.

All he did know for sure was that he would never stop until he found the Viper and made him answer for his crimes.

Chapter Fourteen

As Kino drove toward the safe house, Lea waited for the answer to her question.

Kino's face went hard. "Clay used it once."

The conversation had turned from playful to deadly serious. Lea saw that in his posture and expression. She let go of her irritation and touched his arm. "Do you want to tell me about it?"

"Sometime, maybe."

"Okay, then. What will we do now?"

"I got you some clothes. You can shower up. Get out of that body armor for a while."

She didn't ask him if the vest was necessary. He wouldn't have asked her to wear it if it were not.

"What about you? If I'm wearing yours, then you're not protected."

Kino lifted his shirt, showing her that he, too, was wearing body armor. She didn't know if that revelation made her feel better or worse.

"Tomorrow we go see Chief Scott. I'd like to know he can be relied on in a pinch. In the meantime, if you recognize anyone, Uncle Luke wants me to call him in."

"What did your uncle say about me?"

Kino gave her a rare look of surprise.

"You had him check me out, too, right? I would if I were in your shoes."

"He said you are a hell of a dancer. Won a lot of contests against more experienced women at powwows. He said you have a lot to prove." He glanced at her for a long moment and she felt her belly cramp.

"Lea, why didn't you tell me you have no clan?"

She sucked in a long breath and let it go. The tightness in her stomach remained. To have no clan was to have a mother who was not Apache. He knew.

"My mother is Mexican."

"An illegal, according to my uncle."

"Not anymore. She's married to a full-blood Apache."

"Your father?"

Lea nodded.

"Is that why they're so important to you? The water stations?"

Lea sat back against the seat, listening to the hum of the tires on the asphalt and thinking of all her mother had told her.

"I'm like them. If not for my father, I might be crossing the desert right now."

"How did your mother get in?"

"She worked with a coyote. Only they call themselves *pollero*—chicken farmers. The people they guide are *pollos*—chickens. The man was experienced and had a good reputation for not…not bothering the women. There was supposed to be a truck. The truck was going to meet them on some highway and take them to Dallas. But my aunt fell on a rock and banged up her knee. It swelled and she couldn't keep up, so the *pollero* left them."

"Texas border?"

"Yes," said Lea. "Texas." She spit the word as if the taste were unpalatable. "My mother was pregnant with my older sister. That's why they had to leave. Her father threw her out. She was sixteen. That's why they made the journey, took the risk. They had no supplies. Just the clothes they wore. My mother tried to find water but she thinks she just walked in circles for two days in the July heat. They had no food, no water. Nothing." Lea felt the familiar twist of her heart at this point, thinking of what had happened next. Imagining the choice her mother had faced. "My mother knew she could stay with her sister and die or try to get help."

Lea lowered her head. "She left her."

Lea felt the tears gliding down her cheeks, falling to her lap. The Apache in her would not cry, but the Mexican side wept for the aunt she would never know.

"My aunt said…said she'd catch up. But they both knew it was a lie. My mother followed the trail of the others. She walked through the night and she found a road. Do you know who finally picked her up?"

"An aid worker?"

"No, an Apache. My father. He was a bull rider touring on the rodeo circuit. He gave her water. And he saved her life."

Kino glanced at her.

"Did they go back for her sister?"

Lea nodded. "My father is also a good tracker." She bowed her head. "Or he was. He followed the trail. My aunt was still there. But she was gone."

Lea wanted to tell him the rest of it, but something made her hold her tongue. Her intuition told her that Kino would not approve of what her mother had done to pay for her freedom.

Lea could see little of his expression in the light from the dash. What did he think? Was he wondering how a man could marry a woman with no clan? A woman outside the tribe whose children would also be without clan. For some it was impossible to think of marrying anyone other than an Apache. Her father said that a person could not always choose the calling of their heart.

"It must have been hard for you. On the rez, I mean."

It had been. The differences were subtle, but they were there. Her nose wasn't quite right, her skin color was different and then there was her size.

"I was the smallest in my class."

Kino nodded. "Doesn't explain the pacifism. So I asked him about that specifically. Luke says you started that after…" His words fell off.

"My dad is in a wheelchair. He doesn't work for HUD anymore."

"Uncle Luke says it was a drive-by."

Lea nodded, thinking of that day. Seeing her father in the hospital when she was thirteen, his big body propped up on pillows in the narrow bed. His legs still as stone.

"Bullet shattered his spine. L-5," said Kino.

Lea squeezed her eyes shut. "Did the report say that he was just trying to fix an outdoor water line? He was working, making things better for our tribe, and they shot him."

"Why?"

"Why?" she repeated and gave a slow shake of her head. "How can you ever answer that? People were angry over some evictions. After ignoring every warning and plea HUD had sent them for over a year. I know there was some nasty hate mail at HUD. My mother talked about it. She had to go to public meetings that turned into shouting matches."

"I heard about that. The trouble over evictions. Protests. We had them, too."

"My dad was wearing a HUD shirt that day. Maybe that was the reason they shot him in the back."

Kino's fingers flexed upon the wheel as he reasserted his grip. "Did they ever catch the shooter?"

"No."

Kino slowed as they drove along the road dotted with residences tucked back beyond the vegetation. Had he realized that they both had fathers shot in gun violence?

Kino sat forward, peering into the shafts of light from the headlights. His mouth dipped at the corner. "I don't understand. How could that make you a pacifist?"

She stared at him, his face glowing blue in the light of the dashboard. "It was that or follow the path you walk."

His jaw ticked and his brow swept down over his dark eyes. But he said nothing. Lea understood his choice. She had considered it, too, driven by the need for vengeance, battered by the hatred that pounded at her soul. She had prayed and prayed over what to do.

Kino cast her a perplexed look. "Don't you want to know who did this? Don't you want him brought to justice?"

"Of course I do. I think he should be arrested and stand trial. But if you are asking me if I, personally, want to extract justice? The answer is no. I do not. In fact, I have forgiven him."

"But he's still free."

"And he has to live with what he did."

Kino shifted in his seat. His voice was flintlike. "The

man who killed my father is remorseless. He's not losing any sleep. I know he isn't."

"Even worse for him, then," Lea said and meant it.

His brow wrinkled as he cast her a baffled look.

Kino slowed at a cutoff and glanced at the mailbox illuminated in the high beams. The post was that distinctive shade of pale blue favored for entrances because many deemed the color protective against evil spirits. He'd heard it called Virgin Mary blue since it resembled the color often depicted in her robes.

"This is it." He turned the wheel and in a few minutes they'd jostled up the dirt road and to a small ranchero backed up to a rocky outcropping.

"One way in and out," said Lea.

"Easier to secure."

"This is FBI property?"

"A safe house. They have them everywhere. It's fully stocked."

"Nice." She released her seat belt and left the vehicle gratefully, stretching her tired muscles and then following Kino to the porch. There was a wreath of dried peppers beside the door. Kino removed it to reveal a sunken metal box in the wall. There was a keypad and Kino punched in a code that caused a beep and a click. The small metal door swung open.

"Spy stuff," said Lea, impressed as he retrieved a key.

"It's just a lockbox."

She raised her eyebrows. She'd never seen anything like the front door. It appeared to be wood at first glance, but was actually metal. She brushed her fingers over the surface, which still held the warmth of the day even though the temperature was now dropping with the emergence of stars. Her mother had told her of this, the blazing hot days and freezing nights. Lea glanced up at Kino.

"Is this place bulletproof?" she asked.

He nodded, opened the door with the retrieved key and flicked on the lights. Then he stepped aside to let her enter first. Kino closed and locked the door.

She didn't know what she'd expected, but it was not the pleasant, cozy home. The living room had a three-sided sofa unit facing a huge flat-screen television mounted on the wall. The square wooden coffee table filled the space between the horseshoe-shaped couches. Beyond, a solid-pine dining room table sat against the opposite wall. The center of the table held a bowl of fresh fruit that looked so real she had to touch it and discovered a fresh mango right on top.

"How did he do that? You just called him today."

She fingered the colorful serape on the wall and noted the tasteful paintings of adobes and mesas. Kino flipped on the kitchen light. The room was large and open, with a love seat on the back wall by the rear door and a counter with three stools. On the counter sat a glass dome protecting various cheeses, grapes and nuts. Two boxes of crackers sat beside the offering.

Lea's stomach gave a rumble and Kino removed the lid. Then he retrieved two bottles of cold water from the well-stocked stainless-steel refrigerator.

"This place is like a dream," said Lea, accepting the water.

She grabbed two hunks of cheese and followed Kino toward the doorway opposite the refrigerator. It led to a small conference area with laptop computers, a digital projector and fax machines, printers and a large copy machine. It looked as she'd imagined a corporate boardroom might look.

Past that was a hallway with two bedrooms.

Kino walked her into the first. There, on the bed, was her suitcase.

She gasped and flipped open the case to discover nearly all that she had carried with her from Salt River.

"He got everything except my bathroom bag," she said.

"I'd check the bathroom."

She did and there was her bag along with fresh towels and a large, inviting tub.

"Shower or food?" he asked from the door of the bath.

"Shower," she said. She really wanted a bath, a long, hot soak, but promised herself that she would indulge before bed. She pressed her fingers into one of the fluffy white towels stacked on the counter and glanced back at Kino. Their eyes met and held. Her breath caught. His eyes slipped down her body. Was he picturing her in the shower or wrapped in one of those oversize towels?

For a moment she stopped breathing as her attention caught on the strong angle of his jaw and the stubble growing there. She stepped toward him, reaching.

His brow furrowed and he flinched as her hand touched his jaw. But then he pressed her hand against his cheek. His eyelids closed and he turned his head.

At first she thought he meant to drop a kiss on her palm, but instead he dragged his teeth across the fleshy mound at the base of her thumb.

His eyes snapped open, blazing with desire.

Her body quaked and she felt herself grow liquid, quickening with need. He released her with all but his eyes as he stepped back into the hall. It was all she could do not to follow him as he turned and retreated to the door across from hers.

Lea sagged against the counter, realizing that she wanted neither shower nor food. What she really wanted was Kino in her bed wearing nothing but a bath towel and a welcoming smile.

But did she have the courage to pursue what she wanted? What if she walked across the hall and offered herself to him and he pushed her away?

That possibility sent her to the shower, where she scrubbed away all the dirt and dust. But not the desire. That just burned hotter by the second.

She tried to focus on the reasons that sleeping with Kino was a bad idea.

He was working with border patrol, the very people that once hunted her mother.

Lea turned off the taps.

He didn't approve of Oasis or their mission and regarded her efforts as tantamount to assisting the enemy.

She reached for a towel and tamped away the excess moisture from her damp skin, noticing the nubby texture of the fabric.

He upheld the law, while she was apt to break it, feeling she had an obligation to break those laws that were morally corrupt.

She toweled off her hair and dragged a comb through the tangles as she looked in the mirror at her reflection.

"He really believes that those people out there don't matter, that their lives don't matter. And he thinks killing his father's killer will bring him peace. How could you want to share a bed with a man like that?"

It almost worked. She told herself she needed to open

the door to let the steam out that fogged the mirror. But she followed the swirling moisture out, walking straight across the hallway to Kino's room.

They were safe here. For the first time since the shooting she was safe and, regardless of the costs, she needed to feel alive.

The shooting had taught her something her mother already knew. Life was uncertain and time was short.

Kino's shower was running until she rounded his bed. Then it switched off. She could see into the bathroom, because he'd left the door open. His clothing was on the floor. On the sink sat a razor and can of shaving cream, the nozzle still holding a blob of foam. On the opposite side of the sink on the countertop lay his holster and pistol. Here was the evidence of his profession. Her vision danced over the objects, fixing on the gun he used to kill. She looked away. Time enough for that later.

Next came the scraping of the metal rings on the metal bar. She turned to see Kino step from the shower, naked, heavily muscled and dripping wet. He gripped a white towel in one strong hand. He spotted her. His fist tightened on the towel and his eyes widened.

"Lea?"

Chapter Fifteen

Lea stood naked in front of Kino like every fantasy he'd ever had of her. No, better. In his mind she hadn't been wet. Kino adjusted the towel to cover his rising reaction to her.

"You shouldn't be here," he said. His voice had turned to gravel. He glanced past her, calculating the number of steps to the bed.

When he glanced back it was to find her gaze slipping down his body.

"I couldn't stay away," she said.

It's a mistake, he thought. "I'm glad," he said.

"Kiss me."

Oh, he'd do a sight better than that.

He dropped the towel, stepped from the bathroom and swept her up in his arms, propelling them to the large bed.

She landed on the spotless coverlet with a bounce and he landed on top of her, kissing her mouth as his body covered hers, bringing him in contact with all the soft, wonderful places he had no right to feel. As she wrapped her arms around his neck, he thought that nothing in his life would ever be this right and this wrong all at once.

She threaded her hands into his hair, tugging and making the most adorable growl of need as he deepened the kiss. Only when she was breathless, and he on fire, did he pull back. She tried to stop his retreat, but he needed to make sure there was no mistake.

"You sure?" he asked.

She nodded.

He opened the bedside table, finding unopened lip balm, an iPod on a charger, an uncapped bottle of water, an eye mask and…condoms.

Still protecting me, he thought to himself, thinking of his uncle.

She plucked the bright packet from his fingers and tore it open with her teeth. He thought his heart would stop at the sight of those strong white teeth and soft sensual mouth.

He rolled to his side and dragged his knuckles down the curve of her breast and watched her nipples peak. He dipped to tongue the hard nubs and then sucked as his hand caressed her other breast.

Lea trembled as she arched, offering herself to him. Her fingers raked his back and then threaded into his loose, wet hair. She dragged him closer to the soft pillow of her aroused flesh. His hand swept down her back, caressing the soft curve of her hip, her muscular thighs and the warm, wet folds between her legs. Lea moaned and rocked, the condom momentarily forgotten as she stroked his chest, becoming familiar with the broad planes and enticing hollows.

Lea spread her legs and tugged insistently, making her desires known. He handed her the rolled condom and sighed in pleasure as she slipped the sheath into place, her fingers lingering on his sex. He knew that he'd always remember the feel of her fingers on his flesh, nimble and needy. When she finished she glanced up at him, her desire shining in her dark eyes. He smiled and stroked the long hair from her face.

He might not be able to give her much, but he could give her this. He was jaded and she was sweet. Now he saw that he needed that sweetness and optimism more than he needed the air in his lungs. He lowered himself onto her, his face pressed into her wet, fragrant hair as he kissed the slender column of her throat.

He made love to her, urged on by her soft mewing cries of pleasure and the eager, needy way she matched him stroke for stroke.

The next time was slower, more thorough and intimate, as she stared up at him until her eyes widened and her cry of pleasure broke from her open mouth. Her fulfillment triggered his own, leaving them both panting as they lay entangled in the soft bedding and each other. They rested there, flesh to flesh, safe and sated and full of lethargy. Her breathing changed first as Lea drifted off to slumber in his arms, one hand thrown casually across his chest.

He held her tight and wondered what it might be like to keep her, feeling the loss already as he knew he never would. Lea was like a light in a cavern, showing him a way out of the darkness and hatred he wore around him like body armor. If he let it go, what would be left?

Kino was not so exhausted that he didn't have time to realize what he'd just done. *Never get personal with a witness.* It was the second rule of law enforcement, behind *Finish your shift alive.*

He clasped Lea to his side and she curled against him like a cat. Then Kino broke the third rule of the night, a personal one. *Never spend the entire night with a woman.*

Kino dragged the coverlet over them both. Then he closed his eyes and held tight to this little clanless woman who really thought she could save the world.

She might just do it, too, he thought.

LEA WOKE TO the feel of Kino holding her against the chiseled perfection of his body. Clearly he did not spend most of his time riding in a police car, judging from all the smooth, hard muscle she found herself pressed beside. Just the weight of his arm across her back felt heavy and warm. She opened her eyes but didn't move. Somehow she sensed the man had an extraordinary ability to detect small changes in his surroundings.

The only light came from the bathroom and streamed out, making a rectangle on the carpeted floor. She glanced toward the curtains, trying to judge the hour, but there was no light, no reference to tell if it was still evening or the middle of the night. There was a clock on the bedside table, but she would have to rise up on an elbow to see it over his chest.

Lea waited a moment, savoring his steady, even breathing and the quiet of the room. She felt safe with him. It was a feeling she didn't take for granted. Not anymore. But how many were out there tonight, in the desert, trying to reach the blue flags that meant their survival?

Kino was a police officer. He upheld the law. But did he ever find a law that was wrong or that he didn't agree with? What did he do then? Somehow she already knew—he enforced it. That was his job, but more than that, it was who he was. While she felt a moral imperative to break this restriction against setting up water stations on federal land. She'd set up more than one, and if they caught her, she'd pay whatever consequences.

She sighed. She and Kino were perfect in bed, but outside of this room, they were still adversaries. Nothing had changed.

His hold upon her strengthened and he opened his eyes.

"What's wrong?" he asked.

"What time is it?" she asked.

He turned his head. "Midnight."

She slipped from his embrace. His grip tightened and she met his gaze.

"Time to let me go," she whispered.

His mouth tightened as if he disagreed. But then he released her.

Lea padded silently from the room on bare feet, returning to her own bed. They were now separated by a few yards and a gulf of ideological differences. How could she sleep with a man who didn't believe in the sanctity of human life? Who thought that killing was ever a justifiable choice?

She closed her eyes and remembered the feel of his mouth on her breasts. Lea let out a little moan of need, wanting to return to him again. But why? They had no future together.

Lea walked to the window to look out at the night, but when she parted the curtain she found a metal gate covering the opening. Suddenly her little peaceful retreat turned into what it was: an FBI safe house only used when the occupants were in terrible danger.

She pressed a hand to the cold metal, knowing the Viper was out there, with the migrants, hunting her. Lea crawled into the clean bed, the scent of Kino and their lovemaking still clinging to her skin. Despite her fatigue, it took her some time to finally doze off because, although her body was replete, her mind spun like the devil winds in the desert.

Her dreams were as troubled as her thoughts. She woke groggy and more exhausted than when she'd tumbled into slumber. What had awoken her? She glanced around the dark, unfamiliar room, which was illuminated only by the bluish glow of the clock radio. She realized it was 7:00 a.m. Morning, though she could not tell in this cage of a room.

Groping, she found the nightstand and lamp. A moment later she sat up and inhaled. The aroma of bacon and coffee helped her rally. She showered and dressed quickly, the lure of food more powerful than her embarrassment about last night. Why had she walked right into his room like that? Apache women were supposed to be modest, strong and stoic. She'd learned that and more from her Sunrise Ceremony. She'd also learned that although the tribe recognized her as Apache, many in the community did not. Certainly her classmates never had. Was Kino like them?

Why did it matter what he thought? When this was over, he'd go back to his tribe and she'd go back to trying to prove herself worthy of membership in hers and trying to keep the women and children crossing this desert from dying of thirst.

Lea padded down the hallway, dressed in jeans and her Oasis T-shirt. Kino's smile vanished when he saw what she was wearing.

He offered her coffee and an omelet so overstuffed she nearly dropped the plate when it landed upon it. But she ate every bite. Nothing had ever tasted so good.

"Told you I could cook."

"And the coffee is great, too," she said.

His smile wavered and died. "Lea, why did you do that—last night?"

She lowered her gaze and sipped her coffee. "I messed up," she admitted. "Tired and lonely and…it never should have happened." She met his stern expression. "Have I ruined your investigation?"

"Normally, yes. But I'm not planning to bring this particular suspect to trial."

Her stomach dropped at the thought. "What does that mean?"

"It means I'm going to find him and kill him."

"But you're an officer of the law."

"I'm an Apache and he killed my father."

"So you just get to press Pause and do what you like?"

"It won't be murder, if that's what you mean. I'll give him fair warning. But he won't take it. I know him well enough to know that."

"What if he kills you instead?" she asked, still hardly believing she was having this conversation.

"Well, then I guess I'll have a rattle shoved in my guts. Which reminds me—you need your body armor and the tan shirt today."

Lea knew they couldn't stay here forever, but she had somehow hoped that they could.

"Where are we going?"

"First, I want to see that third water station. The one on your GPS."

"My phone is dead."

He pointed to the charging station in the dining room.

Lea retrieved her phone, found the appropriate charger and then returned to her coffee.

"Where do we go after the water station?" she asked.

"My uncle forwarded information on Moody, DeClay and Scott. They're on the dining room table."

Lea hesitated and rose, abandoning her coffee to go look. She recognized the photos of Moody and another of Anthony DeClay and one of the tribal chief, Charlie Scott.

"Still not him," she said, lowering the last of the three images to the table.

Kino slid her a third sheet. The document at first looked like a résumé for Anthony DeClay. Then she realized it was a list of criminal offenses. Was this what they called a rap sheet?

"He's got drug arrests," said Kino.

"What, did he smoke a joint in college?"

"Dealing on campus. He was eighteen and his father got him a very good attorney. He got off with community service. Care to guess what service he selected?"

She narrowed her eyes at him. Kino was entirely too suspicious.

"Isn't it possible that he saw the error of his ways and turned his life around?"

"Isn't it equally possible that he found the perfect vehicle for transporting drugs and moved right up the chain of command? He's not dealing anymore. He's smuggling."

"You don't know that." But now she wasn't sure. She didn't know her boss personally and she didn't know his business. She did know that he was responsible for all regional programs in New Mexico, Arizona and Texas.

"I don't, but I do know these killings have put him on the FBI's interest list."

"What do we do now?" she asked.

"Go get changed so we can check that third station."

Lea retreated down the hallway. If anything, she now felt worse than before she'd decided to tiptoe across the hall to Kino's bedroom. How had she thought that sleeping with a Shadow Wolf would be anything but trouble?

Thirty-five minutes later, they rode to the third station. Lea again wore Kino's extra vest and now-familiar shirt. Kino pulled into the site and they saw that this one had not yet been removed, either. He asked her to remain in the vehicle until he cut for sign. She watched him walk this way and that, squatting to check the ground and then standing to retrace his steps.

Finally he came back for her.

"Okay, I still need to run some tracks, but I have all I can get from this spot. I'd like you to come with me while I check the trail."

For a moment she felt useful, but then he added, "It's not safe to leave you here alone."

So she trailed after him wondering what he saw.

When they reached a patch of thornbush, he paused to examine a branch. Lea glanced around and caught a flash of pink fabric beneath an ironwood. It was common for immigrants to discard clothing, empty bottles—anything, really, that would lighten their loads. As she moved closer she noted the fabric was not rubbish but the garment covering the body of a girl, reclining in death, her head upon the root of the tree. The corpse had already begun to swell in the heat.

Lea gave a cry and staggered back.

KINO CAUGHT LEA as she scuttled away from the body and set her outside the circle of brush.

"Wait here," he said.

But she didn't. Couldn't. She recovered and followed him right through the thornbushes. The girl could not have been more than twelve or thirteen, judging from her size.

"They left her," said Kino.

"What? Who did?"

"Her party. There were six of them. Two women, three men, all carrying heavy packs. See how the toe prints are deeper? They were leaning forward under the weight. But one had his hands free, probably for his weapons. Paramilitary, their guard. Right here." He pointed to a boot track. "Six sets in. But only five sets of tracks leave in that direction." He pointed at what was invisible to her.

It was like staring down at her aunt. Was this what her mother had found when she'd finally made it back?

"Why?" she whispered.

Kino looked at the body but didn't touch it. She wondered if that was for hygienic reasons or because of the Apache people's general prohibition against touching the dead.

Before the Americans came, her people did not reside near dead bodies. In the old days, before the reservation, when a person died, the family would bury the body and then burn the deceased's house with everything inside. The family then moved away, to keep the ghost from following. Of course, back then the houses were made by the women over several days and the encampments were never permanent. Now they lived mostly in BIA housing, and burning them down after a death was generally discouraged. But old traditions died slowly, and some houses were still burned, especially after the evictions.

"Injury, likely. Or maybe she just couldn't go on."

Lea knew what that meant. No water.

Kino touched her shoulder, and she tore her gaze from the dead girl and stared at him.

He nodded his head, as if just deciding something.

"I get it now, Lea."

"What?"

"What you do. I understand why you would break the law to set up water stations."

She felt the flicker of a smile as their gazes held. "Thank you."

Chapter Sixteen

Lea knelt beside the girl and prayed. It was a prayer her mother had taught her. A prayer to the Virgin Mary to guide this girl home.

When she had finished, Kino helped her to her feet and then moved away from the child who had died here alone in the desert.

Kino pointed to the prints on the ground.

"They didn't fill up at the water station. They stopped there but there were only two sets of prints. One from this group and, before that, someone who came in a truck. Prints are a match for the Viper. He was here recently."

"How do you know?" she asked, peering at the tracks.

Kino squatted and pointed. "Right here. There is a chunk missing from the back of his left heel. Same tracks as the ones he left by those bodies."

The bodies that had lain in a row after he had shot them execution style. His human mules who'd had no further value after they had delivered their cargo.

She rose. Suddenly she wanted to find this man as much as Kino. And in that moment she understood Kino's quest for justice and his need to kill this man. And that terrified her.

She'd forgiven her father's shooter. And she'd tried to be merciful and to help those in need. But that wasn't enough. Not when there were predators like this in the desert. What chance did a rabbit have against a rattlesnake?

"What's wrong, Lea?"

"I'm tired of this! Tired of Americans just throwing these people away as if they were nothing. Tired of this Viper killing the people who bring him his cargo. Tired of people having to choose between carrying these filthy drugs and a future with no hope. I don't know what to do anymore."

Kino offered his hand, but she launched into his arms instead. He held her for several moments while she reined in her trembling, impotent fury and slowed her breathing. It was the behavior of an Apache woman, holding in her pain so that none could tell what sorrow she held in her heart. Their history was full of proof that it had been necessary to build that kind of toughness and it seemed it still was.

He shook his head. "I want this guy stopped. But I wonder if my brother Clyne was right."

"What did he say?"

"Same as you. That our father is dead and gone, but my sister is out there and that is where my duty lies. Not here among the dead."

She couldn't answer such a question, so she didn't try.

"Maybe you're right to help anyone who needs it. I don't know. I'm all mixed up inside. And that could get us killed."

She understood that he was not being dramatic. He needed to make split-second decisions. Shoot. Don't shoot. He couldn't hesitate.

Lea looked up at him, this protector, whom she trusted with her life but not her secrets. Now she wanted him to know everything but still feared his reaction. They had just formed a sort of truce and what she was about to tell him would jeopardize that. Still, she needed him to know.

"I have to tell you something else," she whispered.

His expression became cautious as he pulled back far enough that he could gently clasp each elbow, giving her the silent support of his body and his attention.

"Do you remember me telling you about my mother and her sister?"

Kino nodded. She dropped her chin, avoiding his eyes, the shame of their choices somehow reflecting on her. His hands tightened, giving her the silent encouragement she needed to tell him this next part, the part that had brought her to this time and place.

"I know I'm helping the smugglers. I'm willing to help them along with the others. They're all the same to me."

Kino's hands dropped away. Now he looked at her as if she had become the enemy.

"They're *not* the same."

"Kino, listen. Those people who bring the drugs, they don't have the money to pay the coyotes' fee. Without it, their only choice is to carry. They have to earn their passage. The cartel tells them, 'Here, you bring this backpack over the border and we'll get you across, no charge.' They either carry the drugs or stay behind."

"So they *do* have a choice."

She gave him a plaintive look, praying he would understand. "Everyone has a right to survive. Even if it means breaking a law. You should understand that.

The border, it's drawn by the Americans. Before that it was drawn by the Mexicans. Before that it was the Spanish. It's not real. It doesn't exist. This? All this?" She pointed to the ground. "This is Tohono O'odham land. This—the border?—northern Mexico. All of it."

"You're helping the cartels."

"I'm helping people. People like my mother and her sister."

"They were mules?"

"Yes." Lea registered the look he gave her, absorbing it like a blow.

"Lea, do you know if DeClay is moving product?"

"I don't know."

"Are you mixed up in all this?"

"No."

"You have to tell me if you are."

"I'm not. But we all know that the mules stop for water with the illegal immigrants. I don't distinguish. I can't. To deny one is to deny the other."

The silence stretched as they regarded each other—strangers again. She could see from his frigid expression that anything they had shared had died with her confession.

"Kino, I'm sorry I didn't tell you about my aunt and mother. What they did, I mean. But you don't understand the choices they faced."

"I understand that your mother was a smuggler and an illegal. I understand about your giving those like her assistance."

"I'm giving them water."

"You're no better than the coyotes. You're not Apache." That cut clean through her like the long blade of a hunting knife. But she found that even when accused of the worst, she still endured. She lifted her chin and met the condemnation in his eyes.

"At least I'm not a vigilante."

"I'm taking you back to Oasis. You can do what you want from there."

She stood motionless as the fear slowly rose until it hit her nervous system, setting off tiny shocks of panic. That killer knew who she was and Kino was preparing to cut her loose, throw her into the snake pit. Without him, what chance did she have? Who would help her?

"I'm checking the water station," said Kino.

He returned his attention to the water barrels and tried the spigot.

"No water," he said.

"That's why she died. That little girl. Because this station was empty."

"She died because someone convinced her she had a chance crossing the desert in June."

He lifted the barrel with one hand. It seemed too heavy to be empty. He dropped it back to the wooden platform and heard the familiar rattle just as the entire lid popped off and dozens of rattlesnakes poured from the opening.

Lea screamed.

"Get back," he ordered as rattlesnakes spilled out onto the ground as if from an overturned cup.

Lea jerked beside him, her arms flying wide as she arched. An instant later he heard the gunshot. Lea fell toward him and he caught her as she collapsed.

Shot, he realized. Lea had been shot.

Kino didn't hesitate. He lifted Lea, now deadweight, and ran through the snakes, feeling the strike of more than one on his leather moccasins. Their fangs didn't puncture the hide, and he thanked his ancestors for knowing a thing or two about snakes. He reached the SUV and tugged open the passenger's-side door. Once he had Lea inside, he searched the landscape for the shooter, judging his position from the direction of Lea's fall. But he saw nothing. Surely the shooter had had time to take a few shots at him, unless *he* wasn't the target. His witness was. It was the Viper. Kino felt it in his soul.

Was he watching them through a scope right now?

Kino stood on the running board, resisting the tug of need to go after him. Then he looked down at Lea and knew in that instant that she was more important to him than the shooter. More important than his quest to find his father's killer. Lea's life was worth more to him than anything in this world.

He didn't have to support her efforts to help the very people he hunted in order to care for her, did he?

Lea slumped in the seat. She didn't seem to be breathing.

Kino grasped her shoulder. "Lea!"

Their last conversation flashed into his mind. He'd told her he'd abandon her. He'd said she wasn't Apache. He'd spoken out of anger, but now he feared he'd never have the chance to make things right.

"Please, God, let her be alive."

She gasped as if surfacing from beneath deep water. Then she coughed, her breathing labored and unnatural. He needed to check for injuries and he needed to get her out of here.

Kino closed the door and ran to the opposite side of the vehicle. Then he swung up and into the driver's seat as the snakes wriggled past in all directions. He threw the SUV into gear and took off, driving all the way to the highway before pulling up short. Then he threw the SUV into Park and checked on Lea, praying for her life.

He tugged open the overlarge shirt and found the body armor in place. Kino muttered aloud his prayer of thanks as he pulled apart the fastenings and lifted her gently forward, tugging away the shirt and vest. There, in the center of her back, just below her scapula and over her heart, a purple bruise was forming. Lea had been shot and, although the force of the bullet had been absorbed, the impact was the equivalent to being kicked by a horse. A damned big horse.

"You're all right, Lea. I've got you." He laid her on her side, her head in his lap. Then he set them in motion. Her respiration was shallow and her color bad. But she was breathing.

How had the Viper known where they'd be? How had he found them?

Kino lifted the mike and then replaced it, unsure if he should call for help, take Lea to the hospital or to the safe house. He needed Clay. But for now he had to get Lea some help.

With his destination in mind, Kino accelerated. He stroked Lea's head as he drove. "Wake up, Lea," he begged.

If anything happened to her, it would be his fault.

En route he got a call on the radio. He would have ignored it, but it was his brother.

"Cosen here," replied Kino automatically as he glanced at the speedometer, which read 95 miles per hour.

"Updating you," Clay returned. "We just got a call from tribal. They found Bill Moody dead at his residence."

"Cause?"

"Homicide."

What was going on? Who had killed Moody? Was it the Viper taking out possible leads?

"Need to speak to you," said Clay. Clearly he meant not over the radio.

"Yeah."

"Where?"

"Hospital," said Kino.

"Roger that. ETA is twenty. Got Gomez with me."

Kino told Clay about the shooting and asked him to call it in.

"You got it. Be safe," said Clay. Just as always, his big brother perpetually tried to keep him safe and out of trouble. At nineteen, Clay had been arrested, convicted and then served time. His brother knew about trouble firsthand. Seemed it just wasn't in the Cosens' DNA to stay clear of trouble.

"Roger. Out." Kino put both hands on the wheel and the pedal to the floorboard.

Lea gave a soft moan.

"Hang in there, sweetheart."

His mind tumbled like dried sagebrush in a windstorm. What did Clay have that he couldn't say on radio? What if they were followed?

He had to keep Lea safe. Not because he needed a witness, but because he needed Lea.

That was it. He couldn't play roulette with Lea's life any longer. This had to stop and he had to stop it.

Chapter Seventeen

Kino pulled into the small regional hospital just after 11:00 a.m. and parked in the turnaround in front of the ER. Lea's eyes were fluttering and she blinked up at him, her brow wrinkling in confusion. "Kino?"

"Yeah." He stroked the soft curtain of hair from her face. "I got you. You're all right."

She smiled, struggled to sit upright and then flinched and closed her eyes, breathing through her mouth in short, uneven breaths. That scared him enough to get him running from his side of the SUV to hers. There he slipped his arms under her knees and around her back. Her color was gray and he didn't like the blue tinge of her lips. She gasped as he lifted her and her breath came in little pants.

He ran the rest of the way through the electric doors and past the nurses' station, heading for the treatment rooms he had visited when one of the Shadow Wolves had needed stitches. Someone yelled but he didn't stop until he reached an empty, curtained exam area.

Lea didn't open her eyes, but her forehead wrinkled and her panting was faster, as if she were the one running. He stretched her out on an examination table. Her eyes were pinched shut and her face registered pain. She curled into a ball on her uninjured side. Her skin had a gray cast that made him want to run for help, but instead he stayed by her. He stroked her head.

"Lea, we're at the hospital. You're safe."

A nurse dressed in blue scrubs was the first to arrive. She washed her hands as she barked questions at him, then checked Lea's eyes with a penlight and took her blood pressure. Others arrived and they tried to get him to go to the waiting room but succeeded in getting him only as far as the end of her bed.

He flashed his tribal police shield. "She's my witness. She doesn't leave my sight."

"I'm taking off her clothing, Officer Cosen. You want to see that?"

He shook his head, but instead of looking away, he helped the nurse until together they'd stripped her out of her jeans, outer shirt and vest. The nurse cut off the T-shirt and the spaghetti-strap tank top beneath. The nurse unfastened Lea's bra but left on her pink cotton panties.

Lea opened her eyes and tried to lift her arms but cried out.

"It hurts so much," she whispered.

"I know, sweetie," said the nurse. "We need to figure out what's wrong. Then I can give you something for the pain. Just a few minutes longer. Hold on." The nurse tied the gown in the back as Lea gripped Kino's hand so tight his fingers tingled. The nurse and an orderly transferred Lea to a gurney and the nurse eased Lea to a reclining position that seemed to make her breathing less labored. Up went the rails and an orderly arrived to take Lea for a CT scan.

Kino walked beside her—even though the technician tried to get him to wait outside.

"Someone just shot her. So she doesn't leave my sight while she's here."

"I'm sure the perpetrator isn't in the hospital."

"Are you? I'm not."

He got no further argument as the woman now seemed anxious to get Lea processed as quickly as possible.

He thought he heard Lea call for him as he stood with the technician behind the barrier staring at Lea and the computer screen where the images appeared.

Clay and Nesto Gomez found him as they wheeled Lea back to the ER.

"Her heart and lungs are okay," said Kino. "But she cracked two ribs. Not sure about her spleen yet."

"What happened?" asked Clay.

"Somebody shot her in the back. Rifle."

Clay looked down at Lea as her gurney wheeled past with the help of one orderly.

"Even with the vest that should have killed her."

"I put extra ceramic panels all around."

Clay looked Kino over. "They didn't shoot at you?"

He shook his head and fell into step behind the gurney.

"Strange."

When they reached the cubicle, one of the nurses tried to get them out of the hall and all three flashed badges. She gave up and opened the curtain that separated them from Lea, telling them not to get in her way.

Clay glanced at Kino. "Gomez was at Cardon Station." He turned to Gomez. "Tell him what you told me," he said.

Kino leaned against the examination table, switching his attention from Lea to Nesto as he spoke.

"I was there when Captain Barrow called Mulhay from the scene. That night when Mulhay was questioning Miss Altaha." Gomez motioned over his shoulder at Lea's prone figure. "Mulhay was typing, so he put the call on speaker. The thing is, I heard from the guys that the captain suspended Mulhay for letting Altaha leave the station when he'd given orders that they hold her until he got back from the homicide at the water station. But I *heard* Barrow tell Mulhay to release her."

Kino straightened and glanced at Clay.

"So is Captain Barrow lying to cover his ass or is he lying because he's got something to hide?"

"Or maybe he suspended Mulhay for some other reason," offered Gomez.

"But we'll never know because Mulhay is dead. Maybe that overdose wasn't an accident. We got anything back on his COD?"

"Nope," said Clay.

"Something stinks," said Kino.

"I also got word from our uncle." Clay glanced at Gomez. "He's FBI." Then he returned his attention to his brother. "He said he ran the information we gave him on Rosa Keene. She's a dental hygienist, which is odd since she owns three new-model pickups, two ATVs but drives a 2003 Ford Escort. She rents a two-bedroom in Tucson but owns a climate-controlled storage unit in town free and clear. It's worth 2.2 million dollars."

"What?" asked Kino.

"Yeah. That's what I thought, too. Doesn't make any sense."

"Any word from Gabe? Did he send someone to interview her?"

Clay stretched his neck. "Yeah. I talked to Gabe. He said he's a little busy talking to the BIA up there in South Dakota, but he has a request in with Tucson PD. He also said that the BIA lists a three-year-old girl, orphaned the same month as the accident."

Clay had switched topics from their current hunt for the Viper to his family's hunt for their missing sister. For the first time Kino did not resent the reminder of his older brother's quest. Instead of the familiar gnawing frustration at this problem, he felt a new understanding of what his real mission should be. But first he had to get Lea out of this alive.

"The same month? Not week or day?"

Clay watched him with a look of curiosity as Kino switched subjects, too. Had his brother expected him to keep his attention only on the Viper? Yes, of course he had, because that was all Kino had thought about or seen since they'd arrived. But not anymore. Now he saw Lea and Jovanna. And he wanted to save them both.

"That's when they filed the paperwork," said Clay. "Could be Jovanna. They listed the child as Sioux, tribe and parents unknown. Then they placed her in a foster home off the rez."

"She alive?"

"Looks that way. Gabe says he's got to get back to Black Mountain. There's been some trouble. He wants you back, too. Said to tell you leave of absence is over."

Kino worked for the tribal police, which meant he worked for their chief—his brother Gabe. They were short-staffed as it was and now he and their chief were both off the rez.

Kino blinked and stared at Lea. She was now connected to an IV drip, with an EKG monitoring her heart. They had her on her side and he could see that the nasty bruise was purple and black and had spread from her shoulder to the middle of her back.

"I'm staying," said Kino.

Clay nodded. "I figured. What if we don't find him?"

"He'll find her. She's seen his face. He can't let her go."

"You want me to stay?" asked Clay.

Kino debated and then made his decision. Clay had been up all night on patrol. "Get some rest. I'll call if I need you."

"You better."

Gomez shook Kino's hand and Kino thanked him for the information. Clay patted his shoulder. "Let me know how she's doing."

"I will. And, Clay?"

"Yeah?"

"Be careful."

Kino watched the two stride away and then turned his attention back to Lea.

The doctor arrived. She was heavyset with thick glasses, short, wavy brown hair and deep-set lines flanking her mouth. She checked the CT images on a laptop then ordered medication to be injected into Lea's IV. Kino watched the muscles of Lea's face relax as her body slackened.

"You her husband?" asked the doctor.

Kino hesitated, suddenly speechless, but he found his voice a moment later. "Bodyguard."

He showed her his shield.

"Remind me not to hire you should the opportunity

arise." She pointed at the laptop. The screen was filled with a colorful image that Kino could not interpret. The doctor returned her attention and her hands to Lea's abdomen, which looked flat. Kino had seen spleen ruptures in some of the more horrific auto accidents on the rez and he knew what a distended stomach meant. So the sight of Lea's smooth cinnamon skin was a relief.

"I'm ordering an ultrasound to check her spleen. Two ribs broken but not displaced. I gave her a painkiller, but no sedation. Her breathing is shallow enough. It's going to hurt to breathe, but she needs to or risk getting pneumonia."

"You admitting her?"

"We'll see. Depends on the blood work."

He edged closer, slipping in beside Lea as the doctors came and went. He took her hand.

The nurse who had first treated Lea reappeared through the curtain circling Lea's bed.

"How is she doing?" he asked.

"Blood pressure and heart rate are all good. I'd say that body armor saved her life."

"Is she awake?"

"The pain meds are making her a little out of it, I'd imagine. But she's conscious." The woman's gruff exterior was belied by the twinkle in her eyes and the slight twitch at the corners of her mouth. "I've got other patients to check on."

With that, she hurried down the corridor and into another curtained examination area. He could hear her speaking to a patient.

Kino sat on the plastic stool and wheeled up beside Lea.

"I'm still here. Lea? Can you hear me?"

She nodded and then flinched.

"I'm sorry for everything I said. I admire you for helping them on their journey. And I've got no right to judge what your mother and aunt had to do. Given the same circumstances, I might do the same thing. I'm sorry I didn't protect you better. We should have stayed at the house where you were safe. If anything happens to you I'll never forgive myself."

Her hand was limp in his and her fingers were cold. He pulled the thin cotton blanket up over her body. This time when he took her hand, she squeezed back. Some of the fear left him, replaced by hope. She'd be okay. But what about the next time?

Chapter Eighteen

Kino settled beside Lea's hospital bed as she dozed, attuned to the shallow drawing of her breath and the slight tension at her open mouth. The machines beeped and hummed; the shuffle of rubber soles came and went. He kept the curtain open, his gaze shifting from Lea to the corridor. As afternoon wore into evening, they moved Lea to an observation room in the ER. This room had a door, which he kept shut, and blinds that he kept open.

The doctor came back and reported that Lea's blood work was good, but that they wanted to keep her a few more hours for observation. She'd be going home with a prescription for pain pills. Kino settled in. He called Clay, who told him he'd decided to keep an eye on the entrance to the ER. Kino felt much better knowing that Clay was close. Still, he kept alert.

Lea woke in pain and was given more medicine in her IV, which made her groggy and helped her sleep. Each time she woke her eyes went wide and shifted across the room until she found him. Then she smiled and relaxed.

"I got you," he said.

"I know you do," she answered, her words slightly slurred.

It was nearly four in the afternoon by the time Lea got her release papers and a prescription for the pain medication. Kino paid attention as they wrapped Lea's ribs with an ACE bandage and then he helped her dress.

"This is a switch," he joked. "Trying to get you *into* your clothes."

She gave a sound that started as a laugh and ended as a groan as she clutched her ribs. She was sweating from just the effort of tugging on her jeans.

"Don't make me laugh," she chided.

He lifted the vest, considering. Their eyes met.

"I don't think I can stand the weight," she said.

Before leaving, Kino called Clay, who met them at the observation room.

"How does it look out there?" asked Kino.

"Sunny. Hot. Like always. Man, I miss the trees. The shade and the lakes."

Clearly, Clay had understood what his brother was asking and was just busting chops. Kino scowled.

"Looks clear," said Clay, finally consenting to answer the question.

An orderly wheeled Lea to the exit and Kino helped Lea to her feet, his hand on her elbow. Lea's face was grim and determined as she made slow, shuffling forward progress to the SUV Clay had pulled into the ER roundabout.

They had Lea nearly to the door when Kino's and Clay's radios both sounded at once. It was Dispatch. Border patrol had called from the site of the shooting. They had found tracks and had spotted the shooter. They were in pursuit of the suspect, who had escaped in a large ATV. They needed the Shadow Wolves' help.

Captain Rubio was en route. Dispatch gave the location that Kino knew all too well and radioed out.

Kino got Lea into the passenger seat.

"A sighting," said Clay. "That's our guy."

Kino nodded. "Yeah."

"You coming?" asked Clay.

"Nope." Kino couldn't believe what he was saying, and from the shock registering on his brother's face, Clay couldn't believe it, either.

"But it's him," said Clay, his voice incredulous.

"She's worth a hundred of him."

Clay glanced at Lea and then back to his brother, a look of open speculation on his face. "Maybe we'd better take her back to Black Mountain. At least there we have home-field advantage."

"Yeah," said Kino. "I like the sound of that."

"What do you want me to do?" asked Clay.

"I want you to catch him," said Kino.

Clay gave a lazy smile and thumped Kino's shoulder. "Will do. Then we can get back home. Should be easy, not having to watch your back."

"Just watch your own."

"You going to the safe house?"

"Yeah."

"I'll see you there." Clay hesitated. "Maybe I better stay with you."

Kino considered that then shook his head. "Go take him into custody."

"Custody? Really?"

Kino nodded and Clay smiled. "I'm only good at shooting animals anyway."

The two embraced and Kino watched Clay meet up with Nesto Gomez and stride away, feeling a slight tug of envy. He'd wanted to see the Viper captured. To be there when he went down. But now all he wanted was to see Lea through this and, if she'd let him, to protect her for the rest of their lives.

Kino rounded the SUV. His phone vibrated and he lifted it from his pocket, checking the caller ID. It was Gabe. He might be calling to order him back to work, but Kino knew he might have information. He paused beside the driver's-side door and took the call.

"Hi, Gabe."

"Just got the word on that suspect, the one with the storage unit. Rosa Keene?"

"Yeah. What'd they turn up?"

"The detective who interviewed her said that she denies any knowledge. He also said she still owes eight months on her used Escort and rents a shitty apartment, so he's inclined to believe her. She said it might be her ex-husband. The guy retired, according to Keene, when they threatened to charge him with a felony. The detective my guy spoke to didn't know him or anything about her allegations but reports that Mrs. Keene said her ex-husband was under investigation for taking bribes and involvement with drug smuggling. She told us that the department let him go with his pension in exchange for his resignation."

"What department?"

"Tucson PD. He was a detective."

Kino let the dust from that bombshell settle. His suspect was a retired cop.

"You got a name?" Kino thought about the new tribal police chief, Charlie Scott. He was retired from someplace.

"Yes. His name is Gus Barrow. That mean anything to you?"

Kino nearly dropped the phone. The border patrol captain, the one who'd just got Captain Rubio to order his men to the scene of Lea's shooting. The surge of adrenaline made his ears ring and his skin tingle. Kino turned to Lea and heard her door open.

Kino looked over the roof at Gus Barrow, gun drawn and pointed at Lea's head.

Gabe's voice came through the phone. "Kino? You there?"

"Yeah."

Barrow pressed the barrel of the gun to Lea's head and lifted his chin toward Kino.

"I gotta go. Tell Tessa I send my love." Kino disconnected.

He faced Barrow.

"You," he said.

Barrow nodded. "Get in."

Kino hesitated. It would be better to confront him here. But not better for Lea.

Barrow gripped Lea's arm and she grimaced as Barrow turned the gun on Kino.

"Make up your mind. I can kill you both here."

Kino got in the driver's side.

"Toss me the keys."

He did.

Then the captain climbed into the backseat and threw the keys up on the dash.

"Drive."

Kino started the engine and drove as directed, his fingers itching for a chance to reach for his gun, but when he tried to release the wheel, Barrow noticed.

"Hands at nine and three, Cosen. I don't really need you, you know."

They left town, driving south into the desert. Kino glanced at Lea to find her face pale and her eyes huge. He'd promised to protect her, to keep her safe, and he'd failed. He knew what would happen next. Barrow would take them somewhere remote and shoot them both.

"Sure wish you'd responded to that call. Didn't think you could resist a chance to catch… What do you call me? The Viper? I like it. It has a certain superhero ring to it."

"Villain," said Kino.

"What?"

"Supervillain."

"Whatever. Why are you so interested in my business?"

Kino snorted. "You killed my father."

"Well, I've killed a lot of people."

"My mom said my dad used to pick up drugs from a plane drop and take them to Tucson."

"Yeah. Tractor-trailers. We used to do it that way. Before all the damned homeland security. Drones are hell. Plus, they got choppers up the wazoo. They stop one trailer and they get the whole 50,000 pounds of pot. We lose it all. So it's back to old school. Human mules, each with a fifty-pound pack. Harder to catch a minnow than a whale. You know? They catch maybe one train out of ten. Acceptable losses."

"And the people?" Kino asked. "The ones they leave behind to die."

He saw Barrow smile. "Like I said, 'acceptable losses.'"

Kino's hands fisted the wheel. "Like my dad, Henry Cosen? You shot him ten years ago in his kitchen."

"I remember your dad. Don't you think I checked you out? Couldn't keep you off the Shadow Wolves, unfortunately. Your dad would be mighty surprised to see two of his boys working for the tribal police. Ironic, when you consider his choices. An ex-con with two cops in the family. Funny old world."

Kino's jaw tightened. It was something he never spoke about. But it was true. His dad had been in once for drugs and once for arson. "You shot him in his kitchen."

"It's business, kid. Your dad was an addict and he was shorting me. Had to make an example. You should have let it go. You could be pulling over drunks at Black Mountain. Instead, you'll end up just like dear old dad. You think he would have wanted that?"

"You left a rattle in the wound."

"How do you know that?"

"I was under the table."

Barrow's brows lifted. "You don't say. Why didn't you recognize me, then?"

"Just saw your feet and hands."

Barrow shrugged. "Lucky for me. Unlucky for you."

"Why a rattle?" asked Kino.

"Yeah, that's my calling card. Though I don't always leave them. Especially if I don't want credit. Credit helps in my business. But not all the time. People give you more respect. Funny. A man might not be afraid of dying. But that rattlesnake rattle, it just creeps them right out. And I do love rattlesnakes. Got a special treat for the two of you. Found a nest. Big one. Parked a stash truck right nearby."

Kino checked the rearview, staring at the face of the man he'd hunted all his life. Kino tried to think of something, but the best he came up with was flipping the car. With her ribs already compromised, he was afraid that might kill Lea.

Kino knew that Gabe had got his message. Mentioning their mother would send the cavalry, or in this case, the Apache. But he didn't know if they'd find them in time. For now, Kino and Lea were on their own.

Chapter Nineteen

Lea could see his face in the side mirror. It was him, the one Kino called the Viper. The one she had seen that day in the desert. And he had been right there with Kino all along. A border patrol captain collaborating with the Shadow Wolves. He called the trackers whenever they needed help and could have put Kino down on so many occasions it made Lea's blood freeze in her veins.

She had no doubt that Barrow was the one who had murdered Ernesta, shot at her and now was leading them to their deaths. And despite the pain in her ribs and the aching in her heart, she did want to live. But more than that, she wanted Kino to live.

All this time she had allowed him to protect her and that had brought him to this. She wondered if she could reach across for Kino's gun without Barrow seeing or if she should open the passenger door and simply throw herself out of the vehicle. It would give Kino two things he needed: time to make a move and the benefit of not having to consider her safety first.

She glanced at Kino and his eyes shifted to her and then slid away. He gave a slight shake of his head. He couldn't know what she considered, but he seemed to know she was up to something.

She cast her gaze to the right, where the cactus and scrub brush flashed by as she imagined rolling along the sandy shoulder of the road. Just the anticipation of the pain in her ribs made her nauseous. She reached for the door handle.

"Why don't you just shoot me now?" she asked. Each word caused a knife blade of pain.

Barrow made a tsking sound. "Not on the road. Anyone might happen along. They'd see the blood on the windshield. I need privacy. Besides, I've been working all day to organize this. Nice of the hospital to give me hourly updates on your condition."

Lea slipped her phone from her front pocket with the hand Barrow could not see and prayed the battery wasn't completely dead. She swiped the mobile phone awake and used her thumb to flick it to Silent. Then she punched in her personal code.

"How did you know where we were?" she asked and then hit the phone icon and the star for favorites.

"Tracking device. All my vehicles have one. It keeps me updated on the whereabouts of my men."

Kino glanced at her and then back to the road.

Barrow continued. "But the Shadow Wolves' vehicles, I didn't have them rigged. I've since corrected that mistake." Barrow rested his gun hand on Lea's seat, just beside her left ear. "Cosen here left his vehicle behind that day. Didn't you? Followed my mules right to me. I told your captain I wanted notice if his men were on tribal land. But Rubio isn't any better at communication than lover boy here. Plus, the Shadow Wolves have special permission to come on Tohono O'odham land, right? *Mi casa es su casa.* Indian thing. You should have called that in, Cosen. Told your captain you'd heard gunfire. Man, you almost had me there. Didn't you?" He didn't wait for an answer. "You know why I operate there, right? Harder to prosecute on Indian land. Bureaucratic nightmare. That's what. It's why your father was so handy. Moving product. Stashing product. We've got others on your reservation now. Plenty to replace him."

Kino made no reply, but his hands inched down the wheel.

Lea glanced at her phone and hit the first name on her favorites list. Her mother.

"You don't check in often. That will work in my favor now," said Barrow. "And you didn't report for duty last night. Your brother did, but not you. You've been off course and out of communication a lot over the past few days. Telling everyone about the Viper. Well, won't they be surprised when they discover that you're the one behind this."

She saw the words *calling mobile* appear on the screen.

"Been running drugs up in Black Mountain," said Barrow, "where the local police have no jurisdiction. Same reason you've been running drugs out of this reservation. Chip off the old block, right? Won't be hard to pin this on you. Might even have enough to implicate your older brother, the police chief."

Kino's hands clenched the wheel and his jaw muscles popped. Lea could only imagine how much that threat hurt him.

Her phone clock started, timing the call. Seconds ticked. Three, four, five. Her mother was on the phone. Lea used her thumb to turn down the volume.

Kino's phone rang. He reached to answer.

"Nope," said Barrow. "Let it go to voice mail. You're done talking."

Lea glanced down to see the red "low battery" warning. When she pressed Ignore, the phone disconnected. Could Kino's older brother find them from that call?

"Pull off here," said Barrow.

Kino slowed and turned off the road onto a cutoff. The SUV jostled and Lea cried out in pain as muscle pulled against fractured bone.

"Stop there," Barrow said, pointing with his gun.

Kino stopped.

"Out."

This time Kino did not comply.

"Both of you," Barrow said.

Kino waited for Lea to open the door and ease gingerly from the seat. Her painkillers were wearing off and the prescription had not yet been filled. Not that it would matter. In a few minutes she'd be way beyond painkillers.

Barrow used his radio and Lea caught the faint hum of an engine that grew in volume by the second. Up the road came a large ATV with four seats, a metal cage to protect the passengers against rollovers and the frame specially designed to go where a truck could not. The driver looked familiar. Lea recognized the slicked-back hair and the mirrored sunglasses first. Her mouth dropped open as she realized the driver was the regional director of Oasis, Anthony DeClay.

Kino had been right about him. He was dirty, too.

He did not look as cocky or self-satisfied as Barrow. Instead his expression was set in a kind of grim determination, as if undertaking an unpleasant but necessary chore.

“Lea,” he said, “we are sure going to miss you.”

“You snake,” she said, stepping forward and lifting a hand to slap him. Barrow grasped her elbow and shoved her against the ATV. The air left her lungs as she folded on the hood for a moment. Kino was at her side, supporting her as she tried and failed to straighten.

“I’m so sorry to have mixed you up in this,” she whispered.

“You didn’t,” said Kino.

“Weapons, radio, phone,” said DeClay. “On the seat.”

Kino laid down his knife, gun, radio, phone, Taser as directed. But not the knife she knew he kept in his moccasin.

“Your phone, Miss Altaha.”

Just lifting the phone clear of her pocket hurt so badly that sweat popped out on her upper lip and brow.

Barrow collected all the discarded items and smashed each phone with the butt end of his radio. Then he threw the mangled electronics into the desert. Kino’s gun went in the waistband of his uniform, and the Taser he handed to DeClay, who anchored it under his belt.

Lea knew there was some way or another to track cell phones, but thought they had to be on and functioning and someone with that technology had to be looking. Gabe, she hoped. She had heard Kino tell him to give his love to Tessa. She was certain Gabe was sending help, but his older brother was in South Dakota and they were here. If Gabe called Clay, he would start at the hospital. But then where?

She looked at the mangled mobile phones and her hope flagged. How would they find them now? Her gaze fixed on the ATV and the tire tracks. The Shadow Wolves would track them. But would they find them in time?

"Front seat, Cosen," said Barrow, motioning with his gun toward the ATV. "Miss Altaha will sit in the back with me."

Kino helped Lea in and then Barrow waited as he climbed into the front seat. Only then did he take his place beside Lea directly behind Kino.

"Hold on, you two. Wouldn't want you to fall out." He aimed the comment at Kino and the gun at Lea. "If you do, I shoot her first, then come back for you."

Kino clenched his jaw and he stared straight ahead. Lea could only imagine how much he wanted to get his hands on Barrow.

She did not recall much of the ride except that each jarring jolt and jostle sent a knife blade of pain through her ribs. Her stomach heaved.

"I'm going to be sick," she said.

"Go ahead," said Barrow without a shred of compassion.

Lea knew in that moment that she was surely going to die. Clay would not arrive in time to rescue them.

They approached a rocky outcropping rising some thirty feet from the desert.

"That's it," said Barrow.

DeClay slowed and then stopped. "Get this over with."

"Out," said Barrow.

Kino did as he was told, his body tense. But Barrow was a former police officer with the same training as Kino. He had more experience and he had a gun. Kino had desperation and a younger physique.

"You, too," said Barrow to Lea.

She walked beside Kino, just ahead of their captors.

"Where are we going?" asked Kino.

"Oh, *your* stash. The truck was about half-full with weed. There's a nest of rattlers I have had my eye on.

Planned to harvest some of the larger ones this fall, but, you know, it occurred to me that a smuggler, bitten by a snake or two that was right next to his stash car…well, that smuggler might not get out alive. There must be fifty rattlers in there. You know even one bite can kill a man. Once you're hit, you need to get that antivenin quick or it's lights out.

"So, you and Lea, your willing companion, have been moving product through the Apache reservations for years. Salt River and Black Mountain. Cosen, you've been recently promoted in the organization, just like I was, so you're down here to help move product and the Viper was only an excuse for you to go off on your own program. You weren't hunting illegals. You were moving product, because you knew exactly where the Shadow Wolves were and where they would not be. Didn't you?"

Kino made no reply.

"Of course, I'll drag your brother into this. You didn't seem to mind, so why should I? Probably kill Clay. No loose ends."

Lea feared that Kino was willing to die to save her and she was shaking with the anticipation of what he might try. As they walked the final few yards she realized that they would be murdered or die trying to escape. But she saw no outcome where an unarmed man and a woman with two cracked ribs would overcome two armed gunmen.

Lea reconciled that she was going to die, but the lump in her throat came when she thought of Kino lying out here in the baking sun.

He didn't deserve it.

Chapter Twenty

Kino walked beside Lea, his hand light on her elbow. As he walked, he surveyed the desert, searching for some weapon, and found only patchy rock and sparse, tufted grass. The stash pickup was parked beside the outcropping, covered with camo tarps to make it less visible from the air.

His eye caught movement and then he saw it, his chance. Rattlesnakes. A whole lot of them, writhing and undulating over one another. And there at the base of the outcropping, one or two of the serpents had slithered out to sun themselves. One large one sat with the surety of a creature well camouflaged and with few enemies. Kino's idea blossomed in his mind. The irony of using a snake to fight a viper was not lost on him. If it worked, that was, and he figured the chances were fifty-fifty.

The rattlesnake was coiled with its great diamond-shaped wedge of a head resting on its body. Only its tongue moved, flicking in and out as it checked the air for the heat and taste of warm prey. Kino estimated it was three inches in diameter at the center and might be up to four feet in length. Most important, it was still silent and Kino would reach it first.

"Nest is right there," said Barrow.

He hoped Barrow's attention was momentarily directed toward the shallow rock den of snakes as Kino released Lea's elbow using two fingers to push her gently away. Her eyes flashed to him, but she moved as he directed, giving him a narrow gap between them. Under ordinary circumstances, Kino would never willingly engage a snake this big or this deadly.

"Far enough," said Barrow.

Kino didn't stop. He needed two more steps.

"Stop."

He did but he slid his foot into the sand as the rattlesnake gave a warning shake of its tail. But Kino already had his foot under the closest coil. The snake hit the side of his knee-high moccasin and released with such speed, Kino didn't see or feel the strike. As the snake recoiled, Kino got his foot under its thick ropelike body. He whirled on the other foot and kicked. The snake sailed into the air, twisting as it flew in a high arch right in the direction of Captain Barrow.

Barrow's attention shifted from Kino to the imminent threat of the snake. The gun tracked the reptile, and Kino launched himself at the captain. The snake, Barrow and Kino all landed in a heap together. Kino rolled, wrestling for the gun. Barrow screamed and his hand went slack. Had he been bitten? Kino hoped so as he wrenched the gun away and rolled to his feet.

A quick glance toward Lea gave him a glimpse of DeClay dragging her toward the ATV. When Kino flashed his attention back to Barrow, it was to see that he had already drawn Kino's semiautomatic from the waistband of his trousers and was scrambling behind the pickup. It was the stash truck, the one he had parked dangerously close to the nest of rattlers. A moment later

Barrow fired from beneath the truck. The rock beside Kino's foot sparked as the bullet ricocheted off the stone.

Kino had no shot at Barrow but he did have a shot at the rattlers' nest tucked into the low ledge beside the truck. He fired at the rock above the den, knowing snakes, although deaf, were highly sensitive to vibration. In response, rattlers began pouring out of the nest and onto the ground behind the pickup.

Barrow gave a shout.

Kino expected battling the serpents would keep him busy.

Kino took off after Lea. DeClay had her around the throat and was holding her in front of him as a human shield. Kino aimed Barrow's pistol but did not shoot. There was too much chance of hitting Lea. DeClay turned the handgun on Lea, pressing the barrel against her temple.

Kino's heart slammed into his ribs at the thought that DeClay might kill Lea. Was this how it was going to end? Two more bodies in the desert?

He had to stop DeClay and rescue Lea. But DeClay already had Lea at the ATV.

Her eyes met his as he closed the distance between them.

"Stop right there," ordered DeClay.

Lea's attention swung from Kino to the pickup.

"He's behind the gate," she yelled.

Kino rolled as the pistol shots began again with steady rhythmic cadence. Kino made it to the opposite side of the ATV from DeClay, giving him good cover from Barrow's barrage of bullets. With the metal frame now shielding him from attack, he turned his attention to

Lea. She struggled, her face red from the effort and lack of air. DeClay swung the pistol in Kino's direction. He heard the sound of banging, as if someone was pounding on the side of the truck. A quick glance showed Barrow scrambling over the camo tarp that covered the pickup bed. Kino took a shot, but Barrow managed to swing through the cab's open rear window and into the truck. The engine started a moment later.

Kino stood and saw DeClay shove Lea into the ATV. Lea's head was down as she fell against the wheel well.

"Get up!" roared DeClay as he hoisted her by her collar.

Lea screamed as she rose. Kino saw something black gripped in her hand. A gun?

No, he realized. His stun gun. She only had to pull the trigger, but if one of the electrodes missed, the weapon would be useless.

The pickup barreled toward them with Barrow behind the wheel. Kino had time to dive away as the truck hit the back of the ATV, rolling the vehicle. DeClay and Lea tumbled out and away as the truck dragged the mangled vehicle for several yards before pushing it clear.

DeClay stood and dragged Lea up in front of him once again. But this time Lea's face showed no pain. Instead her expression was as stoic as any Apache woman engaged in the Sunrise Ceremony. Unlike most women, Apache females had to prove their toughness through action. Kino had no doubt what she would do.

She raised the stun gun and flicked the safety up to the armed position with her thumb, just as he had shown her. Then his little Apache pacifist pressed the contacts to DeClay's biceps, which even now encircled her neck, set her jaw and squeezed the trigger.

DeClay went rigid and fell.

Lea remained standing, a shocked expression on her face, as DeClay's nervous system went haywire. She seemed to remember then that the current continued until the trigger was released. She dropped the unit and DeClay's body went from twitching in the sand to complete stillness. Lea fell to her knees, hunching as she clutched her ribs.

Kino ran in their direction as the pickup turned in a wide half circle.

He took a low, ready stance, squatting in front of Lea as the captain barreled toward them. Kino raised the pistol and took aim. The first shot went right through the windshield and through the space where Barrow's head had just been. But Barrow had ducked down. He popped back up and aimed Kino's weapon out the side window at them, squeezing the trigger with one hand and holding the wheel with the other. The truck was barreling straight at them.

Kino had time for one single shot. But this time he aimed at the tire. The resulting explosion of air and rubber threw the truck into a skid that sent Barrow broadside to Kino's position. Barrow released the pistol in favor of a two-handed grip on the pickup's steering wheel as it careened out of control.

Kino aimed high and fired. Blood sprayed and Barrow slumped. Had he hit him or grazed him? The truck rolled on, stopping only when it collided with the rock face where the snakes now slithered in front of their earlier-disturbed nest.

Kino looked at the crumpled hood and steam that

billowed from the engine block. Then he glanced over at Lea. She lay on her side on the ground and her stillness frightened him into motion.

Kino scrambled to Lea, lifting her into his arms. Her body sagged and her head lolled. Her eyes rolled back in their sockets as her body went slack. Kino's heart pounded so hard it deafened him.

"Lea?" He lowered his head to listen to her heart but could hear nothing beyond the roar of his own blood in his ears. His stomach roiled as he pressed two fingers against the vessel at her neck. He could feel her pulse, steady and fast. Kino slumped.

Had she fainted?

Beside him, DeClay moaned. Kino left Lea for as long as it took to retrieve DeClay's gun and tie his wrists and ankles, leaving the stun gun, which could be fired only once.

When he returned to Lea, he found her breathing shallow and her color chalky. Her ashen face bore an eerie resemblance to the white paint used to turn a young girl into the representation of Buffalo Woman in the Sunrise Ceremony. Only this wasn't paint; it was shock.

He glanced toward the ruined truck and then the mangled ATV. How would he get them out of here before the desert heat killed them both?

A RATTLESNAKE SLITHERED by and Kino decided Lea could not remain on the ground. He lifted her into his arms and set her in the passenger seat of the ATV. The vehicle was ruined, but the metal frame had done its job, protecting the passenger compartment.

"I have to check on Barrow. I'll be right back." He

received no reply from Lea but knew he had to see if Barrow was still a threat.

He held the gun at the ready as he approached the stillness of the truck cab. His gun lay in the dirt beside the back tire. Kino used his toe to bring it well clear of the range of a striking snake before stooping to retrieve it. He tucked Barrow's gun into his waistband and reclaimed the familiar semiautomatic. Rattlesnakes continued to undulate across the sand, seeking alternative shelter from the morning heat. Some rattled from beneath the truck, their tails lifted near the back tires.

Kino walked with a slow, careful step.

He could not see Barrow through the window, but he knew he was in there because he hadn't seen him exit. When he moved close enough to look into the compartment, Kino found Barrow slumped to the right. He was tempted to put an insurance bullet in the back of his head. He knew if the situation was reversed, that was just what he could expect from this man. Before he'd met Lea, he would have taken Barrow out. No question. But now he questioned everything he'd once wanted.

He reached in with the gun and poked Barrow. A low moan issued from the downed captain. Then Kino saw the man's hand. The snake that had hit Kino first in the leg had obviously got Barrow, too, when he'd raised his hand to defend his face. Judging from the swollen purple flesh, Barrow had got a fair share of venom. The soft tissue was now already twice its normal size. No wonder his aim had been off. Kino was surprised Barrow had even been able to hold the gun. He grasped Barrow by the shoulder and heaved him upright in his seat. He needed to get back to Lea.

Barrow's forehead showed the deep gouge of Kino's

bullet. Blood poured down his face, but the wound was superficial. Barrow opened his eyes and Kino met the cold terror glimmering there.

"Twice," he whispered.

"What?"

Barrow tried to lift his arm. "Hand and shoulder. Twice. You have to get me help."

One snake bite was hard to survive, especially from a snake as big as the one Kino had kicked at Barrow. Two? Well, you'd have to be very close to the antivenin and very, very lucky.

"You took my radio. You trashed the ATV and the truck."

Barrow groaned. "My phone."

Kino took it from the captain's front pocket and flicked it on. "No service. Radio? Satellite phone?"

"No." Barrow's head fell back to the headrest. Blood continued to flow from his head wound down his neck, soaking into the cotton of his shirt. "It wasn't supposed to end like this."

"No?" said Kino. "Looks about right to me."

"Get me out of here." Barrow's eyes closed and he started panting like a rabid dog.

Kino knew he'd be lucky to get Lea out of this alive. He wasn't dragging Barrow along, too. He stepped away from the truck.

Barrow's eyes flashed open. He must have understood Kino's intention to leave him because he struggled to rise, reaching his swollen hand toward Kino. The skin had stretched tight. The wound around the bite marks oozed clear fluid. Soon the tissue would begin to rot.

"Don't leave me here like this."

Kino knew a few people who had been bitten. Each said it was the worst pain of their life.

"I can't take you and Lea. I'll send help."

Their eyes met and both knew it would be too late.

"Then shoot me," said Barrow through gritted teeth. "It's what you wanted. Shoot me to avenge your old man."

Kino's jaw ticked as he raised his weapon and aimed. Barrow relaxed into his seat. Kino lowered his weapon. All Kino wanted was Lea's life and he was wasting precious seconds with a dead man.

Kino holstered his pistol and stepped slowly away through the settling snakes.

"No!" howled Barrow. His words became curses and then moans.

Kino kept walking toward Lea so he could get them out of the desert.

As he walked he thought how strange that he had come to kill this man and now, when it would be so easy, he had lost his will to do so. Lea said she had forgiven her father's shooter. Could he find the strength to do the same?

Kino returned to the truck. Barrow stopped screaming, panting as he stared at him, his face dripping with sweat.

"I forgive you," Kino said.

Barrow squinted at Kino through bloodshot eyes. Kino left him, trailed by animallike shrieks mixed with curses.

LEA WOKE TO the sound of screams. She opened her eyes to find she sat in the ATV. Kino stood beside the truck, returning his gun to its holster before pivoting and heading toward her. Her eye caught movement and she turned her head, the simple motion making her ribs throb to life with a pain so fierce it turned her stomach. She gagged and folded at the waist, thinking she would be sick. Even the pain was momentarily forgotten as her eyes came to rest on the wiggling, squirming body.

Beside her, on the dusty ground, her Oasis director writhed uselessly, his hands secured behind his back and his ankles pinned together with what looked like white plastic bands. A snake slithered from beneath the ATV, straight at DeClay, who screamed "Get me up!"

Lea realized another voice came from the direction of the pickup. But the sound was barely human. It was hoarse, feral and full of agony. Lea clamped her hands over her ears as Kino approached. He glanced at the advancing snake and the retreating man and stepped over the snake as he continued toward her.

"You okay?" asked Kino.

"What is that? That howling?" she asked.

"Barrow. He's been bitten by a snake. Twice."

Her hands slid away as she looked in the direction of the truck.

"Can we help him?" She didn't say the obvious, which was that he had brought them here to murder them.

"I've got nothing but my weapons. He smashed my radio and our phones." Kino met her gaze and held it.

"He needs a hospital. Antivenin."

"Within six hours. I know. It was part of my training. He can't walk, shouldn't. It will only make the venom effect faster. We have no transport. You understand? We have to walk out."

Lea felt the cold fingers of fear breaking through the

pain. The truck was wrecked and the ATV a tangle. It was clear to her from the angle of the front wheels that the axle was broken.

She tried to remember how far they'd come and recognized it was too far. Kino might make it, but she never would. Realization hit hard.

She had become her aunt, a burden, holding back the one who had a chance.

Lea's gaze slipped to Anthony DeClay, the man she'd once respected. Her disappointment mixed with the agony of breathing as emotional and physical pain merged.

"He's ruined Oasis. The funding will dry up with the water and more people will die."

"Possibly. This will shed media attention on an important problem."

"Important?" she asked, dark brows rising at his words as if searching for sarcasm in his voice.

"Yes. It's important."

Her mouth twitched in a smile.

"Maybe the right person could turn the media blitz into an opportunity to get the word out. Get government support and more funding."

"The right person?" she whispered.

"You, Lea." He took her hand. "I'll help."

Perhaps she could if she had a chance of walking out of here. "I thought you disapproved."

"No. Not anymore. And even if I did, I'd support anything you felt this strongly about." He glanced at DeClay, who continued his caterwaul. "Guess I better get him up and out of the sun."

Kino left her to assist DeClay. He stooped and dragged the downed man to his feet and then put an arm around his middle, tipping him over his shoulder. DeClay was begging and threatening and shouting about his rights as Kino took him to the pickup. Lea couldn't hear what Kino said, but she did hear the door open and close.

He walked back to her amid the chorus of cries.

"You can't leave him tied up like that," she said.

"Nope. I didn't." She noticed Kino now held DeClay's boots. He carried them by the laces, swung them and released his grip. The boots sailed a good thirty feet before falling into a patch of cactus. "I cut loose his legs. He can get his hands free with a little effort and then go after his boots. I told him that I'd shoot him if he followed us."

"You have to leave me," she said.

"That's not going to happen."

"You can make it out and send help."

He gave her a stern look. "No. You're coming with me."

"Kino, I can't walk."

Chapter Twenty-One

Kino collected a tarp, some rope and one empty gallon jug. He left everything else to ensure they could move as quickly as possible. He wanted to carry Lea, but she insisted on walking. He let her try, but it was impossible. As her face turned chalky he put his foot down.

"You're going to faint again," he said. "Then I'll have to carry you anyway."

"You should go get help and bring them back."

"We don't separate."

"I know." She lowered her head. "I know. My mother and my aunt knew, too."

"They didn't have a choice. I do. I can get us both out of here, Lea. I can."

She took his hand. "My aunt sent her sister away out of love and I'm sure my mom left for the same reason: Love for the child she carried."

"But I'm not leaving."

"We could both die out here," she said.

"I can find water."

"There isn't any."

"Yes, there is. I've spent time with the O'odham. This is their land. They survive here without streams, lakes, rivers or water stations."

Lea's expression showed hope. "Really?"

Kino nodded and lifted her into his arms. She flinched but then set her expression in grim determination. Kino had a decision to make. He could follow the road the truck had taken or he could retrace their route out. He did not know how long the road leading here might be, so he took the known route, through the uneven ground taken by the ATV. Following the path was simple enough, but his pace was slow and he knew they both were losing water as they went.

Within an hour he found a downed, dried-out saguaro. The hull was just what he needed. He set Lea on the sand and harvested four of the ribs from the once mighty cactus. He used them to make a travois and wrapped the carrying platform with the camouflage tarp Barrow had used to disguise the stash truck. When he finished, he thought the Plains Apache might even be proud of his efforts.

Lea seemed much more comfortable stretched out in the cradle of the tarp than curled in his arms. He propped one end up on a rock to ease her breathing as he set to work. He used two of the remaining ribs, cutting one short and tying it to the top second-longer pole to form a vee.

"What is that?" she asked.

"Harvesting pole. The saguaro fruit is ripe now ten to fifteen feet up. I just need to find one and we find water."

But he needed to find one fast. He knew exactly how much fluid they needed.

He placed the harvesting pole beside Lea and lifted the end of the travois, setting them in motion. As he walked the winds began to pick up. He removed his

T-shirt and used it to cover his face and then placed the tarp over Lea to keep the swirling, stinging sand from attacking her.

She used one arm to lift the end and stare up at him.

"How can you see?" she asked, raising her voice to be heard and then grimacing as she paid for her lapse in judgment.

"I know the direction. We'll be all right."

She wrapped an arm around her ribs and lowered the tarp. She gripped the end to keep it in place.

He raised the travois, slowed again by the terrain and the stinging wind.

The storm blew and blew, making the sun a hazy orb and making his progress painfully slow. Finally he was forced to take shelter and wait with her under the tarp.

"I'm getting you out of here," he whispered.

She huddled next to him, clutching his arm but saying nothing. Finally the shrieking wind died and the sand fell back to the desert floor. When he raised the tarp it was to see the haze remaining in the sky. They watched the storm sweep away like a thunderstorm of earth.

Kino reconstructed the travois and recovered his cactus pole. Then he set them off again, searching all the while for a saguaro topped with the ripening red fruit enclosed in green pods or bursting from the pods. When he found what he was after, he set Lea's travois down. Using the pole, he knocked several of the pods to the ground. The pink, ripening tip showed the fruit was ripe.

With his knife he slit open the pods, and he and Lea ate the sweet red pulp and black seeds. The moisture was a welcome relief. Once they were no longer thirsty, Kino knocked down a dozen more pods, taking some and leaving some where they had fallen. Then he handed off the pole and lifted the end of the travois.

"Are you just going to leave them?" she asked.

He resumed their journey, speaking as he moved slowly along, refreshed now by the moisture and sweet sticky fruit, but worried by the sun's descent.

"That's how it's done. You need to leave some for the birds and animals. It's rude to take it all. The O'odham believe that these giant cactus are relatives and for centuries this fruit was vital to survival."

As he walked he told her the story as he recalled it, of the boy struggling across the desert who was helped by the animals and birds. In time he took root and lifted his arms and became the cactus to shelter and protect the creatures who had safeguarded him.

"Well, I've seen the woodpeckers nest in them," Lea said.

He smiled, glad to take her mind from her pain and their peril. With the cactus in bloom they would not die from thirst. Still, her injured ribs and the trauma of their capture worried him greatly.

"Owls, too," he said. "Have you had the syrup made from saguaro fruit? It's great."

The sun was low on the horizon when he stopped a second time. He figured they had made half the distance to the SUV.

He sat beside Lea and split open more of the saguaro fruit.

Lea sat stiffly on the ground beside him, accepting what he offered.

"Will we make it out?" she asked.

Kino nodded and glanced at the sky. "Few more

hours, maybe." If not…well, they'd be in even more trouble.

He offered her another fruit.

"You eat it," she said, pushing it back toward him.

He did, and when he had finished the sticky red pulp, he found Lea staring at him.

"It's finished, isn't it? He won't be after me anymore."

He nodded.

Lea's ribs hurt her so much she could barely breathe past the pain, but she had to say something before they reached help and their lives returned to normal.

"I'm proud of you," she said.

"Yes? Why?"

"Because you didn't kill him."

"I think the snakes did that. He just hasn't accepted it yet."

"But you could have finished him. What I want to know is…did you leave him out of mercy or vengeance?"

Kino glanced away, his stare as distant as the horizon. "I forgave him, Lea." His gaze returned to her. "I think you are right. My hate for him was a kind of blackness inside me. I thought I had a duty to my father. But this hunt was bad, because it kept me from doing my duty to my family, my clan and to my tribe."

At the word *clan*, her hope fell. She was only half Apache, a fact that few of her peers let her forget. And for Kino, his tribe and clan were everything. What would happen if they reached safety? His promise to her had been fulfilled. She'd no longer need his protection from the Viper. But still, she yearned for him in the very depth of her soul.

"Kino, I know how important your family and tribe are to you. I know you deserve a strong Apache woman and that I…well, that I don't even have a clan."

He cocked his head and she felt insecure, embarrassed and unworthy all at once.

"Lea, what are you talking about?"

"My mother is Mexican. I have no clan and my children will have no clan."

He frowned. "Children?"

She was going about this all wrong. Her timing; her words. She lowered her head, unable to meet his dark, searching gaze.

He took her hand and gave it a light squeeze. "Lea?"

She met his eyes and let the words pour from her. "Oh, Kino, I'm in love with you."

He could not have looked more shocked if she had struck him in the face.

"Well, say something."

"Your timing is bad," he said at last.

Lea's face went hot and her skin prickled as embarrassment momentarily overcame her pain.

"I'm sorry. I just wanted you to know in case…"

He scowled. "I'll get you back safe."

She nodded as if she believed him. But already her thirst was becoming more intolerable than her painful ribs.

Even if they made it, he would leave her and return to Black Mountain. She wanted him to know what he meant to her before that. What for her had been an experience that filled her with the hope and promise of a future with this wonderful man, for him was an obligation to be fulfilled and then put behind him. She accepted her loss with as much grace as she could manage.

"And then you'll join your brothers and find Jovanna."

He nodded. "Yes."

Lea swallowed her pain and disappointment. "I understand."

"No. You don't. Lea, I—" Kino stopped in midsentence as he cocked his head.

Lea listened, fearing another rattlesnake. Kino's attention shifted to the sky and then she heard it, the faint *womp, womp, womp* of a helicopter.

Chapter Twenty-Two

Kino forgot what he was saying as he jumped to his feet, staring up at the cloudless sky. He could hear that a helicopter was near. It was likely one of the border patrol units searching for traffickers. But it might be someone looking for them. He didn't know. What he did know was that Lea was failing. Her color was bad and her breathing was worsening. He had to get her out of here and that meant the chopper had to see them.

Kino grabbed the pole he had used to collect saguaro fruit and dragged it across the soft sand, making a giant X. Then he traced it again as the chopper appeared in the distance. If they saw them, they were saved. Unless it was Barrow's men.

Kino drew his pistol.

He didn't want to scare Lea, but her admission that she loved him had scared him right down to his gut. It was exactly what he'd wanted to hear, but he wondered if it was the pain and the fear talking and not her heart. Did she think she was dying? He knew he loved Lea and that to him her origins mattered not at all. She was more Apache woman than anyone he knew, except for possibly his grandmother.

If he could get Lea to safety and see her well and *if*

she still had feelings for him when she was not staring down her own mortality, then he would be only too glad to take her at her word. The number of ifs in that line of reasoning frightened him almost as much as having the chopper miss them altogether. But the helicopter headed right for them almost as if they were the object of search and the pilot knew exactly where to look.

Clay, he realized. Only Clay could have tracked them through this sand. The high winds would have all but obliterated their tracks. But not to his older brother. Kino knew how good Clay was. But how would he have known where to begin? How could he possibly have found the SUV, their origin?

He didn't know, but the certainty took route and bloomed as the chopper hovered and then made for a landing some fifty yards off on a flat stretch amid the saguaros. Kino holstered his pistol and returned to Lea. Then he shielded their eyes as the chopper touched down and the dust spiraled outward in all directions.

He had expected Clay but found Nesto Gomez and Rick Rubio hopping down from the interior compartment and running in their direction. Kino's grip on his gun tightened. Was it possible that Nesto and Captain Rubio were working with Barrow, too?

"Where's Clay?" asked Kino.

Gomez noted the position of Kino's hand and kept his hands in plain sight.

"Tracking on foot," said Rubio. "Should be here in about thirty minutes. Anyone hurt?"

"Yeah. Lea's ribs are broken. Barrow was snake bit and Anthony DeClay was stunned." Kino gestured over his shoulder.

"Barrow?" said Rubio, his voice echoing surprise.

"Captain Barrow?" asked Gomez.

Kino nodded.

"He did this?" asked Rubio.

Kino understood the astonishment he saw reflected in their faces. He'd never seen it coming, either. "Yeah. He's been trafficking through here for years. Used to work up in Tucson and they moved him here. Thought having a man in border patrol would help their success rate."

"No wonder we were always in the wrong place," said Nesto. "He was sending us on wild-goose chases."

"Explains why he was always trying to get me to check in," said Rubio. "I thought he was just a control freak."

"He put homing devices on all our vehicles," said Kino.

The two Shadow Wolves exchanged a glance.

Rubio lifted an arm and gestured. "Come on, son. Let's get you two out of here. We'll bring Miss Altaha to the hospital and then swing back for DeClay and Barrow."

Kino took a look at the helicopter and realized it wasn't one of theirs. It was larger and it was armed. One of the pilots glanced at him and nodded. The sleeve of his navy blue jacket was emblazoned with yellow letters. FBI.

"Whose chopper?" he asked Rubio.

"A Fed. Luke Forrest. He your boss?"

Kino had always thought of Gabe, Clay and his uncle as his bosses. But not anymore. Now he saw them for what they were and had always been. The most important thing a man could have—his family—and they had his back in good times and bad.

"He's my uncle."

Clay again, realized Kino, or Gabe, getting him what he needed, as always. And his uncle, who had helped him so many times, had now sent him the resources to get Lea out fast. The gratitude choked him and his vision blurred.

Kino wiped his eyes on his shirt and then helped Lea into the chopper. They lifted off a moment later. The journey that would have taken hours would now be only minutes.

"Destination?" asked the pilot.

"Regional hospital in Pima," answered Kino.

"Yes, sir."

Below them, Kino spotted Clay on the ground and waved. Clay signaled back and turned around. Clearly, he was interested in finding his brother and not the man who had abducted him. It was Kino who had come here for the Viper. Clay had come here only to watch over his little brother. Family first, his father had always said. Why hadn't Kino realized that meant the living? Clyne, Gabe, Clay, Jovanna, his uncle Luke and now Lea. That was who mattered because that was who he loved.

They reached the road and Kino looked down to find a legion of vehicles including DEA, FBI and border patrol. Even if Barrow had succeeded in his plan, he was not getting away this time.

Nesto handed Kino his radio and Kino spoke to Clay.

"Heading to the hospital," Kino said.

"Meet you there, little brother. How is Lea?"

"Banged up. Clay?"

"Yeah?"

"Thanks, brother. You saved me. Out."

Lea's color continued to drain from her skin and

now she had a cough. Each spasm made her sweat and grimace. He tried to get her to drink, but she said she felt too nauseous. They touched down in the parking lot and a crew rushed out to meet them, transferring Lea to the gurney.

At the ER, Lea was stripped of clothing, hustled into a hospital gown and wrapped in white sheets that emphasized that her usually cinnamon skin was an unnatural gray. He knew she was dehydrated and was relieved when they started the IV. They tried to usher him to the waiting room, but he said she was his witness. But now she was not just a witness. She was the love of his life and he would stay with her through this and anything else that threatened her.

Her condition scared him more than snakes or guns or the dangers of the desert. Because Lea was the one thing he could not afford to lose.

Kino did leave her briefly to give the FBI agents a quick rundown of events before he left them so they could board the helicopter back to the scene. In his absence Lea had been taken to Radiation. He found her in a familiar curtained cubicle. He searched her face and noted her color returning.

"What did they say?" he asked.

"More of the same. The fractures are a little worse."

That news caused him physical pain.

"But the lungs are fine. It's just hard to breathe and talk." She smiled and her eyes seemed less bright. "They gave me something for the pain."

He took hold of the hand that was clear of medical equipment and leaned in to kiss her forehead. "I'm so sorry."

He pressed his forehead to the place he had just kissed. She squeezed his hand.

"I'm not."

Kino pulled back, surprised.

"We got him. You did it. You avenged your father and your family, caught the bad guy and a second one, to boot. You should be so happy."

Kino frowned.

Lea narrowed her eyes. "So why don't you look happy?"

"Because I was all wrong. Chasing after that guy. You almost died, and convincing my brother to come down here with me and join the Shadow Wolves put him in danger, too. What was I doing it for? You heard him—my father was exactly the kind of man that I arrest. Why couldn't I see what was right in front of me?"

"He was your dad. It's natural to put him on a pedestal."

Kino now recognized what he hadn't been willing to admit, even to himself. His dad had loved him, but he had been one of the bad guys. Kino thought of all the people who had tried to tell him that and the fights he'd got into because of their words. Yeah, he had a blind spot where his dad was concerned and it had almost got Lea killed. How would he have lived with that?

Kino sat on the stool beside her bed and pressed her hand to his face. "If anything had happened to you, I'd never forgive myself."

"You got him. He won't be hiring any more men and women to risk their lives as mules, and they won't have those filthy drugs to sell, either. You did that."

"There will be another one to replace him."

She nodded. "That's true."

"So what have I accomplished?"

"You saved my life."

He smiled. If he never did a thing again, it made everything worth doing.

"And it's a life to be proud of," he said.

Her smile faded and she looked tired and drawn once more.

"I don't know what to do now. The migrants will keep coming. They need water. But I don't think I belong here anymore. What does the military call it? Shell shock?"

"PTSD—post-traumatic stress disorder."

"Yeah. Well, just thinking about going out there now makes me feel sick."

Kino knew what he wanted and he prayed that what she'd said to him out there in the desert hadn't just been the pain and the fear and the exhaustion. Lea had said she loved him. He sucked in a breath, determined to find out if she meant it.

Chapter Twenty-Three

Lea stared at this beautiful, driven man who sat beside her bed. She was grateful, but she knew that their time together was drawing short. He had done as he had promised. She was safe. But his life was in Black Mountain and hers… Well, where did she belong? Not here. Not anymore. Back at Salt River, her mother and father had made a life, but her older sister had already left, unwilling to live where she was merely tolerated.

Kino was Apache. Not just by blood but by every measure of what it meant to be one of his tribe.

And she wasn't, not wholly. She wished she could take back the words she had spoken to him. Not because they were untrue but because they would make him feel sorry for her and sorry for having to leave her. What else could she do? She had shown him and told him, and though she was not full-blood Apache, she knew the meaning of pride and stoicism. She would not weep or beg him to stay. And she would not try to hold what could not be held.

"Lea, what you said out there. Was it true?"

She squeezed her eyes shut, wishing she could disappear. The humiliation was almost as deep as the pain.

Only there was no medication for this kind of pain, was there?

When she opened her eyes it was to find him staring anxiously at her. Lea took a painful breath and set her face in the mask of unreadable stoicism learned through long practice.

"I'm sorry," she said. "I had no right to just blurt that out. Please forget I ever said that."

He straightened and his expression changed. He shifted his weight and, for a moment, looked unsettled.

"Oh" was all he said. His eyes scanned the room. "Forget it," he said, as if to himself. Then his eyes flashed back to hers and she saw that intensity, that maddening and wonderful passion that showed in everything he believed in and everything he loved.

They stared as the medical machines all around them chirped and bleeped and pinged.

"Forget it because it is not true," he asked, "or because this is a difficult truth?"

"Kino, I know we have differences. Lots. Too many, maybe. And nothing about that has changed. Not really."

"I disagree. I think everything has changed."

She felt a stab of hope between her ribs, right over her heart. "Everything?" she whispered.

He rested a broad callused hand on her forearm and stroked all the way down to her fingertips.

Despite the pain and the medication and the exhaustion, her skin tingled and her body zipped to full sexual awareness of him.

He leaned forward and pressed his lips to hers, taking her mouth in a kiss filled with possession and promise.

When he withdrew, her heart monitor was bleating and her face flushed.

"I need you, Lea, all of you."

"Why?"

"Lea, I know we are different, but those differences are good. I ground you to the earth and you lift me to the sky. You bring out my humanity and I bring you reality. I am practical and you dream of possibilities." He traced her hand across his jaw and pressed a kiss into her palm. "I am hard and you are soft. You bring me balance and love."

She could not keep the astonishment from her voice. "I thought that you would be leaving. That this was all finished."

"This is only just beginning," he said.

"But I'm Mexican, half-Mexican."

"It doesn't matter."

"Of course it does. Because it's my mother. Have you thought about this, really thought? I have no clan. If we stay together, if…"

"If we have a family?"

"Yes. They will have no clan."

"But they will have you as a mother. I can think of nothing better for my children."

"But…but you said that being Apache was who and what you are. That it was more than nationality. It was a way of being. You said you couldn't imagine ever being with someone who wasn't Native."

"Lea, are you saying that you don't think you are Apache?"

It was hard to say out loud, so she held his gaze as she nodded.

"But you *are* an Apache woman. You're stoic, brave, resourceful, enduring. And you care for your family… only, for you, Lea, your family is the entire world. Don't ever say you aren't one of us. You are. In fact, you are the best of us."

Lea kept her expression blank but the tears of joy gave her away. Perhaps she was not as stoic as he'd thought.

"You believe that?" she whispered, hope rising to push away her sorrow.

"With all that I am or will ever be." He stroked the back of her forearm with an easy, gentle touch and finally captured her hand. "Once I thought that finding my father's killer was the most important thing in my life. It isn't. The most important thing, Lea, is you. I want to spend every day for the rest of my life proving that to you."

Lea sagged back in the bed.

"Really?"

Kino kicked the stool away and knelt at her bedside, her hand now trapped in both of his.

"Lea, will you marry me?"

CLAY AND KINO filed their paperwork and finished their last report for the Shadow Wolves. Their captain, Rick Rubio, was there to shake their hands.

"You both are welcome back anytime. We need more guys like you. And if you got any more like the two of you up there in Black Mountain, send them my way."

"Will do," promised Clay.

They exited the small station. All that was left was to pick up Lea at the Oasis office where she had been helping Margie Crocker transition from area supervisor to regional director. Kino had been right about the media coverage. They had descended like the locusts of old, but Lea was a charismatic spokesman and, given her recent experiences, she was in high demand. In every interview she managed to bring the subject away from her and onto the people crossing a desert without water. And just as they had hoped, donations had flooded in and new volunteers were applying daily.

Clay walked with Kino out into the dry desert heat.

"Look at that," said Clay, pointing.

There over rocky cliffs, white clouds billowed.

"It's not the rainy season yet," said Kino, stopping to look at the unfamiliar sight.

"Might just rain, though."

"I miss the rain," said Kino as they reached Clay's battered brown truck and swung up into the front bucket seats.

"I miss a lot of things," said Clay.

Kino paused. "Hey, I never asked you. How did you find our trail? From the hospital, I mean?"

"There aren't that many ways out of town. Rubio had called in everyone and we started running the highways. He'd also called Barrow, but couldn't reach him. About that time we got the trace on both of your phones. That put us right at the spot you left the road. I took over the tracking from there."

"You're the best tracker I know."

"Captain said that, too. I'd even consider staying if not for the heat."

"Save a lot of lives, catching them before they die out there in that desert."

"Yeah. I'll think on it. For now, I want to get back home and help Gabe and Clyne." Clay started the truck. "I heard from Gabe. They're back in Black Mountain. Grandma is dyeing leather again."

Oh, boy. That meant she was back at preparing the

all-important traditional buckskin dress for the Sunrise Ceremony.

"But what if we don't find Jovanna by next July?" asked Kino.

"We'd better. She's started a guest list and she's enlisted her sister and her sister's daughters for the cooking."

"Don't get me wrong—I want to find her. But she's been missing for nine years."

"She's alive," said Clay.

"She was alive when they placed her in foster care," corrected Kino.

"Gabe says he can't take any more time off. There was a spike in crime while he was gone."

"I've got a few more days of leave left," said Kino.

"I thought those were for your honeymoon."

"We will honeymoon—in South Dakota."

Clay laughed. "Most folks go to Vegas or Sedona. Lea is all right with that?"

"It was her idea."

Clay's eyebrows rose at this information. "I think she will be good for you."

"I hope Grandma agrees," said Kino.

"Will it make a difference?"

"Not to me. But it's important to Lea. She's worried about the no-clan thing."

Clay nodded.

"You coming back to testify against DeClay?"

"If they call us."

"I heard that Barrow's family didn't even claim the body. He was cremated."

Clay glanced at Kino.

Kino knew the look. Clay had something on his mind. "Spit it out."

"Did you know when you left him that he'd die?" asked Clay.

"You taught me all I know about rattlesnakes," Kino said.

"Is that why you left him?"

Kino thought back to the last time he'd seen Barrow. There had been no more threats, no smugness or air of authority. Just cold fear in those eyes as he'd faced his own mortality.

"I left him because I'd lost the need to kill him. I just wanted Lea safely away."

"Terrible death, that," said Clay.

"Yeah," agreed Kino.

"No worse than he deserved," said Clay.

Clay pulled up and Kino jumped out. Lea emerged from the Oasis office as if she'd been looking out for them. He kissed her long and deep and she melted against him. His hold was light, deferential to her healing body. Even with the bandage wrapped around her ribs he knew that she was very tender. But with time she would mend and they would marry.

He stepped back and she stared up at him dreamily.

"I've missed you," she sighed.

"It's only been three hours."

"Too long. Way, way too long."

Clay already had Kino's duffels out of the back of his truck and beside Lea's car. From here Clay would head to Black Mountain and Kino and Lea would visit her home in Salt River, where Kino would meet her family.

Clay and Kino embraced, each thumping the other on the back.

"See you at home," said Clay. He then kissed Lea gently on the cheek before returning to his truck alone.

"Ready?" Lea asked Kino.

To begin the rest of his life with her? Yes, he was more than ready and willing and eager.

"You bet," he said and lifted his bags into Lea's car. "Let's go home."

* * * * *